THE Archies® IN INDIA

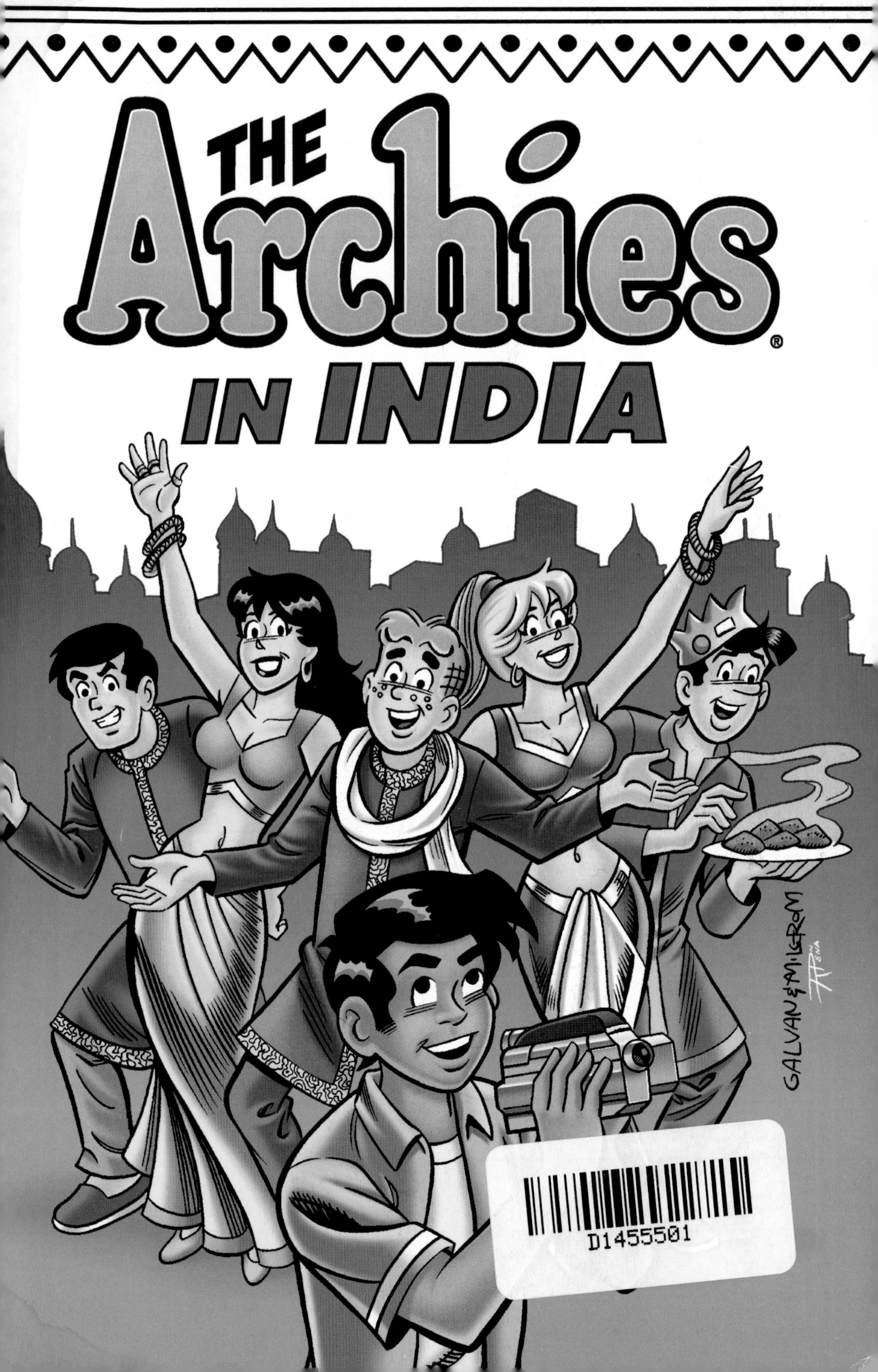
GALVAN & MILGROM

Publisher / Co-CEO: Jon Goldwater
President / Editor-In-Chief: Mike Pellerito
Chief Creative Officer: Roberto Aguirre-Sacasa
Chief Operating Officer: William Mooar
Chief Financial Officer: Robert Wintle
Director: Jonathan Betancourt
Senior Director of Editorial: Jamie Lee Rotante
Production Manager: Stephen Oswald
Art Director: Vincent Lovallo
Lead Designer: Kari McLachlan
Associate Editor: Carlos Antunes
Co-CEO: Nancy Silberkleit

WRITTEN BY

Bill Golliher, Dan Parent,
Michael Uslan, Tania Del Rio,
Fernando Ruiz, & George Gladir

ART BY

Dan Parent, Bill Galvan,
Fernando Ruiz, Rich Koslowski, Bob Smith,
Hy Eisman, Glenn Whitmore, Digikore Studios,
Carlos Antunes, Barry Grossman, Jack Morelli,
Rosario "Tito" Pena, Tom Orzechowski,
Al Milgrom, & Mindy Eisman

CONTENTS

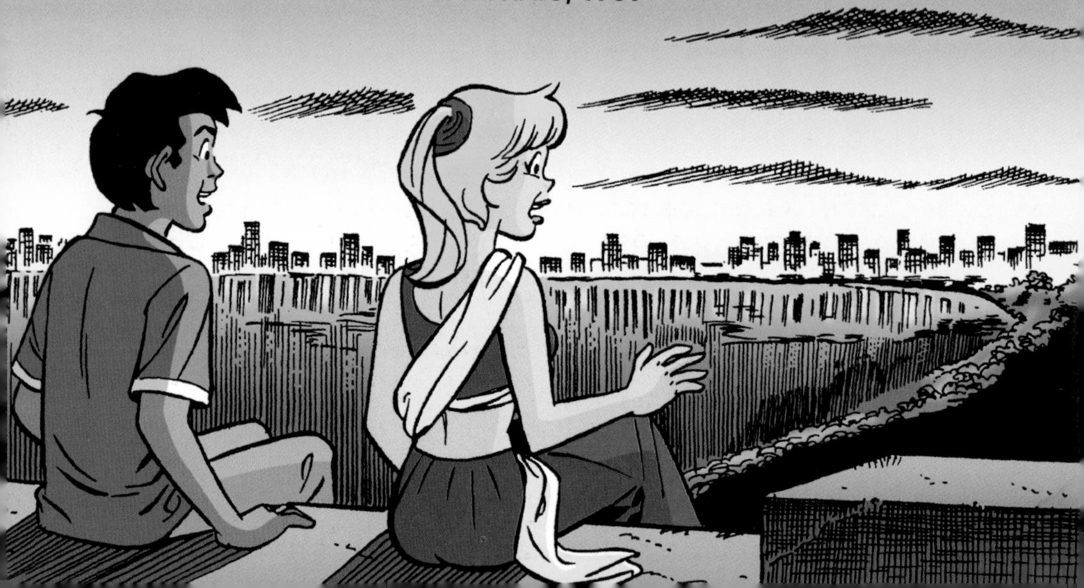

THE ARCHIES FROM NETFLIX

In Conversation with Director Zoya Akhtar and Archie Comics CEO Jon Goldwater

ZA: Hi, I'm Zoya Akhtar, and along with Reema Kagti, I'm the co-founder of Tiger Baby Films. I'm also the director of *The Archies.*

JG: And I'm Jon Goldwater, CEO of Archie Comics. Archie has been a global icon for many years. Archie Comics is a group of iconic characters that were created in 1941. They live in the town of Riverdale. I've been enamored with doing something in India for many, many years. And then my good friend, Sharad (Devarajan of Graphic India), mentioned to me that he had spoken to you about doing an Archies movie. And when he mentioned that it was you who was interested, I immediately said, "Oh my God, we have to try to make this happen." And then, of course, the confluence of you being with the best streaming company in the world in Netflix, it seemed like a no-brainer for *The Archies.*

ZA: I have to say it's such a pleasure and an absolute honor to be asked to make the Indian adaptation of this very iconic comic. It's a huge part of my childhood. I've grown up reading it. And it's very exciting to be able to take the characters and introduce them to a new generation and, at the same time, keep that nostalgia and the essence of the comic alive for people like me that grew up on it. We've set it in the Anglo-Indian community of India. And it's in a magical, fictional hill station town in our country. I mean, the town's called Riverdale. It's fictional.

JG: And I should mention that the film is set in the 1960s. And there's a lot of friendship and love and conflict and community and the music. Music is such a big part of Archie's heritage throughout the decades. The '60s for Archie were also such an important part as we transitioned from what Archie was to where Archie is now. The '60s were the gateway between the classic Archie and the new Archie.

HI GUYS, WHAT'S GOING ON?
NOT MUCH, JUST HEADING OVER TO POP'S!
HEY, LOOK AT THAT!
A NEW MOVIE BY ZOYA AKHTAR COMING TO NETFLIX! COOL!
COMING TO NETFLIX
A film by Zoya Akhtar
I LOVE HER MOVIES!
I WONDER WHO'S STARRING IN IT?
WOW! IT LOOKS LIKE WE ARE!!
The Archies
A FILM BY ZOYA AKHTAR
NETFLIX

The Archies*, a feature film adaptation of the comics, will be produced by Tiger Baby, Graphic India, Archie Comics, and will premiere worldwide exclusively on Netflix in 2023.*

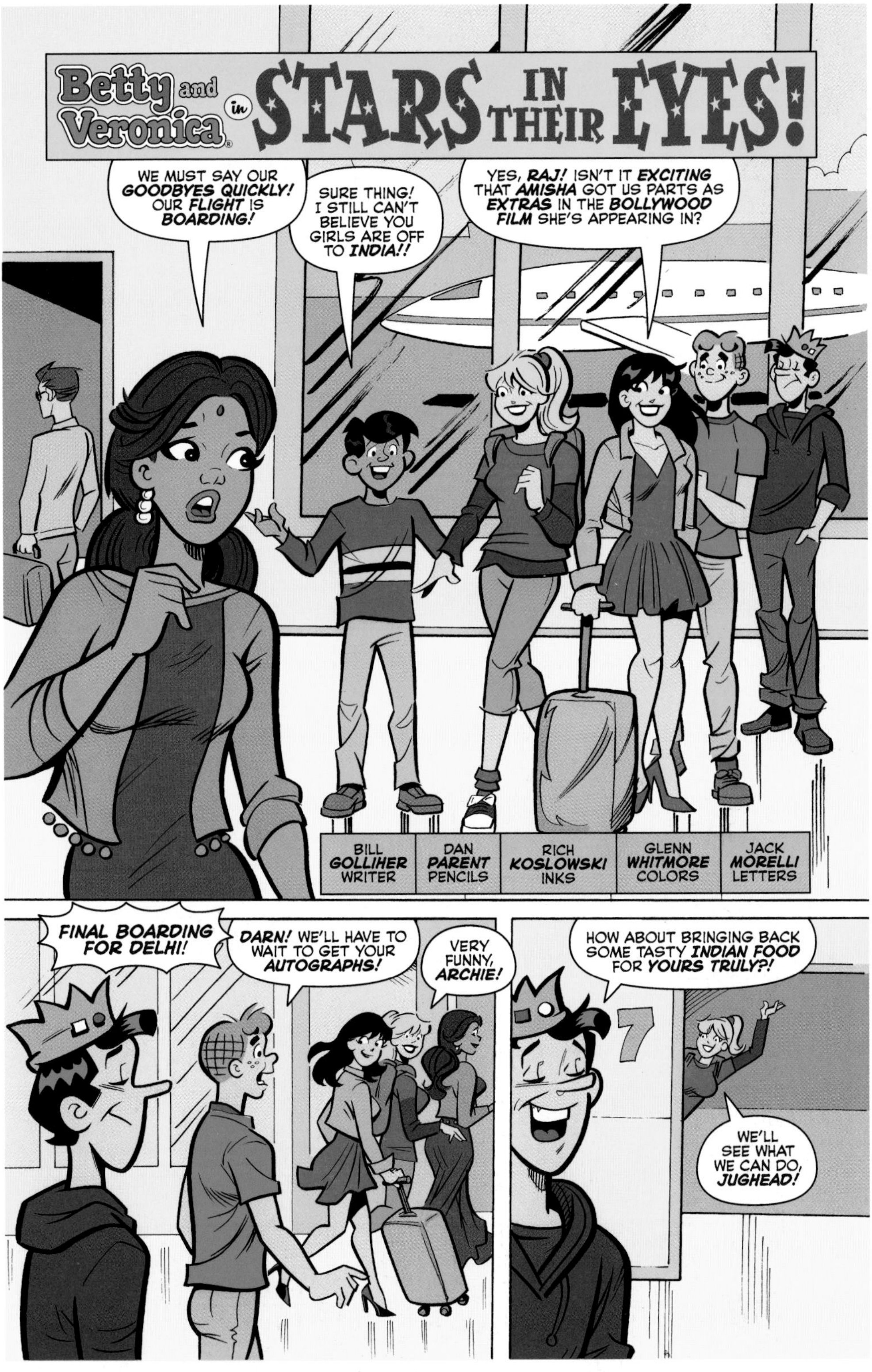
Betty and Veronica in STARS IN THEIR EYES!
WE MUST SAY OUR GOODBYES QUICKLY! OUR FLIGHT IS BOARDING!
SURE THING! I STILL CAN'T BELIEVE YOU GIRLS ARE OFF TO INDIA!!
YES, RAJ! ISN'T IT EXCITING THAT AMISHA GOT US PARTS AS EXTRAS IN THE BOLLYWOOD FILM SHE'S APPEARING IN?
BILL GOLLIHER WRITER
DAN PARENT PENCILS
RICH KOSLOWSKI INKS
GLENN WHITMORE COLORS
JACK MORELLI LETTERS
FINAL BOARDING FOR DELHI!
DARN! WE'LL HAVE TO WAIT TO GET YOUR AUTOGRAPHS!
VERY FUNNY, ARCHIE!
HOW ABOUT BRINGING BACK SOME TASTY INDIAN FOOD FOR YOURS TRULY?!
7
WE'LL SEE WHAT WE CAN DO, JUGHEAD!

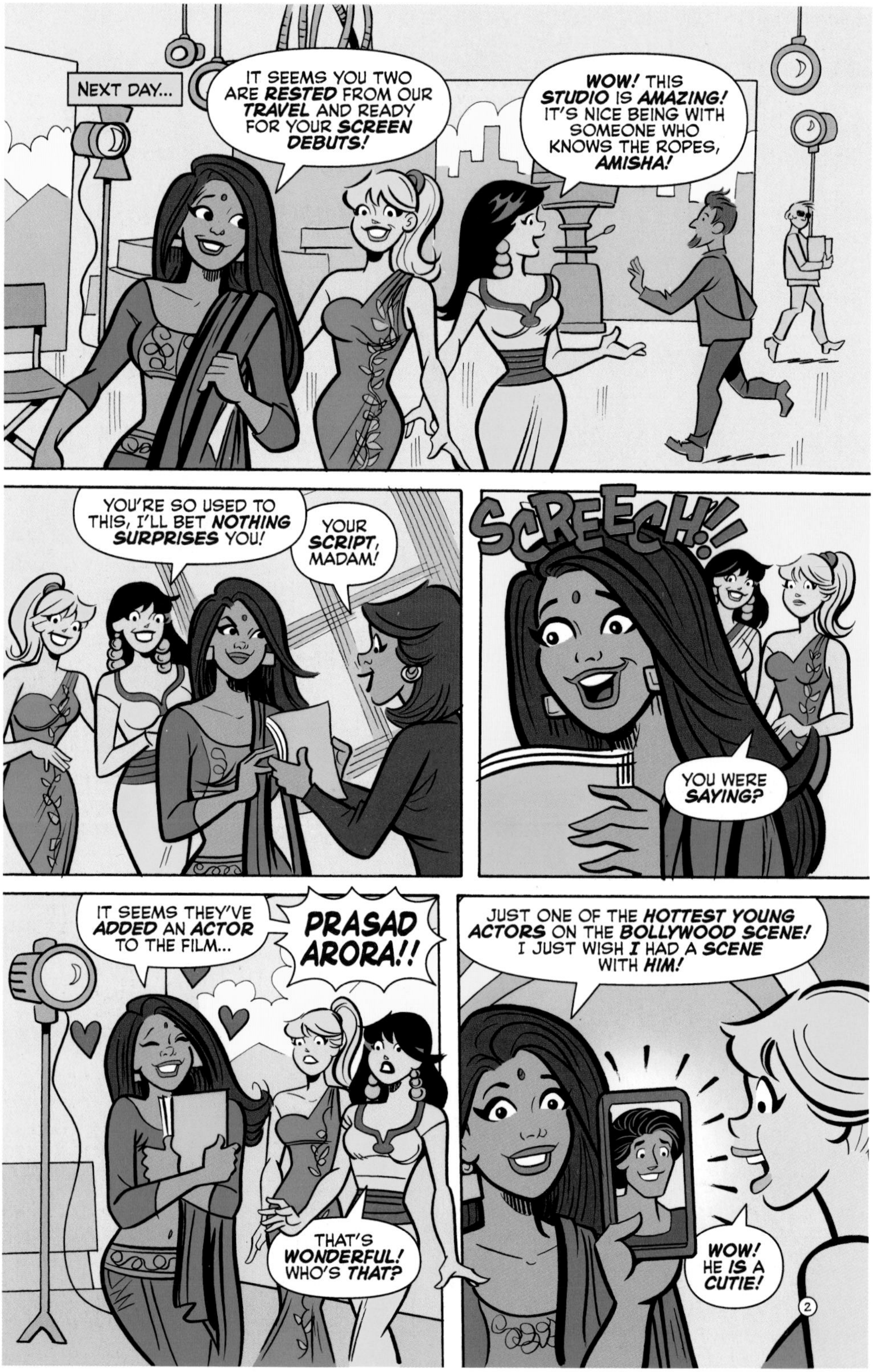

NEXT DAY...
IT SEEMS YOU TWO ARE RESTED FROM OUR TRAVEL AND READY FOR YOUR SCREEN DEBUTS!
WOW! THIS STUDIO IS AMAZING! IT'S NICE BEING WITH SOMEONE WHO KNOWS THE ROPES, AMISHA!
YOU'RE SO USED TO THIS, I'LL BET NOTHING SURPRISES YOU!
YOUR SCRIPT, MADAM!
SCREECH!!
YOU WERE SAYING?
IT SEEMS THEY'VE ADDED AN ACTOR TO THE FILM...
PRASAD ARORA!!
THAT'S WONDERFUL! WHO'S THAT?
JUST ONE OF THE HOTTEST YOUNG ACTORS ON THE BOLLYWOOD SCENE! I JUST WISH I HAD A SCENE WITH HIM!
WOW! HE IS A CUTIE!
2

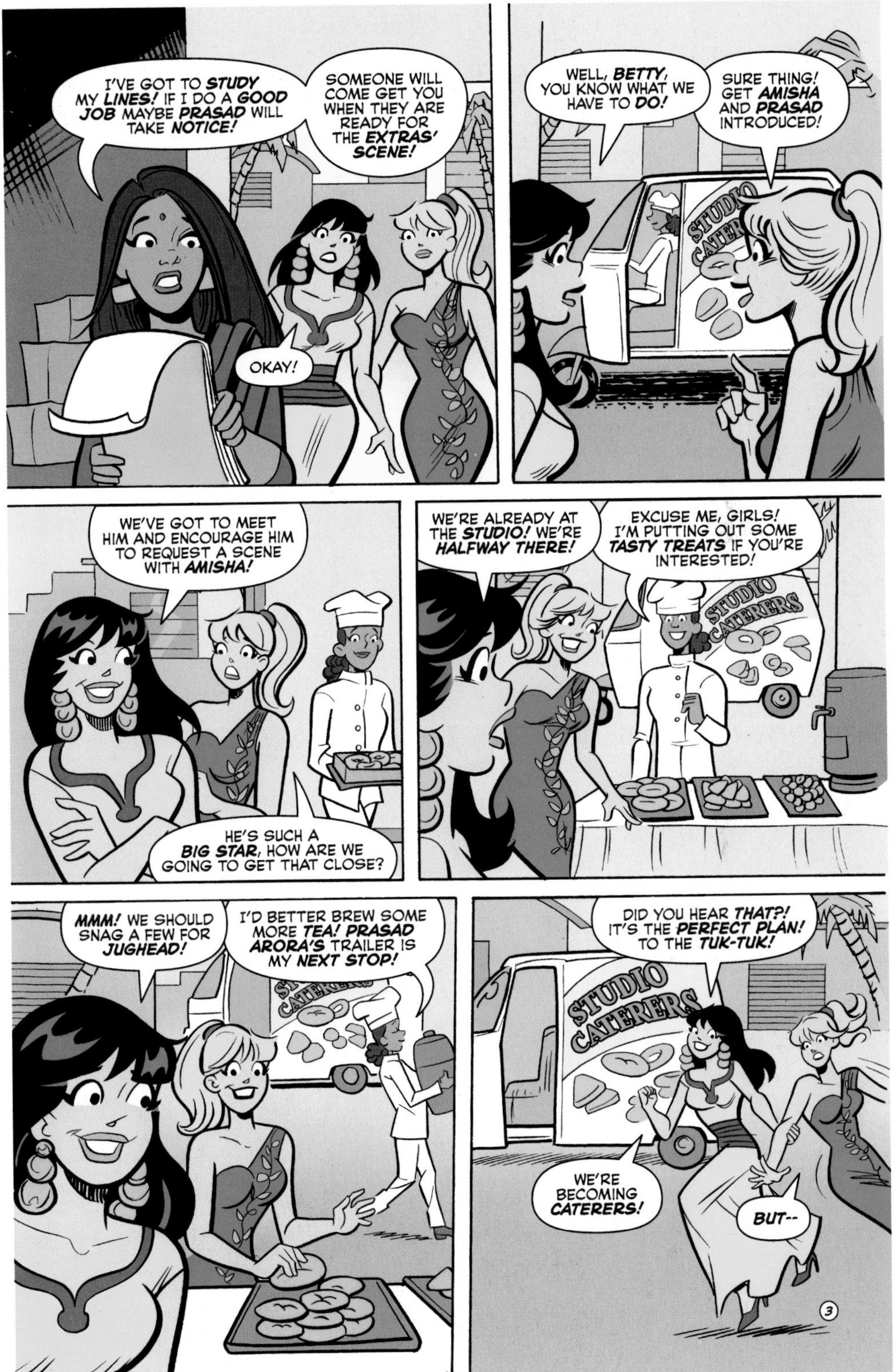
I'VE GOT TO STUDY MY LINES! IF I DO A GOOD JOB MAYBE PRASAD WILL TAKE NOTICE!
SOMEONE WILL COME GET YOU WHEN THEY ARE READY FOR THE EXTRAS' SCENE!
OKAY!
WELL, BETTY, YOU KNOW WHAT WE HAVE TO DO!
SURE THING! GET AMISHA AND PRASAD INTRODUCED!
STUDIO CATERERS
WE'VE GOT TO MEET HIM AND ENCOURAGE HIM TO REQUEST A SCENE WITH AMISHA!
HE'S SUCH A BIG STAR, HOW ARE WE GOING TO GET THAT CLOSE?
WE'RE ALREADY AT THE STUDIO! WE'RE HALFWAY THERE!
EXCUSE ME, GIRLS! I'M PUTTING OUT SOME TASTY TREATS IF YOU'RE INTERESTED!
STUDIO CATERERS
MMM! WE SHOULD SNAG A FEW FOR JUGHEAD!
I'D BETTER BREW SOME MORE TEA! PRASAD ARORA'S TRAILER IS MY NEXT STOP!
DID YOU HEAR THAT?! IT'S THE PERFECT PLAN! TO THE TUK-TUK!
STUDIO CATERERS
WE'RE BECOMING CATERERS!
BUT--
3

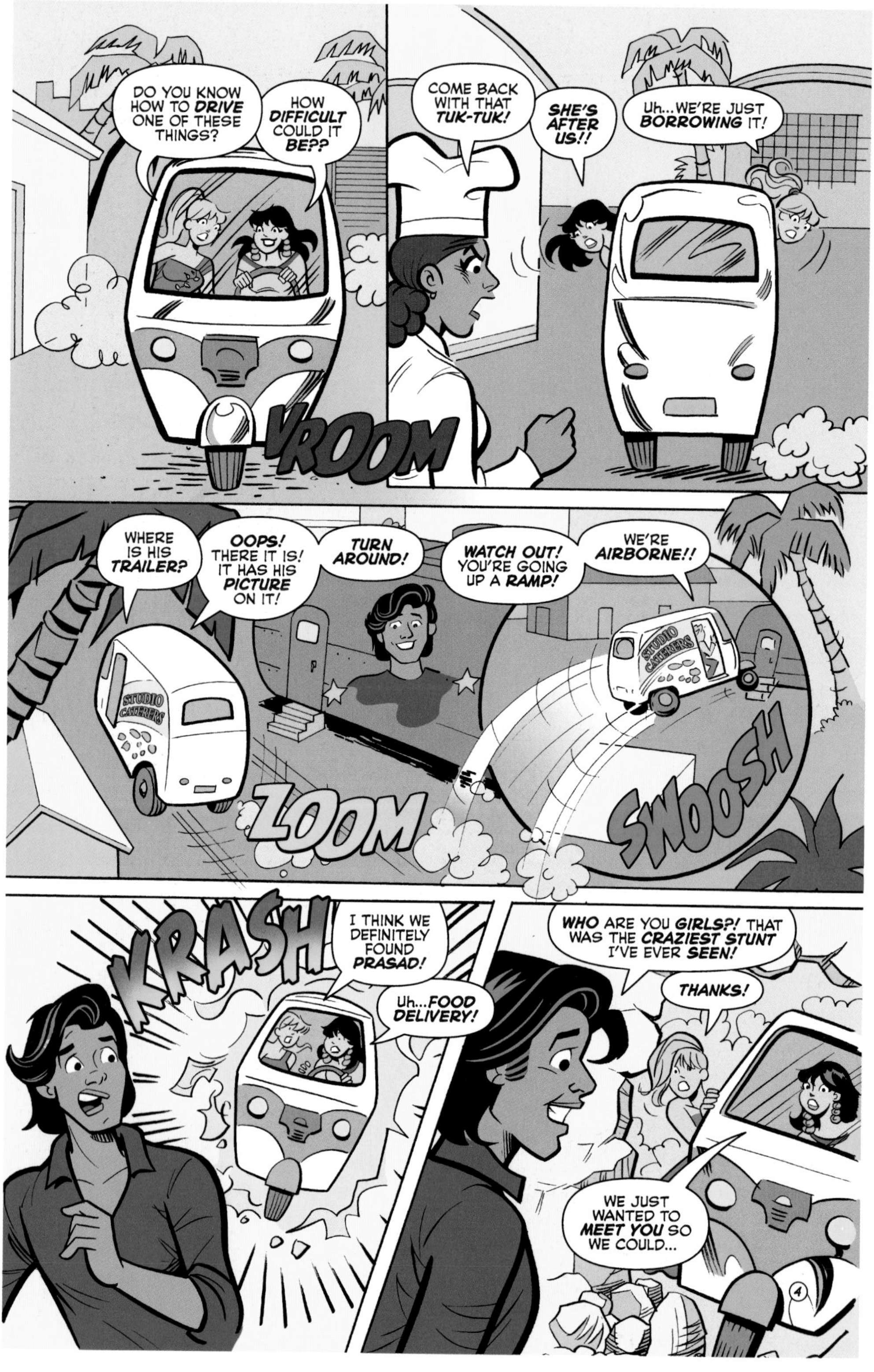

DO YOU KNOW HOW TO DRIVE ONE OF THESE THINGS?
HOW DIFFICULT COULD IT BE??
VROOM
COME BACK WITH THAT TUK-TUK!
SHE'S AFTER US!!
Uh...WE'RE JUST BORROWING IT!
WHERE IS HIS TRAILER?
OOPS! THERE IT IS! IT HAS HIS PICTURE ON IT!
TURN AROUND!
WATCH OUT! YOU'RE GOING UP A RAMP!
WE'RE AIRBORNE!!
STUDIO CATERERS
ZOOM
SWOOSH
KRASH
I THINK WE DEFINITELY FOUND PRASAD!
Uh...FOOD DELIVERY!
WHO ARE YOU GIRLS?! THAT WAS THE CRAZIEST STUNT I'VE EVER SEEN!
THANKS!
WE JUST WANTED TO MEET YOU SO WE COULD...

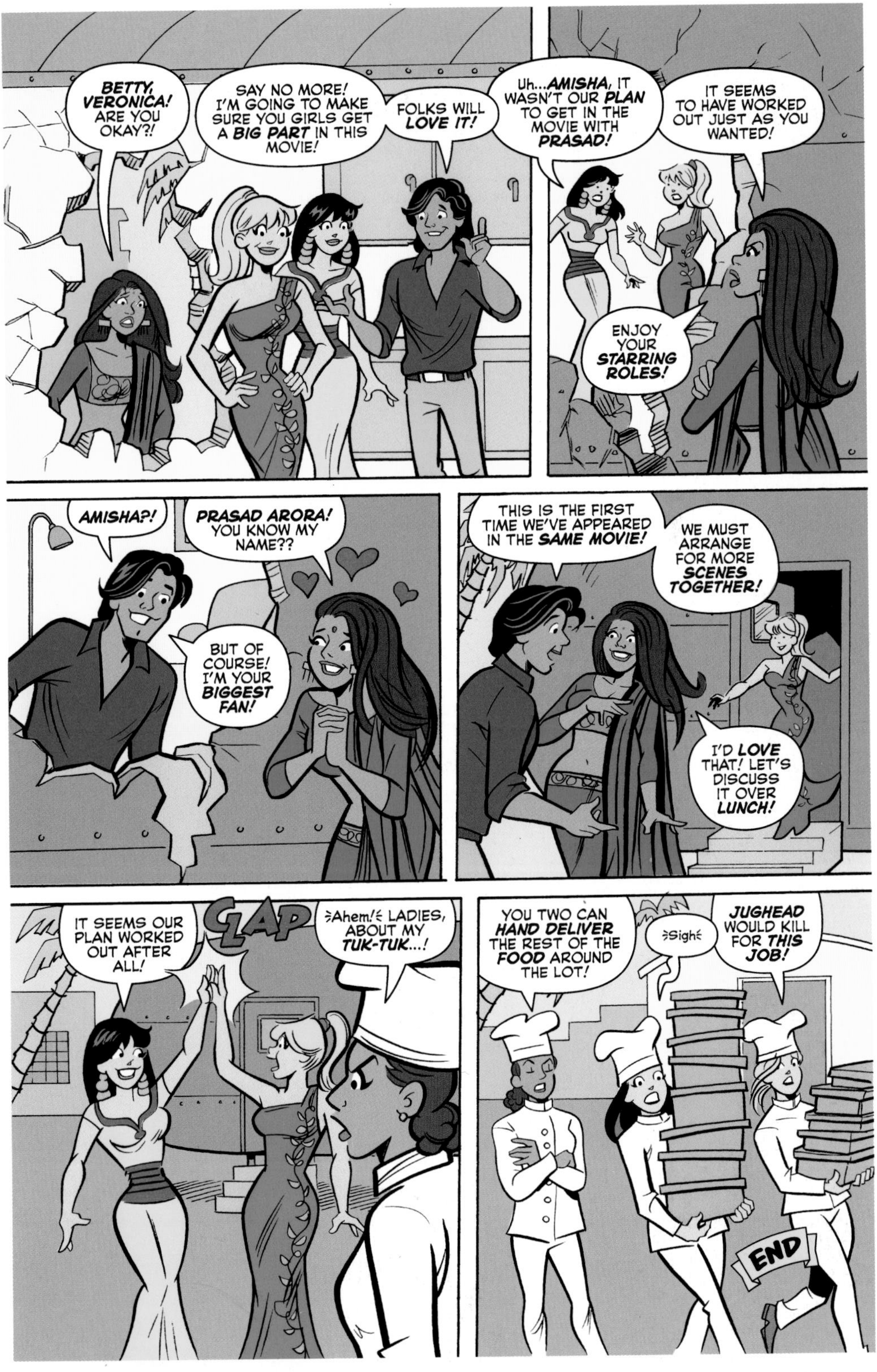
BETTY, VERONICA! ARE YOU OKAY?!
SAY NO MORE! I'M GOING TO MAKE SURE YOU GIRLS GET A BIG PART IN THIS MOVIE!
FOLKS WILL LOVE IT!
Uh...AMISHA, IT WASN'T OUR PLAN TO GET IN THE MOVIE WITH PRASAD!
IT SEEMS TO HAVE WORKED OUT JUST AS YOU WANTED!
ENJOY YOUR STARRING ROLES!
AMISHA?!
PRASAD ARORA! YOU KNOW MY NAME??
BUT OF COURSE! I'M YOUR BIGGEST FAN!
THIS IS THE FIRST TIME WE'VE APPEARED IN THE SAME MOVIE!
WE MUST ARRANGE FOR MORE SCENES TOGETHER!
I'D LOVE THAT! LET'S DISCUSS IT OVER LUNCH!
IT SEEMS OUR PLAN WORKED OUT AFTER ALL!
CLAP
Ahem! LADIES, ABOUT MY TUK-TUK...!
YOU TWO CAN HAND DELIVER THE REST OF THE FOOD AROUND THE LOT!
Sigh
JUGHEAD WOULD KILL FOR THIS JOB!
END

Archie in From India with Love!

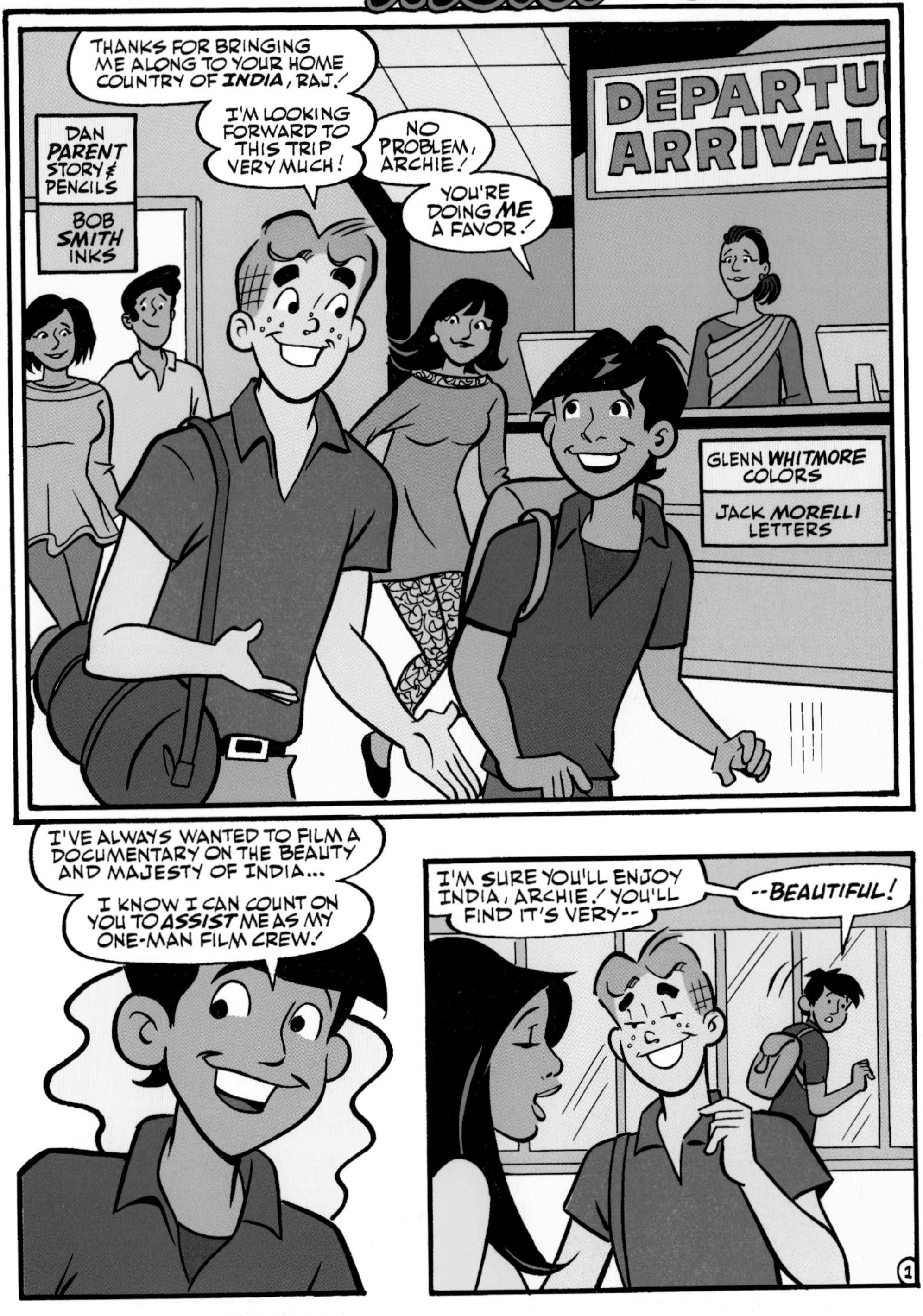

THANKS FOR BRINGING ME ALONG TO YOUR HOME COUNTRY OF INDIA, RAJ!
I'M LOOKING FORWARD TO THIS TRIP VERY MUCH!
NO PROBLEM, ARCHIE!
YOU'RE DOING ME A FAVOR!
DAN PARENT STORY & PENCILS
BOB SMITH INKS
DEPARTU
ARRIVALS
GLENN WHITMORE COLORS
JACK MORELLI LETTERS
I'VE ALWAYS WANTED TO FILM A DOCUMENTARY ON THE BEAUTY AND MAJESTY OF INDIA...
I KNOW I CAN COUNT ON YOU TO ASSIST ME AS MY ONE-MAN FILM CREW!
I'M SURE YOU'LL ENJOY INDIA, ARCHIE! YOU'LL FIND IT'S VERY--
--BEAUTIFUL!
1

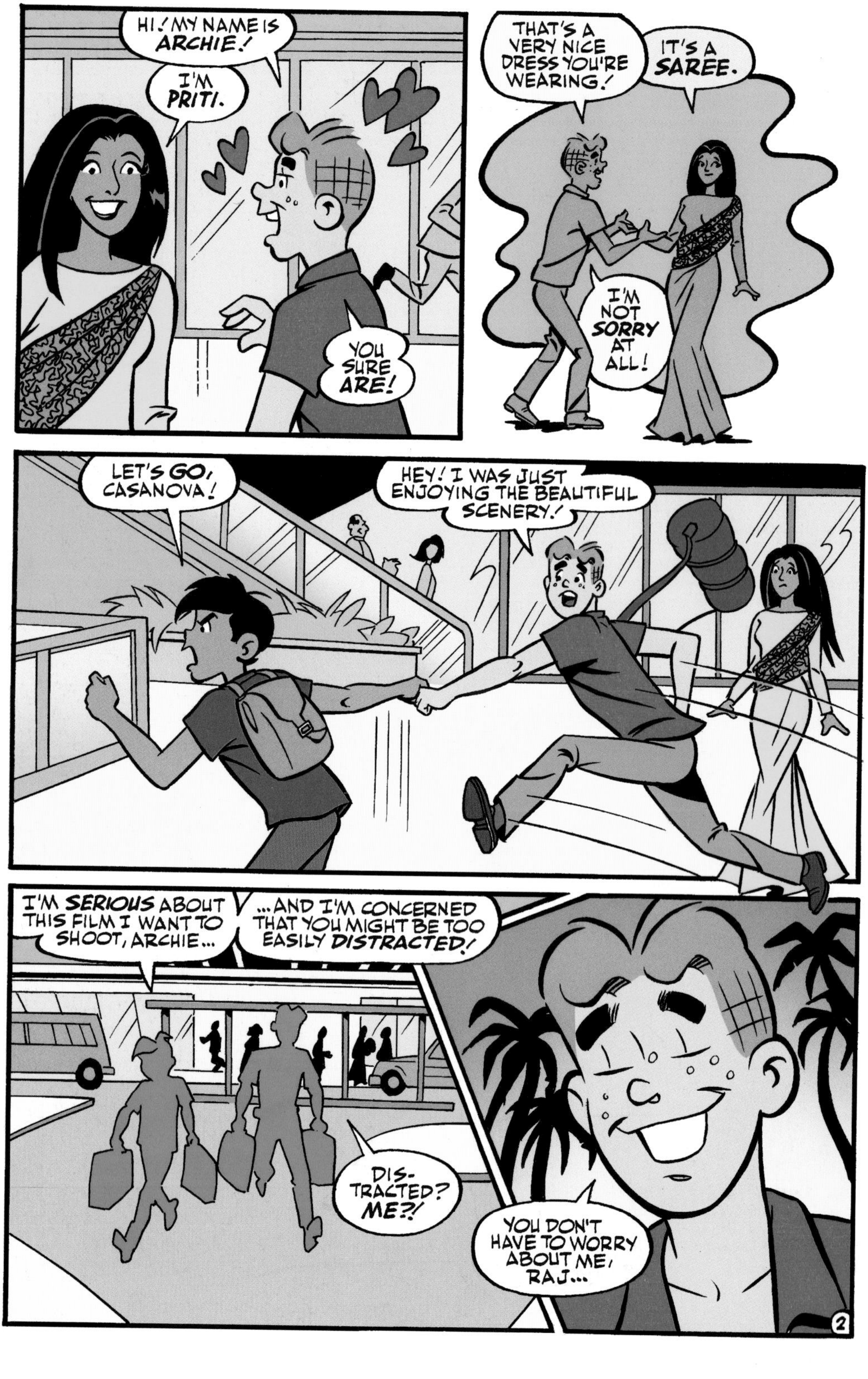
HI! MY NAME IS ARCHIE!
I'M PRITI.
YOU SURE ARE!
THAT'S A VERY NICE DRESS YOU'RE WEARING!
IT'S A SAREE.
I'M NOT SORRY AT ALL!
LET'S GO, CASANOVA!
HEY! I WAS JUST ENJOYING THE BEAUTIFUL SCENERY!
I'M SERIOUS ABOUT THIS FILM I WANT TO SHOOT, ARCHIE...
...AND I'M CONCERNED THAT YOU MIGHT BE TOO EASILY DISTRACTED!
DIS-TRACTED? ME?!
YOU DON'T HAVE TO WORRY ABOUT ME, RAJ...
2

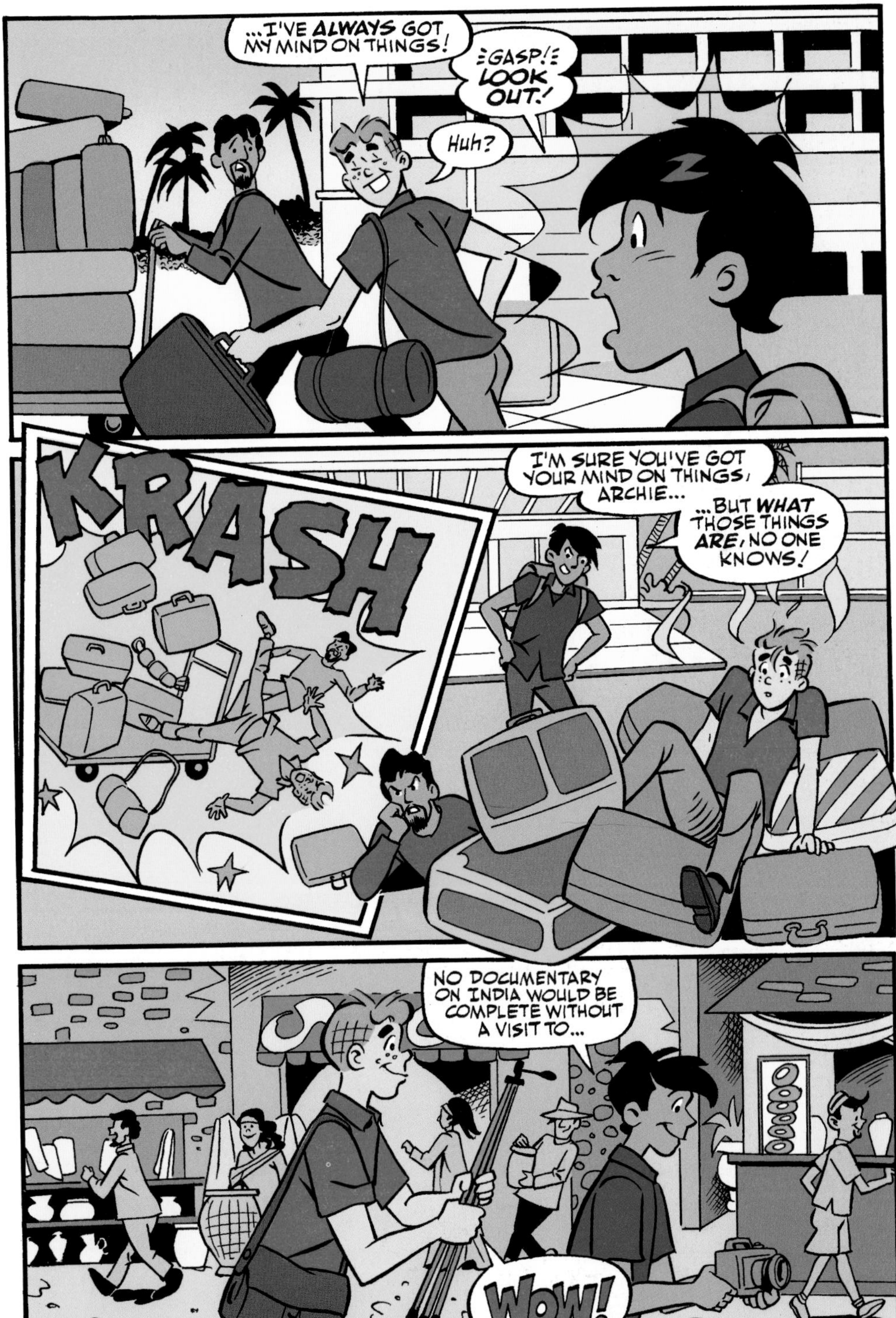
...I'VE ALWAYS GOT MY MIND ON THINGS!
GASP! LOOK OUT!
Huh?
KRASH
I'M SURE YOU'VE GOT YOUR MIND ON THINGS, ARCHIE...
...BUT WHAT THOSE THINGS ARE, NO ONE KNOWS!
NO DOCUMENTARY ON INDIA WOULD BE COMPLETE WITHOUT A VISIT TO...
WOW!
3

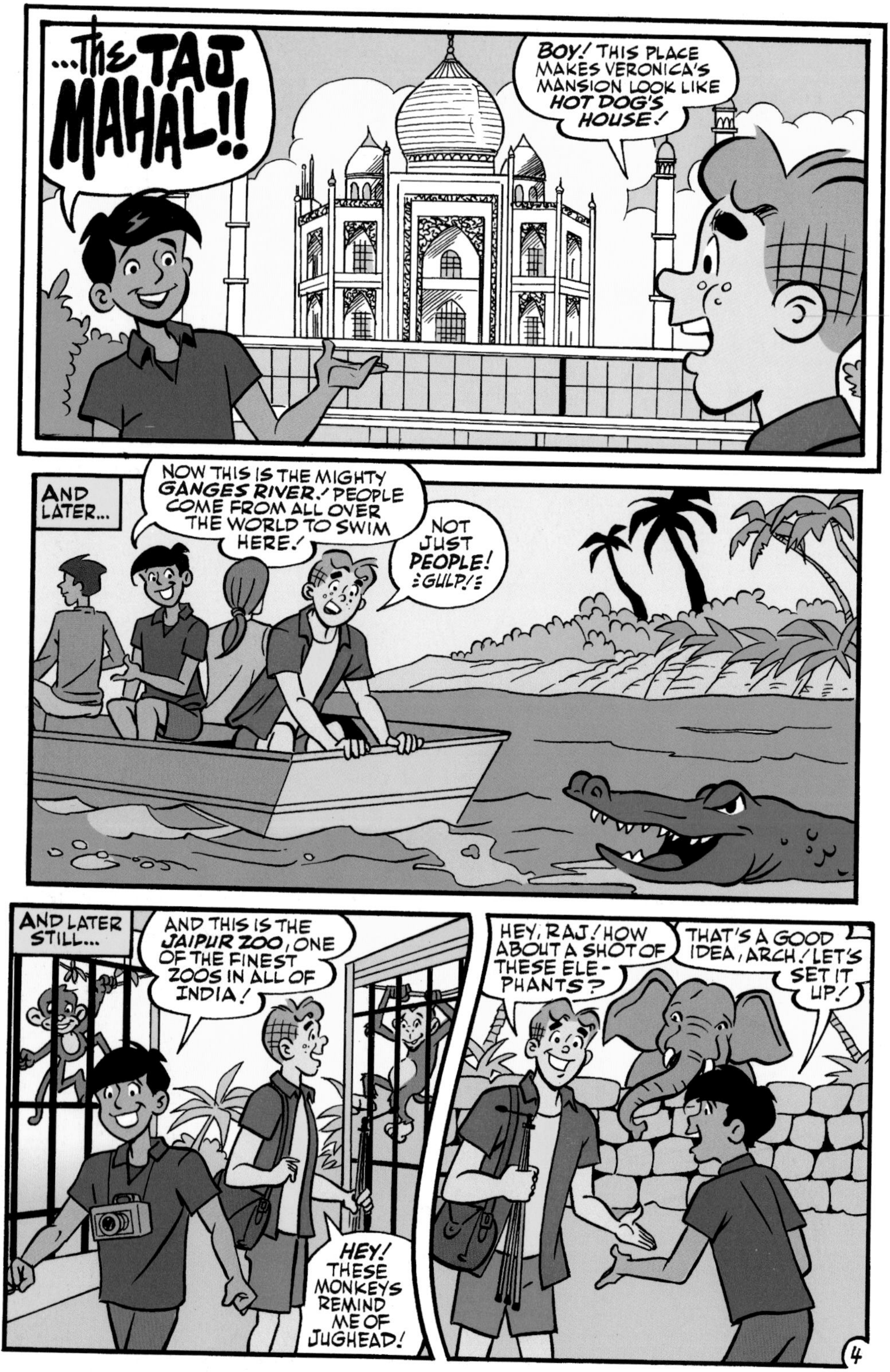
...THE TAJ MAHAL!!
BOY! THIS PLACE MAKES VERONICA'S MANSION LOOK LIKE HOT DOG'S HOUSE!
AND LATER...
NOW THIS IS THE MIGHTY GANGES RIVER! PEOPLE COME FROM ALL OVER THE WORLD TO SWIM HERE!
NOT JUST PEOPLE! GULP!
AND LATER STILL...
AND THIS IS THE JAIPUR ZOO, ONE OF THE FINEST ZOOS IN ALL OF INDIA!
HEY! THESE MONKEYS REMIND ME OF JUGHEAD!
HEY, RAJ! HOW ABOUT A SHOT OF THESE ELE-PHANTS?
THAT'S A GOOD IDEA, ARCH! LET'S SET IT UP!
4

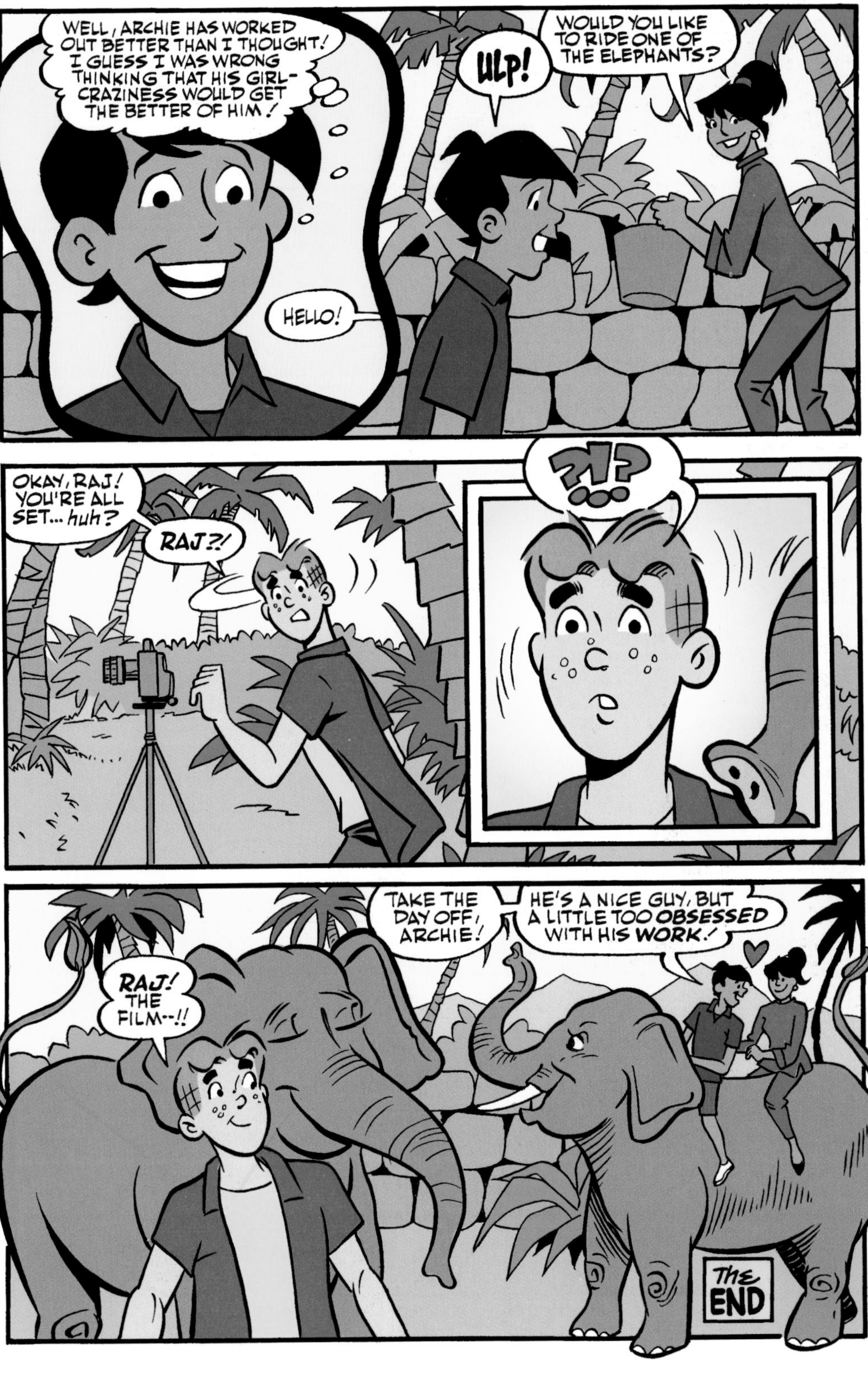
WELL, ARCHIE HAS WORKED OUT BETTER THAN I THOUGHT! I GUESS I WAS WRONG THINKING THAT HIS GIRL-CRAZINESS WOULD GET THE BETTER OF HIM!
HELLO!
ULP!
WOULD YOU LIKE TO RIDE ONE OF THE ELEPHANTS?
OKAY, RAJ! YOU'RE ALL SET... huh?
RAJ?!
?!?
RAJ! THE FILM--!!
TAKE THE DAY OFF, ARCHIE!
HE'S A NICE GUY, BUT A LITTLE TOO OBSESSED WITH HIS WORK!
THE END

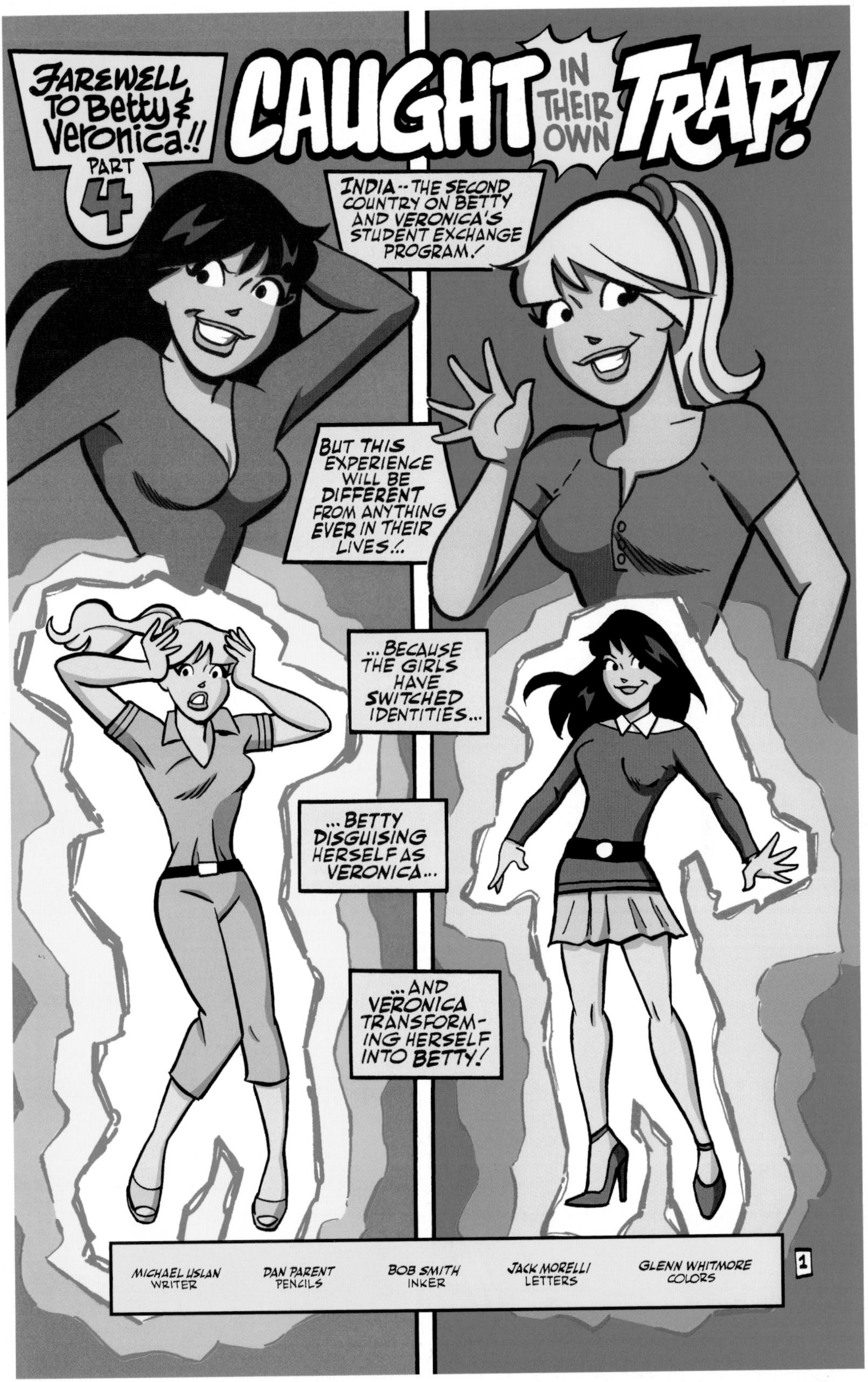

FAREWELL TO Betty & Veronica!! PART 4
CAUGHT IN THEIR OWN TRAP!
INDIA -- THE SECOND COUNTRY ON BETTY AND VERONICA'S STUDENT EXCHANGE PROGRAM!
BUT THIS EXPERIENCE WILL BE DIFFERENT FROM ANYTHING EVER IN THEIR LIVES...
...BECAUSE THE GIRLS HAVE SWITCHED IDENTITIES...
...BETTY DISGUISING HERSELF AS VERONICA...
...AND VERONICA TRANSFORMING HERSELF INTO BETTY!
MICHAEL USLAN WRITER
DAN PARENT PENCILS
BOB SMITH INKER
JACK MORELLI LETTERS
GLENN WHITMORE COLORS
1

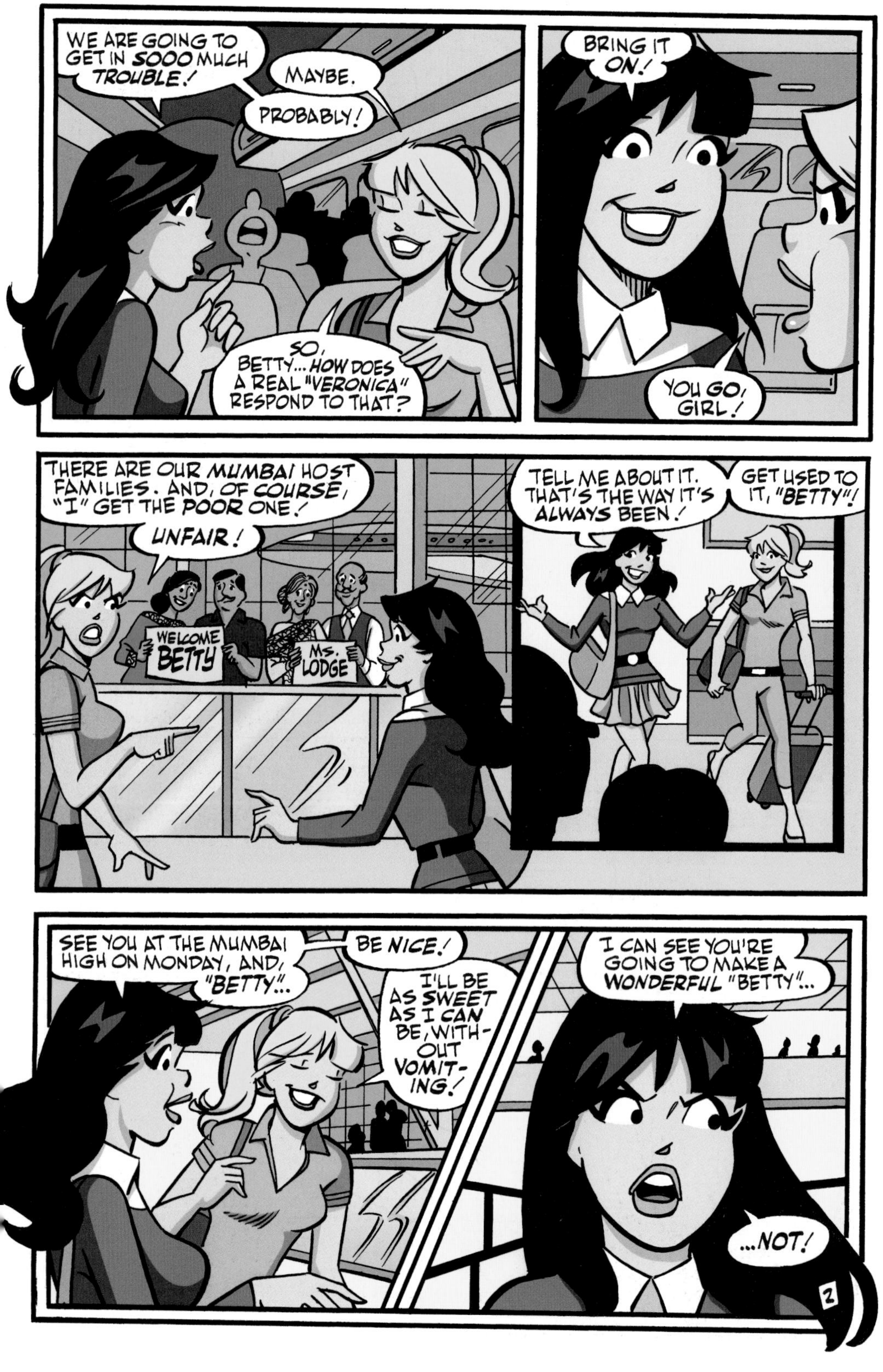
WE ARE GOING TO GET IN SOOO MUCH TROUBLE!
MAYBE.
PROBABLY!
SO, BETTY... HOW DOES A REAL "VERONICA" RESPOND TO THAT?
BRING IT ON!
YOU GO, GIRL!
THERE ARE OUR MUMBAI HOST FAMILIES. AND, OF COURSE, "I" GET THE POOR ONE!
UNFAIR!
WELCOME BETTY
MS. LODGE
TELL ME ABOUT IT. THAT'S THE WAY IT'S ALWAYS BEEN!
GET USED TO IT, "BETTY"!
SEE YOU AT THE MUMBAI HIGH ON MONDAY, AND, "BETTY"...
BE NICE!
I'LL BE AS SWEET AS I CAN BE, WITH-OUT VOMIT-ING!
I CAN SEE YOU'RE GOING TO MAKE A WONDERFUL "BETTY"...
...NOT!
2

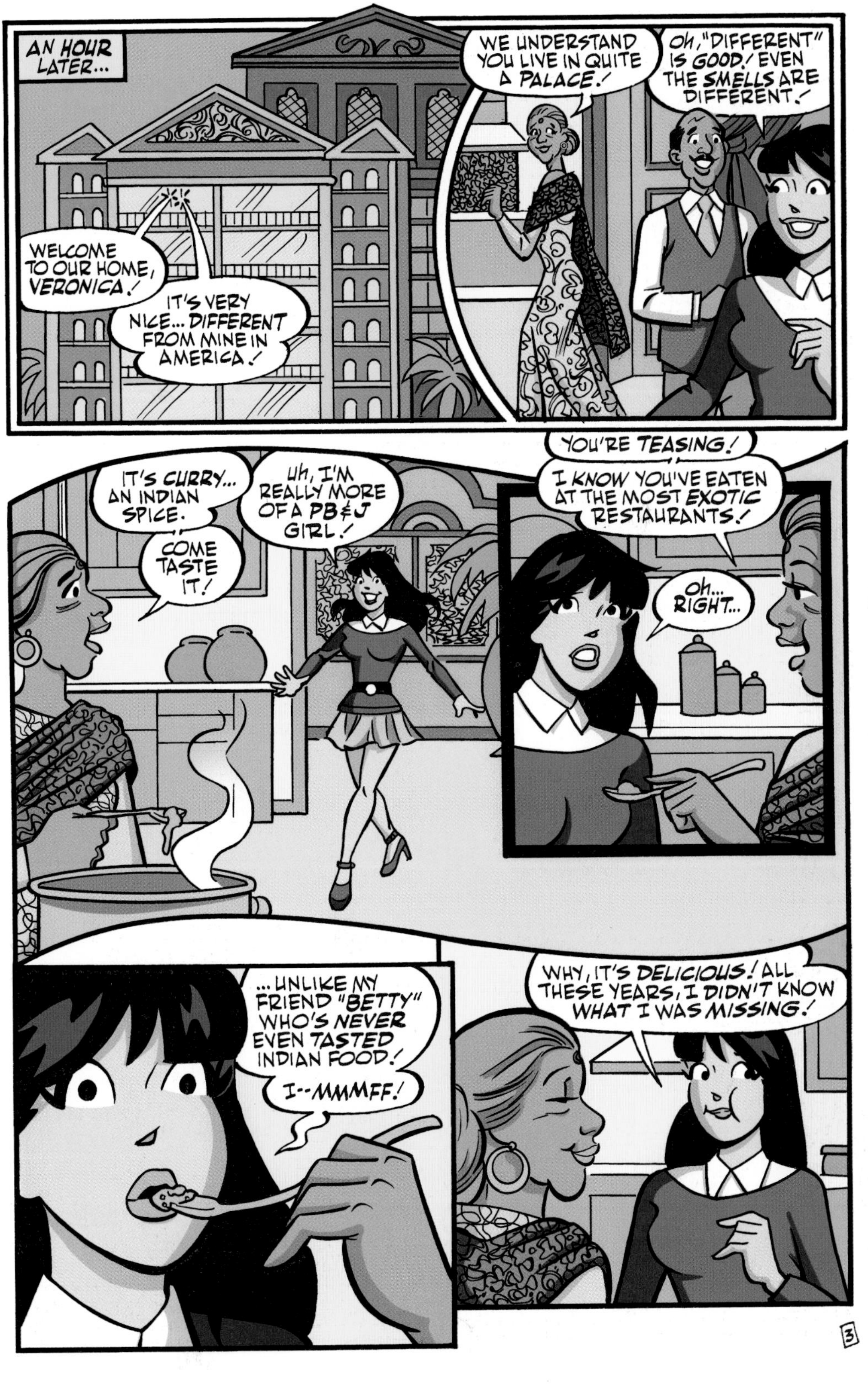

AN HOUR LATER...
WELCOME TO OUR HOME, VERONICA!
IT'S VERY NICE... DIFFERENT FROM MINE IN AMERICA!
WE UNDERSTAND YOU LIVE IN QUITE A PALACE!
Oh, "DIFFERENT" IS GOOD! EVEN THE SMELLS ARE DIFFERENT!
IT'S CURRY... AN INDIAN SPICE.
COME TASTE IT!
Uh, I'M REALLY MORE OF A PB&J GIRL!
YOU'RE TEASING!
I KNOW YOU'VE EATEN AT THE MOST EXOTIC RESTAURANTS!
Oh... RIGHT...
...UNLIKE MY FRIEND "BETTY" WHO'S NEVER EVEN TASTED INDIAN FOOD!
I--MMMFF!
WHY, IT'S DELICIOUS! ALL THESE YEARS, I DIDN'T KNOW WHAT I WAS MISSING!
3

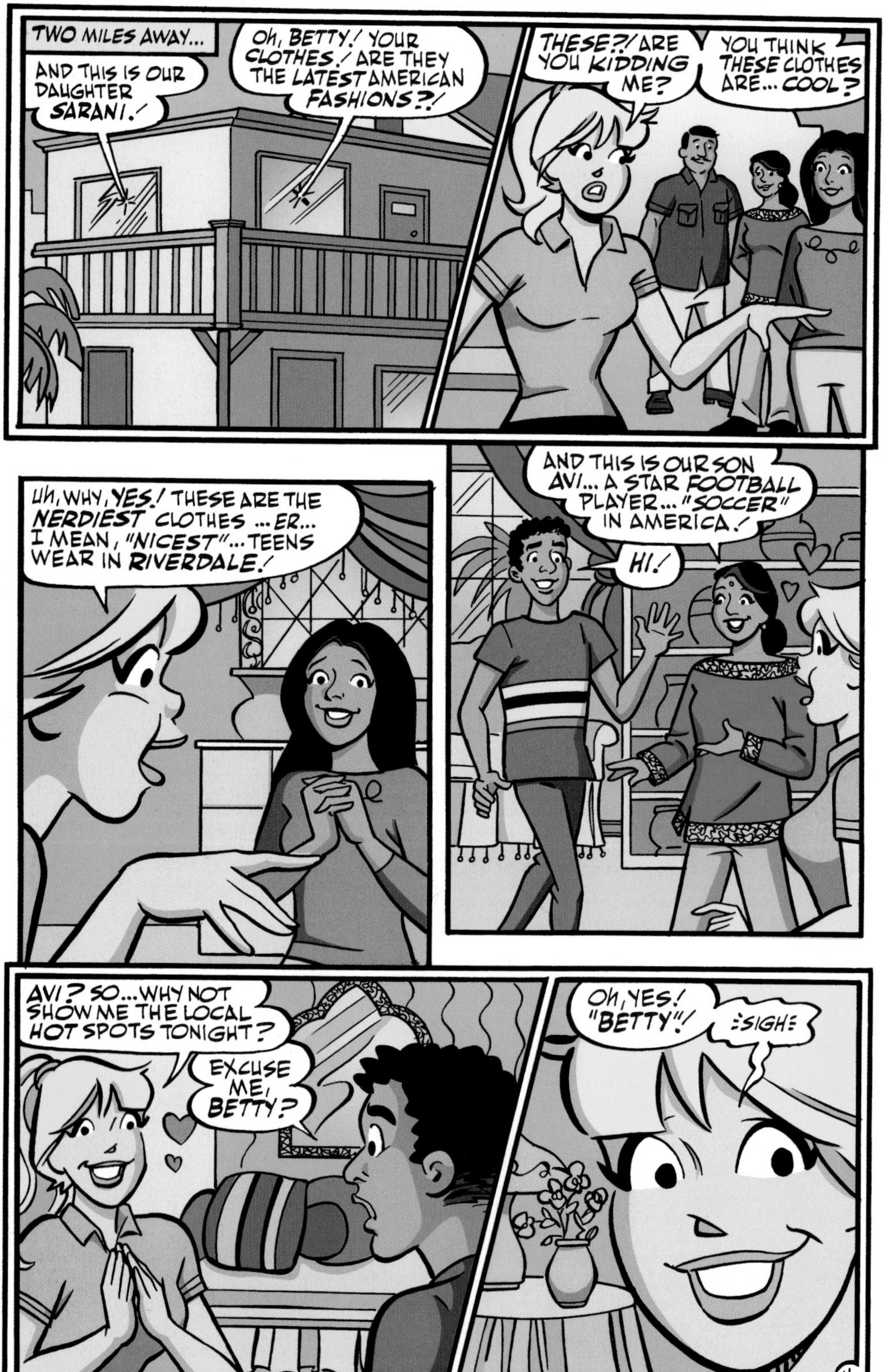
TWO MILES AWAY...
AND THIS IS OUR DAUGHTER SARANI!
OH, BETTY! YOUR CLOTHES! ARE THEY THE LATEST AMERICAN FASHIONS?!
THESE?! ARE YOU KIDDING ME?
YOU THINK THESE CLOTHES ARE... COOL?
UH, WHY, YES! THESE ARE THE NERDIEST CLOTHES ...ER... I MEAN, "NICEST"... TEENS WEAR IN RIVERDALE!
AND THIS IS OUR SON AVI... A STAR FOOTBALL PLAYER... "SOCCER" IN AMERICA!
HI!
AVI? SO...WHY NOT SHOW ME THE LOCAL HOT SPOTS TONIGHT?
EXCUSE ME, BETTY?
OH, YES! "BETTY"!
SIGH
4

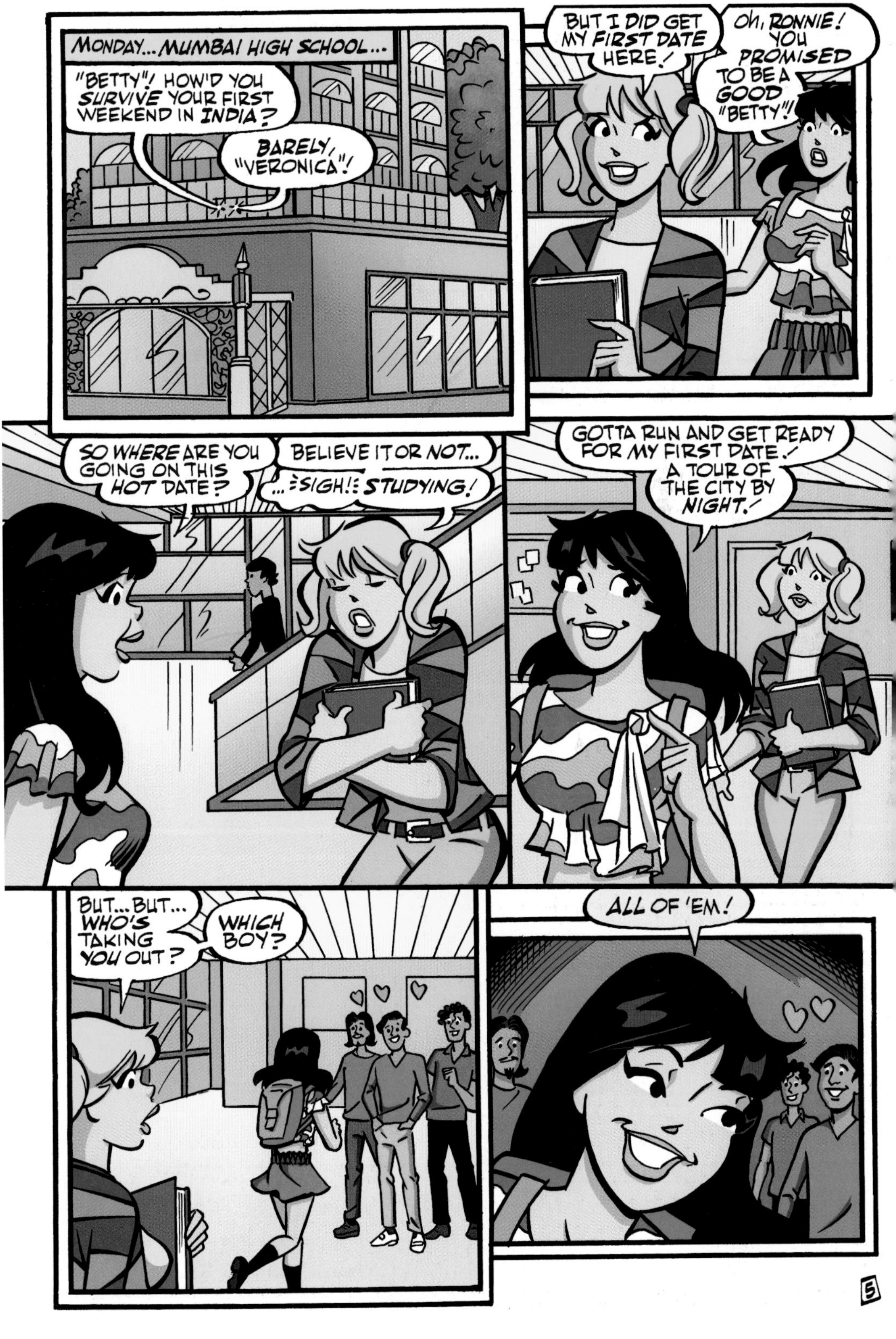
MONDAY... MUMBAI HIGH SCHOOL...
"BETTY"! HOW'D YOU SURVIVE YOUR FIRST WEEKEND IN INDIA?
BARELY, "VERONICA"!
BUT I DID GET MY FIRST DATE HERE!
Oh, RONNIE! YOU PROMISED TO BE A GOOD "BETTY"!
SO WHERE ARE YOU GOING ON THIS HOT DATE?
BELIEVE IT OR NOT... ...SIGH! STUDYING!
GOTTA RUN AND GET READY FOR MY FIRST DATE!
A TOUR OF THE CITY BY NIGHT!
BUT... BUT... WHO'S TAKING YOU OUT?
WHICH BOY?
ALL OF 'EM!
5

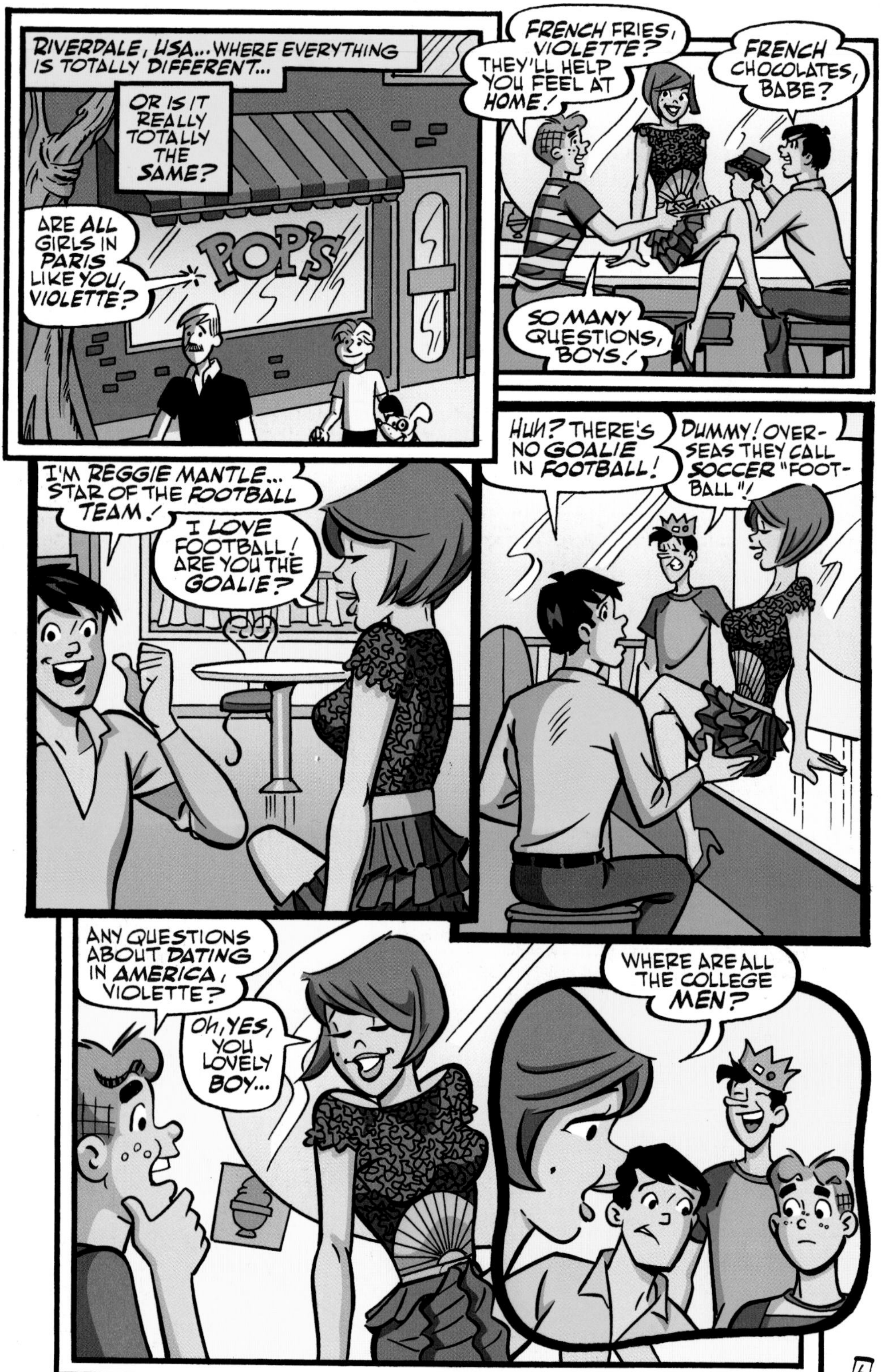
RIVERDALE, USA... WHERE EVERYTHING IS TOTALLY DIFFERENT...
OR IS IT REALLY TOTALLY THE SAME?
ARE ALL GIRLS IN PARIS LIKE YOU, VIOLETTE?
POP'S
FRENCH FRIES, VIOLETTE? THEY'LL HELP YOU FEEL AT HOME!
FRENCH CHOCOLATES, BABE?
SO MANY QUESTIONS, BOYS!
I'M REGGIE MANTLE... STAR OF THE FOOTBALL TEAM!
I LOVE FOOTBALL! ARE YOU THE GOALIE?
HUH? THERE'S NO GOALIE IN FOOTBALL!
DUMMY! OVER-SEAS THEY CALL SOCCER "FOOT-BALL"!
ANY QUESTIONS ABOUT DATING IN AMERICA, VIOLETTE?
OH, YES, YOU LOVELY BOY...
WHERE ARE ALL THE COLLEGE MEN?
6

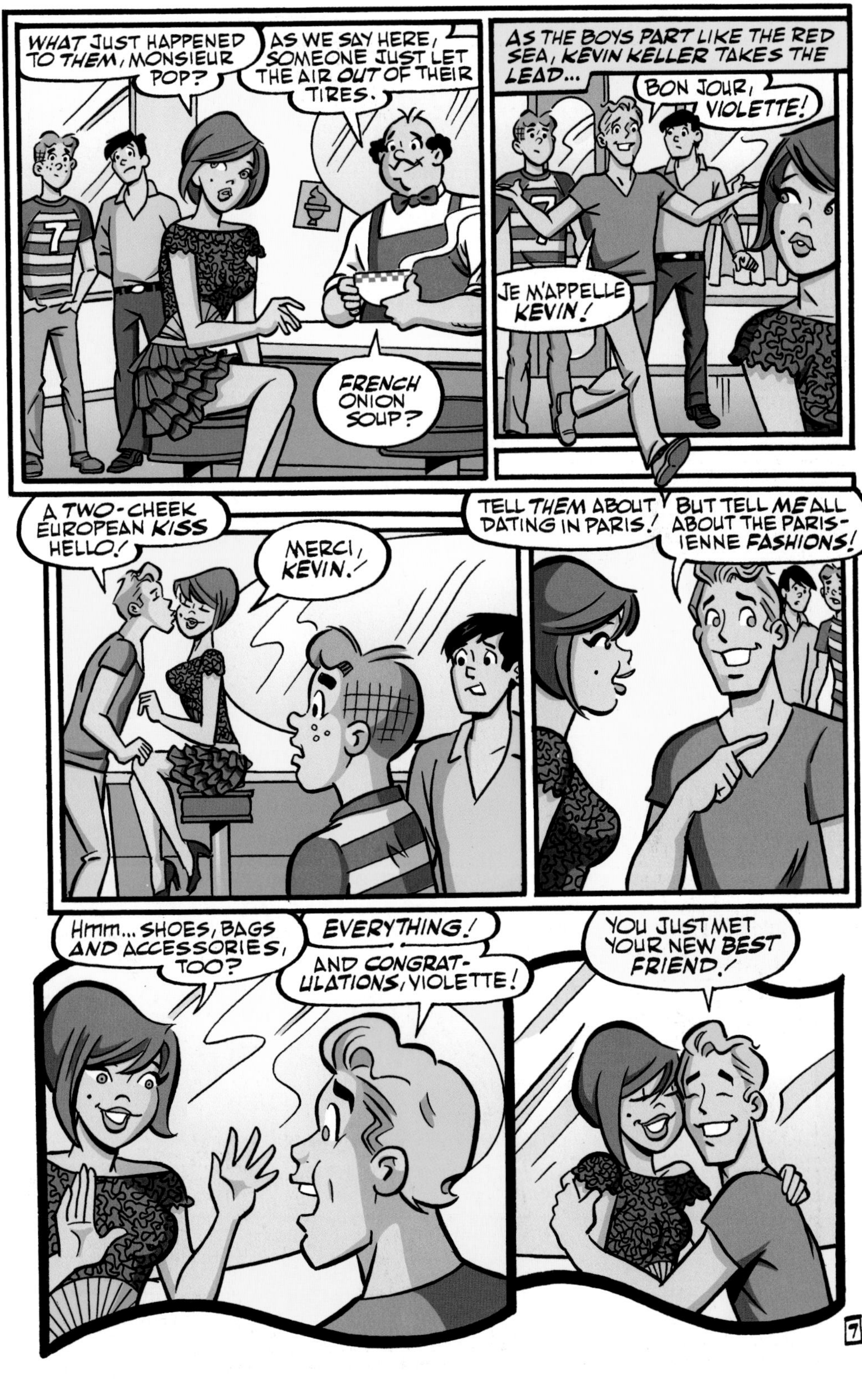

WHAT JUST HAPPENED TO THEM, MONSIEUR POP?
AS WE SAY HERE, SOMEONE JUST LET THE AIR OUT OF THEIR TIRES.
FRENCH ONION SOUP?
AS THE BOYS PART LIKE THE RED SEA, KEVIN KELLER TAKES THE LEAD...
BON JOUR, VIOLETTE!
JE M'APPELLE KEVIN!
A TWO-CHEEK EUROPEAN KISS HELLO!
MERCI, KEVIN.
TELL THEM ABOUT DATING IN PARIS!
BUT TELL ME ALL ABOUT THE PARIS-IENNE FASHIONS!
Hmm... SHOES, BAGS AND ACCESSORIES, TOO?
EVERYTHING!
AND CONGRAT-ULATIONS, VIOLETTE!
YOU JUST MET YOUR NEW BEST FRIEND!
7

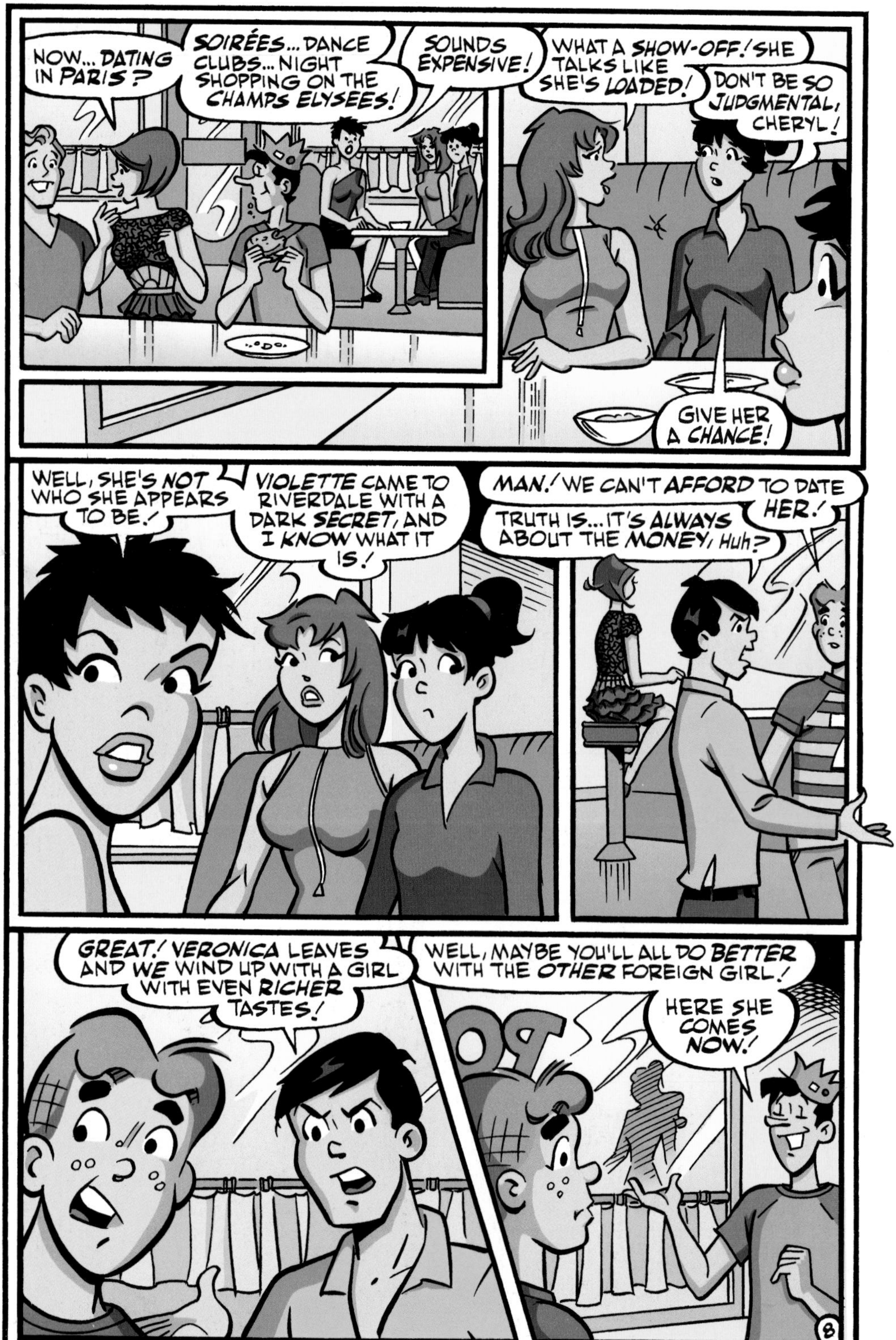
NOW... DATING IN PARIS?
SOIRÉES... DANCE CLUBS... NIGHT SHOPPING ON THE CHAMPS ELYSEES!
SOUNDS EXPENSIVE!
WHAT A SHOW-OFF! SHE TALKS LIKE SHE'S LOADED!
DON'T BE SO JUDGMENTAL, CHERYL!
GIVE HER A CHANCE!
WELL, SHE'S NOT WHO SHE APPEARS TO BE!
VIOLETTE CAME TO RIVERDALE WITH A DARK SECRET, AND I KNOW WHAT IT IS!
MAN! WE CAN'T AFFORD TO DATE HER!
TRUTH IS... IT'S ALWAYS ABOUT THE MONEY, Huh?
GREAT! VERONICA LEAVES AND WE WIND UP WITH A GIRL WITH EVEN RICHER TASTES!
WELL, MAYBE YOU'LL ALL DO BETTER WITH THE OTHER FOREIGN GIRL!
HERE SHE COMES NOW!
8

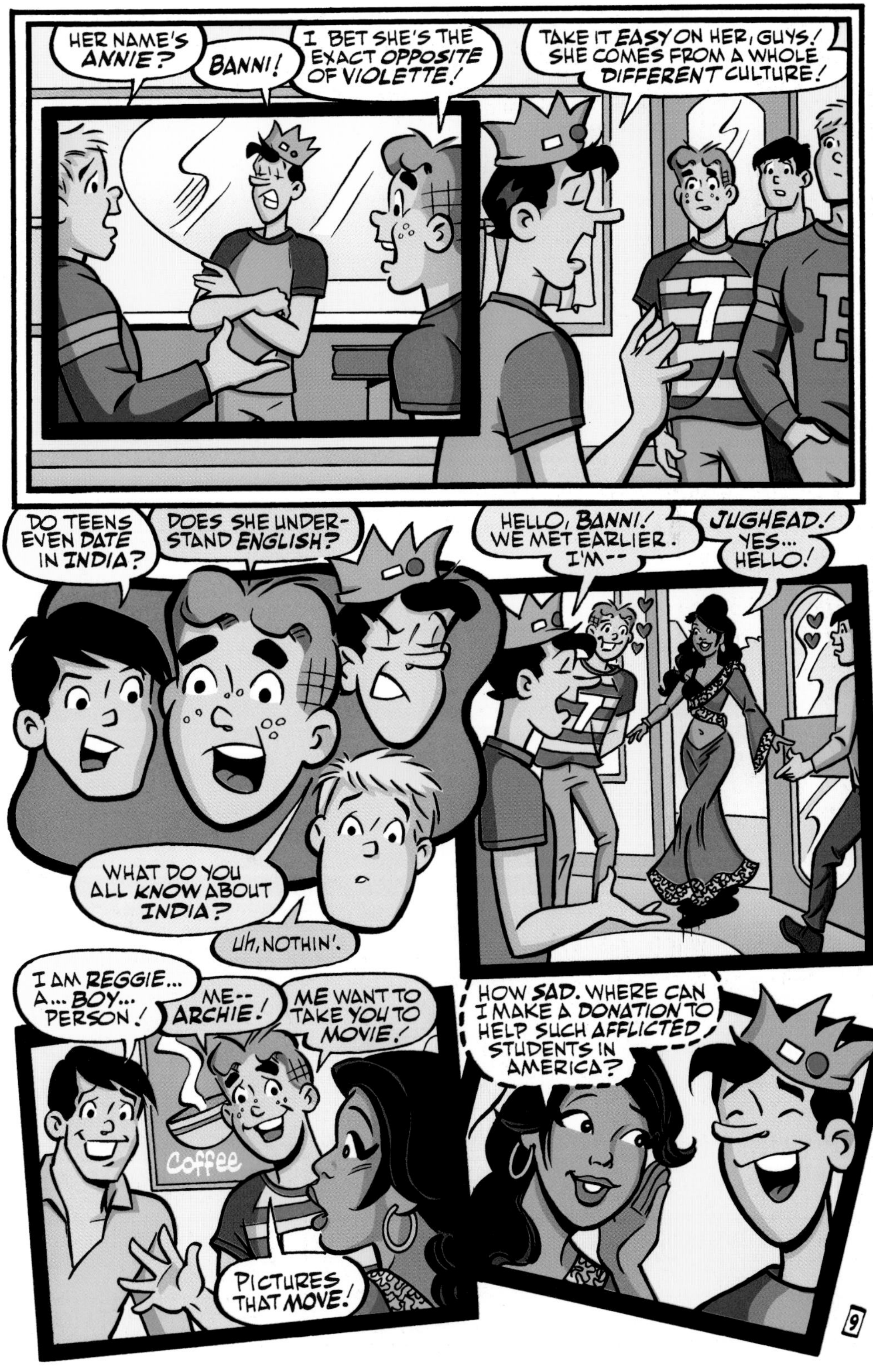

HER NAME'S ANNIE?
BANNI!
I BET SHE'S THE EXACT OPPOSITE OF VIOLETTE!
TAKE IT EASY ON HER, GUYS! SHE COMES FROM A WHOLE DIFFERENT CULTURE!
DO TEENS EVEN DATE IN INDIA?
DOES SHE UNDER-STAND ENGLISH?
WHAT DO YOU ALL KNOW ABOUT INDIA?
UH, NOTHIN'.
HELLO, BANNI! WE MET EARLIER. I'M--
JUGHEAD! YES... HELLO!
I AM REGGIE... A... BOY... PERSON!
ME-- ARCHIE!
ME WANT TO TAKE YOU TO MOVIE!
Coffee
PICTURES THAT MOVE!
HOW SAD. WHERE CAN I MAKE A DONATION TO HELP SUCH AFFLICTED STUDENTS IN AMERICA?
9

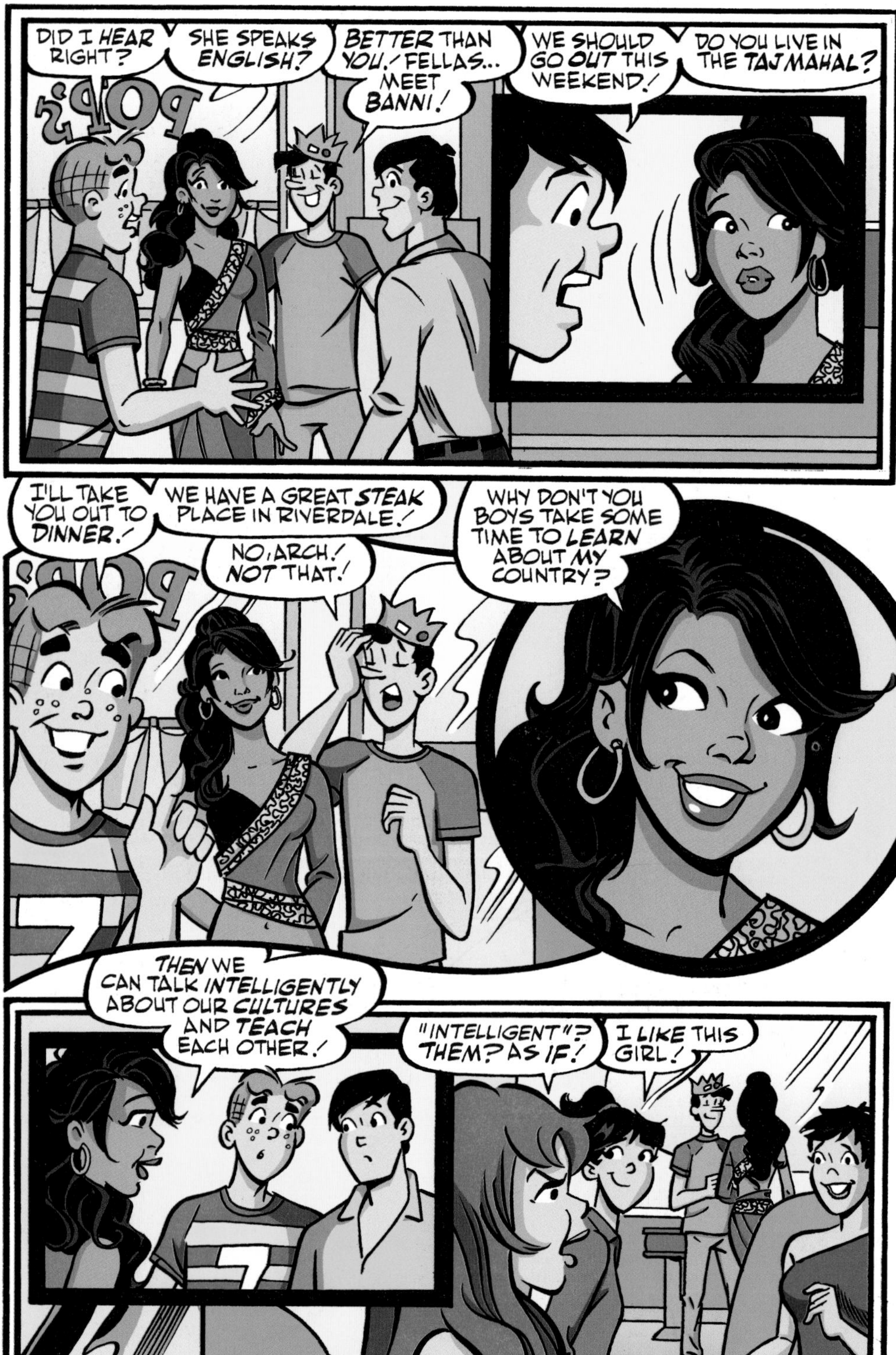
DID I HEAR RIGHT?
SHE SPEAKS ENGLISH?
BETTER THAN YOU! FELLAS... MEET BANNI!
WE SHOULD GO OUT THIS WEEKEND!
DO YOU LIVE IN THE TAJ MAHAL?
POP'S
I'LL TAKE YOU OUT TO DINNER!
WE HAVE A GREAT STEAK PLACE IN RIVERDALE!
NO, ARCH! NOT THAT!
WHY DON'T YOU BOYS TAKE SOME TIME TO LEARN ABOUT MY COUNTRY?
THEN WE CAN TALK INTELLIGENTLY ABOUT OUR CULTURES AND TEACH EACH OTHER!
"INTELLIGENT"? THEM? AS IF!
I LIKE THIS GIRL!
10

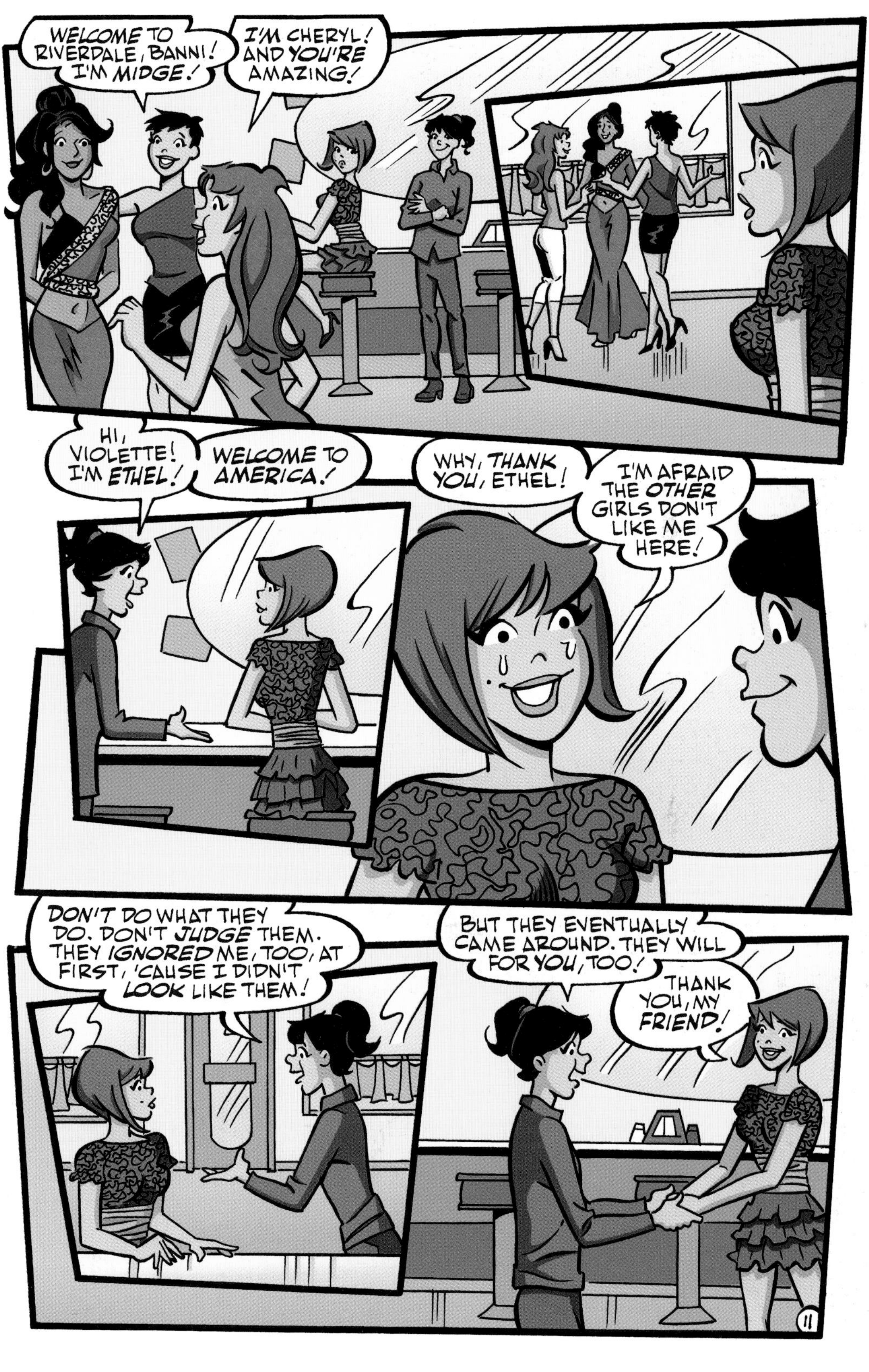
WELCOME TO RIVERDALE, BANNI! I'M MIDGE!
I'M CHERYL! AND YOU'RE AMAZING!
HI, VIOLETTE! I'M ETHEL!
WELCOME TO AMERICA!
WHY, THANK YOU, ETHEL!
I'M AFRAID THE OTHER GIRLS DON'T LIKE ME HERE!
DON'T DO WHAT THEY DO. DON'T JUDGE THEM. THEY IGNORED ME, TOO, AT FIRST, 'CAUSE I DIDN'T LOOK LIKE THEM!
BUT THEY EVENTUALLY CAME AROUND. THEY WILL FOR YOU, TOO!
THANK YOU, MY FRIEND!
11

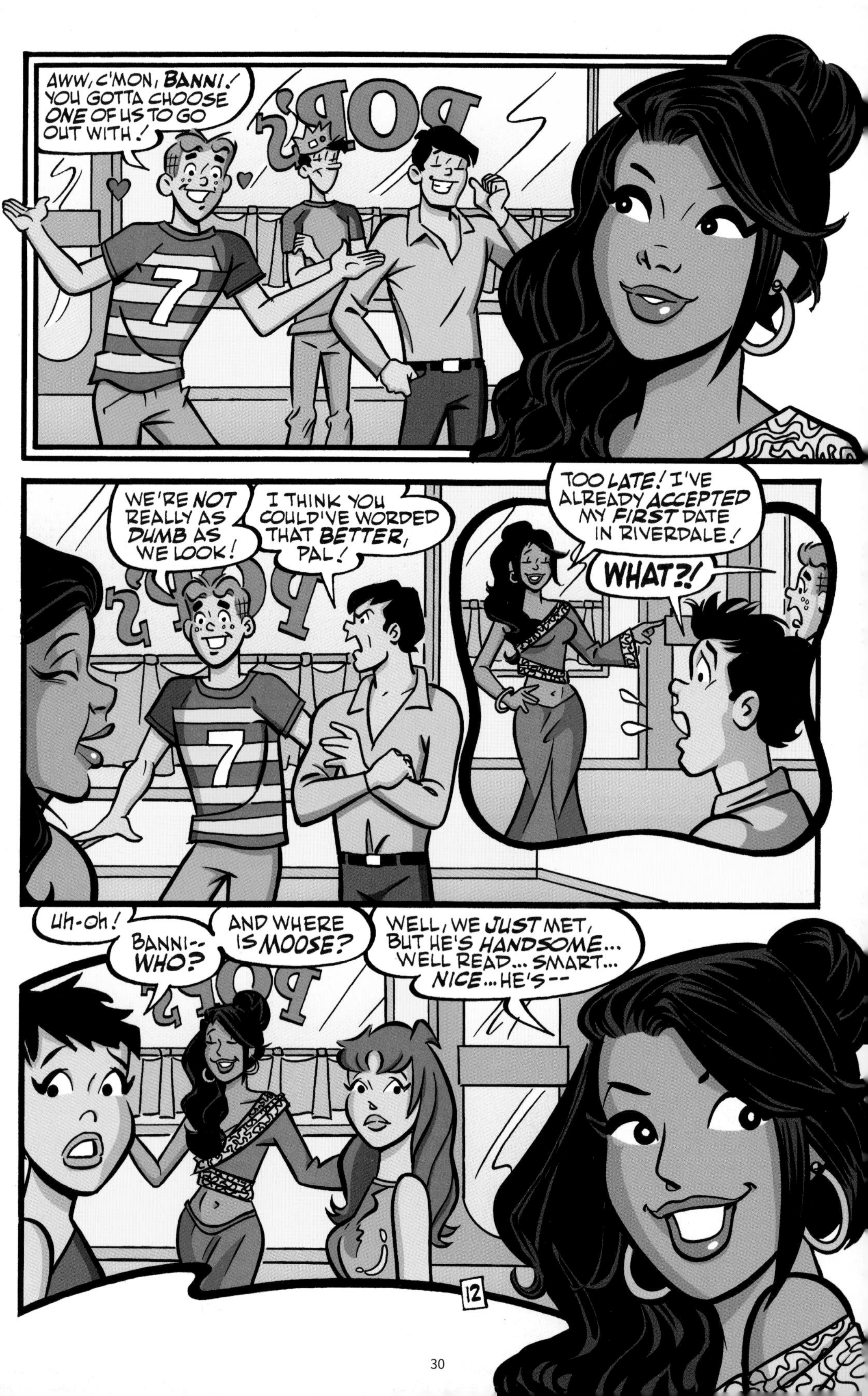
AWW, C'MON, BANNI! YOU GOTTA CHOOSE ONE OF US TO GO OUT WITH!
POP'S
WE'RE NOT REALLY AS DUMB AS WE LOOK!
I THINK YOU COULD'VE WORDED THAT BETTER, PAL!
TOO LATE! I'VE ALREADY ACCEPTED MY FIRST DATE IN RIVERDALE!
WHAT?!
Uh-oh!
BANNI-- WHO?
AND WHERE IS MOOSE?
WELL, WE JUST MET, BUT HE'S HANDSOME... WELL READ... SMART... NICE... HE'S--
12

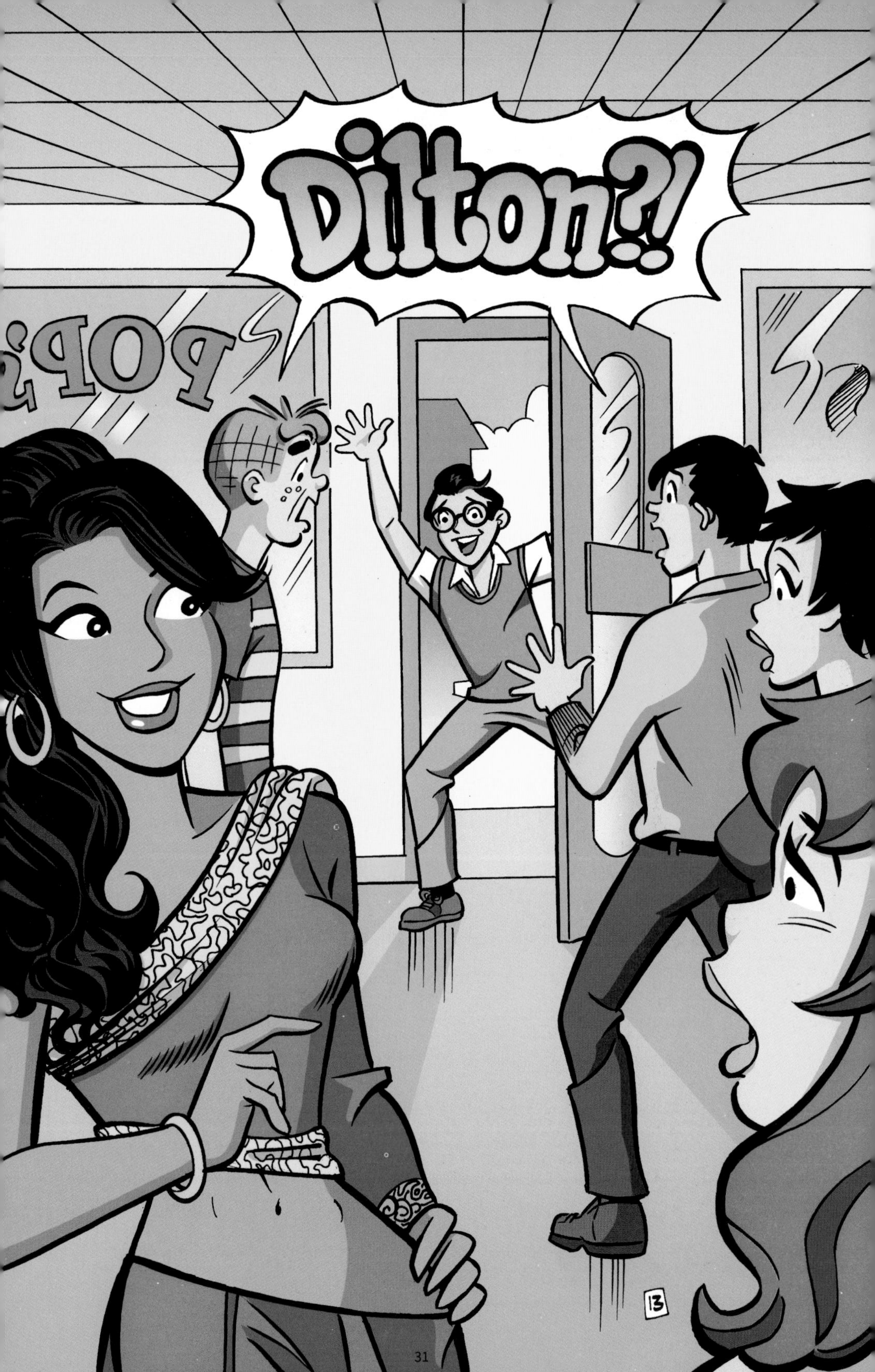
DILTON?!
POP'S
13

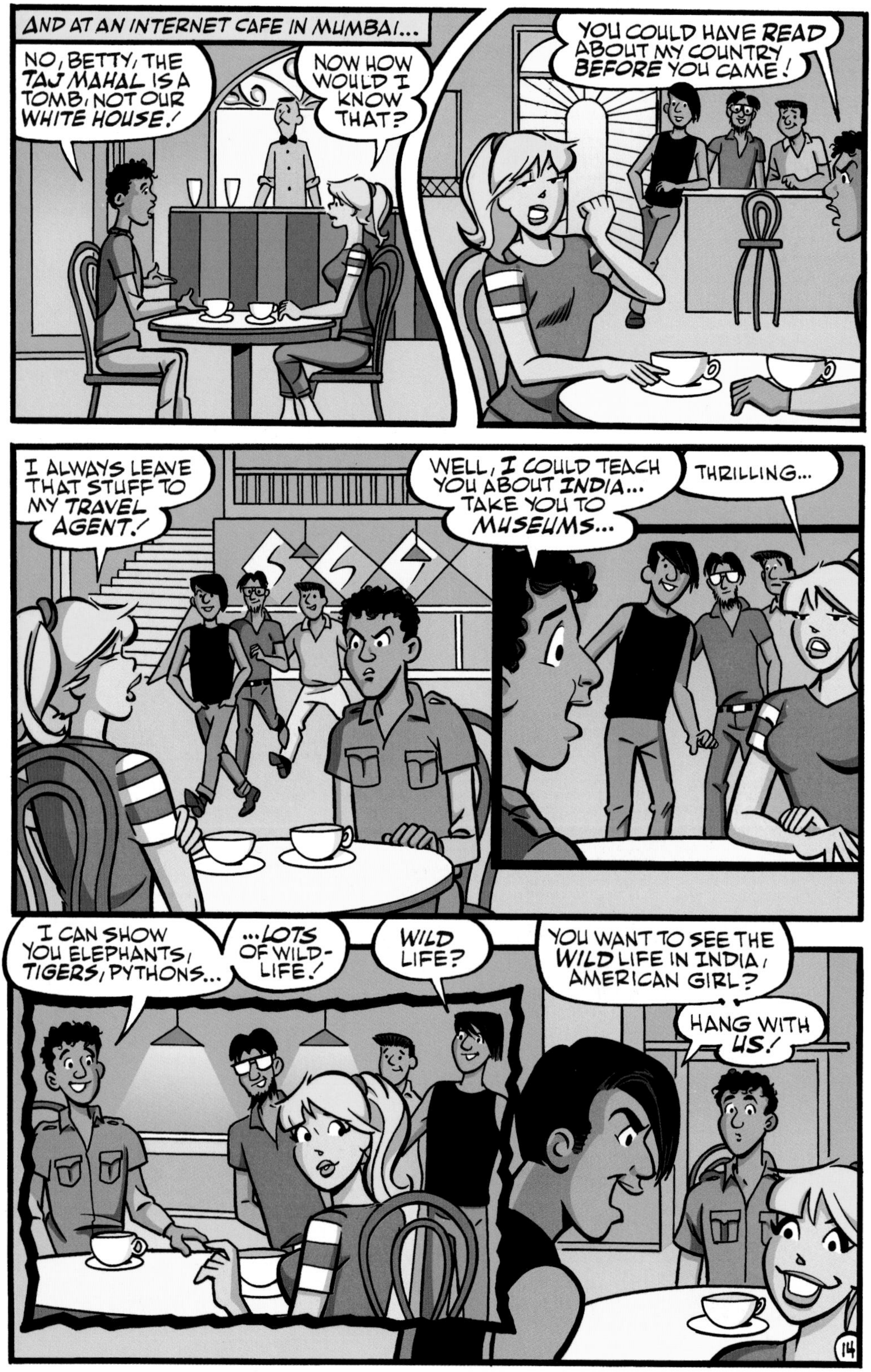
AND AT AN INTERNET CAFE IN MUMBAI...
NO, BETTY, THE TAJ MAHAL IS A TOMB, NOT OUR WHITE HOUSE!
NOW HOW WOULD I KNOW THAT?
YOU COULD HAVE READ ABOUT MY COUNTRY BEFORE YOU CAME!
I ALWAYS LEAVE THAT STUFF TO MY TRAVEL AGENT!
WELL, I COULD TEACH YOU ABOUT INDIA... TAKE YOU TO MUSEUMS...
THRILLING...
I CAN SHOW YOU ELEPHANTS, TIGERS, PYTHONS...
...LOTS OF WILD-LIFE!
WILD LIFE?
YOU WANT TO SEE THE WILD LIFE IN INDIA, AMERICAN GIRL?
HANG WITH US!
14

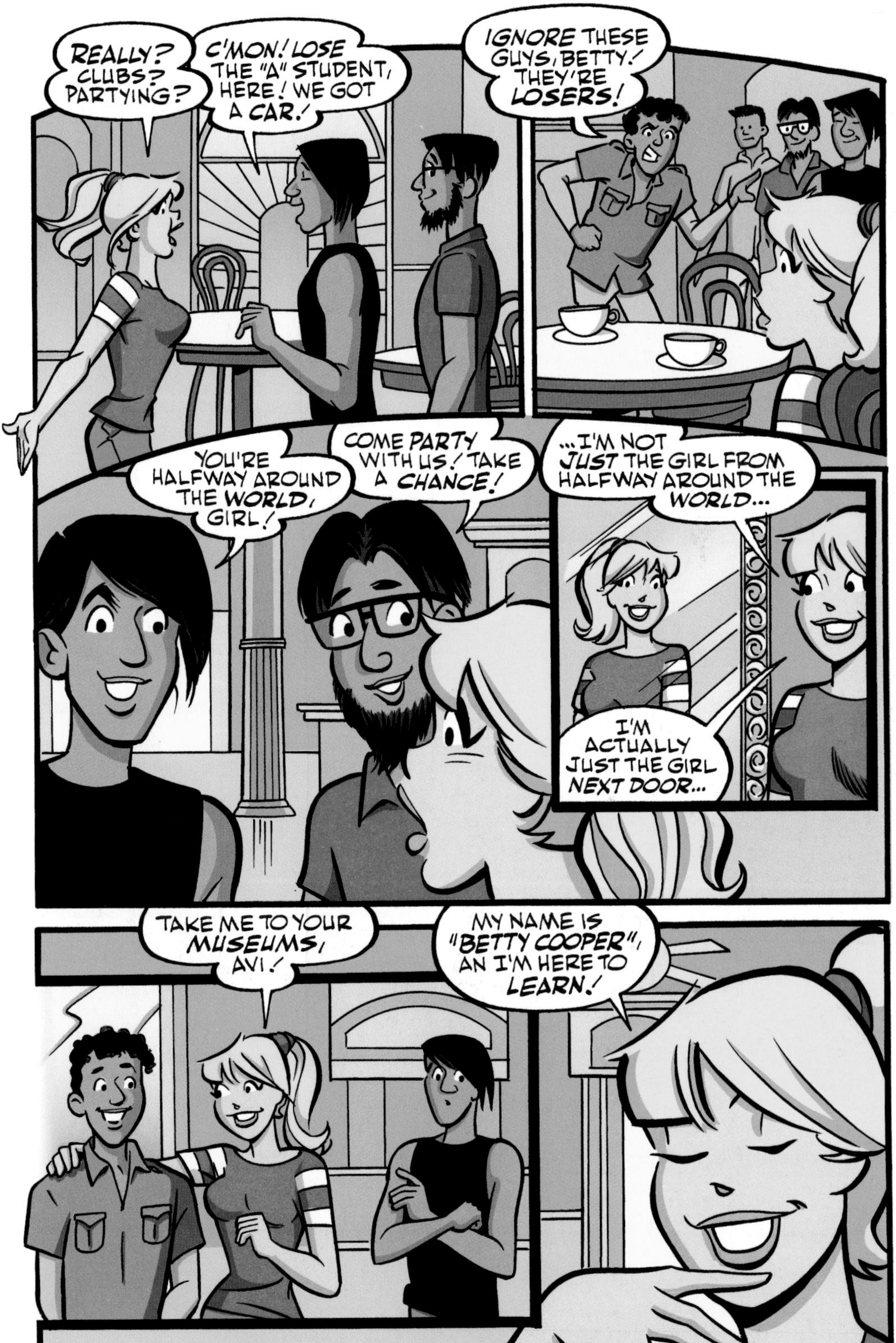
REALLY? CLUBS? PARTYING?
C'MON! LOSE THE "A" STUDENT, HERE! WE GOT A CAR!
IGNORE THESE GUYS, BETTY! THEY'RE LOSERS!
YOU'RE HALFWAY AROUND THE WORLD, GIRL!
COME PARTY WITH US! TAKE A CHANCE!
...I'M NOT JUST THE GIRL FROM HALFWAY AROUND THE WORLD...
I'M ACTUALLY JUST THE GIRL NEXT DOOR...
TAKE ME TO YOUR MUSEUMS, AVI!
MY NAME IS "BETTY COOPER", AN I'M HERE TO LEARN!
15

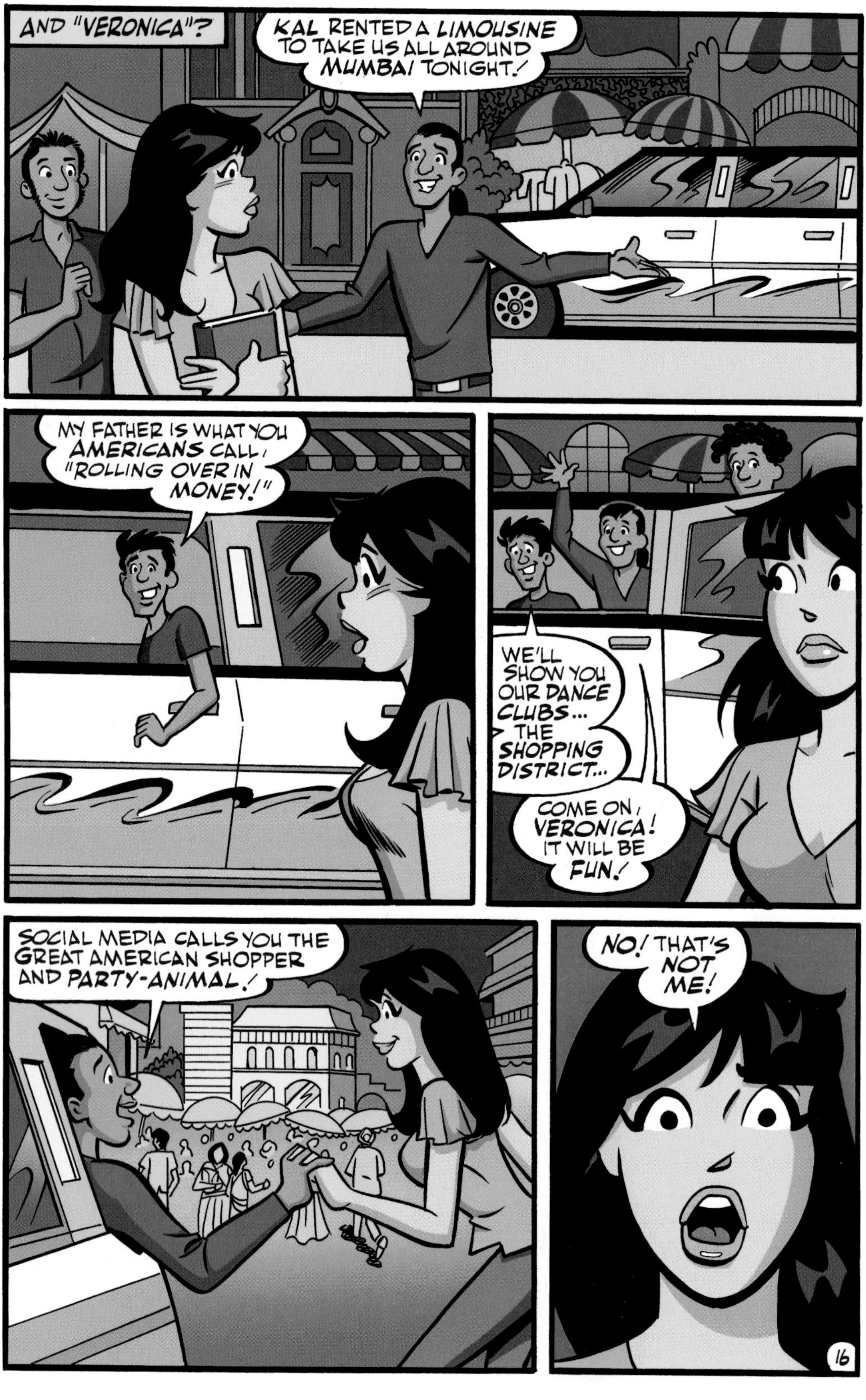
AND "VERONICA"?
KAL RENTED A LIMOUSINE TO TAKE US ALL AROUND MUMBAI TONIGHT!
MY FATHER IS WHAT YOU AMERICANS CALL, "ROLLING OVER IN MONEY!"
WE'LL SHOW YOU OUR DANCE CLUBS... THE SHOPPING DISTRICT...
COME ON, VERONICA! IT WILL BE FUN!
SOCIAL MEDIA CALLS YOU THE GREAT AMERICAN SHOPPER AND PARTY-ANIMAL!
NO! THAT'S NOT ME!
16

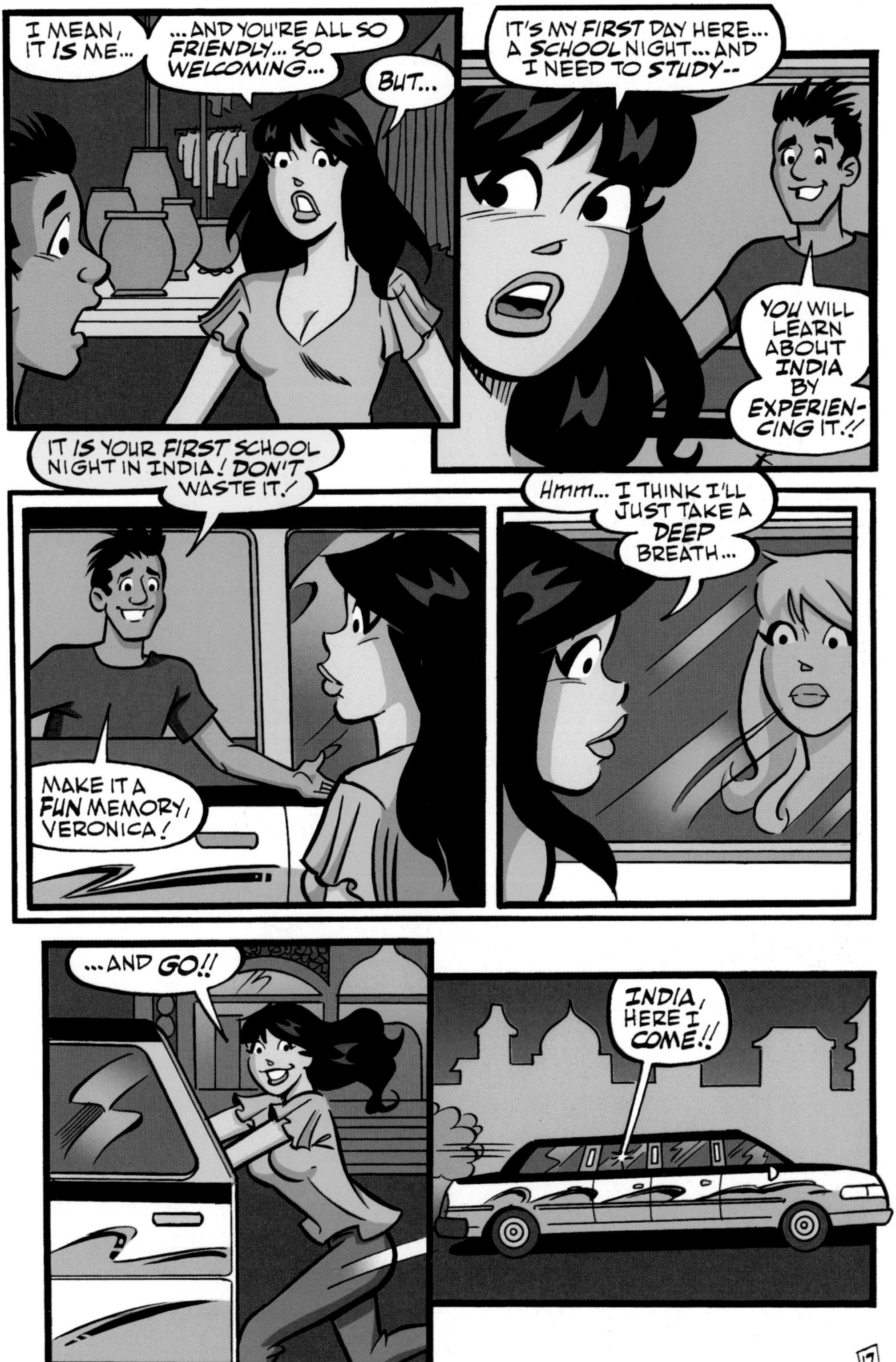
I MEAN, IT IS ME...
...AND YOU'RE ALL SO FRIENDLY... SO WELCOMING...
BUT...
IT'S MY FIRST DAY HERE... A SCHOOL NIGHT... AND I NEED TO STUDY--
YOU WILL LEARN ABOUT INDIA BY EXPERIEN-CING IT!!
IT IS YOUR FIRST SCHOOL NIGHT IN INDIA! DON'T WASTE IT!
MAKE IT A FUN MEMORY, VERONICA!
Hmm... I THINK I'LL JUST TAKE A DEEP BREATH...
...AND GO!!
INDIA, HERE I COME!!
17

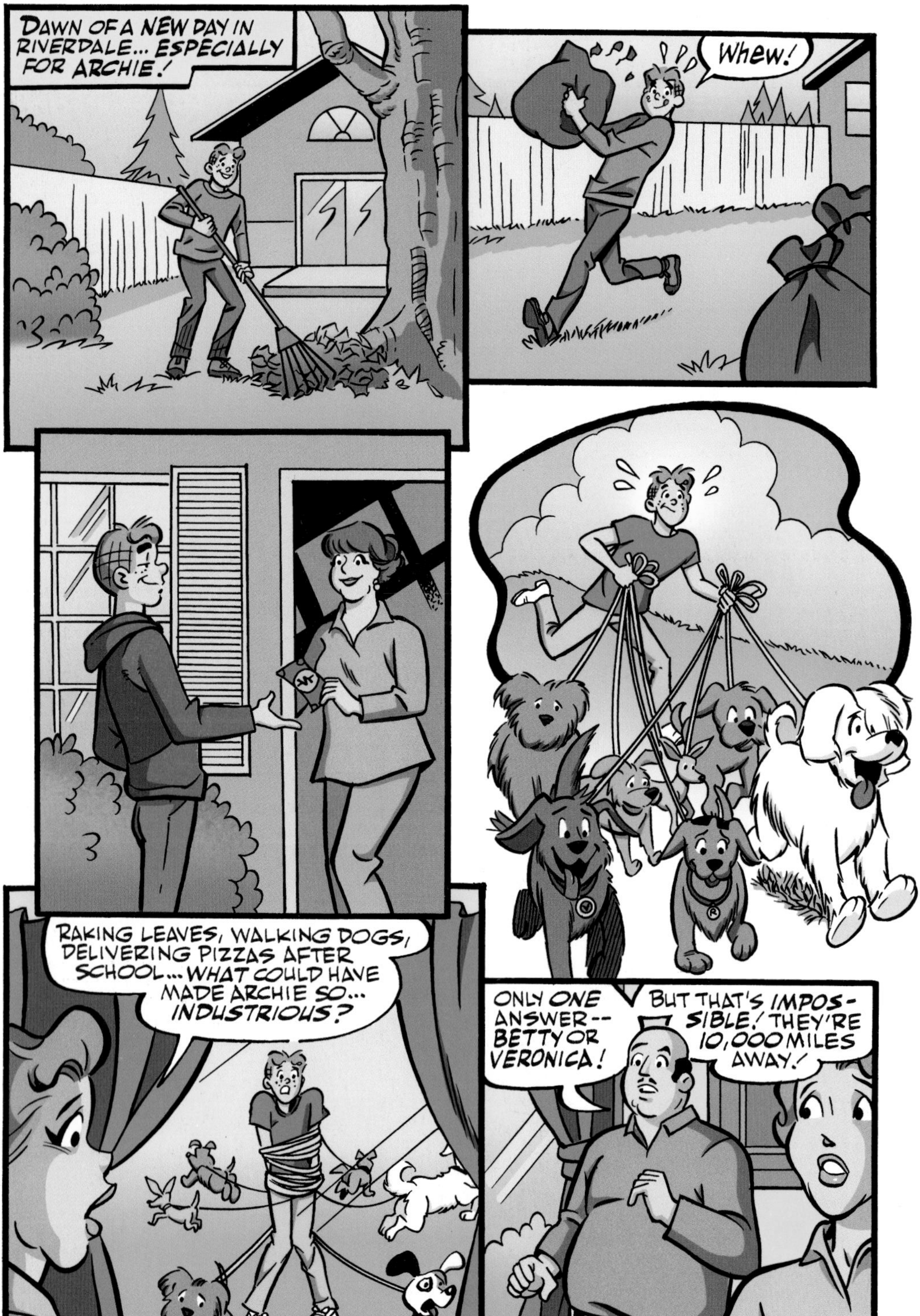
DAWN OF A NEW DAY IN RIVERDALE... ESPECIALLY FOR ARCHIE!
Whew!
RAKING LEAVES, WALKING DOGS, DELIVERING PIZZAS AFTER SCHOOL... WHAT COULD HAVE MADE ARCHIE SO... INDUSTRIOUS?
ONLY ONE ANSWER-- BETTY OR VERONICA!
BUT THAT'S IMPOSSIBLE! THEY'RE 10,000 MILES AWAY!
18

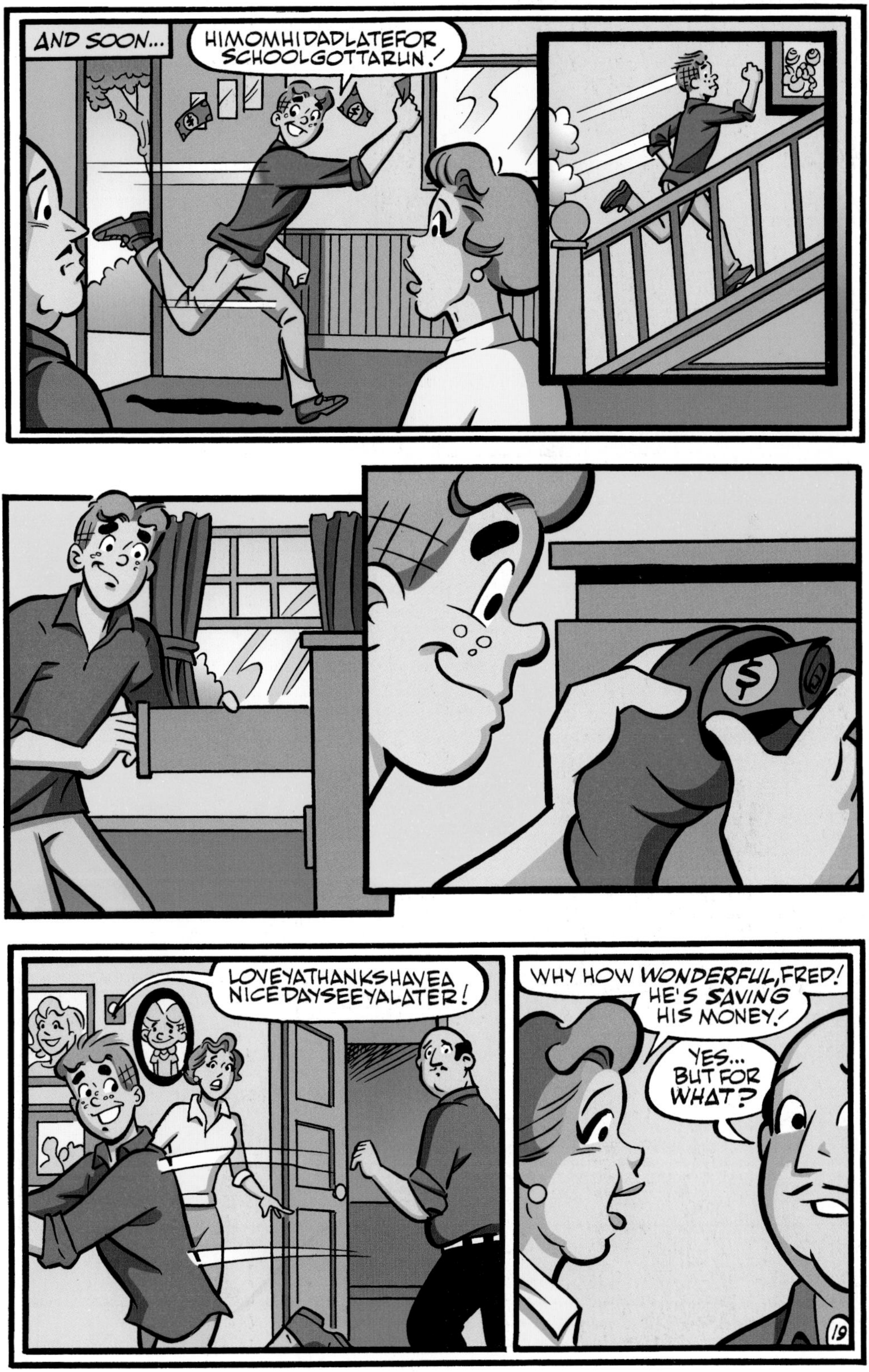
AND SOON...
HIMOMHIDADLATEFOR SCHOOLGOTTARUN!
LOVEYATHANKSHAVEA NICEDAYSEEYALATER!
WHY HOW WONDERFUL, FRED! HE'S SAVING HIS MONEY!
YES... BUT FOR WHAT?
19

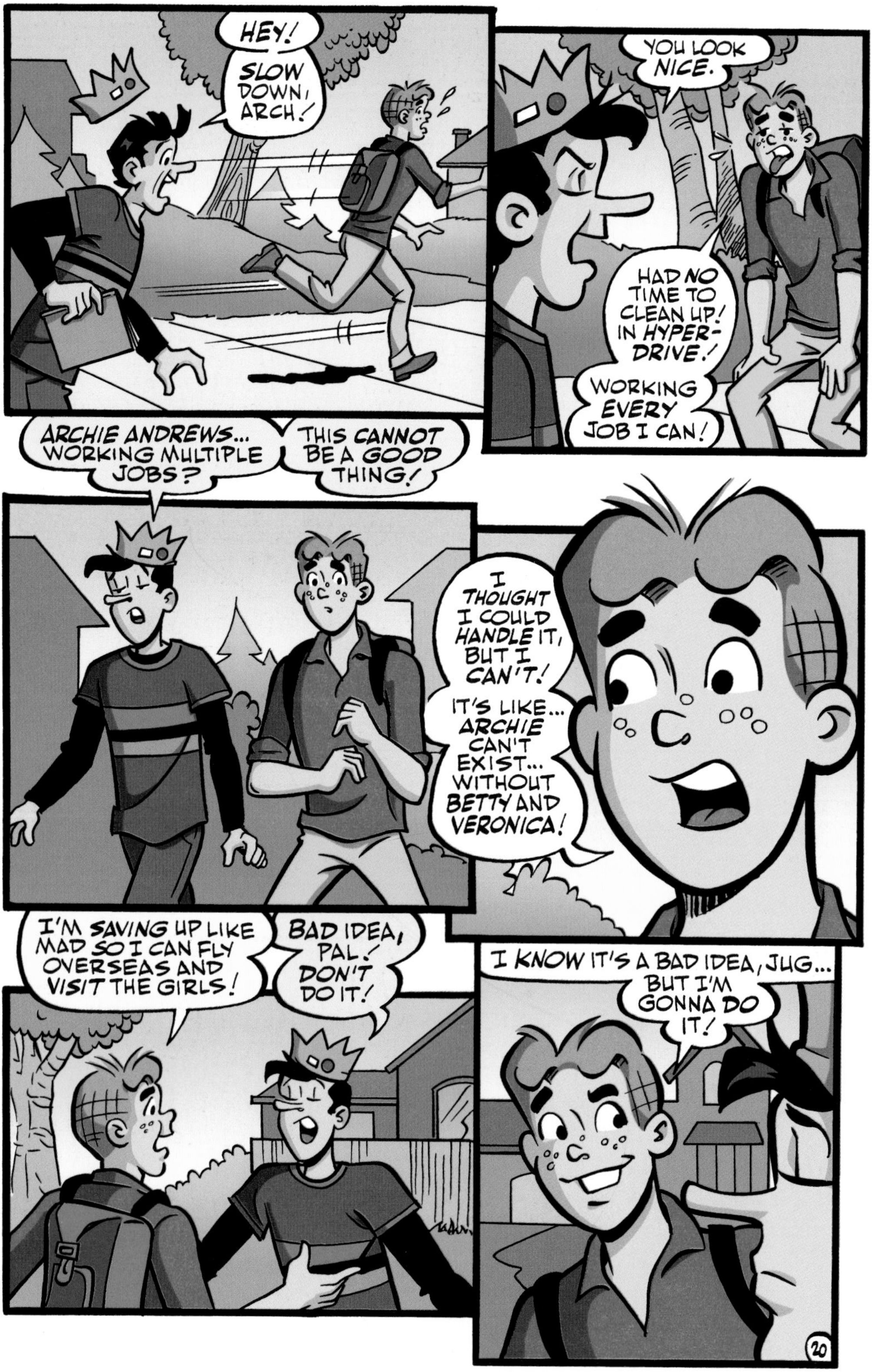
HEY!
SLOW DOWN, ARCH!
YOU LOOK NICE.
HAD NO TIME TO CLEAN UP! IN HYPER-DRIVE!
WORKING EVERY JOB I CAN!
ARCHIE ANDREWS... WORKING MULTIPLE JOBS?
THIS CANNOT BE A GOOD THING!
I THOUGHT I COULD HANDLE IT, BUT I CAN'T!
IT'S LIKE... ARCHIE CAN'T EXIST... WITHOUT BETTY AND VERONICA!
I'M SAVING UP LIKE MAD SO I CAN FLY OVERSEAS AND VISIT THE GIRLS!
BAD IDEA, PAL! DON'T DO IT!
I KNOW IT'S A BAD IDEA, JUG... BUT I'M GONNA DO IT!
20

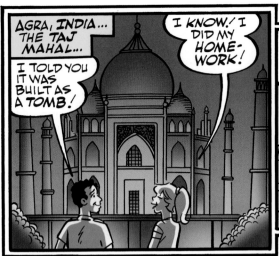

AGRA, INDIA... THE TAJ MAHAL...

I TOLD YOU IT WAS BUILT AS A TOMB!

I KNOW! I DID MY HOMEWORK!

HERE YOU'LL LEARN ABOUT OUR GREAT HERO GANDHI!

ANYONE WHO DEVOTES HIS LIFE TO PEACE AND NON-VIOLENCE IS THE GREATEST HERO!

THE GAME RESERVE...

OUR NOBLE INDIAN ELEPHANT WITH ITS SHORTER EARS... AND LOOK..

LIONS AND TIGERS AND BEARS!

OH, MY!

SO, DOES ALL THIS INSPIRE YOU TO READ...TO LEARN?

WHAT ARE YOU THINKING?

21

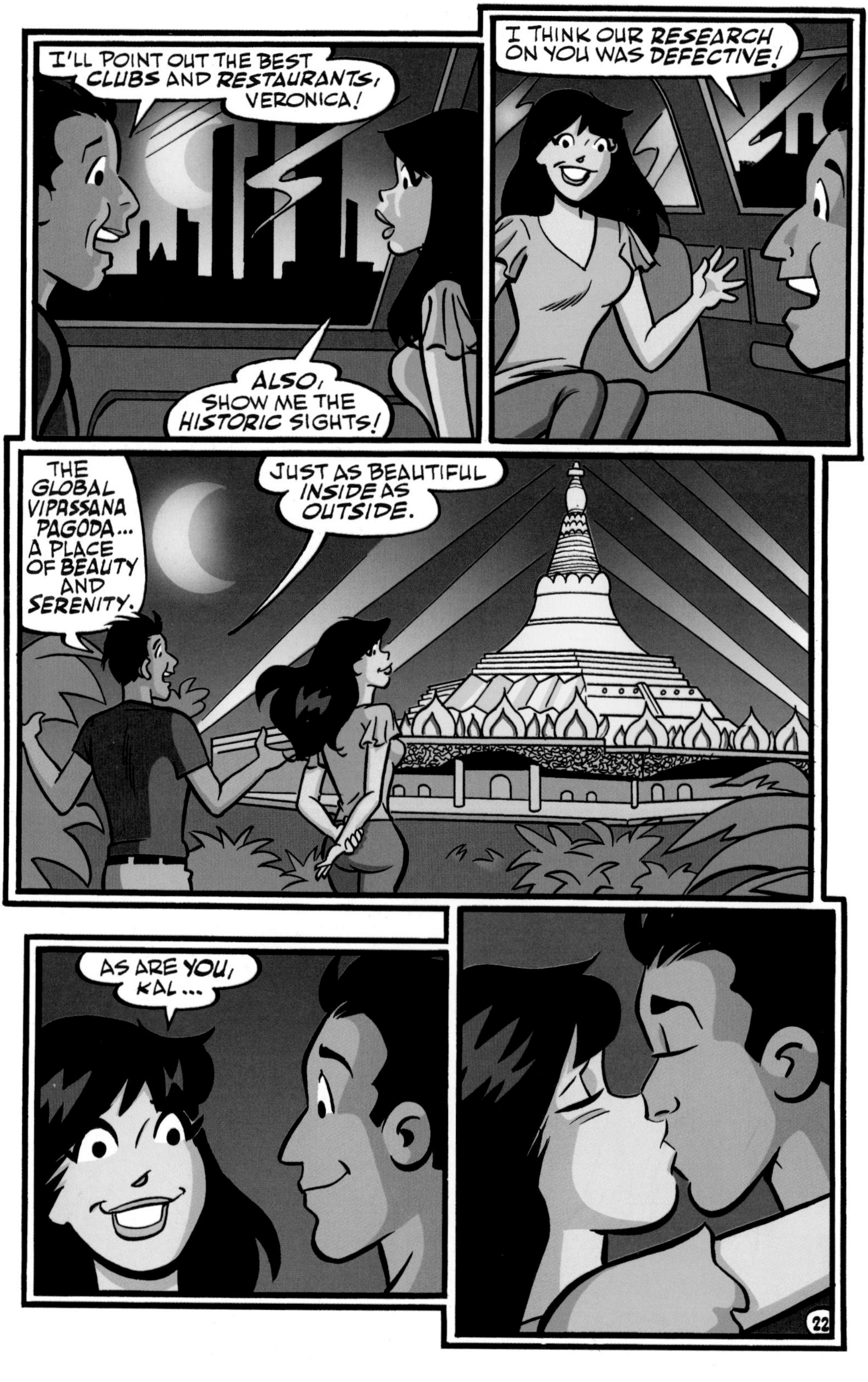
I'LL POINT OUT THE BEST CLUBS AND RESTAURANTS, VERONICA!
ALSO, SHOW ME THE HISTORIC SIGHTS!
I THINK OUR RESEARCH ON YOU WAS DEFECTIVE!
THE GLOBAL VIPASSANA PAGODA... A PLACE OF BEAUTY AND SERENITY.
JUST AS BEAUTIFUL INSIDE AS OUTSIDE.
AS ARE YOU, KAL...
22

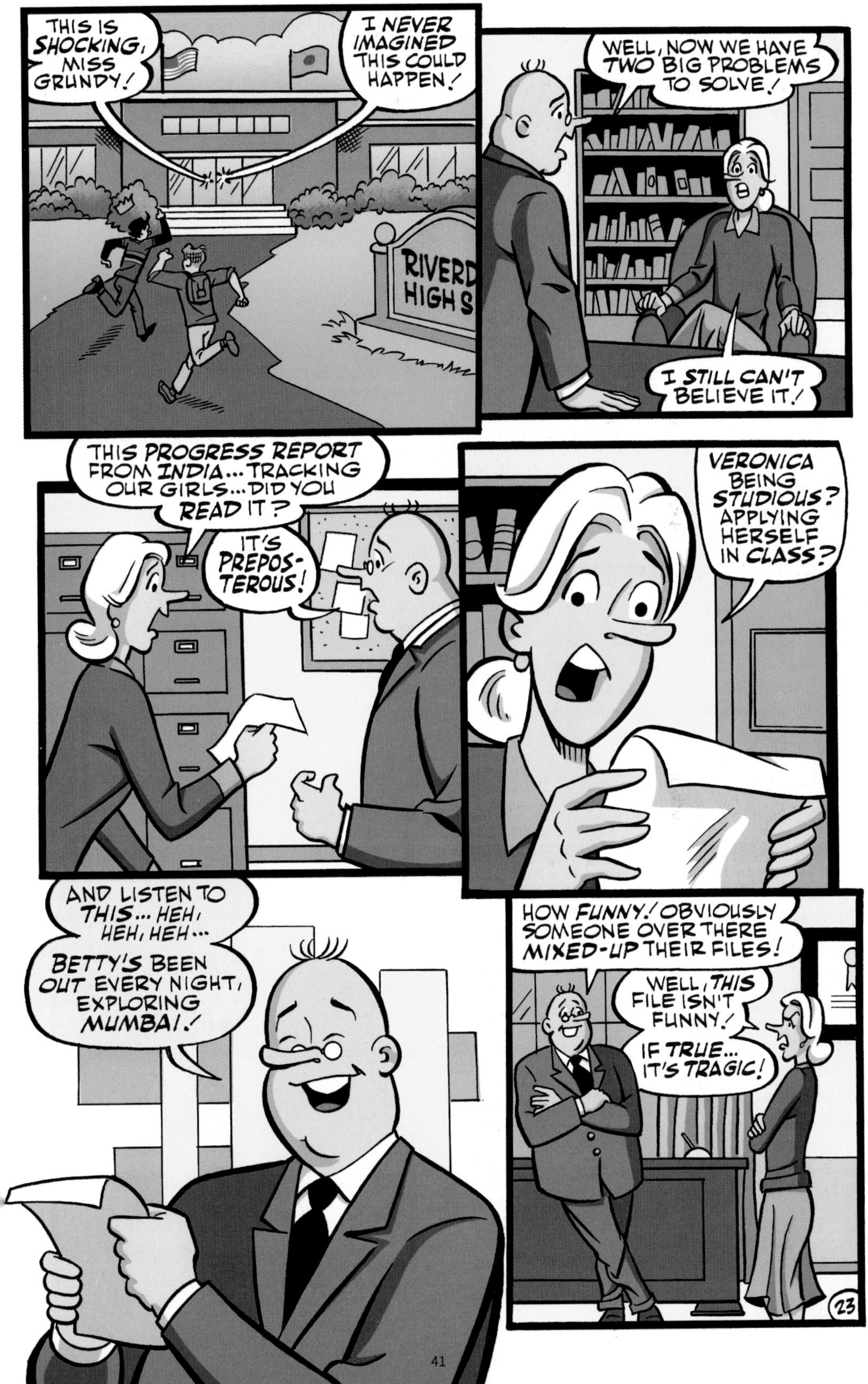
THIS IS SHOCKING, MISS GRUNDY!
I NEVER IMAGINED THIS COULD HAPPEN!
RIVERD HIGH S
WELL, NOW WE HAVE TWO BIG PROBLEMS TO SOLVE!
I STILL CAN'T BELIEVE IT!
THIS PROGRESS REPORT FROM INDIA... TRACKING OUR GIRLS... DID YOU READ IT?
IT'S PREPOSTEROUS!
VERONICA BEING STUDIOUS? APPLYING HERSELF IN CLASS?
AND LISTEN TO THIS... HEH, HEH, HEH...
BETTY'S BEEN OUT EVERY NIGHT, EXPLORING MUMBAI!
HOW FUNNY! OBVIOUSLY SOMEONE OVER THERE MIXED-UP THEIR FILES!
WELL, THIS FILE ISN'T FUNNY!
IF TRUE... IT'S TRAGIC!
23

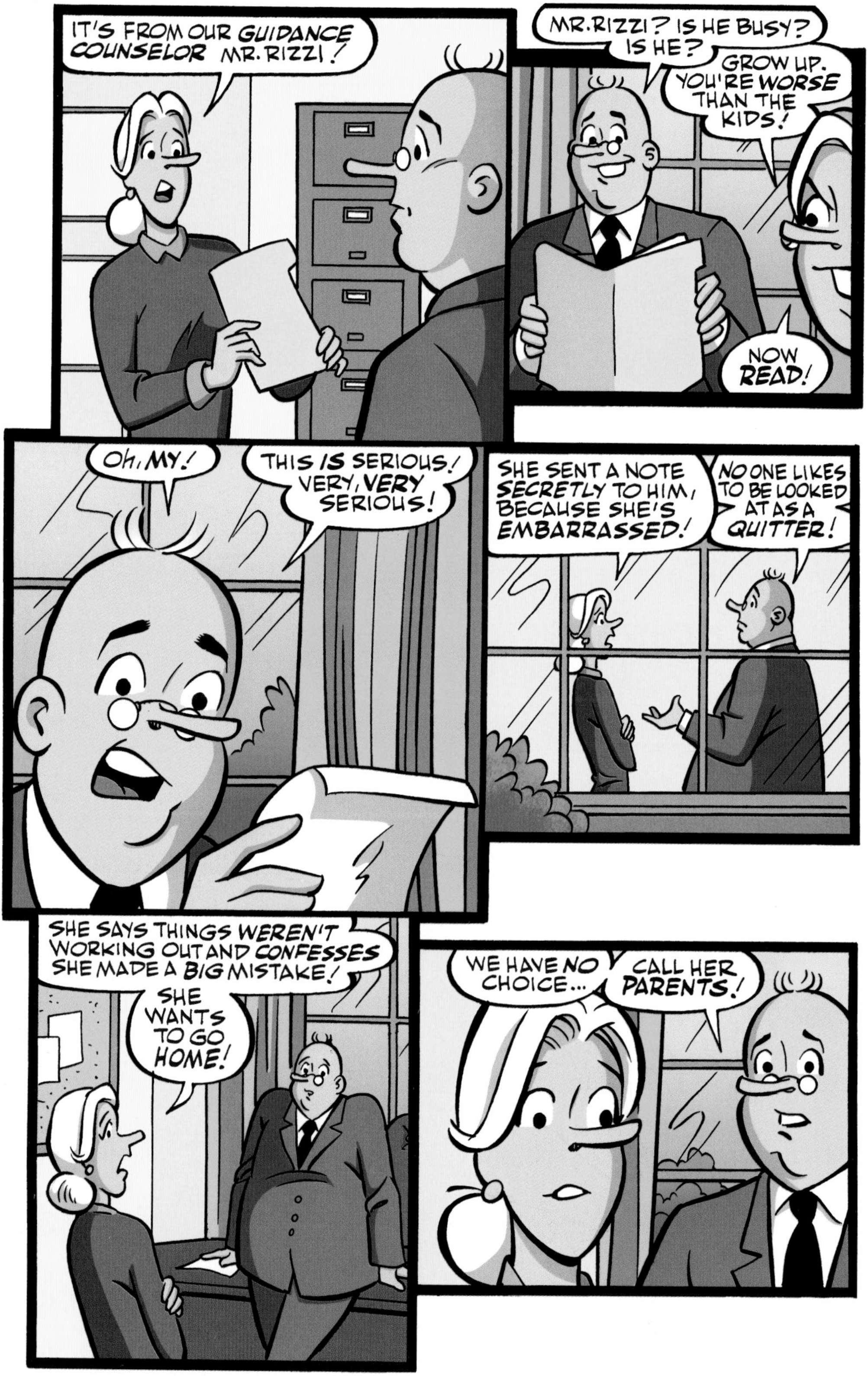
IT'S FROM OUR GUIDANCE COUNSELOR MR. RIZZI!
MR. RIZZI? IS HE BUSY? IS HE?
GROW UP. YOU'RE WORSE THAN THE KIDS!
NOW READ!
Oh, MY!
THIS IS SERIOUS! VERY, VERY SERIOUS!
SHE SENT A NOTE SECRETLY TO HIM, BECAUSE SHE'S EMBARRASSED!
NO ONE LIKES TO BE LOOKED AT AS A QUITTER!
SHE SAYS THINGS WEREN'T WORKING OUT AND CONFESSES SHE MADE A BIG MISTAKE!
SHE WANTS TO GO HOME!
WE HAVE NO CHOICE...
CALL HER PARENTS!

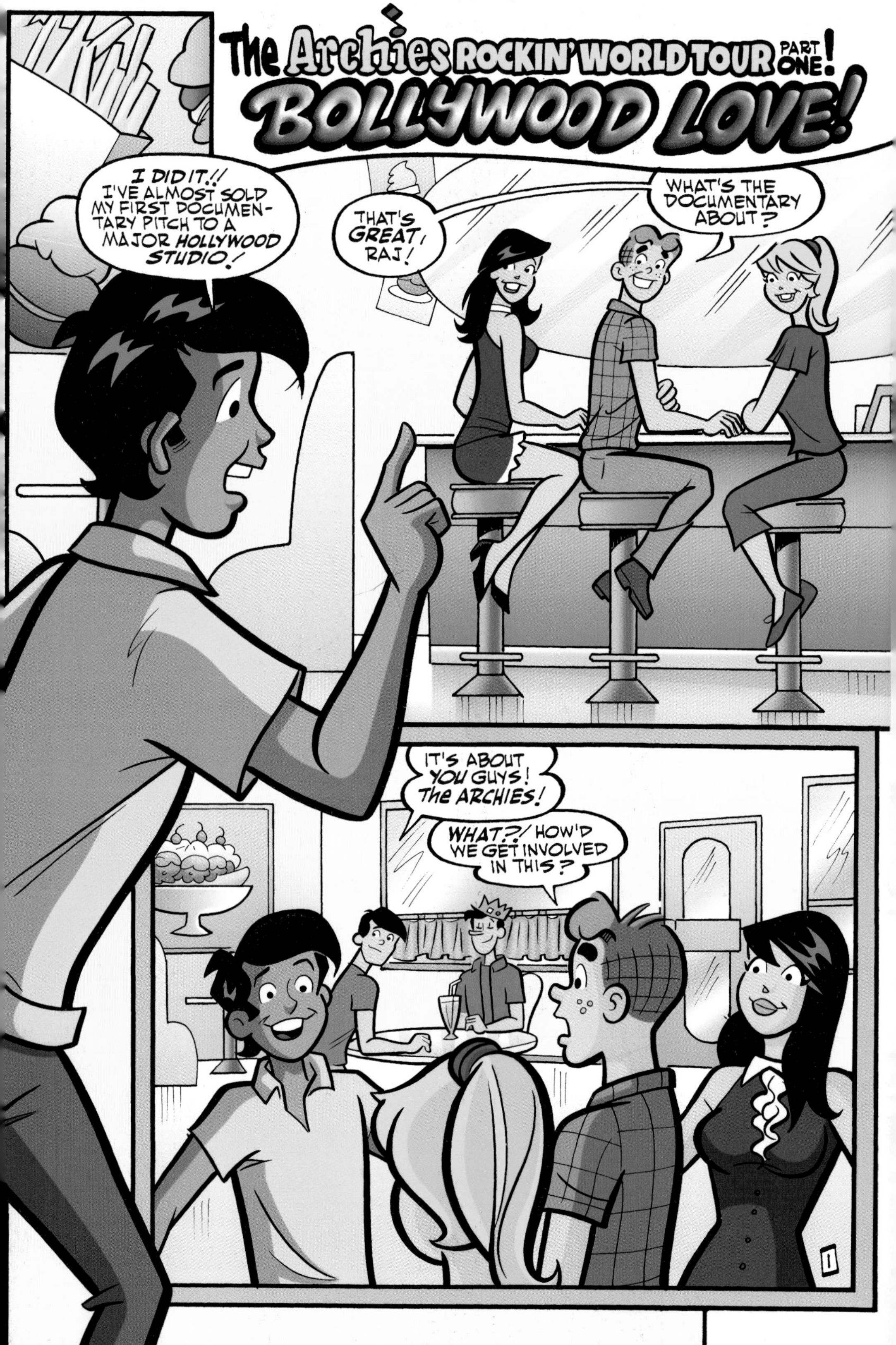
The Archies ROCKIN' WORLD TOUR PART ONE!
BOLLYWOOD LOVE!
I DID IT!! I'VE ALMOST SOLD MY FIRST DOCUMENTARY PITCH TO A MAJOR HOLLYWOOD STUDIO!
THAT'S GREAT, RAJ!
WHAT'S THE DOCUMENTARY ABOUT?
IT'S ABOUT YOU GUYS! THE ARCHIES!
WHAT?! HOW'D WE GET INVOLVED IN THIS?
1

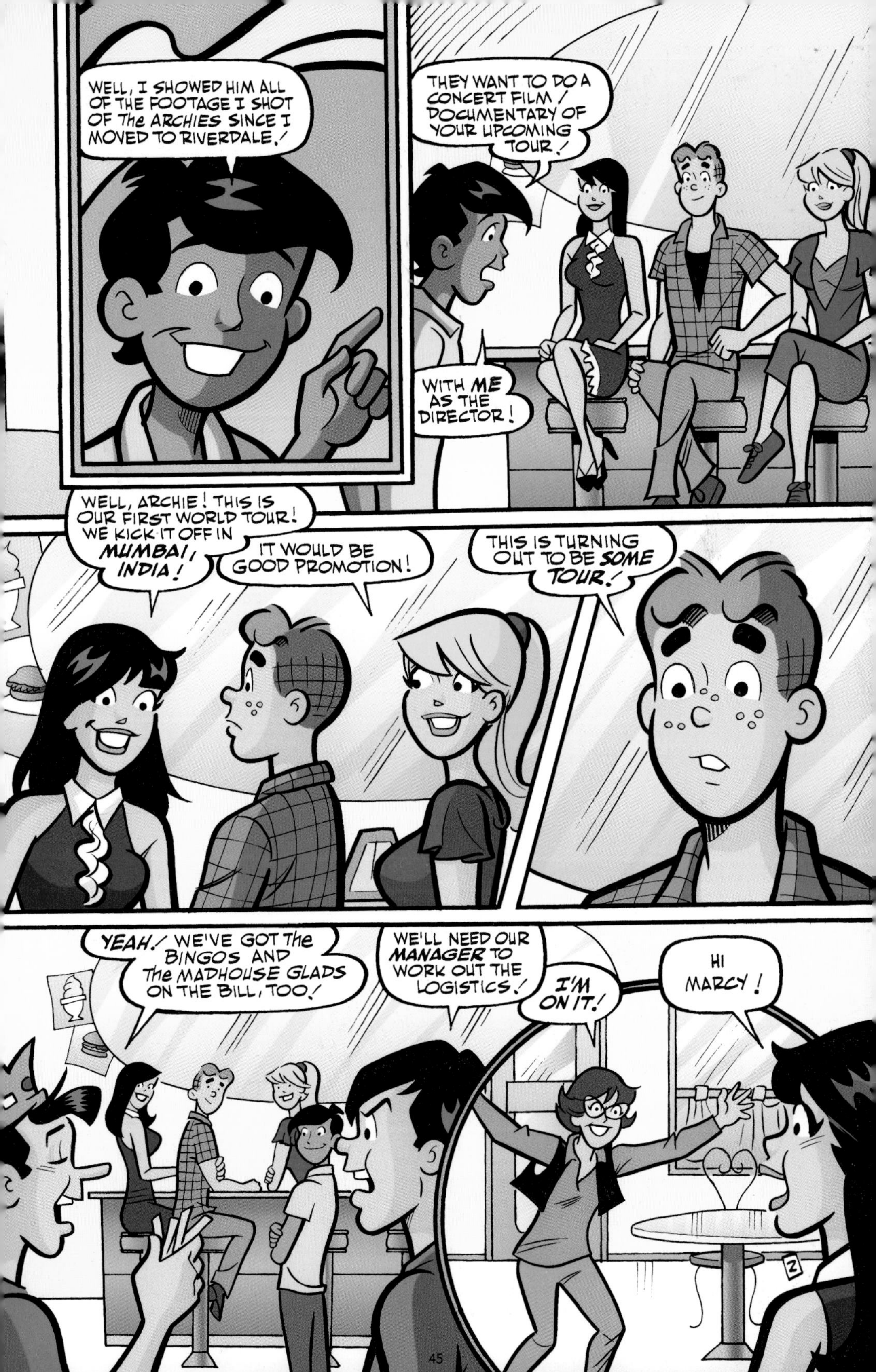

WELL, I SHOWED HIM ALL OF THE FOOTAGE I SHOT OF The ARCHIES SINCE I MOVED TO RIVERDALE!
THEY WANT TO DO A CONCERT FILM / DOCUMENTARY OF YOUR UPCOMING TOUR!
WITH ME AS THE DIRECTOR!
WELL, ARCHIE! THIS IS OUR FIRST WORLD TOUR! WE KICK IT OFF IN MUMBAI, INDIA!
IT WOULD BE GOOD PROMOTION!
THIS IS TURNING OUT TO BE SOME TOUR!
YEAH! WE'VE GOT The BINGOS AND The MADHOUSE GLADS ON THE BILL, TOO!
WE'LL NEED OUR MANAGER TO WORK OUT THE LOGISTICS!
I'M ON IT!
HI MARCY!

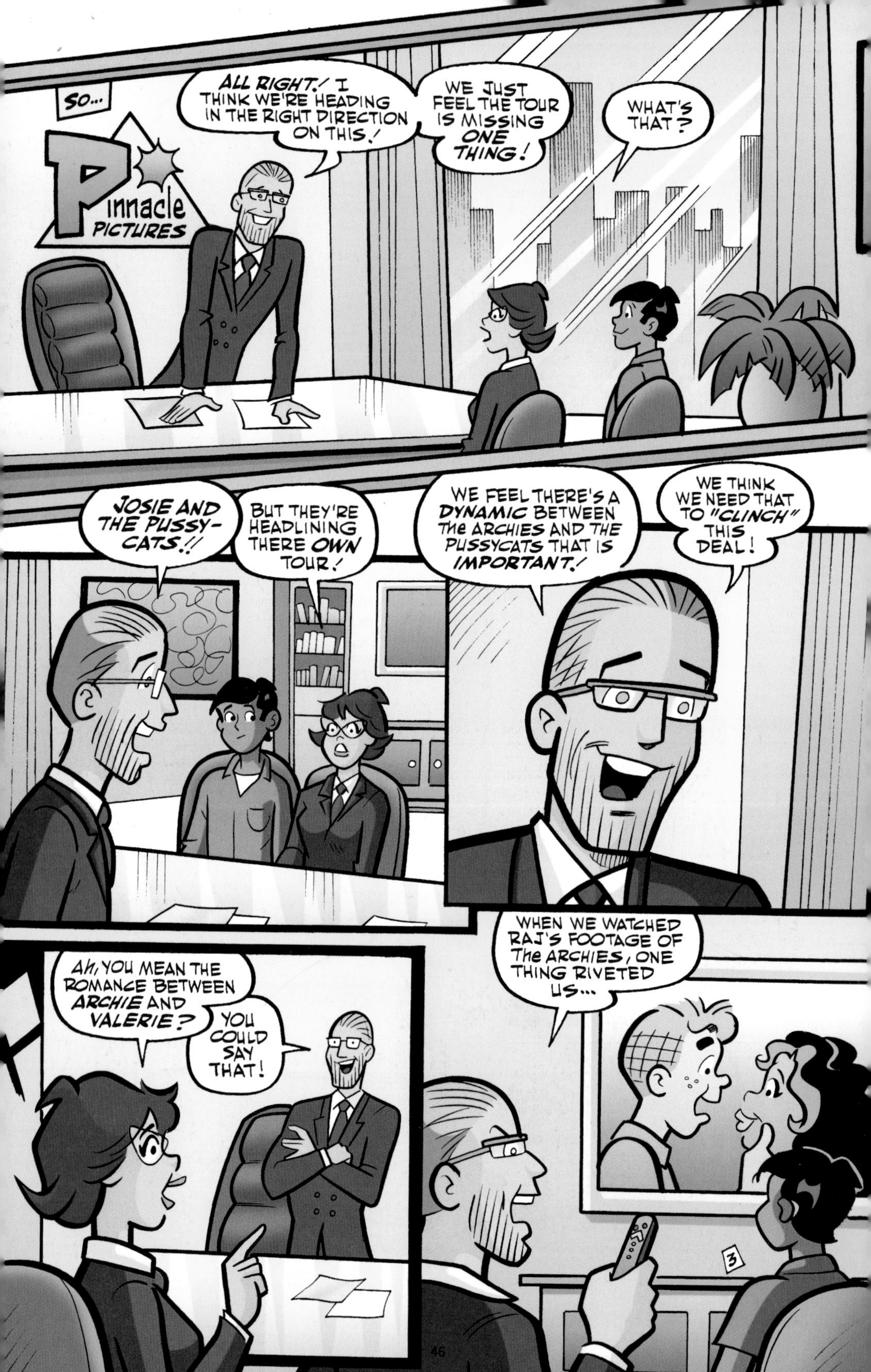
SO...
PINNACLE PICTURES
ALL RIGHT! I THINK WE'RE HEADING IN THE RIGHT DIRECTION ON THIS!
WE JUST FEEL THE TOUR IS MISSING ONE THING!
WHAT'S THAT?
JOSIE AND THE PUSSY-CATS!!
BUT THEY'RE HEADLINING THERE OWN TOUR!
WE FEEL THERE'S A DYNAMIC BETWEEN THE ARCHIES AND THE PUSSYCATS THAT IS IMPORTANT!
WE THINK WE NEED THAT TO "CLINCH" THIS DEAL!
AH, YOU MEAN THE ROMANCE BETWEEN ARCHIE AND VALERIE?
YOU COULD SAY THAT!
WHEN WE WATCHED RAJ'S FOOTAGE OF THE ARCHIES, ONE THING RIVETED US...
3

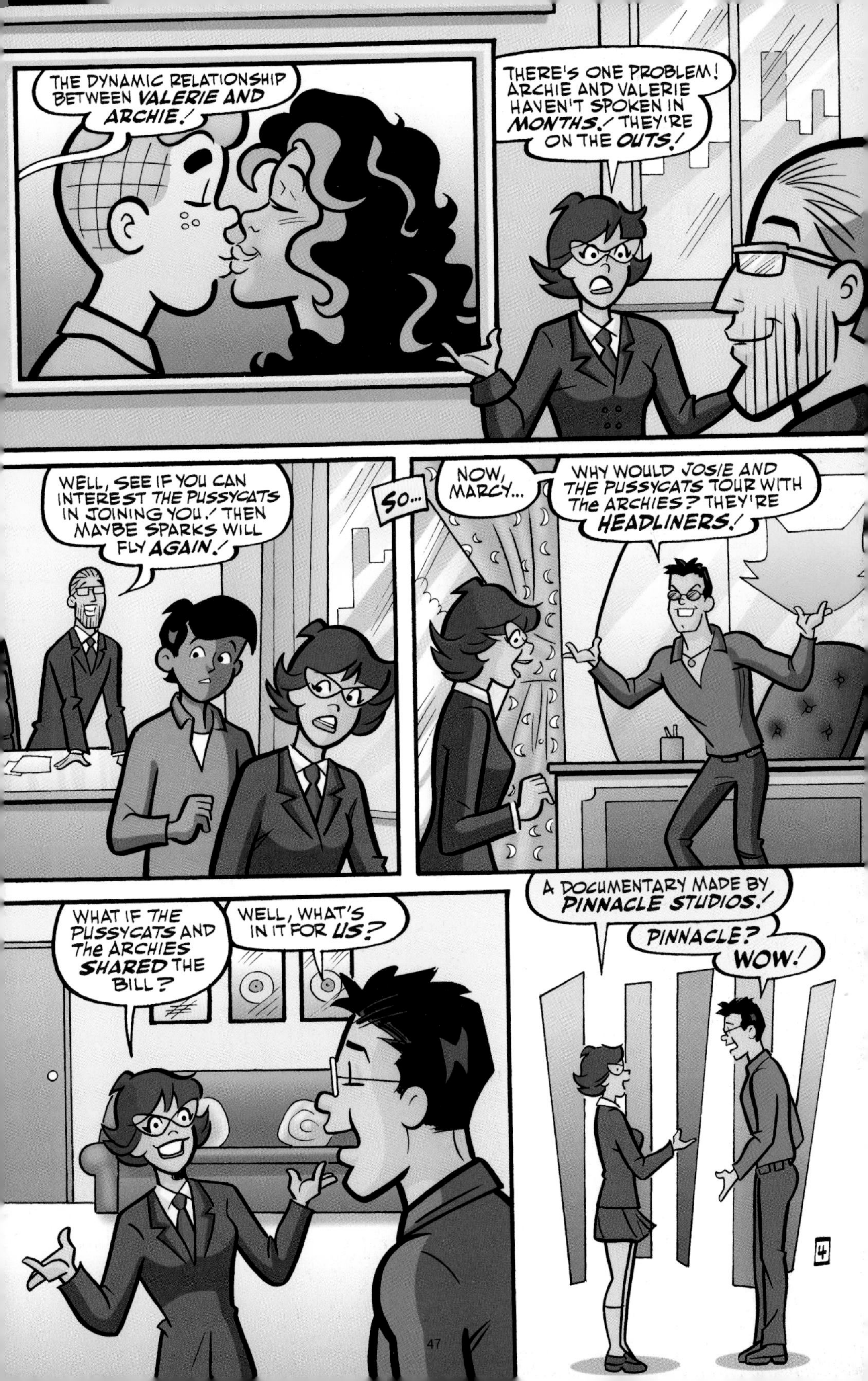
THE DYNAMIC RELATIONSHIP BETWEEN VALERIE AND ARCHIE!
THERE'S ONE PROBLEM! ARCHIE AND VALERIE HAVEN'T SPOKEN IN MONTHS! THEY'RE ON THE OUTS!
WELL, SEE IF YOU CAN INTEREST THE PUSSYCATS IN JOINING YOU! THEN MAYBE SPARKS WILL FLY AGAIN!
SO...
NOW, MARCY...
WHY WOULD JOSIE AND THE PUSSYCATS TOUR WITH The ARCHIES? THEY'RE HEADLINERS!
WHAT IF THE PUSSYCATS AND The ARCHIES SHARED THE BILL?
WELL, WHAT'S IN IT FOR US?
A DOCUMENTARY MADE BY PINNACLE STUDIOS!
PINNACLE? WOW!
4

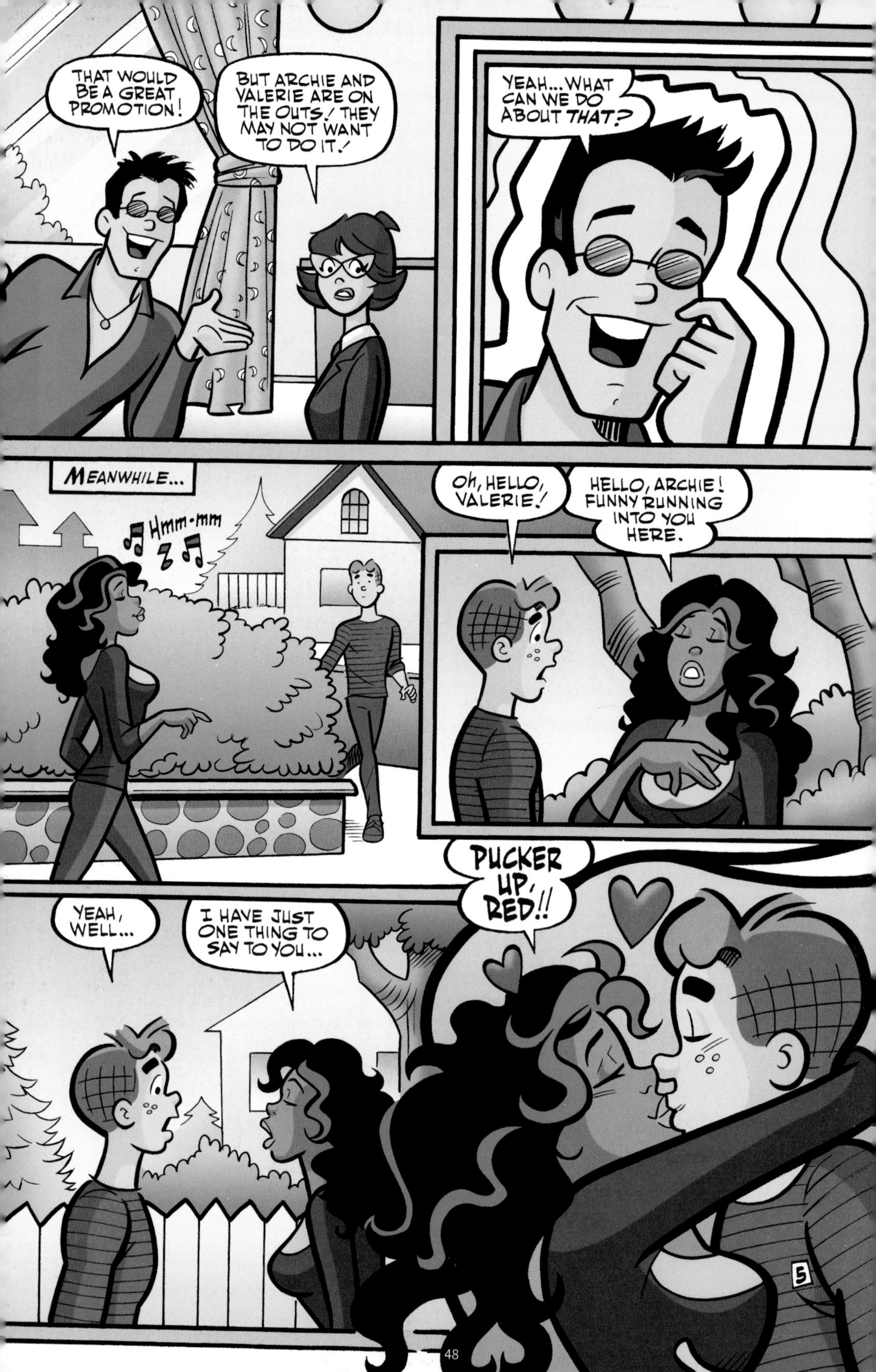
THAT WOULD BE A GREAT PROMOTION!
BUT ARCHIE AND VALERIE ARE ON THE OUTS! THEY MAY NOT WANT TO DO IT!
YEAH... WHAT CAN WE DO ABOUT THAT?
MEANWHILE...
Hmm-mm
Oh, HELLO, VALERIE!
HELLO, ARCHIE! FUNNY RUNNING INTO YOU HERE.
YEAH, WELL...
I HAVE JUST ONE THING TO SAY TO YOU...
PUCKER UP, RED!!

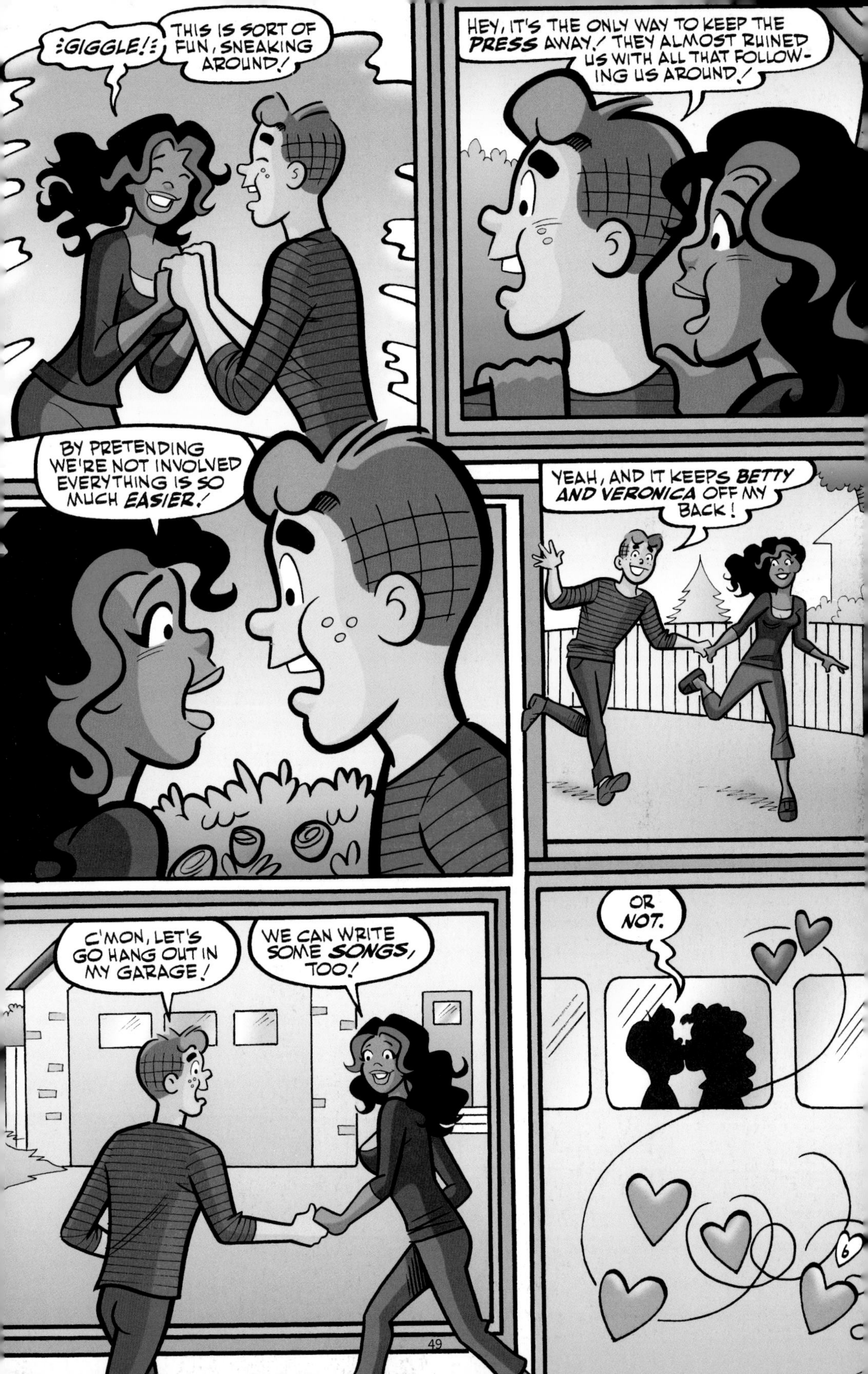
:GIGGLE!:
THIS IS SORT OF FUN, SNEAKING AROUND!
HEY, IT'S THE ONLY WAY TO KEEP THE PRESS AWAY! THEY ALMOST RUINED US WITH ALL THAT FOLLOWING US AROUND!
BY PRETENDING WE'RE NOT INVOLVED EVERYTHING IS SO MUCH EASIER!
YEAH, AND IT KEEPS BETTY AND VERONICA OFF MY BACK!
C'MON, LET'S GO HANG OUT IN MY GARAGE!
WE CAN WRITE SOME SONGS, TOO!
OR NOT.
6

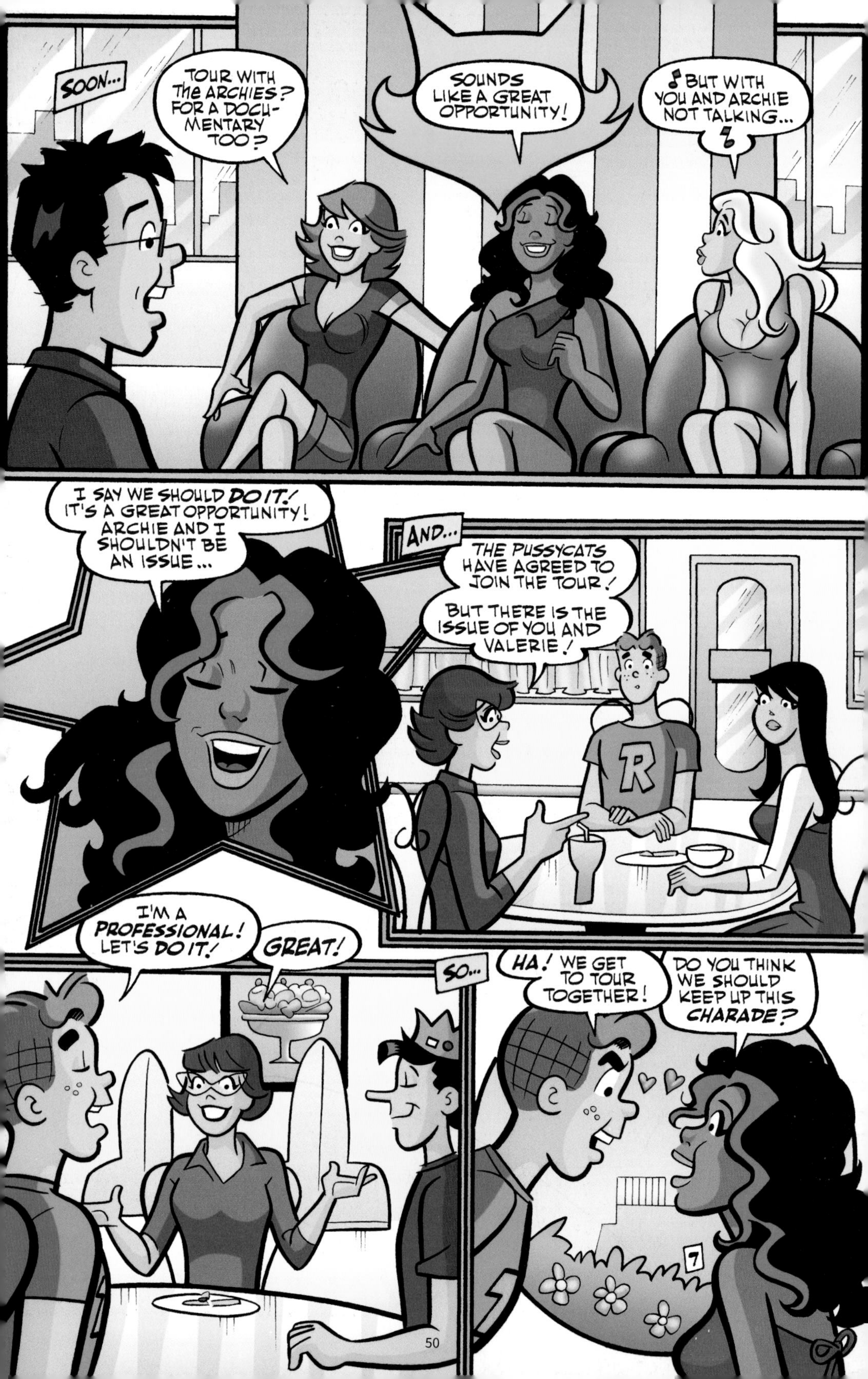
SOON...
TOUR WITH THE ARCHIES? FOR A DOCU-MENTARY TOO?
SOUNDS LIKE A GREAT OPPORTUNITY!
BUT WITH YOU AND ARCHIE NOT TALKING...
I SAY WE SHOULD DO IT! IT'S A GREAT OPPORTUNITY! ARCHIE AND I SHOULDN'T BE AN ISSUE...
AND...
THE PUSSYCATS HAVE AGREED TO JOIN THE TOUR!
BUT THERE IS THE ISSUE OF YOU AND VALERIE!
I'M A PROFESSIONAL! LET'S DO IT!
GREAT!
SO...
HA! WE GET TO TOUR TOGETHER!
DO YOU THINK WE SHOULD KEEP UP THIS CHARADE?
7

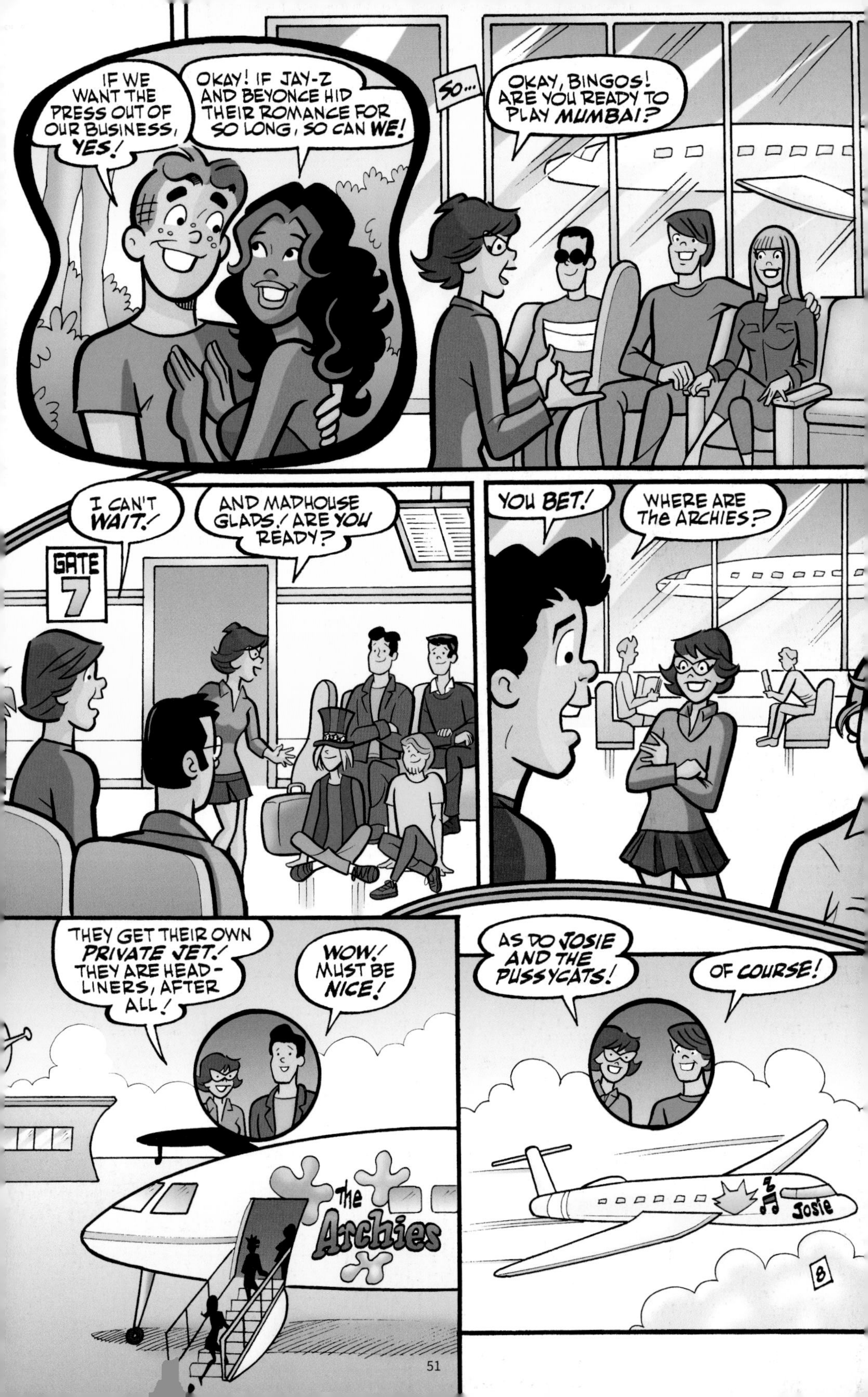
IF WE WANT THE PRESS OUT OF OUR BUSINESS, YES!
OKAY! IF JAY-Z AND BEYONCE HID THEIR ROMANCE FOR SO LONG, SO CAN WE!
SO...
OKAY, BINGOS! ARE YOU READY TO PLAY MUMBAI?
I CAN'T WAIT!
AND MADHOUSE GLADS! ARE YOU READY?
GATE 7
YOU BET!
WHERE ARE The ARCHIES?
THEY GET THEIR OWN PRIVATE JET! THEY ARE HEAD-LINERS, AFTER ALL!
WOW! MUST BE NICE!
The Archies
AS DO JOSIE AND THE PUSSYCATS!
OF COURSE!
Josie
8

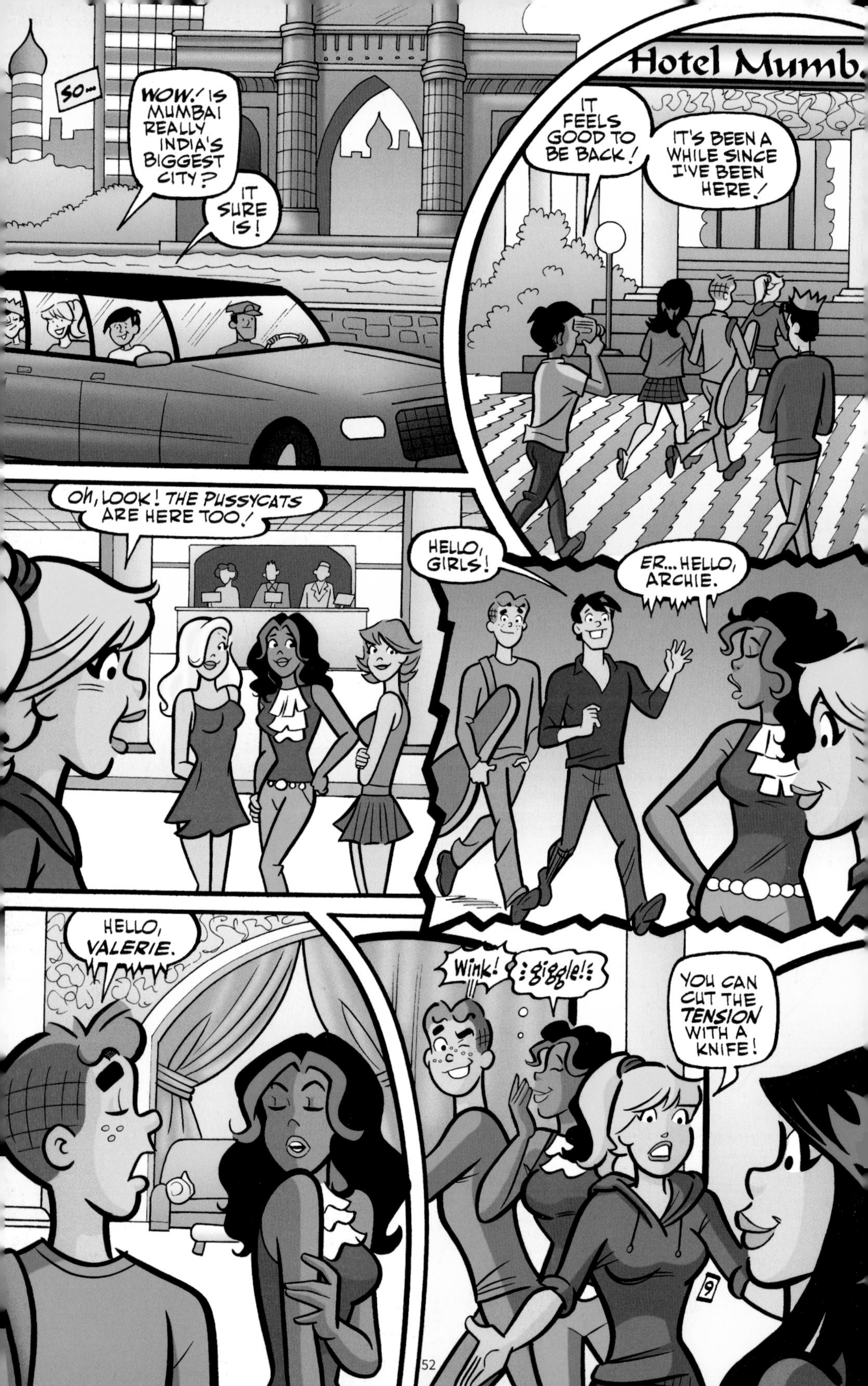

Hotel Mumb
SO...
WOW! IS MUMBAI REALLY INDIA'S BIGGEST CITY?
IT SURE IS!
IT FEELS GOOD TO BE BACK!
IT'S BEEN A WHILE SINCE I'VE BEEN HERE!
Oh, LOOK! THE PUSSYCATS ARE HERE TOO!
HELLO, GIRLS!
ER...HELLO, ARCHIE.
HELLO, VALERIE.
Wink!
giggle!
YOU CAN CUT THE TENSION WITH A KNIFE!
9

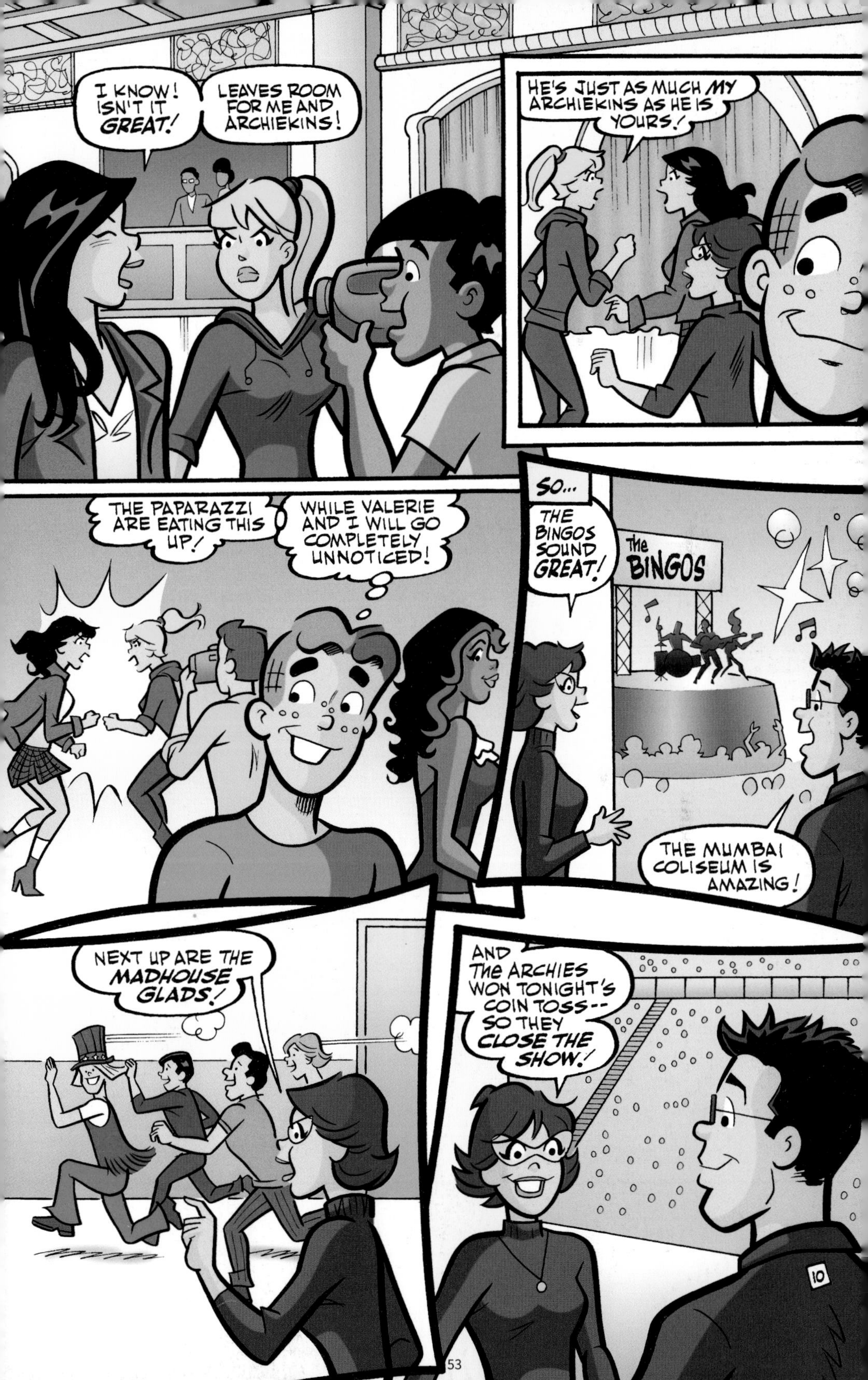
I KNOW! ISN'T IT GREAT!
LEAVES ROOM FOR ME AND ARCHIEKINS!
HE'S JUST AS MUCH MY ARCHIEKINS AS HE IS YOURS!
THE PAPARAZZI ARE EATING THIS UP!
WHILE VALERIE AND I WILL GO COMPLETELY UNNOTICED!
SO...
THE BINGOS SOUND GREAT!
The BINGOS
THE MUMBAI COLISEUM IS AMAZING!
NEXT UP ARE THE MADHOUSE GLADS!
AND The ARCHIES WON TONIGHT'S COIN TOSS-- SO THEY CLOSE THE SHOW!
10

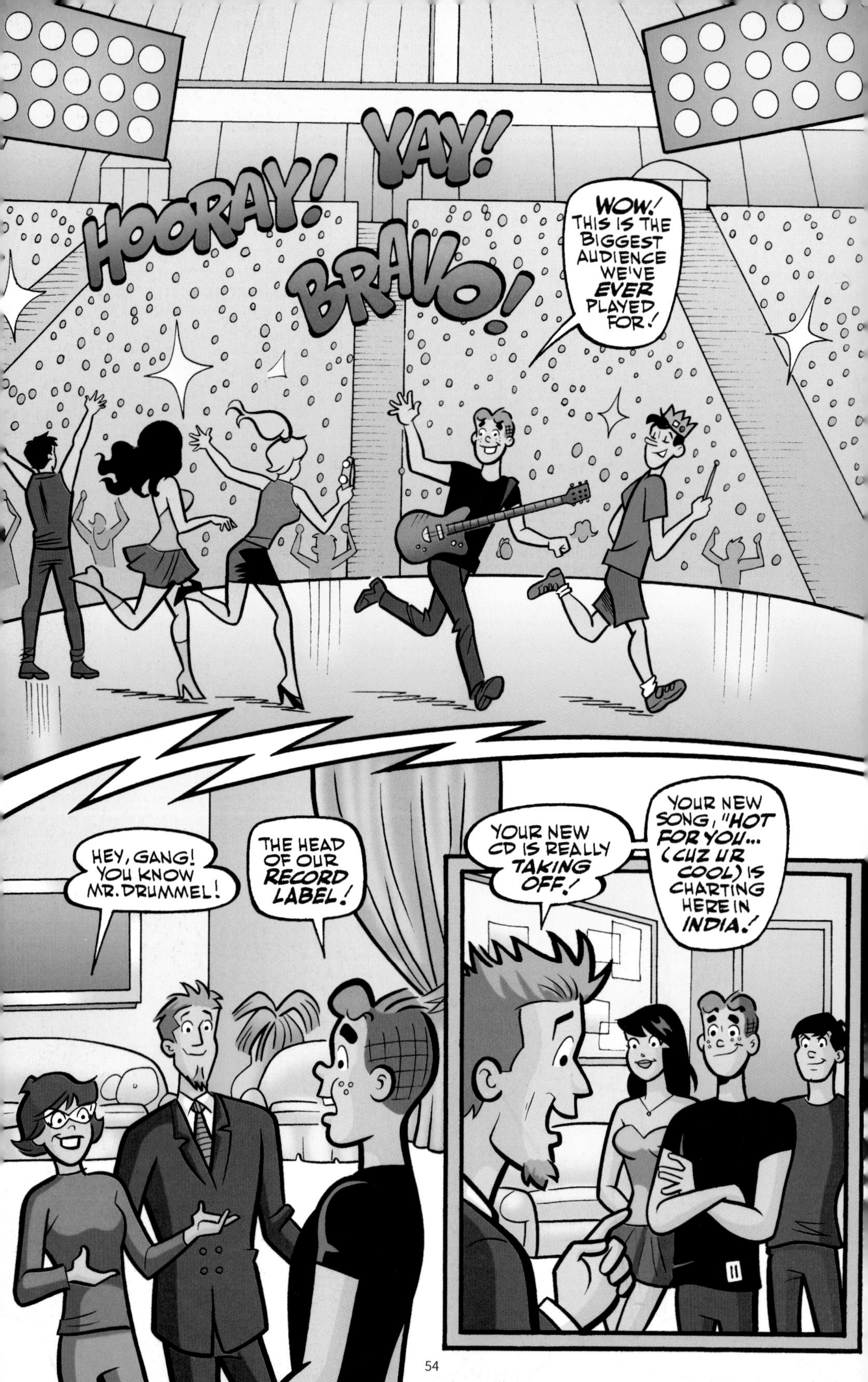
HOORAY!
YAY!
BRAVO!
WOW! THIS IS THE BIGGEST AUDIENCE WE'VE EVER PLAYED FOR!
HEY, GANG! YOU KNOW MR. DRUMMEL!
THE HEAD OF OUR RECORD LABEL!
YOUR NEW CD IS REALLY TAKING OFF!
YOUR NEW SONG, "HOT FOR YOU... (CUZ UR COOL) IS CHARTING HERE IN INDIA!
II

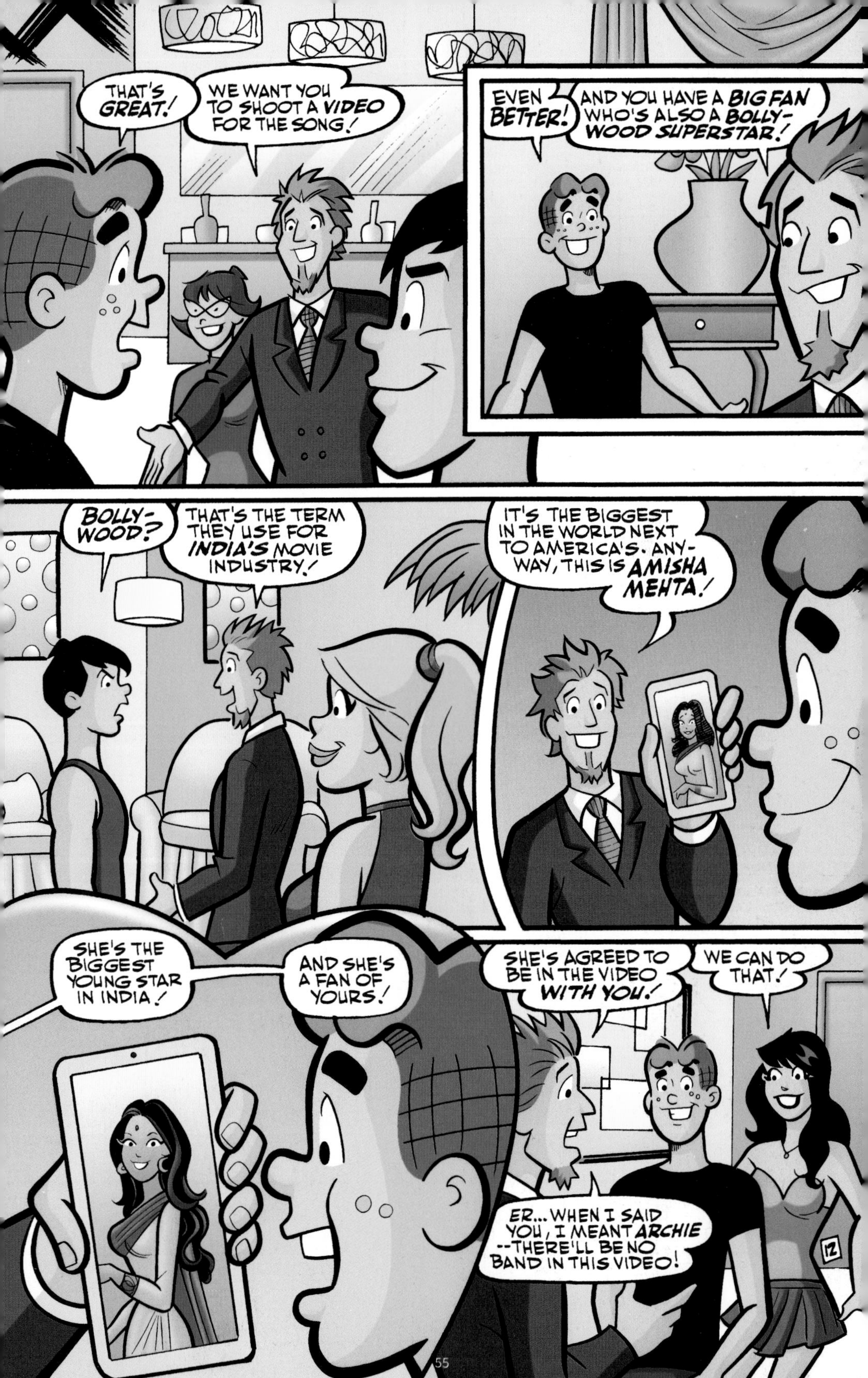
THAT'S GREAT!
WE WANT YOU TO SHOOT A VIDEO FOR THE SONG!
EVEN BETTER!
AND YOU HAVE A BIG FAN WHO'S ALSO A BOLLY-WOOD SUPERSTAR!
BOLLY-WOOD?
THAT'S THE TERM THEY USE FOR INDIA'S MOVIE INDUSTRY!
IT'S THE BIGGEST IN THE WORLD NEXT TO AMERICA'S. ANY-WAY, THIS IS AMISHA MEHTA!
SHE'S THE BIGGEST YOUNG STAR IN INDIA!
AND SHE'S A FAN OF YOURS!
SHE'S AGREED TO BE IN THE VIDEO WITH YOU!
WE CAN DO THAT!
ER... WHEN I SAID YOU, I MEANT ARCHIE --THERE'LL BE NO BAND IN THIS VIDEO!
12

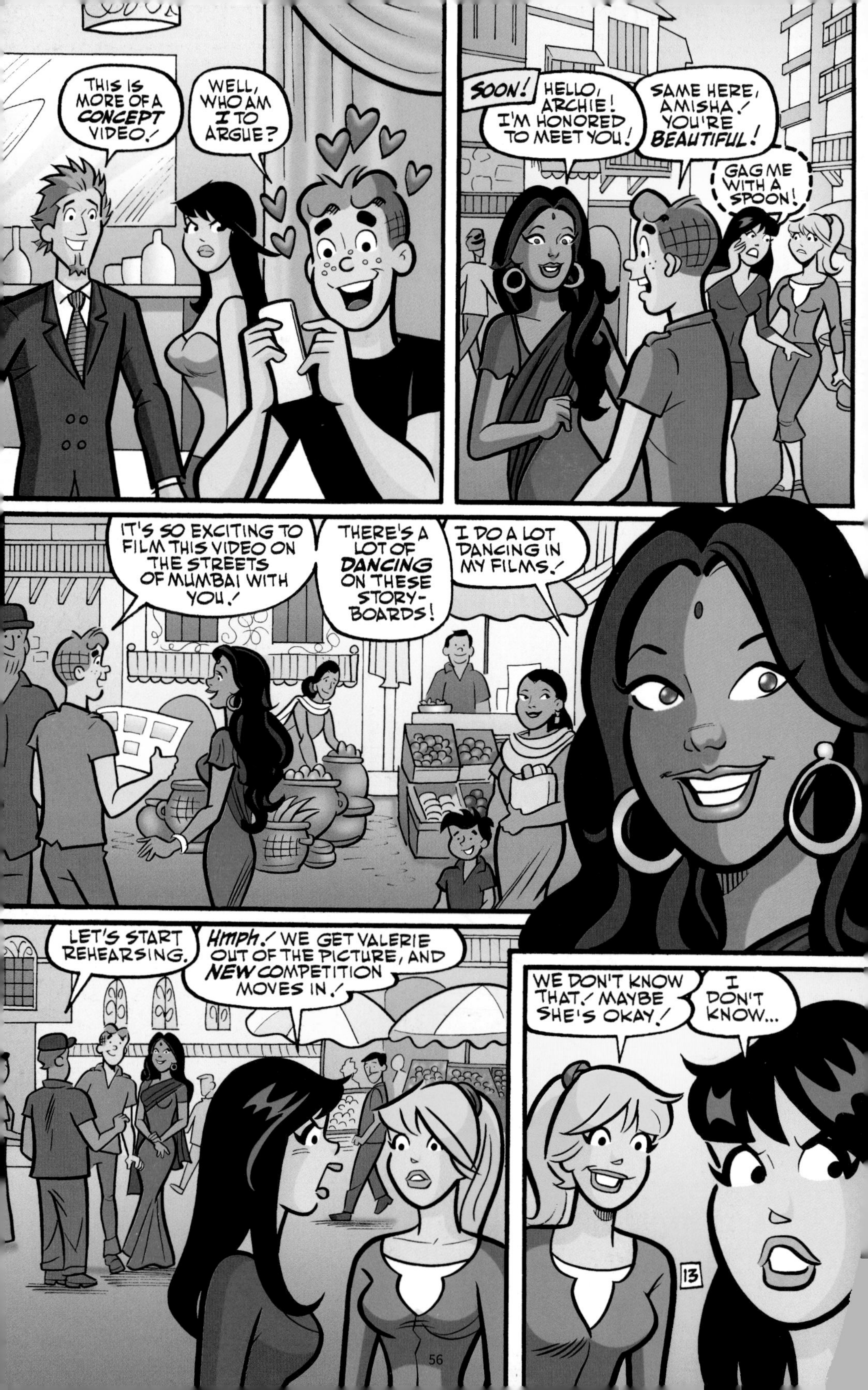
THIS IS MORE OF A CONCEPT VIDEO!
WELL, WHO AM I TO ARGUE?
SOON!
HELLO, ARCHIE! I'M HONORED TO MEET YOU!
SAME HERE, AMISHA! YOU'RE BEAUTIFUL!
GAG ME WITH A SPOON!
IT'S SO EXCITING TO FILM THIS VIDEO ON THE STREETS OF MUMBAI WITH YOU!
THERE'S A LOT OF DANCING ON THESE STORY-BOARDS!
I DO A LOT DANCING IN MY FILMS!
LET'S START REHEARSING.
Hmph! WE GET VALERIE OUT OF THE PICTURE, AND NEW COMPETITION MOVES IN!
WE DON'T KNOW THAT! MAYBE SHE'S OKAY!
I DON'T KNOW...
13

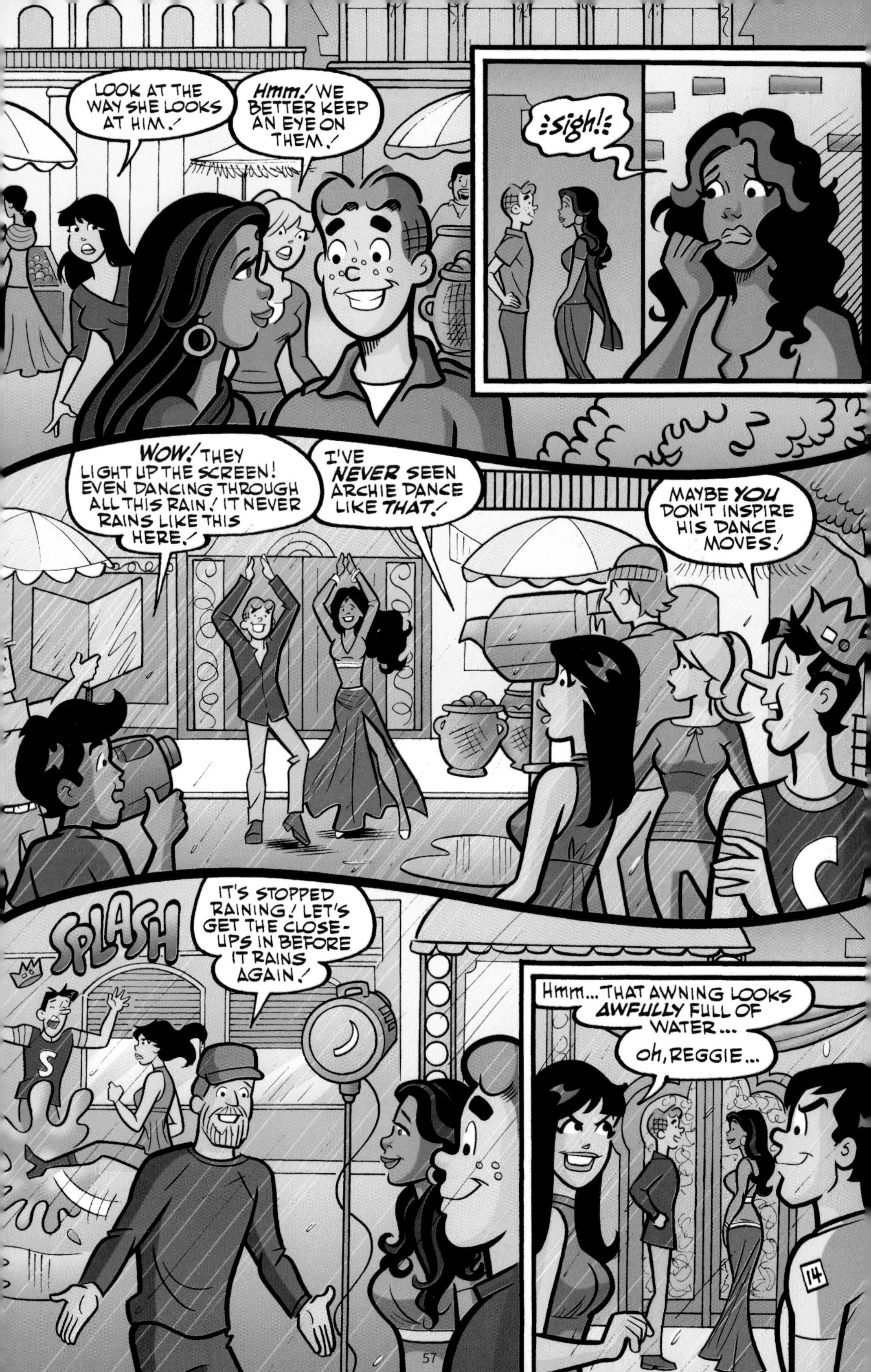
LOOK AT THE WAY SHE LOOKS AT HIM!
Hmm! WE BETTER KEEP AN EYE ON THEM!
sigh!
WOW! THEY LIGHT UP THE SCREEN! EVEN DANCING THROUGH ALL THIS RAIN! IT NEVER RAINS LIKE THIS HERE!
I'VE NEVER SEEN ARCHIE DANCE LIKE THAT!
MAYBE YOU DON'T INSPIRE HIS DANCE MOVES!
SPLASH
IT'S STOPPED RAINING! LET'S GET THE CLOSE-UPS IN BEFORE IT RAINS AGAIN!
Hmm... THAT AWNING LOOKS AWFULLY FULL OF WATER...
oh, REGGIE...
14

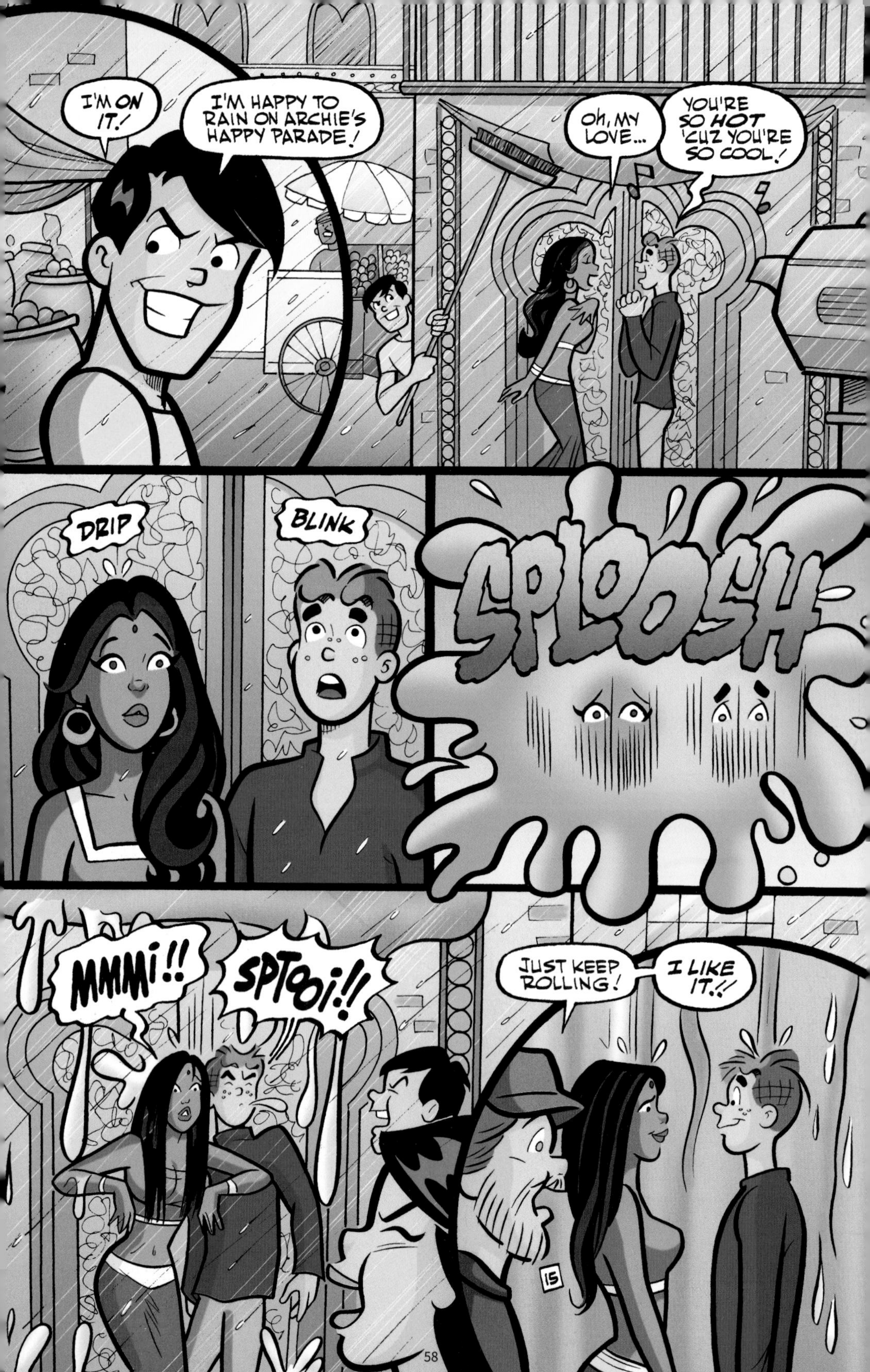
I'M ON IT.!
I'M HAPPY TO RAIN ON ARCHIE'S HAPPY PARADE!
Oh, MY LOVE...
YOU'RE SO HOT 'CUZ YOU'RE SO COOL!
DRIP
BLINK
SPLOOSH
MMM!!
SPTOOi!!
JUST KEEP ROLLING!
I LIKE IT.!!
15

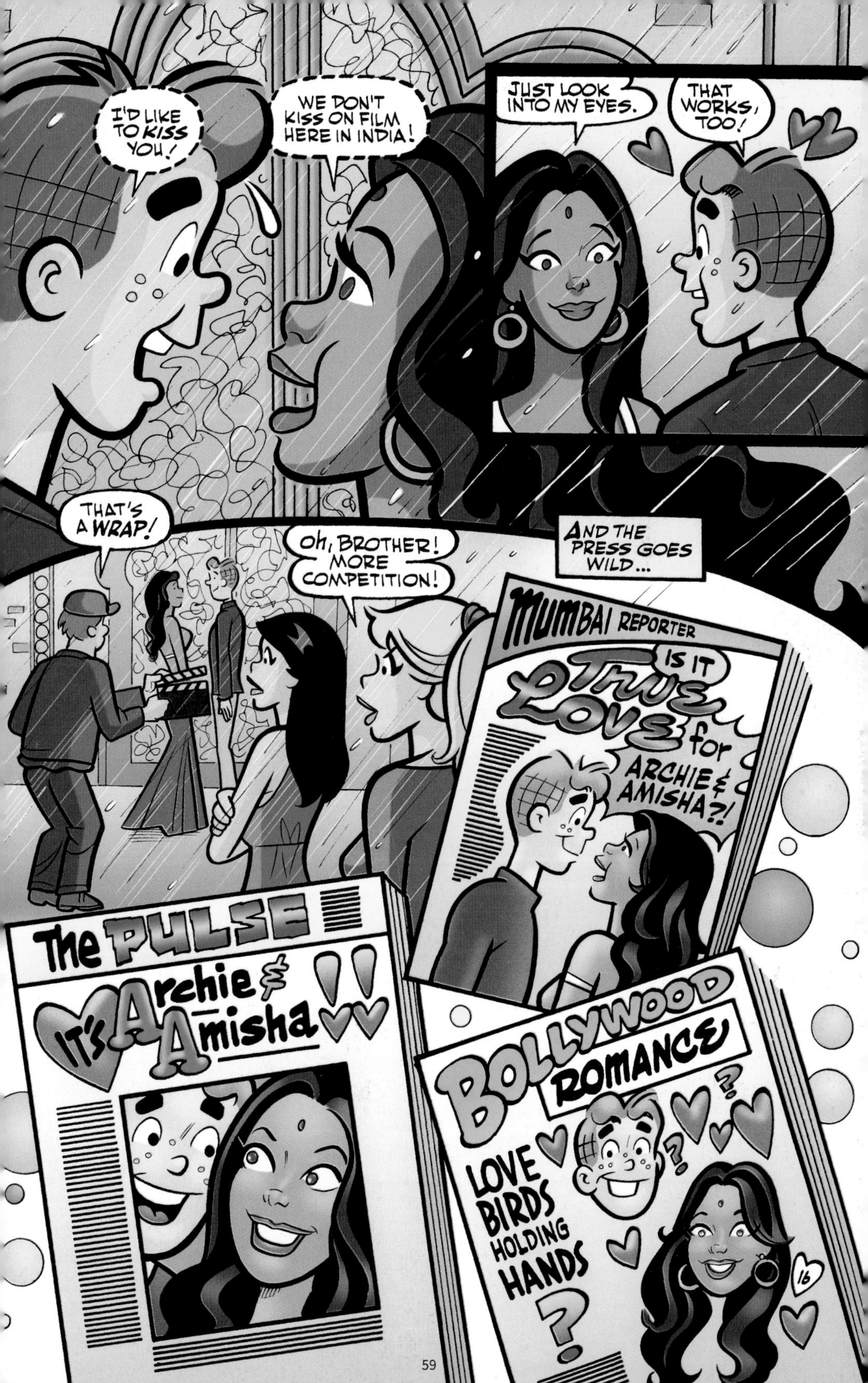
I'D LIKE TO KISS YOU!
WE DON'T KISS ON FILM HERE IN INDIA!
JUST LOOK INTO MY EYES.
THAT WORKS, TOO!
THAT'S A WRAP!
Oh, BROTHER! MORE COMPETITION!
AND THE PRESS GOES WILD...
MUMBAI REPORTER
IS IT TRUE LOVE for ARCHIE & AMISHA?!
The PULSE
IT'S Archie & Amisha!!
BOLLYWOOD ROMANCE
LOVE BIRDS HOLDING HANDS?
16

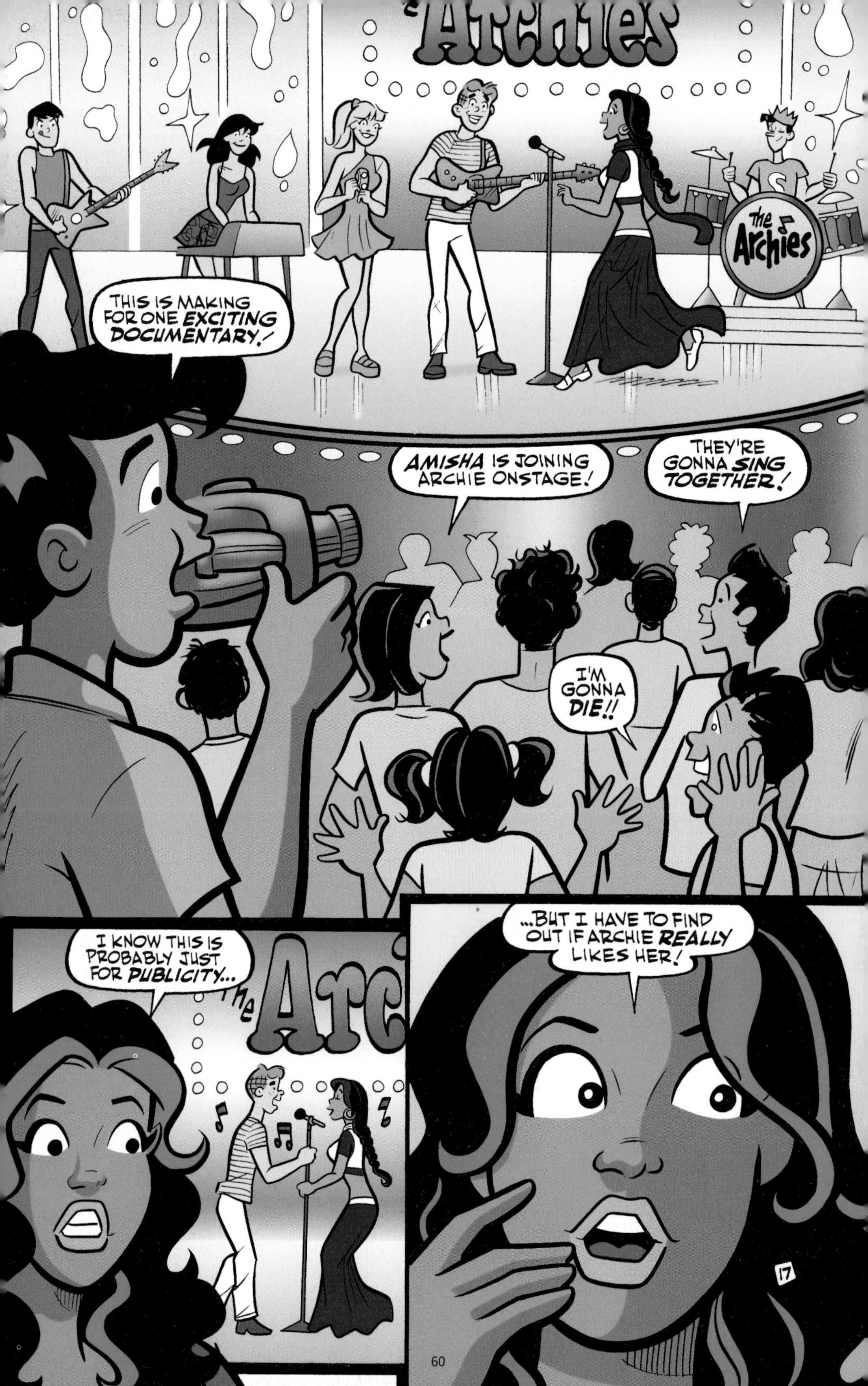

Archies
THIS IS MAKING FOR ONE EXCITING DOCUMENTARY!
The Archies
AMISHA IS JOINING ARCHIE ONSTAGE!
THEY'RE GONNA SING TOGETHER!
I'M GONNA DIE!!
I KNOW THIS IS PROBABLY JUST FOR PUBLICITY...
...BUT I HAVE TO FIND OUT IF ARCHIE REALLY LIKES HER!
17

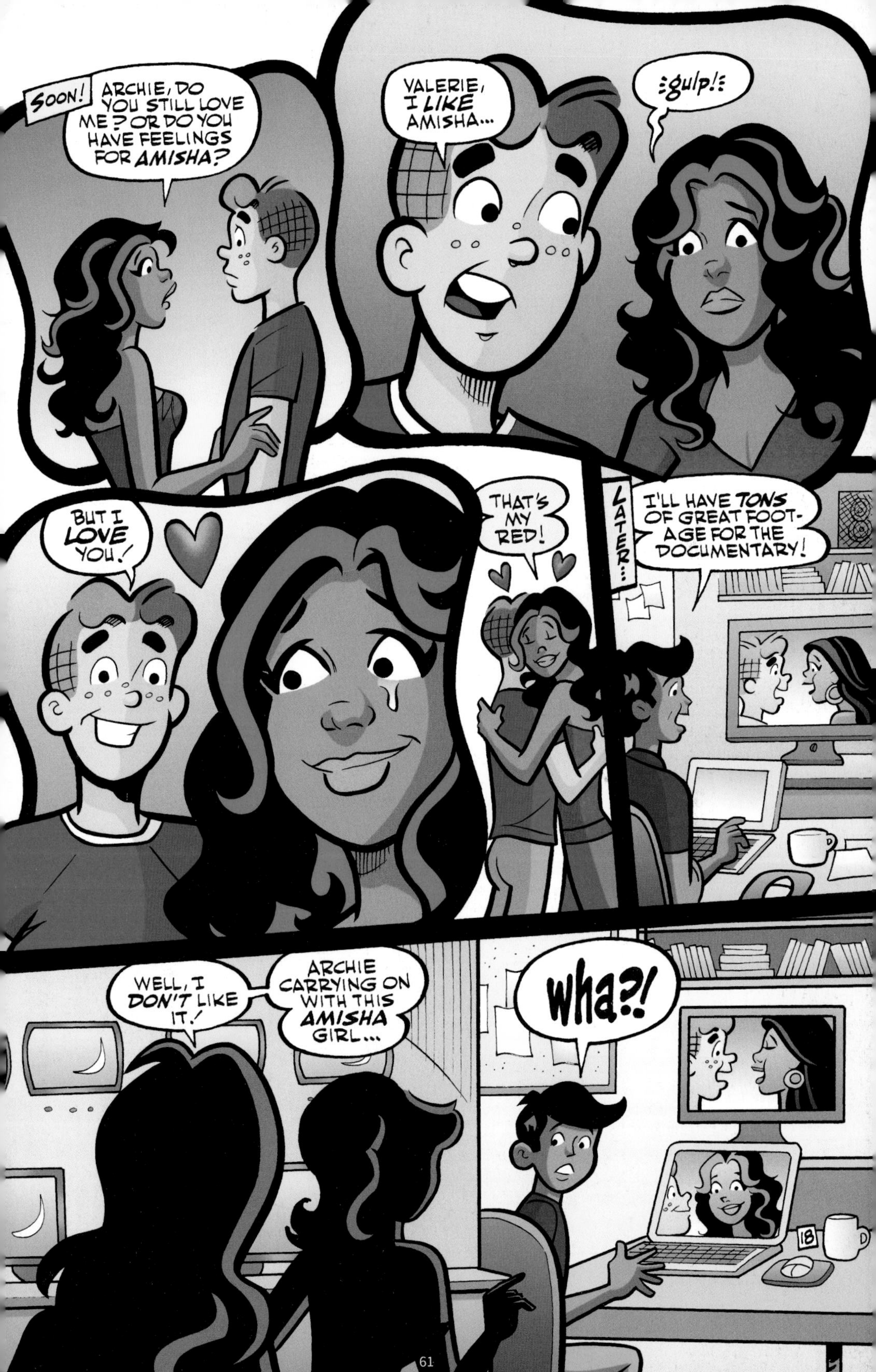
SOON!
ARCHIE, DO YOU STILL LOVE ME? OR DO YOU HAVE FEELINGS FOR AMISHA?
VALERIE, I LIKE AMISHA...
:gulp!:
BUT I LOVE YOU!
THAT'S MY RED!
LATER...
I'LL HAVE TONS OF GREAT FOOTAGE FOR THE DOCUMENTARY!
WELL, I DON'T LIKE IT!
ARCHIE CARRYING ON WITH THIS AMISHA GIRL...
wha?!
18

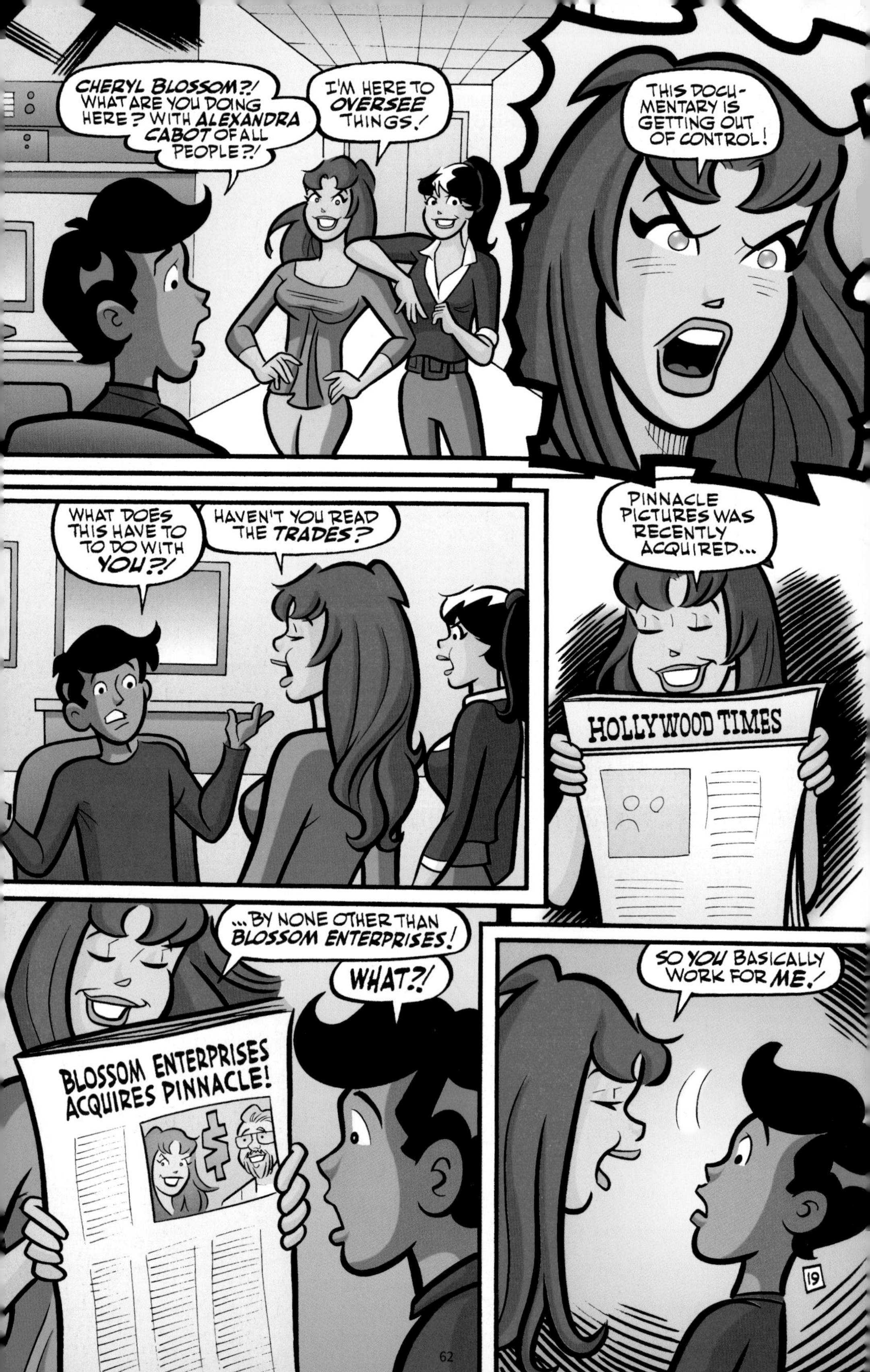
CHERYL BLOSSOM?! WHAT ARE YOU DOING HERE? WITH ALEXANDRA CABOT OF ALL PEOPLE?!
I'M HERE TO OVERSEE THINGS!
THIS DOCUMENTARY IS GETTING OUT OF CONTROL!
WHAT DOES THIS HAVE TO TO DO WITH YOU?!
HAVEN'T YOU READ THE TRADES?
PINNACLE PICTURES WAS RECENTLY ACQUIRED...
HOLLYWOOD TIMES
...BY NONE OTHER THAN BLOSSOM ENTERPRISES!
WHAT?!
BLOSSOM ENTERPRISES ACQUIRES PINNACLE!
SO YOU BASICALLY WORK FOR ME!
19

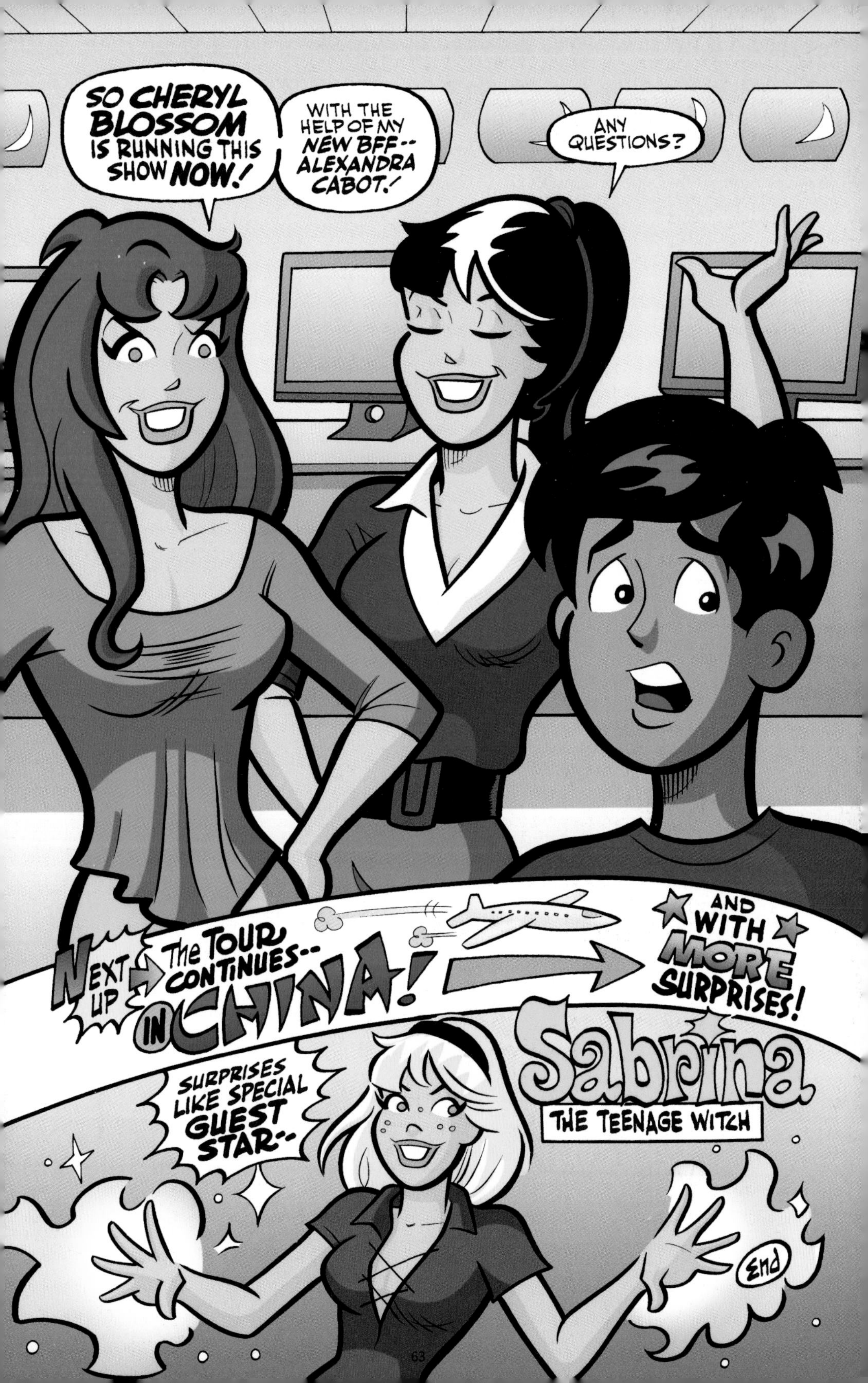
SO CHERYL BLOSSOM IS RUNNING THIS SHOW NOW!
WITH THE HELP OF MY NEW BFF-- ALEXANDRA CABOT!
ANY QUESTIONS?
NEXT UP
The TOUR CONTINUES-- IN CHINA!
AND WITH MORE SURPRISES!
SURPRISES LIKE SPECIAL GUEST STAR--
Sabrina
THE TEENAGE WITCH
End

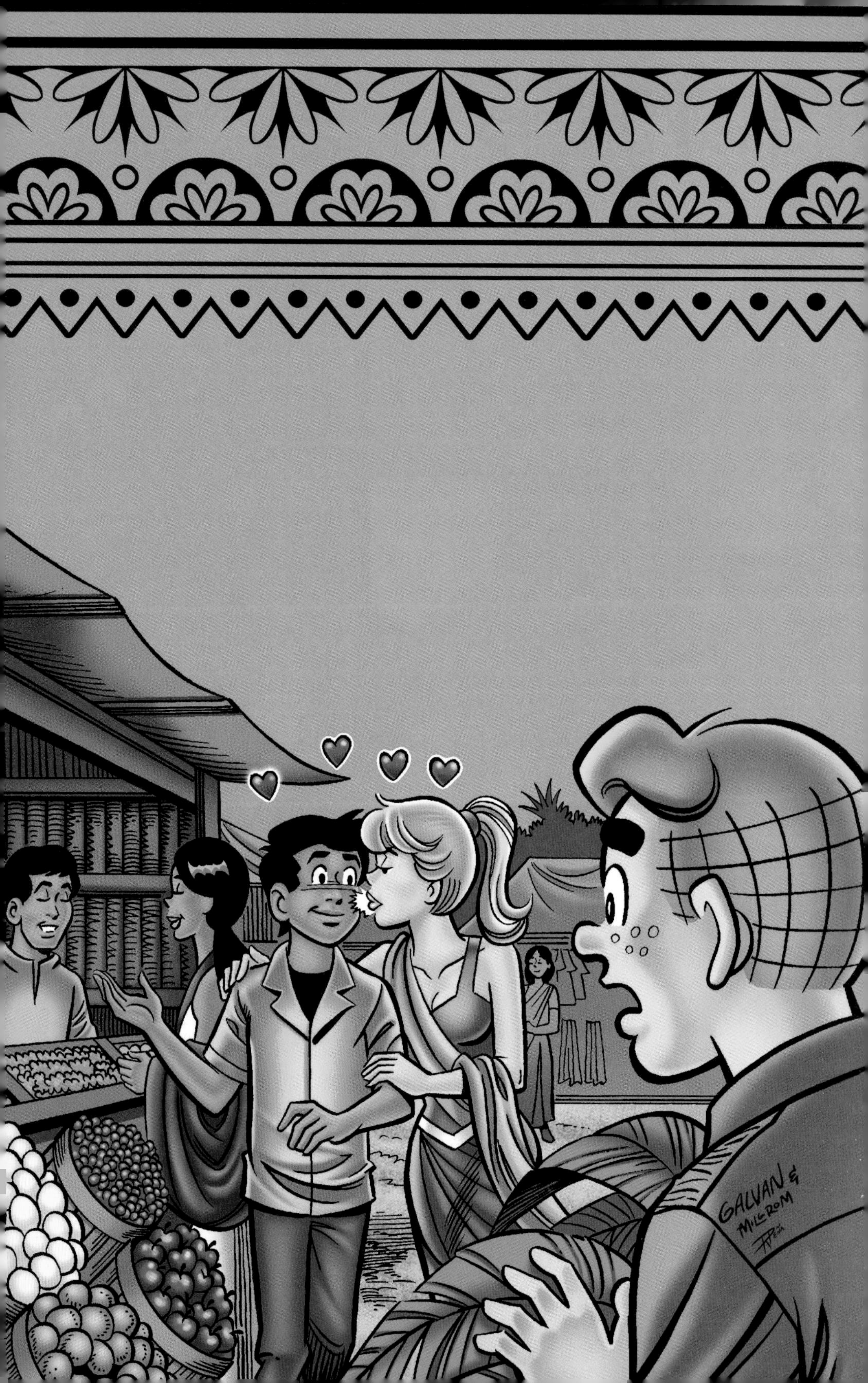

GALVAN & MILGROM

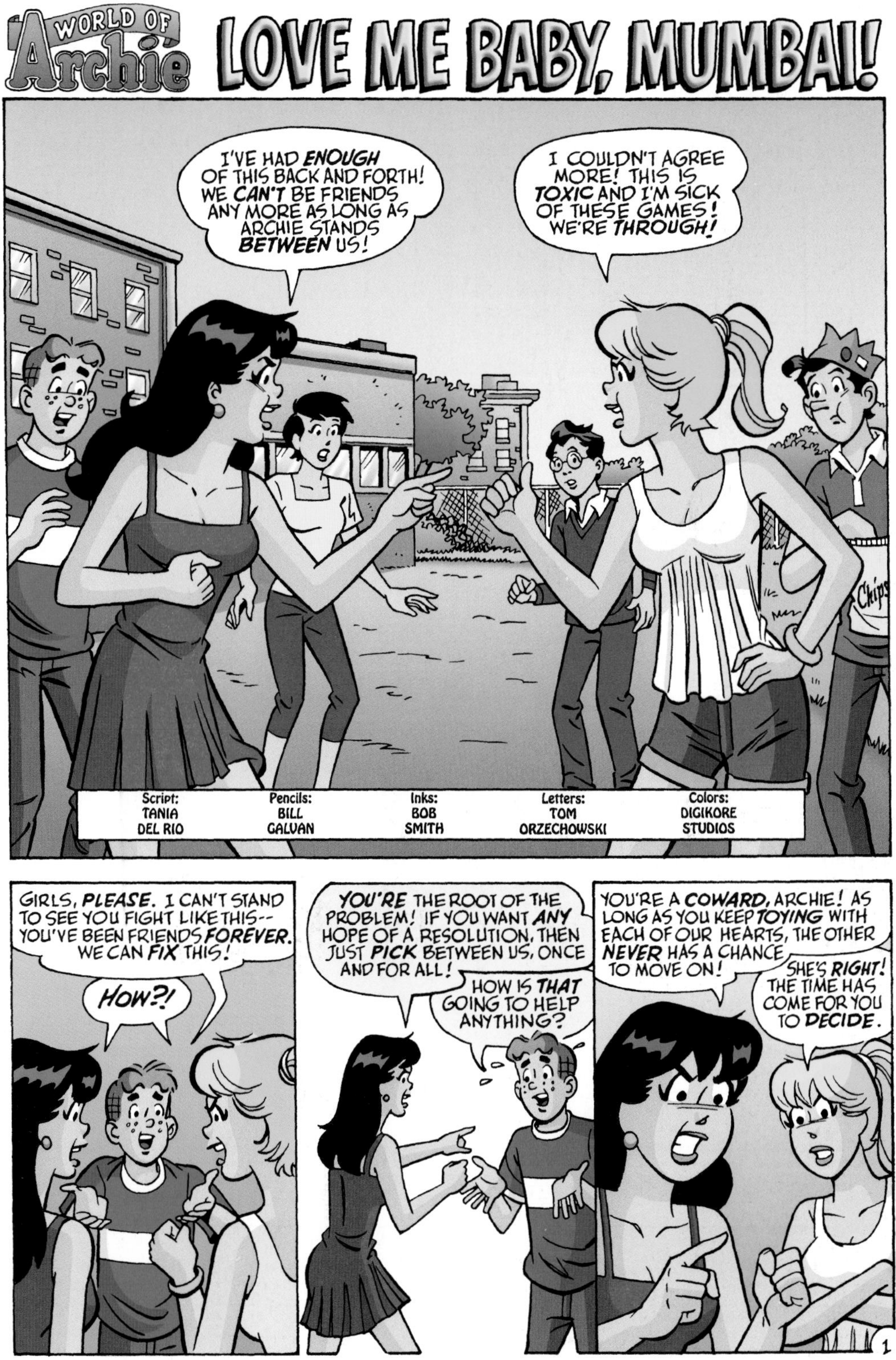
WORLD OF Archie
LOVE ME BABY, MUMBAI!
I'VE HAD ENOUGH OF THIS BACK AND FORTH! WE CAN'T BE FRIENDS ANY MORE AS LONG AS ARCHIE STANDS BETWEEN US!
I COULDN'T AGREE MORE! THIS IS TOXIC AND I'M SICK OF THESE GAMES! WE'RE THROUGH!
Chips
Script: TANIA DEL RIO
Pencils: BILL GALVAN
Inks: BOB SMITH
Letters: TOM ORZECHOWSKI
Colors: DIGIKORE STUDIOS
GIRLS, PLEASE. I CAN'T STAND TO SEE YOU FIGHT LIKE THIS-- YOU'VE BEEN FRIENDS FOREVER. WE CAN FIX THIS!
HOW?!
YOU'RE THE ROOT OF THE PROBLEM! IF YOU WANT ANY HOPE OF A RESOLUTION, THEN JUST PICK BETWEEN US, ONCE AND FOR ALL!
HOW IS THAT GOING TO HELP ANYTHING?
YOU'RE A COWARD, ARCHIE! AS LONG AS YOU KEEP TOYING WITH EACH OF OUR HEARTS, THE OTHER NEVER HAS A CHANCE TO MOVE ON!
SHE'S RIGHT! THE TIME HAS COME FOR YOU TO DECIDE.
1

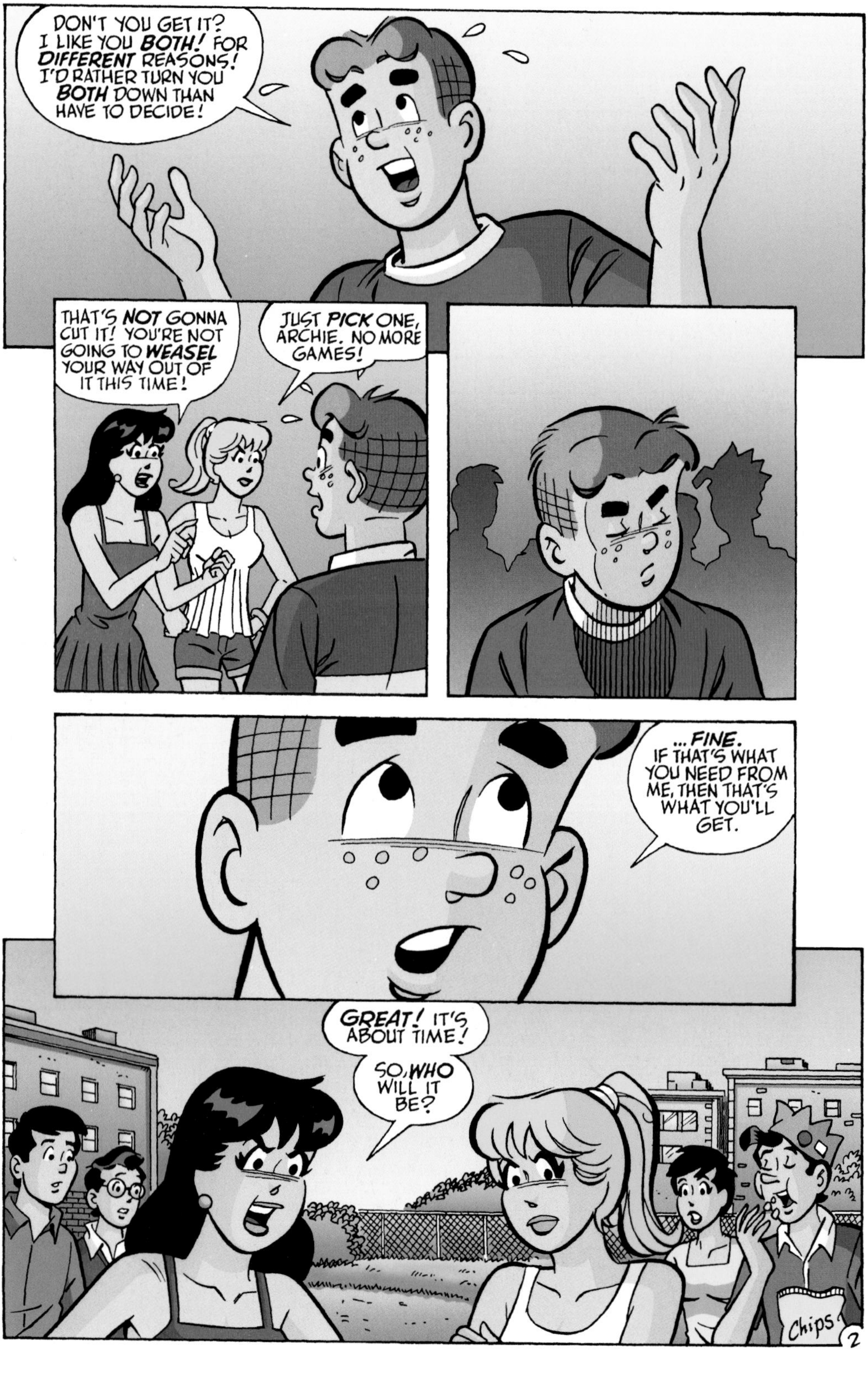
DON'T YOU GET IT? I LIKE YOU BOTH! FOR DIFFERENT REASONS! I'D RATHER TURN YOU BOTH DOWN THAN HAVE TO DECIDE!
THAT'S NOT GONNA CUT IT! YOU'RE NOT GOING TO WEASEL YOUR WAY OUT OF IT THIS TIME!
JUST PICK ONE, ARCHIE. NO MORE GAMES!
... FINE. IF THAT'S WHAT YOU NEED FROM ME, THEN THAT'S WHAT YOU'LL GET.
GREAT! IT'S ABOUT TIME!
SO, WHO WILL IT BE?
Chips
2

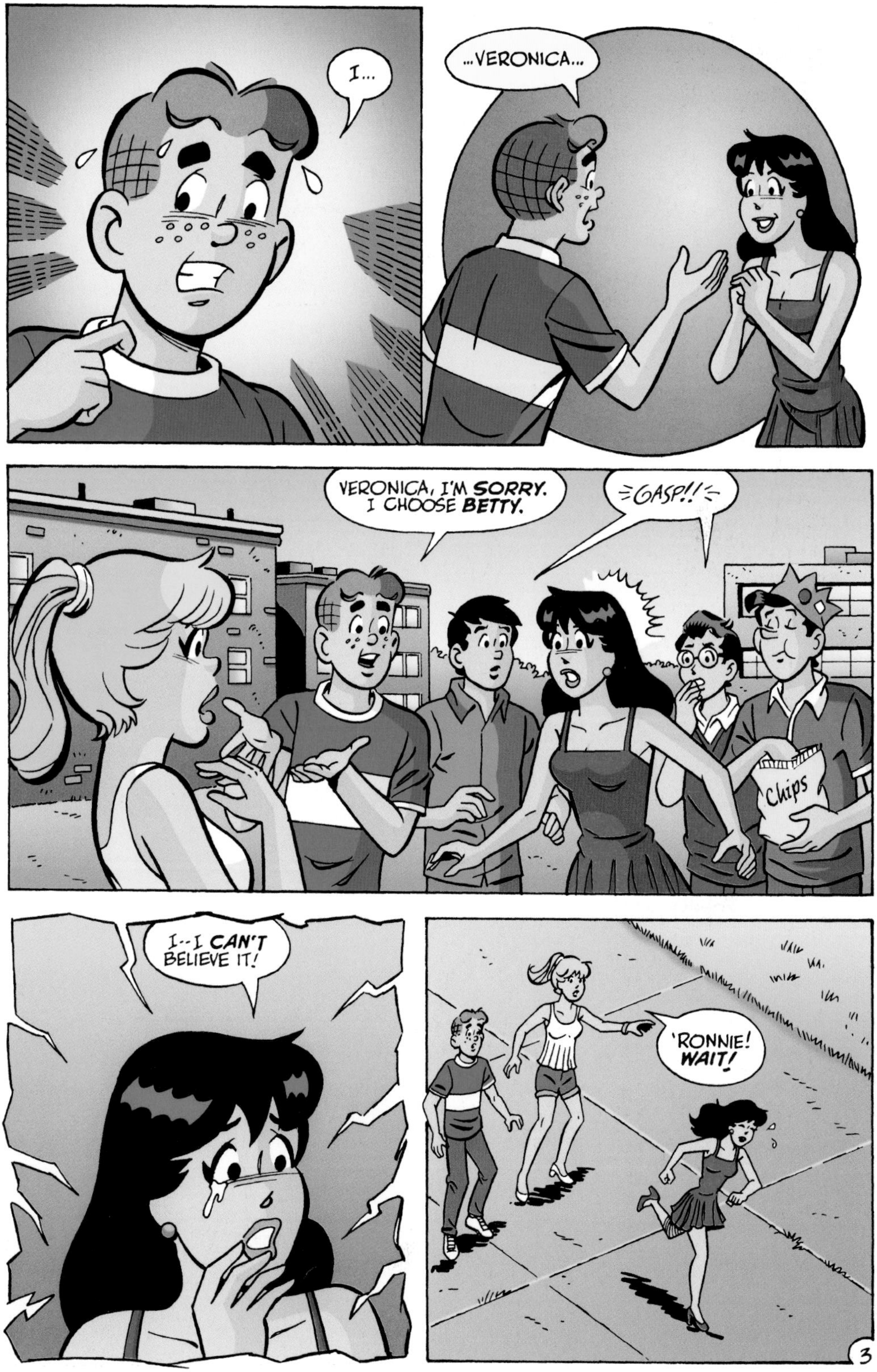
I...
...VERONICA...
VERONICA, I'M SORRY. I CHOOSE BETTY.
GASP!!
Chips
I--I CAN'T BELIEVE IT!
'RONNIE! WAIT!
3

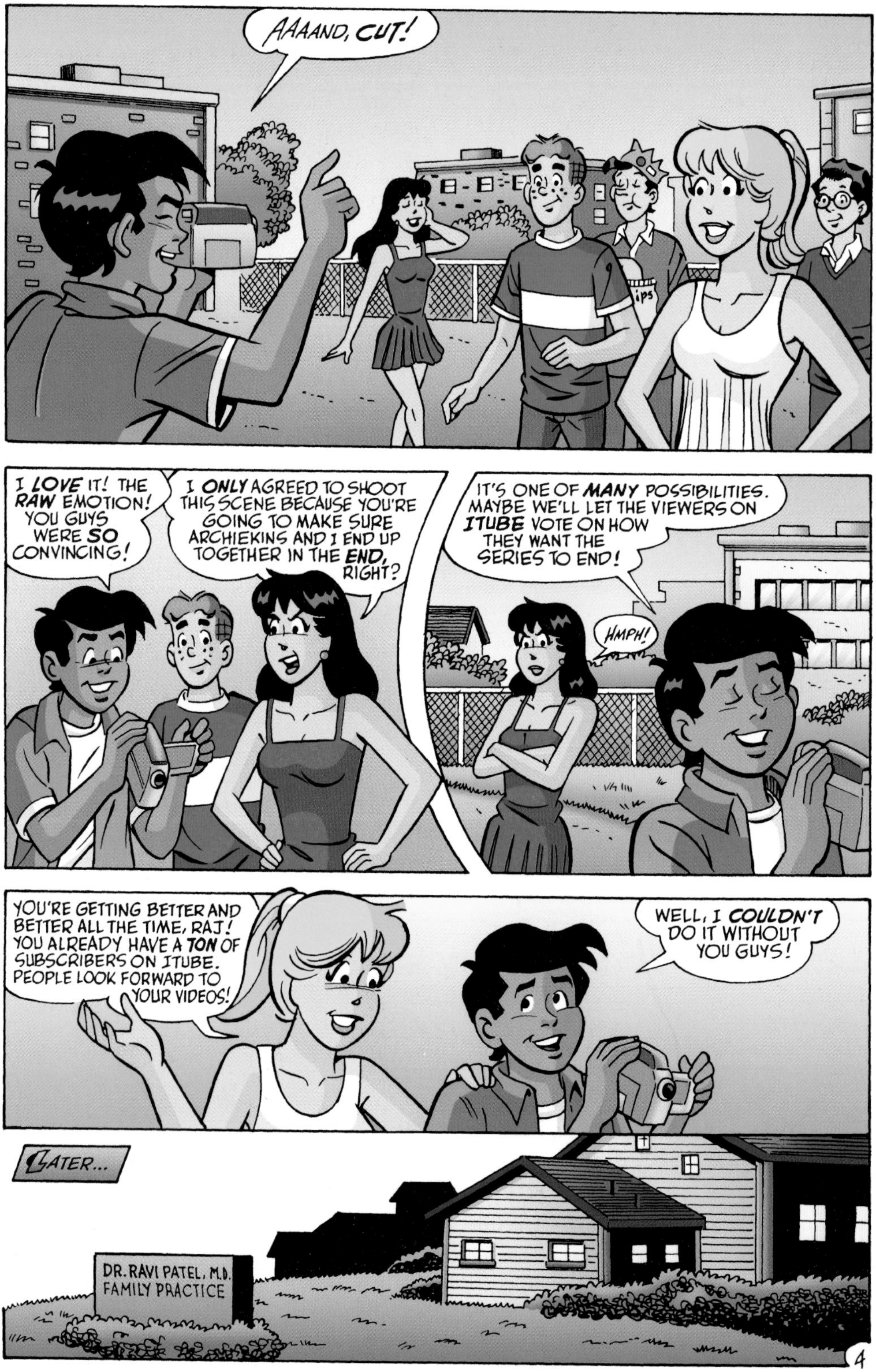

AAAAND, CUT!
I LOVE IT! THE RAW EMOTION! YOU GUYS WERE SO CONVINCING!
I ONLY AGREED TO SHOOT THIS SCENE BECAUSE YOU'RE GOING TO MAKE SURE ARCHIEKINS AND I END UP TOGETHER IN THE END, RIGHT?
IT'S ONE OF MANY POSSIBILITIES. MAYBE WE'LL LET THE VIEWERS ON ITUBE VOTE ON HOW THEY WANT THE SERIES TO END!
HMPH!
YOU'RE GETTING BETTER AND BETTER ALL THE TIME, RAJ! YOU ALREADY HAVE A TON OF SUBSCRIBERS ON ITUBE. PEOPLE LOOK FORWARD TO YOUR VIDEOS!
WELL, I COULDN'T DO IT WITHOUT YOU GUYS!
LATER...
DR. RAVI PATEL, M.D.
FAMILY PRACTICE
4

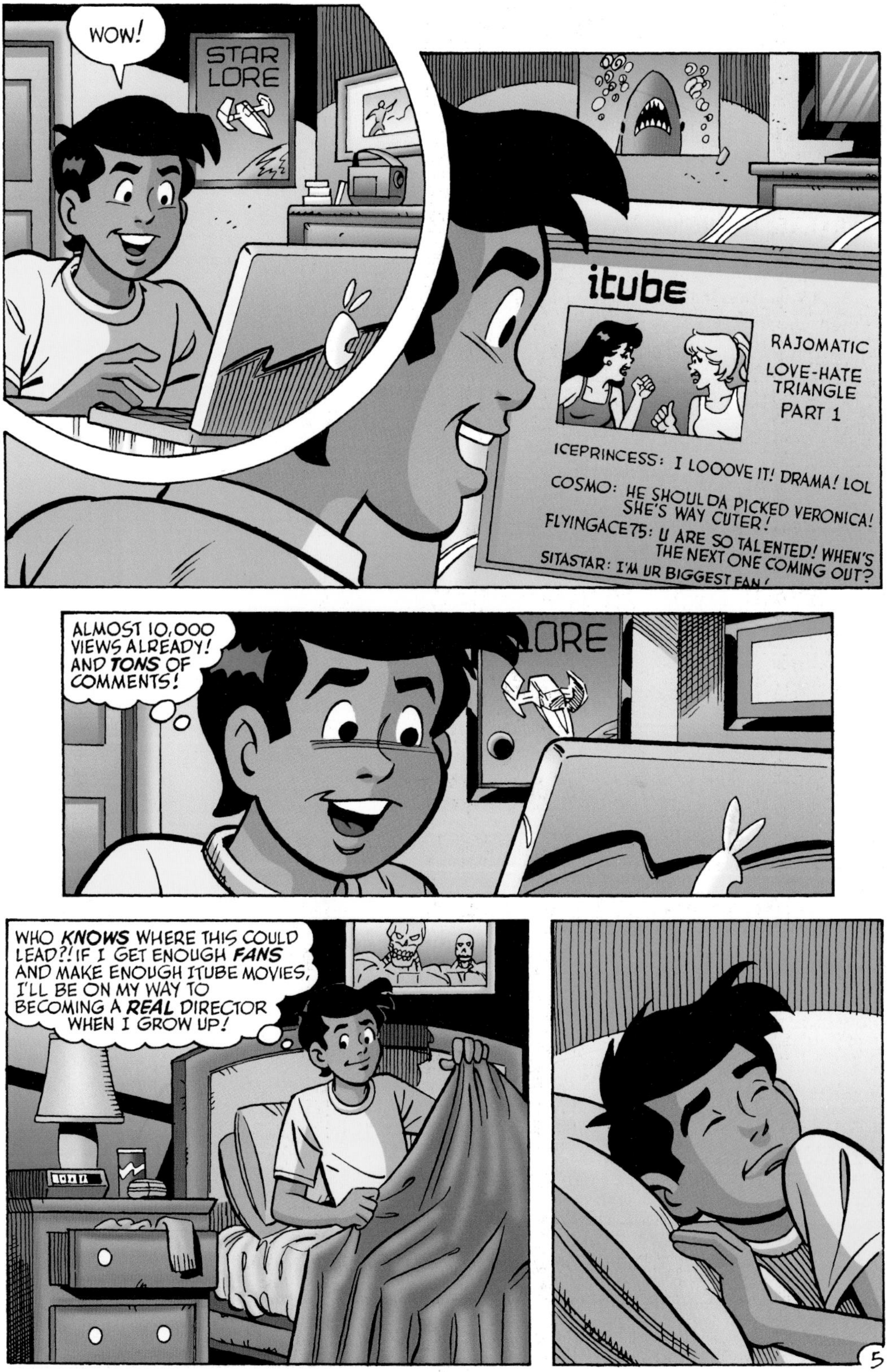
WOW!
STAR LORE
itube
RAJOMATIC
LOVE-HATE TRIANGLE PART 1
ICEPRINCESS: I LOOOVE IT! DRAMA! LOL
COSMO: HE SHOULDA PICKED VERONICA! SHE'S WAY CUTER!
FLYINGACE75: U ARE SO TALENTED! WHEN'S THE NEXT ONE COMING OUT?
SITASTAR: I'M UR BIGGEST FAN!
ALMOST 10,000 VIEWS ALREADY! AND TONS OF COMMENTS!
LORE
WHO KNOWS WHERE THIS COULD LEAD?! IF I GET ENOUGH FANS AND MAKE ENOUGH ITUBE MOVIES, I'LL BE ON MY WAY TO BECOMING A REAL DIRECTOR WHEN I GROW UP!
5

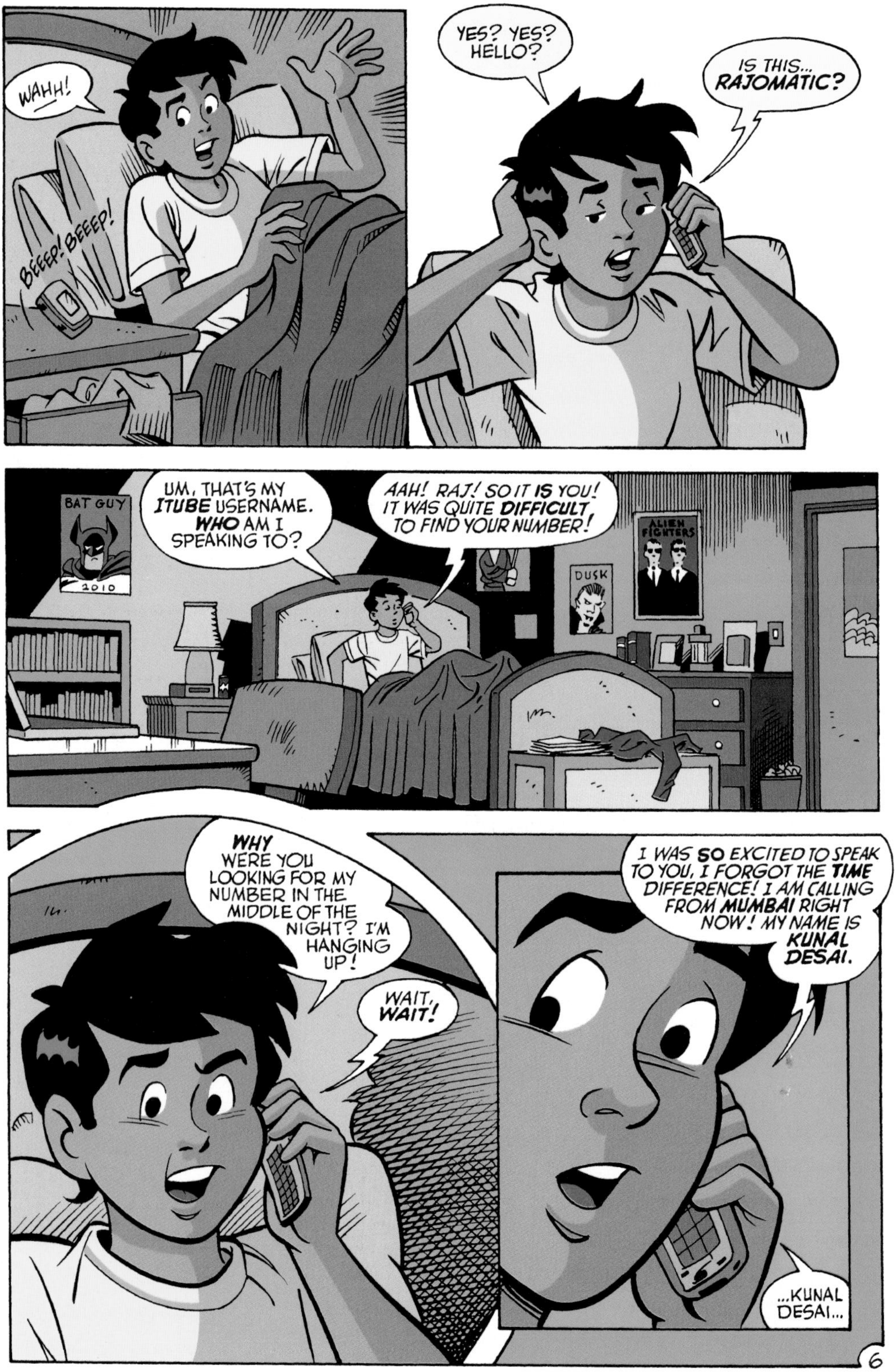
WAHH!
BEEEP! BEEEP!
YES? YES? HELLO?
IS THIS... RAJOMATIC?
BAT GUY
2010
UM, THAT'S MY ITUBE USERNAME. WHO AM I SPEAKING TO?
AAH! RAJ! SO IT IS YOU! IT WAS QUITE DIFFICULT TO FIND YOUR NUMBER!
ALIEN FIGHTERS
DUSK
WHY WERE YOU LOOKING FOR MY NUMBER IN THE MIDDLE OF THE NIGHT? I'M HANGING UP!
WAIT, WAIT!
I WAS SO EXCITED TO SPEAK TO YOU, I FORGOT THE TIME DIFFERENCE! I AM CALLING FROM MUMBAI RIGHT NOW! MY NAME IS KUNAL DESAI.
...KUNAL DESAI...
6

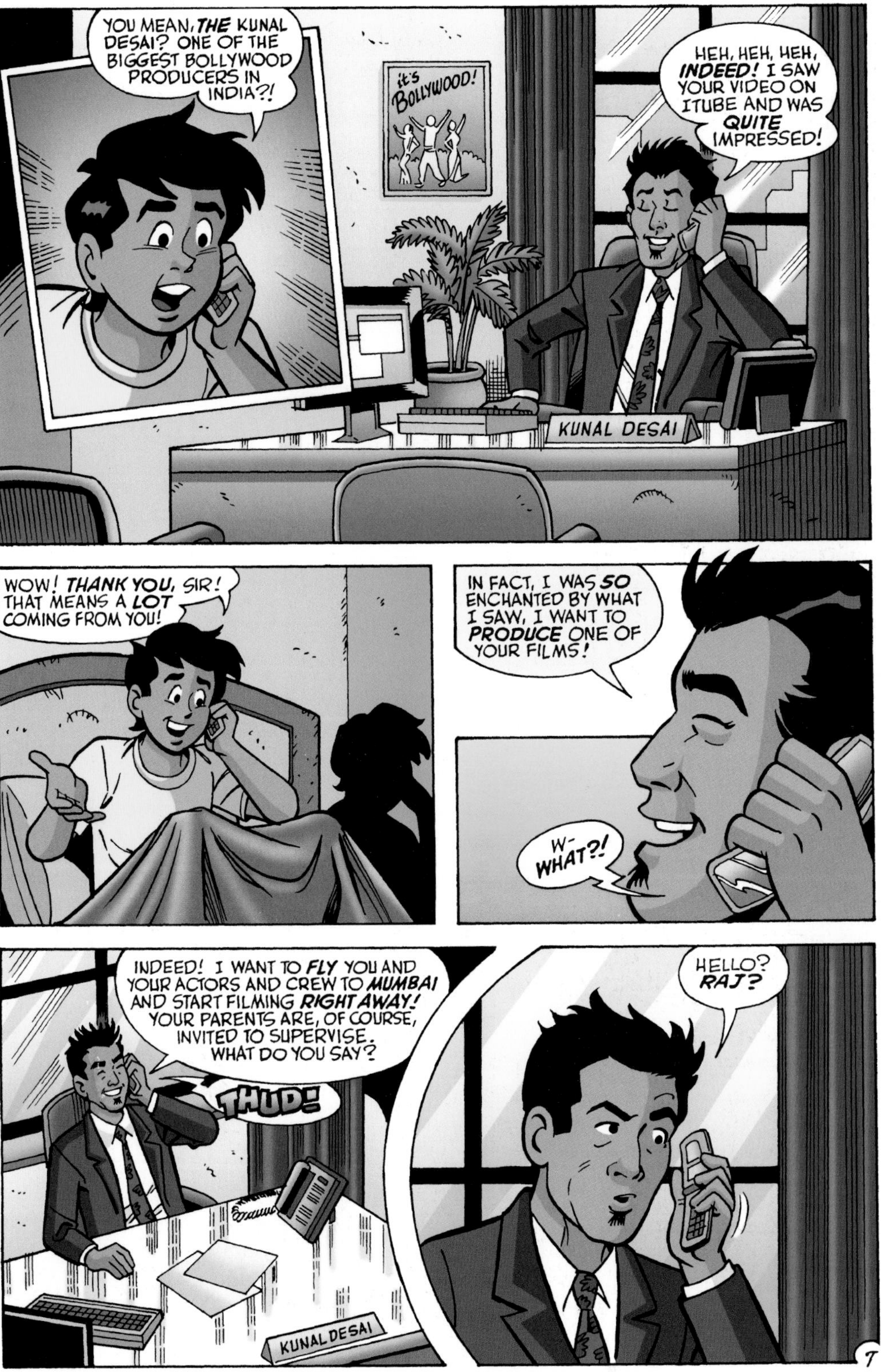
YOU MEAN, THE KUNAL DESAI? ONE OF THE BIGGEST BOLLYWOOD PRODUCERS IN INDIA?!
it's BOLLYWOOD!
HEH, HEH, HEH, INDEED! I SAW YOUR VIDEO ON ITUBE AND WAS QUITE IMPRESSED!
KUNAL DESAI
WOW! THANK YOU, SIR! THAT MEANS A LOT COMING FROM YOU!
IN FACT, I WAS SO ENCHANTED BY WHAT I SAW, I WANT TO PRODUCE ONE OF YOUR FILMS!
W- WHAT?!
INDEED! I WANT TO FLY YOU AND YOUR ACTORS AND CREW TO MUMBAI AND START FILMING RIGHT AWAY! YOUR PARENTS ARE, OF COURSE, INVITED TO SUPERVISE. WHAT DO YOU SAY?
THUD!
HELLO? RAJ?
KUNAL DESAI
7

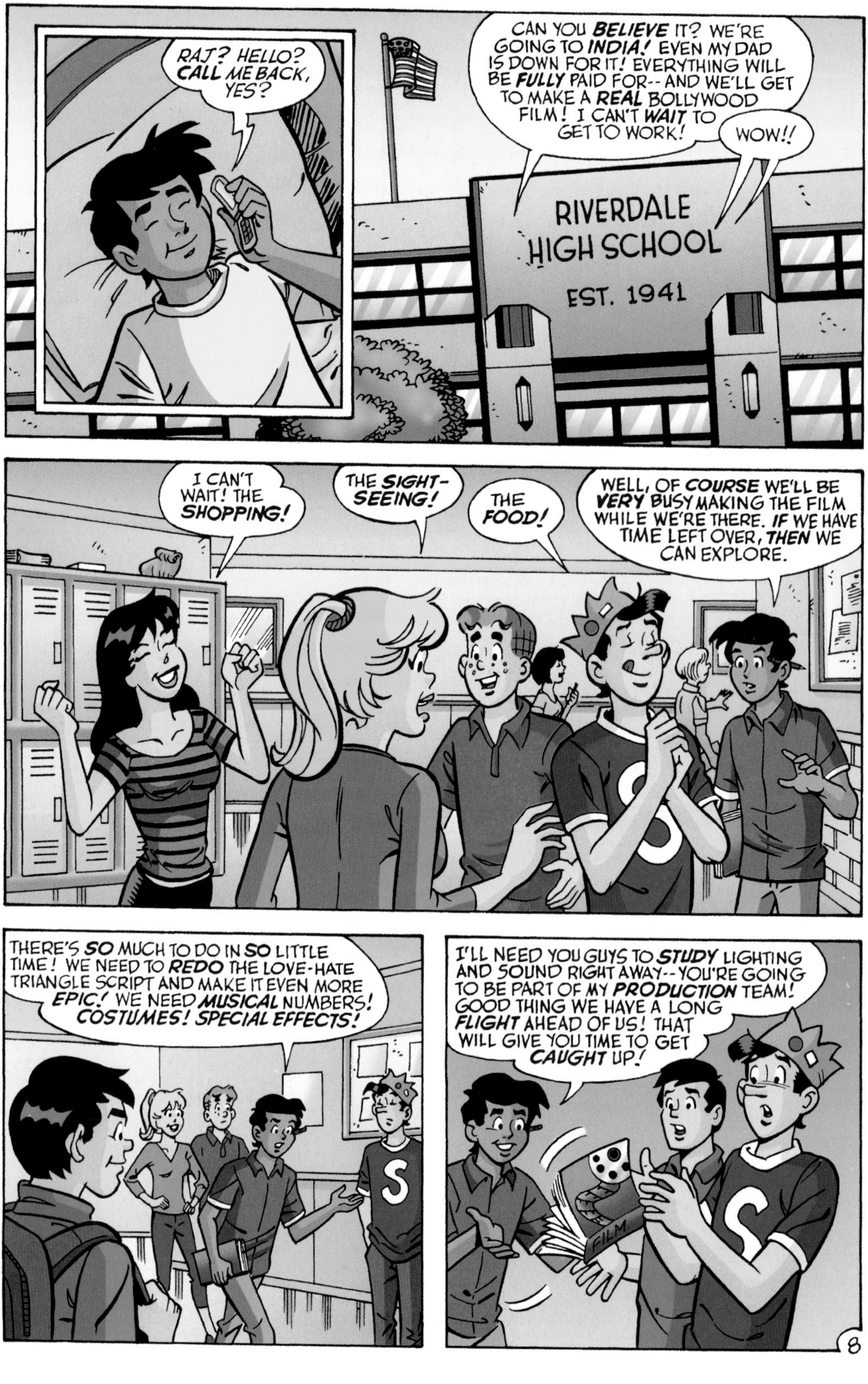
RAJ? HELLO? CALL ME BACK, YES?
CAN YOU BELIEVE IT? WE'RE GOING TO INDIA! EVEN MY DAD IS DOWN FOR IT! EVERYTHING WILL BE FULLY PAID FOR-- AND WE'LL GET TO MAKE A REAL BOLLYWOOD FILM! I CAN'T WAIT TO GET TO WORK!
WOW!!
RIVERDALE HIGH SCHOOL
EST. 1941
I CAN'T WAIT! THE SHOPPING!
THE SIGHT-SEEING!
THE FOOD!
WELL, OF COURSE WE'LL BE VERY BUSY MAKING THE FILM WHILE WE'RE THERE. IF WE HAVE TIME LEFT OVER, THEN WE CAN EXPLORE.
THERE'S SO MUCH TO DO IN SO LITTLE TIME! WE NEED TO REDO THE LOVE-HATE TRIANGLE SCRIPT AND MAKE IT EVEN MORE EPIC! WE NEED MUSICAL NUMBERS! COSTUMES! SPECIAL EFFECTS!
I'LL NEED YOU GUYS TO STUDY LIGHTING AND SOUND RIGHT AWAY-- YOU'RE GOING TO BE PART OF MY PRODUCTION TEAM! GOOD THING WE HAVE A LONG FLIGHT AHEAD OF US! THAT WILL GIVE YOU TIME TO GET CAUGHT UP!
FILM
8

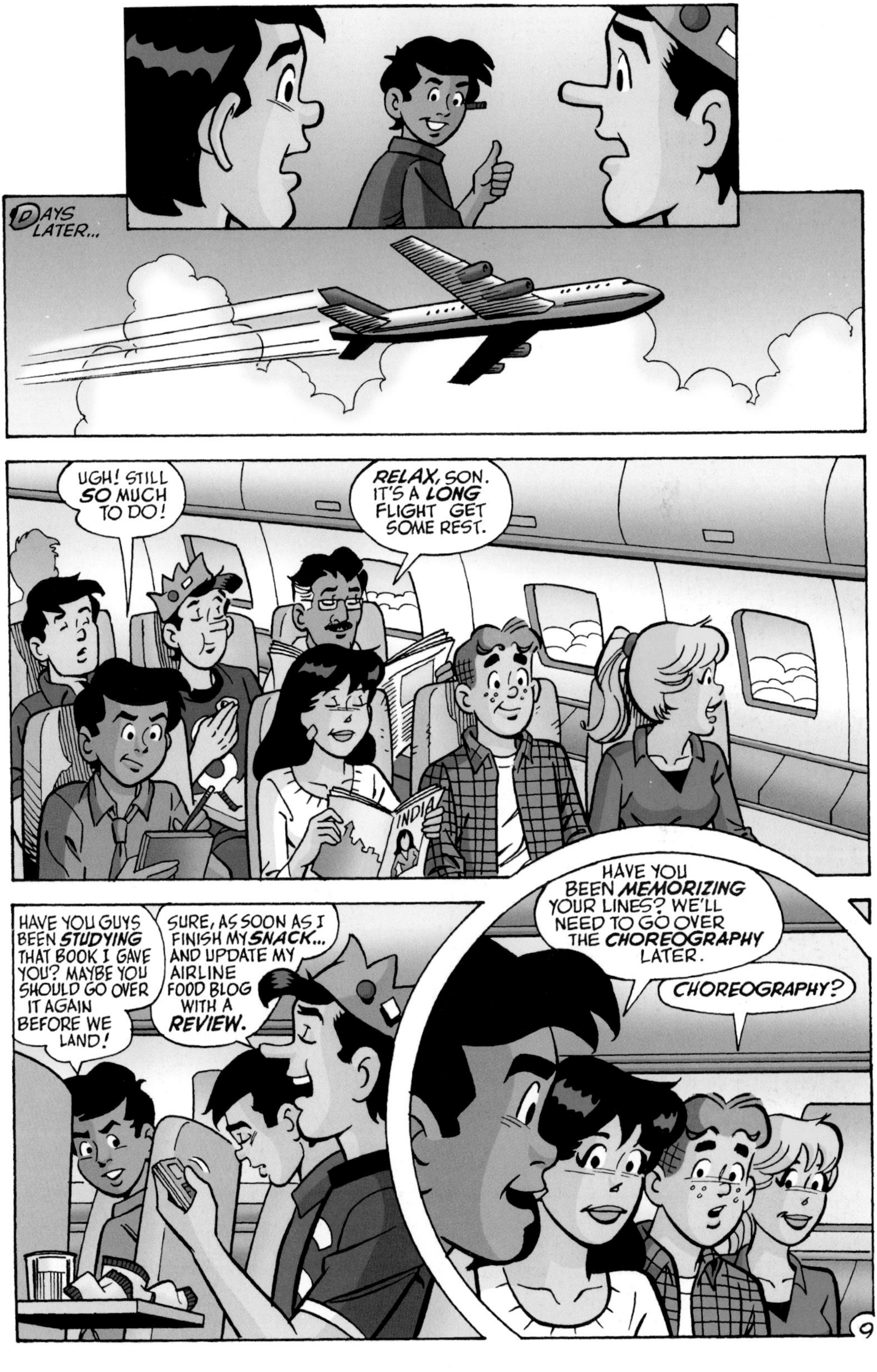
DAYS LATER...
UGH! STILL SO MUCH TO DO!
RELAX, SON. IT'S A LONG FLIGHT GET SOME REST.
INDIA
HAVE YOU GUYS BEEN STUDYING THAT BOOK I GAVE YOU? MAYBE YOU SHOULD GO OVER IT AGAIN BEFORE WE LAND!
SURE, AS SOON AS I FINISH MY SNACK... AND UPDATE MY AIRLINE FOOD BLOG WITH A REVIEW.
HAVE YOU BEEN MEMORIZING YOUR LINES? WE'LL NEED TO GO OVER THE CHOREOGRAPHY LATER.
CHOREOGRAPHY?
9

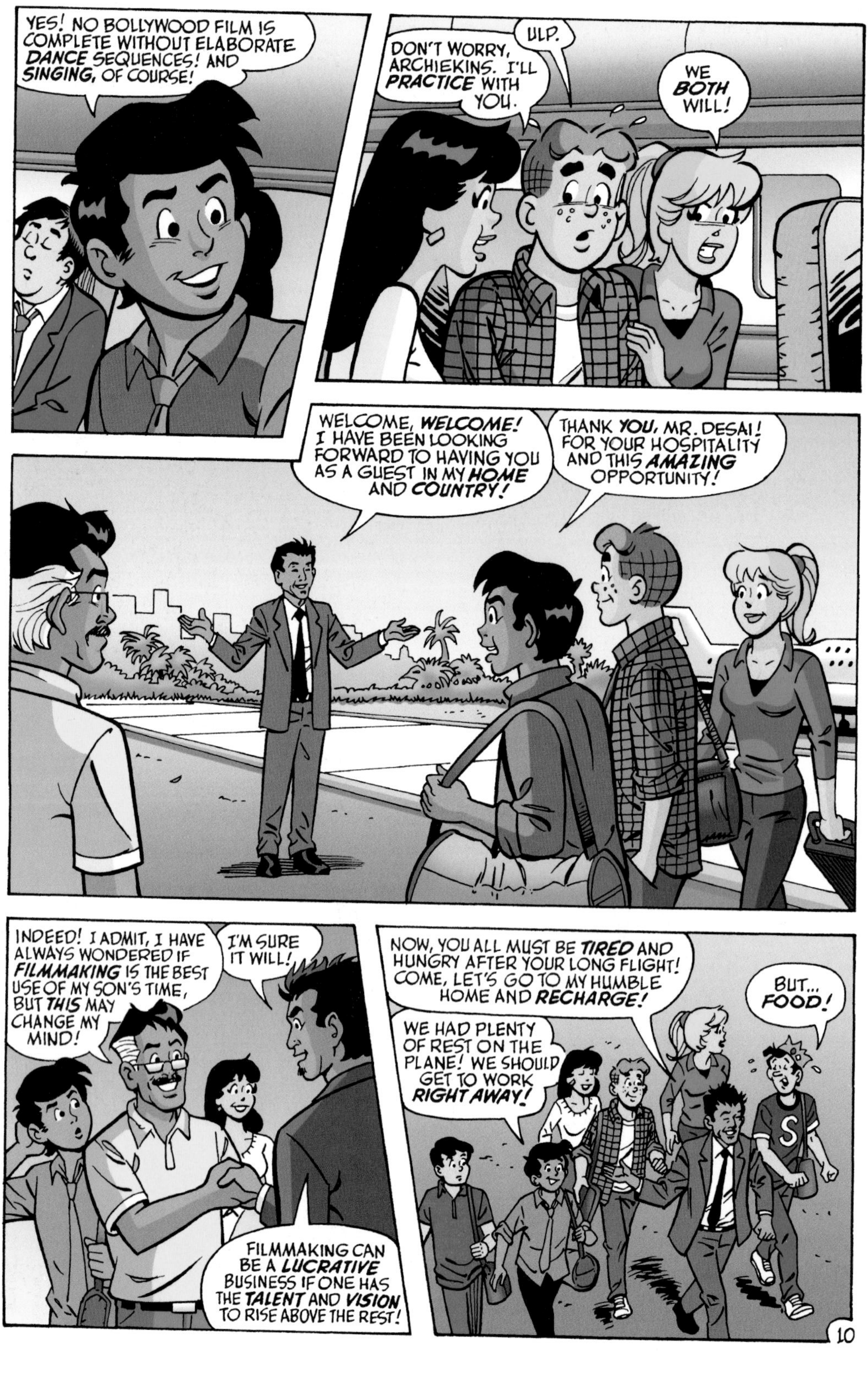
YES! NO BOLLYWOOD FILM IS COMPLETE WITHOUT ELABORATE DANCE SEQUENCES! AND SINGING, OF COURSE!
DON'T WORRY, ARCHIEKINS. I'LL PRACTICE WITH YOU.
ULP.
WE BOTH WILL!
WELCOME, WELCOME! I HAVE BEEN LOOKING FORWARD TO HAVING YOU AS A GUEST IN MY HOME AND COUNTRY!
THANK YOU, MR. DESAI! FOR YOUR HOSPITALITY AND THIS AMAZING OPPORTUNITY!
INDEED! I ADMIT, I HAVE ALWAYS WONDERED IF FILMMAKING IS THE BEST USE OF MY SON'S TIME, BUT THIS MAY CHANGE MY MIND!
I'M SURE IT WILL!
FILMMAKING CAN BE A LUCRATIVE BUSINESS IF ONE HAS THE TALENT AND VISION TO RISE ABOVE THE REST!
NOW, YOU ALL MUST BE TIRED AND HUNGRY AFTER YOUR LONG FLIGHT! COME, LET'S GO TO MY HUMBLE HOME AND RECHARGE!
WE HAD PLENTY OF REST ON THE PLANE! WE SHOULD GET TO WORK RIGHT AWAY!
BUT... FOOD!
10

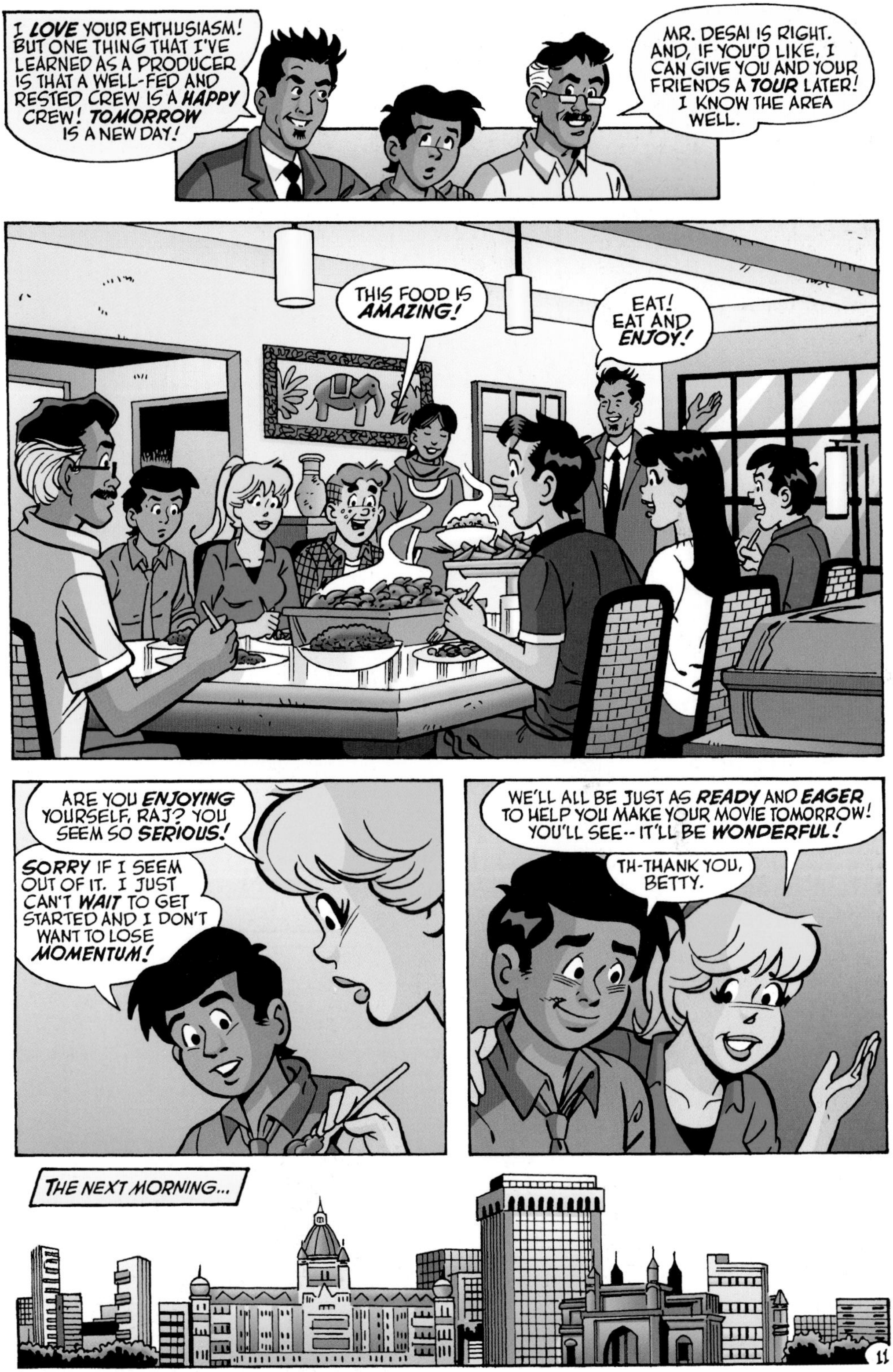
I LOVE YOUR ENTHUSIASM! BUT ONE THING THAT I'VE LEARNED AS A PRODUCER IS THAT A WELL-FED AND RESTED CREW IS A HAPPY CREW! TOMORROW IS A NEW DAY!
MR. DESAI IS RIGHT. AND, IF YOU'D LIKE, I CAN GIVE YOU AND YOUR FRIENDS A TOUR LATER! I KNOW THE AREA WELL.
THIS FOOD IS AMAZING!
EAT! EAT AND ENJOY!
ARE YOU ENJOYING YOURSELF, RAJ? YOU SEEM SO SERIOUS!
SORRY IF I SEEM OUT OF IT. I JUST CAN'T WAIT TO GET STARTED AND I DON'T WANT TO LOSE MOMENTUM!
WE'LL ALL BE JUST AS READY AND EAGER TO HELP YOU MAKE YOUR MOVIE TOMORROW! YOU'LL SEE-- IT'LL BE WONDERFUL!
TH-THANK YOU, BETTY.
THE NEXT MORNING...
11

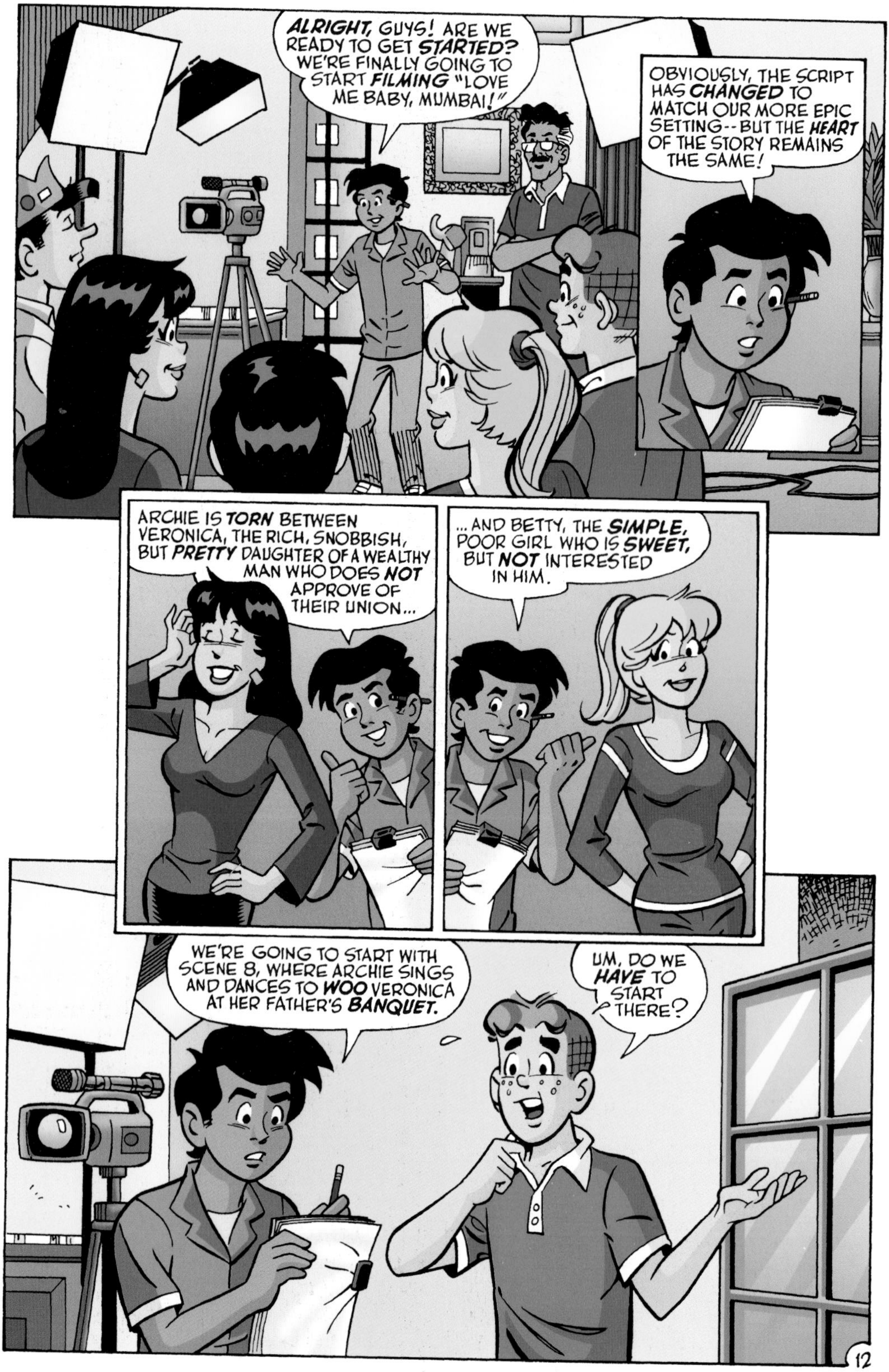
ALRIGHT, GUYS! ARE WE READY TO GET STARTED? WE'RE FINALLY GOING TO START FILMING "LOVE ME BABY, MUMBAI!"
OBVIOUSLY, THE SCRIPT HAS CHANGED TO MATCH OUR MORE EPIC SETTING--BUT THE HEART OF THE STORY REMAINS THE SAME!
ARCHIE IS TORN BETWEEN VERONICA, THE RICH, SNOBBISH, BUT PRETTY DAUGHTER OF A WEALTHY MAN WHO DOES NOT APPROVE OF THEIR UNION...
...AND BETTY, THE SIMPLE, POOR GIRL WHO IS SWEET, BUT NOT INTERESTED IN HIM.
WE'RE GOING TO START WITH SCENE 8, WHERE ARCHIE SINGS AND DANCES TO WOO VERONICA AT HER FATHER'S BANQUET.
UM, DO WE HAVE TO START THERE?
12

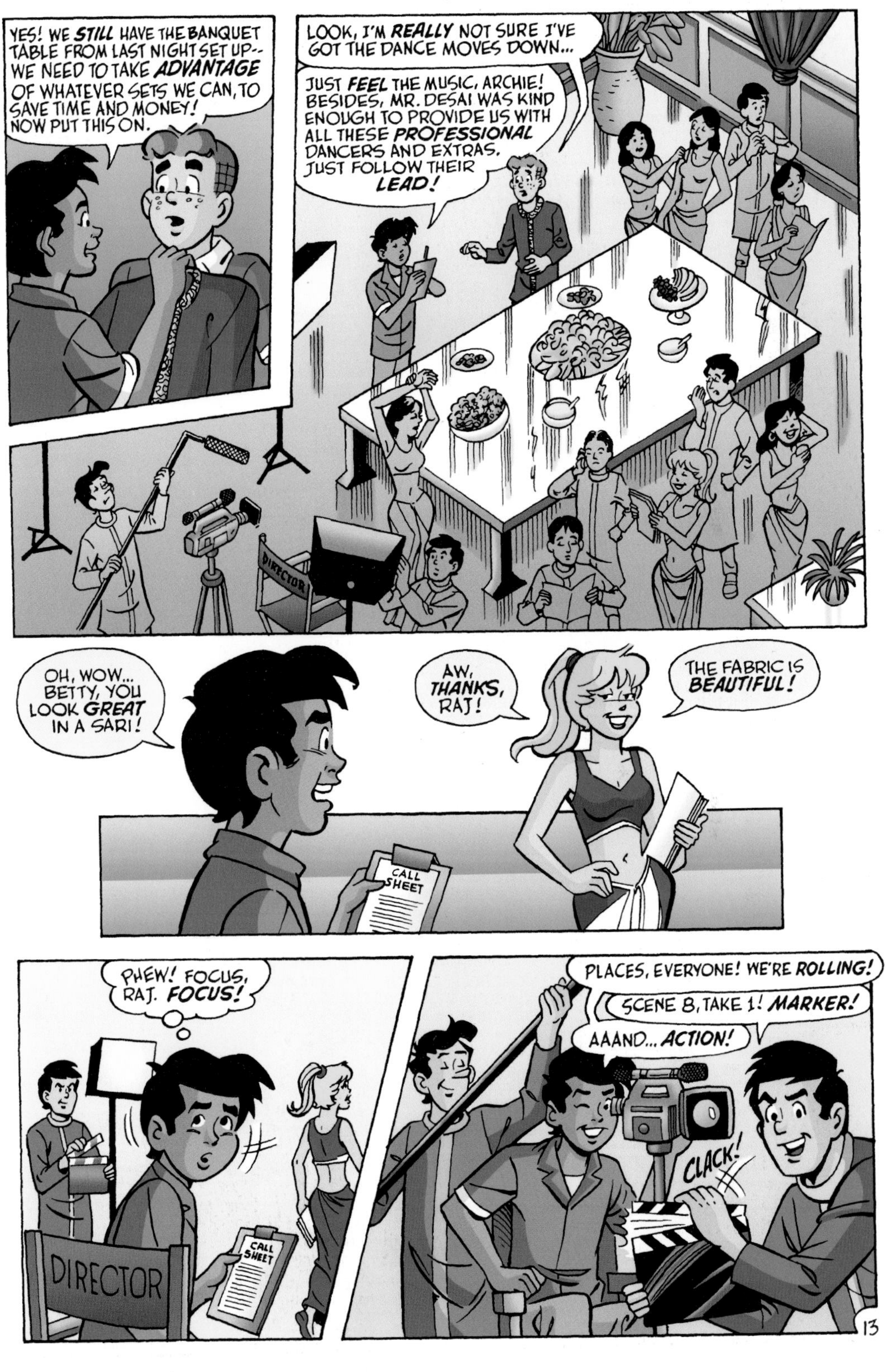
YES! WE STILL HAVE THE BANQUET TABLE FROM LAST NIGHT SET UP-- WE NEED TO TAKE ADVANTAGE OF WHATEVER SETS WE CAN, TO SAVE TIME AND MONEY! NOW PUT THIS ON.
LOOK, I'M REALLY NOT SURE I'VE GOT THE DANCE MOVES DOWN...
JUST FEEL THE MUSIC, ARCHIE! BESIDES, MR. DESAI WAS KIND ENOUGH TO PROVIDE US WITH ALL THESE PROFESSIONAL DANCERS AND EXTRAS. JUST FOLLOW THEIR LEAD!
DIRECTOR
OH, WOW... BETTY, YOU LOOK GREAT IN A SARI!
AW, THANKS, RAJ!
THE FABRIC IS BEAUTIFUL!
CALL SHEET
PHEW! FOCUS, RAJ. FOCUS!
DIRECTOR
CALL SHEET
PLACES, EVERYONE! WE'RE ROLLING!
SCENE 8, TAKE 1! MARKER!
AAAND... ACTION!
CLACK!
13

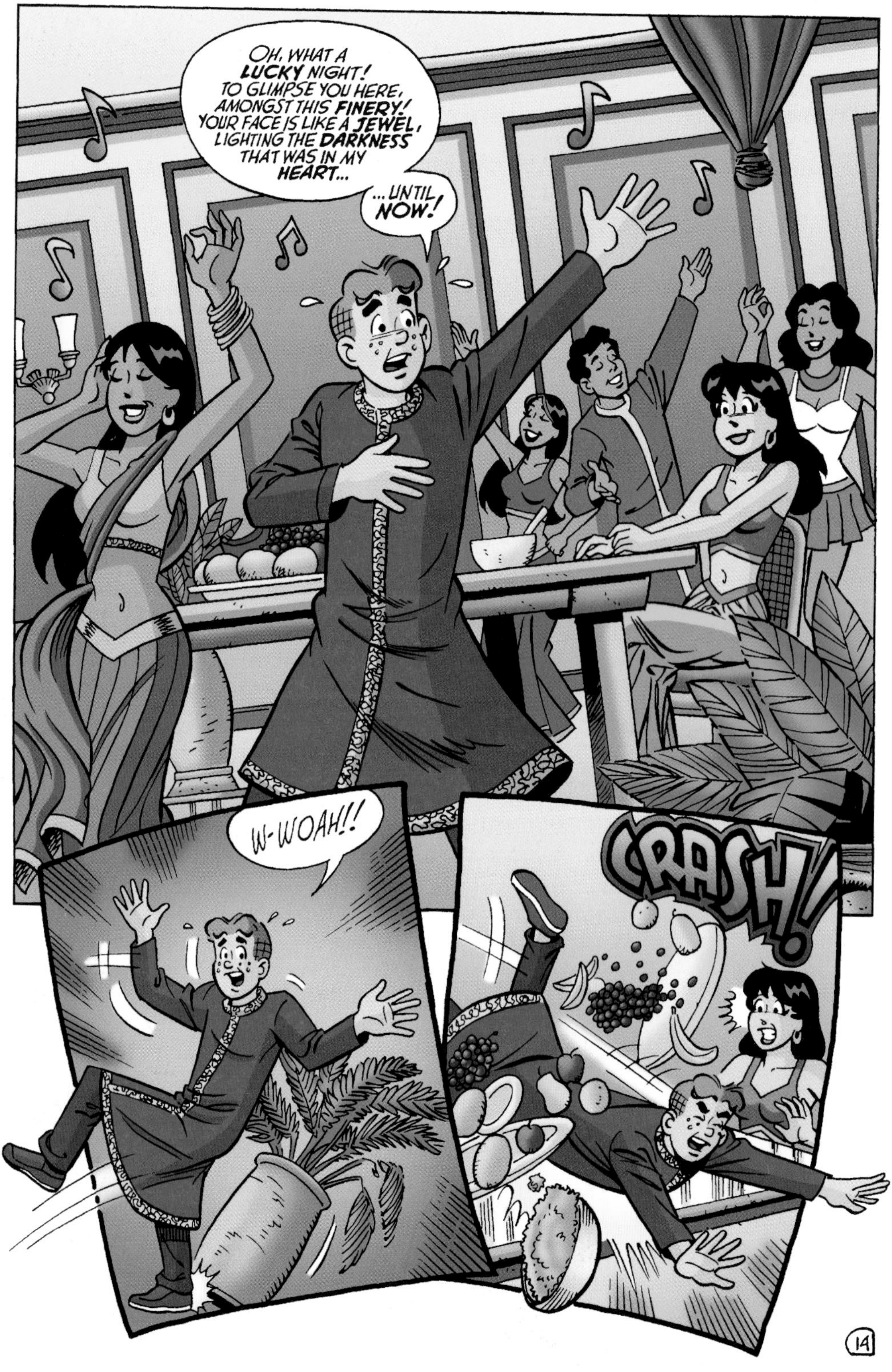
OH, WHAT A LUCKY NIGHT! TO GLIMPSE YOU HERE, AMONGST THIS FINERY! YOUR FACE IS LIKE A JEWEL, LIGHTING THE DARKNESS THAT WAS IN MY HEART...
...UNTIL NOW!
W-WOAH!!
CRASH!
14

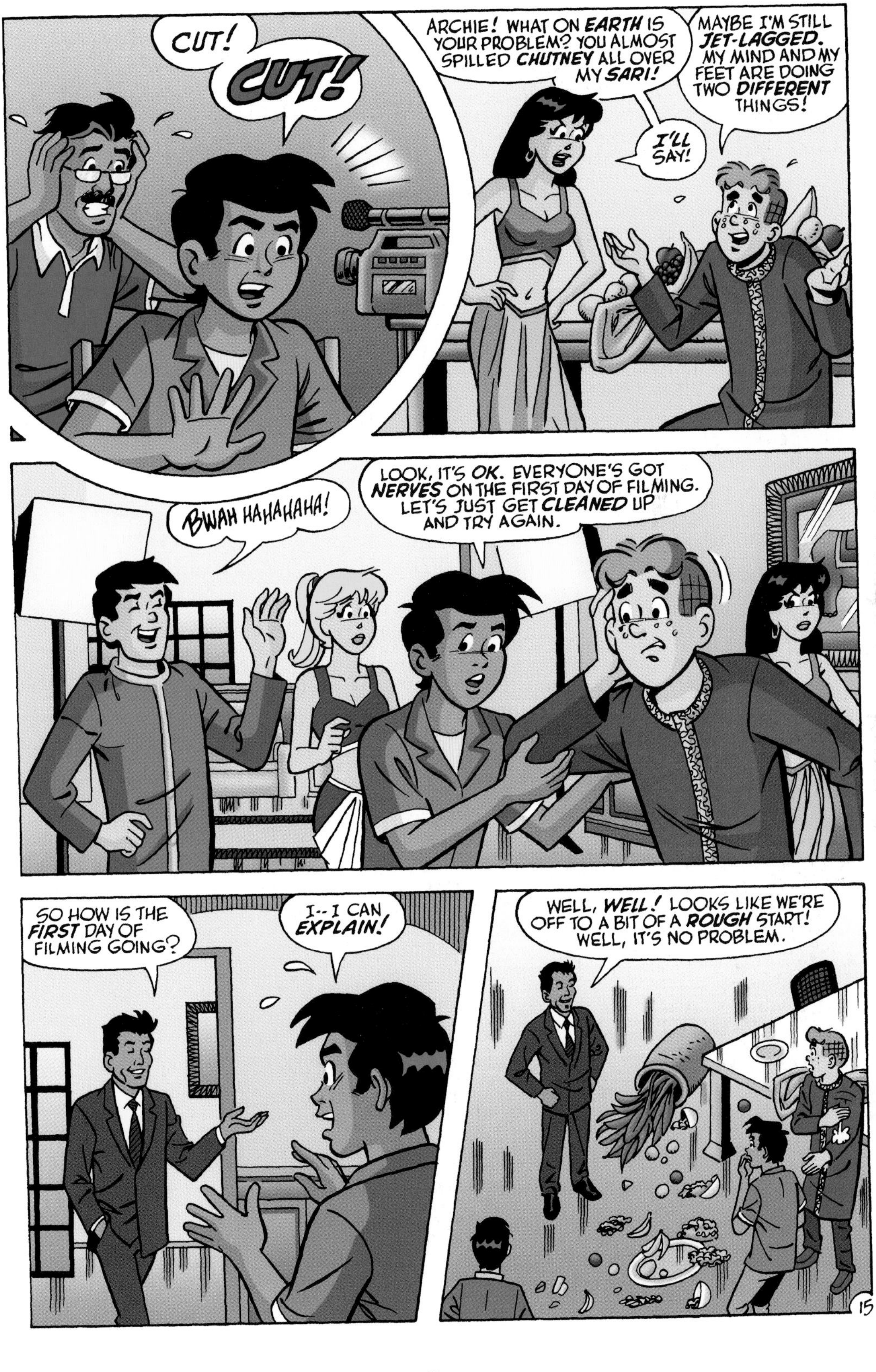
CUT!
CUT!
ARCHIE! WHAT ON EARTH IS YOUR PROBLEM? YOU ALMOST SPILLED CHUTNEY ALL OVER MY SARI!
I'LL SAY!
MAYBE I'M STILL JET-LAGGED. MY MIND AND MY FEET ARE DOING TWO DIFFERENT THINGS!
BWAH HAHAHAHA!
LOOK, IT'S OK. EVERYONE'S GOT NERVES ON THE FIRST DAY OF FILMING. LET'S JUST GET CLEANED UP AND TRY AGAIN.
SO HOW IS THE FIRST DAY OF FILMING GOING?
I-- I CAN EXPLAIN!
WELL, WELL! LOOKS LIKE WE'RE OFF TO A BIT OF A ROUGH START! WELL, IT'S NO PROBLEM.
15

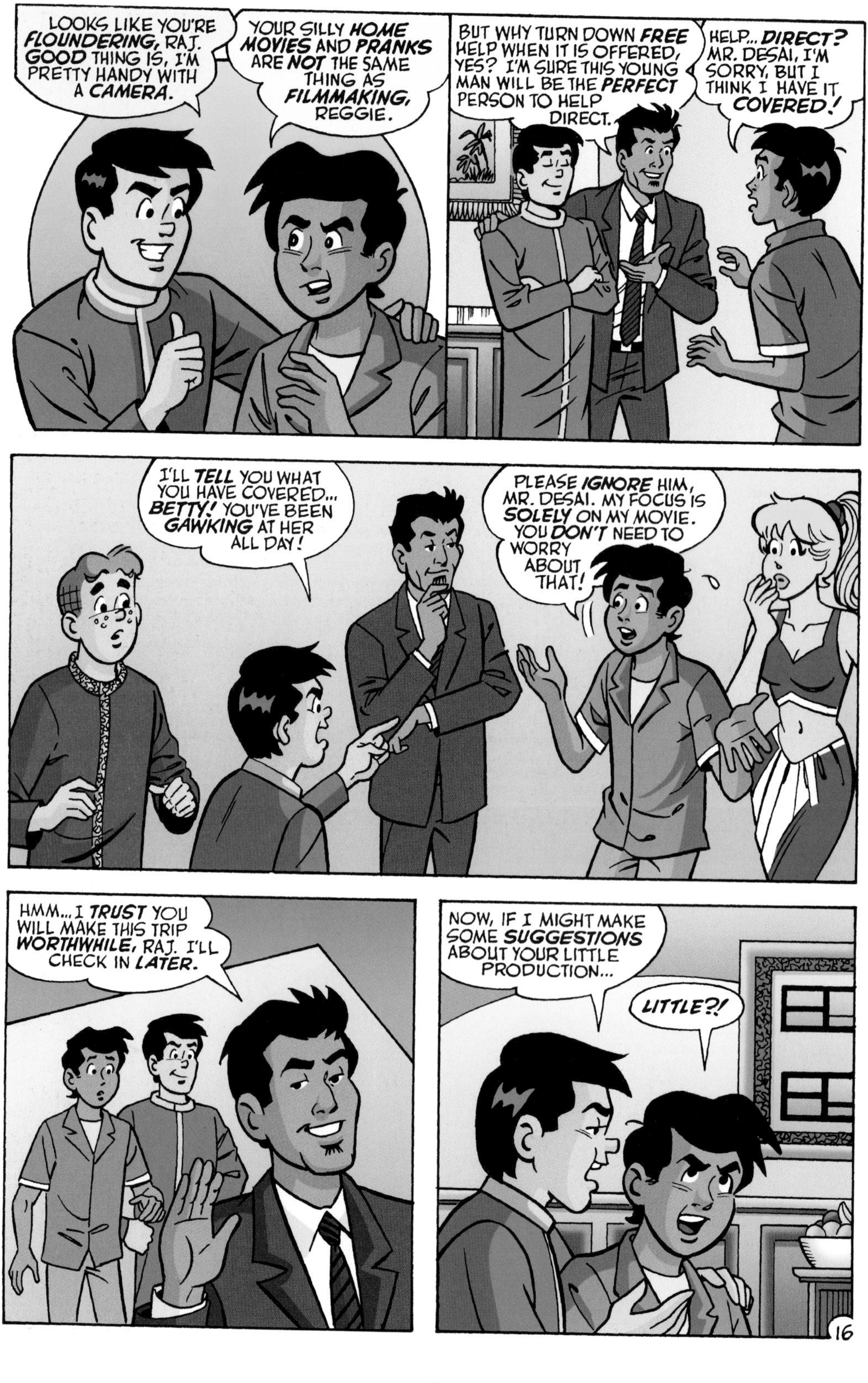
LOOKS LIKE YOU'RE FLOUNDERING, RAJ. GOOD THING IS, I'M PRETTY HANDY WITH A CAMERA.
YOUR SILLY HOME MOVIES AND PRANKS ARE NOT THE SAME THING AS FILMMAKING, REGGIE.
BUT WHY TURN DOWN FREE HELP WHEN IT IS OFFERED, YES? I'M SURE THIS YOUNG MAN WILL BE THE PERFECT PERSON TO HELP DIRECT.
HELP... DIRECT? MR. DESAI, I'M SORRY, BUT I THINK I HAVE IT COVERED!
I'LL TELL YOU WHAT YOU HAVE COVERED... BETTY! YOU'VE BEEN GAWKING AT HER ALL DAY!
PLEASE IGNORE HIM, MR. DESAI. MY FOCUS IS SOLELY ON MY MOVIE. YOU DON'T NEED TO WORRY ABOUT THAT!
HMM... I TRUST YOU WILL MAKE THIS TRIP WORTHWHILE, RAJ. I'LL CHECK IN LATER.
NOW, IF I MIGHT MAKE SOME SUGGESTIONS ABOUT YOUR LITTLE PRODUCTION...
LITTLE?!
16

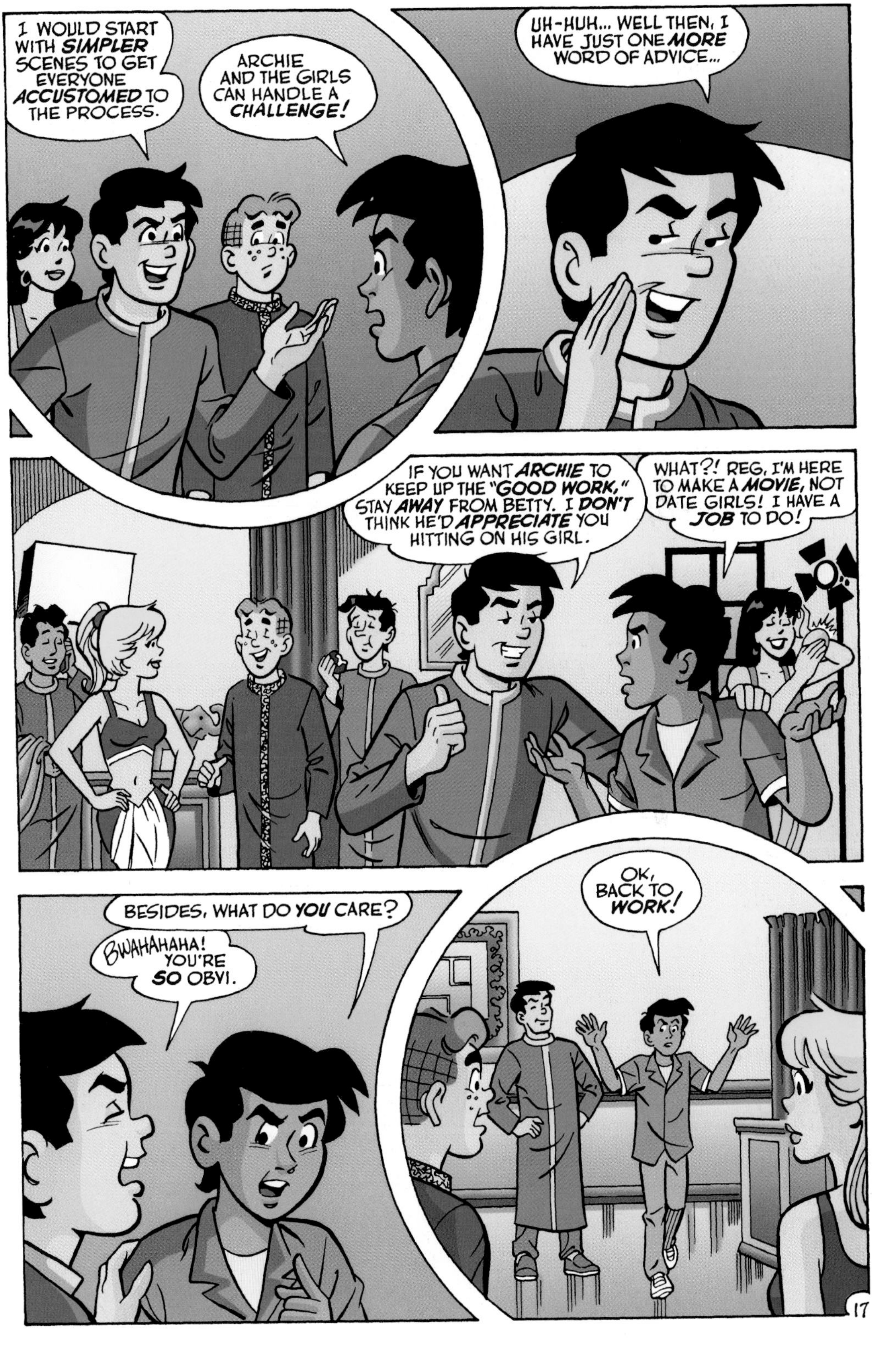
I WOULD START WITH SIMPLER SCENES TO GET EVERYONE ACCUSTOMED TO THE PROCESS.
ARCHIE AND THE GIRLS CAN HANDLE A CHALLENGE!
UH-HUH... WELL THEN, I HAVE JUST ONE MORE WORD OF ADVICE...
IF YOU WANT ARCHIE TO KEEP UP THE "GOOD WORK," STAY AWAY FROM BETTY. I DON'T THINK HE'D APPRECIATE YOU HITTING ON HIS GIRL.
WHAT?! REG, I'M HERE TO MAKE A MOVIE, NOT DATE GIRLS! I HAVE A JOB TO DO!
BESIDES, WHAT DO YOU CARE?
BWAHAHAHA! YOU'RE SO OBVI.
OK, BACK TO WORK!
17

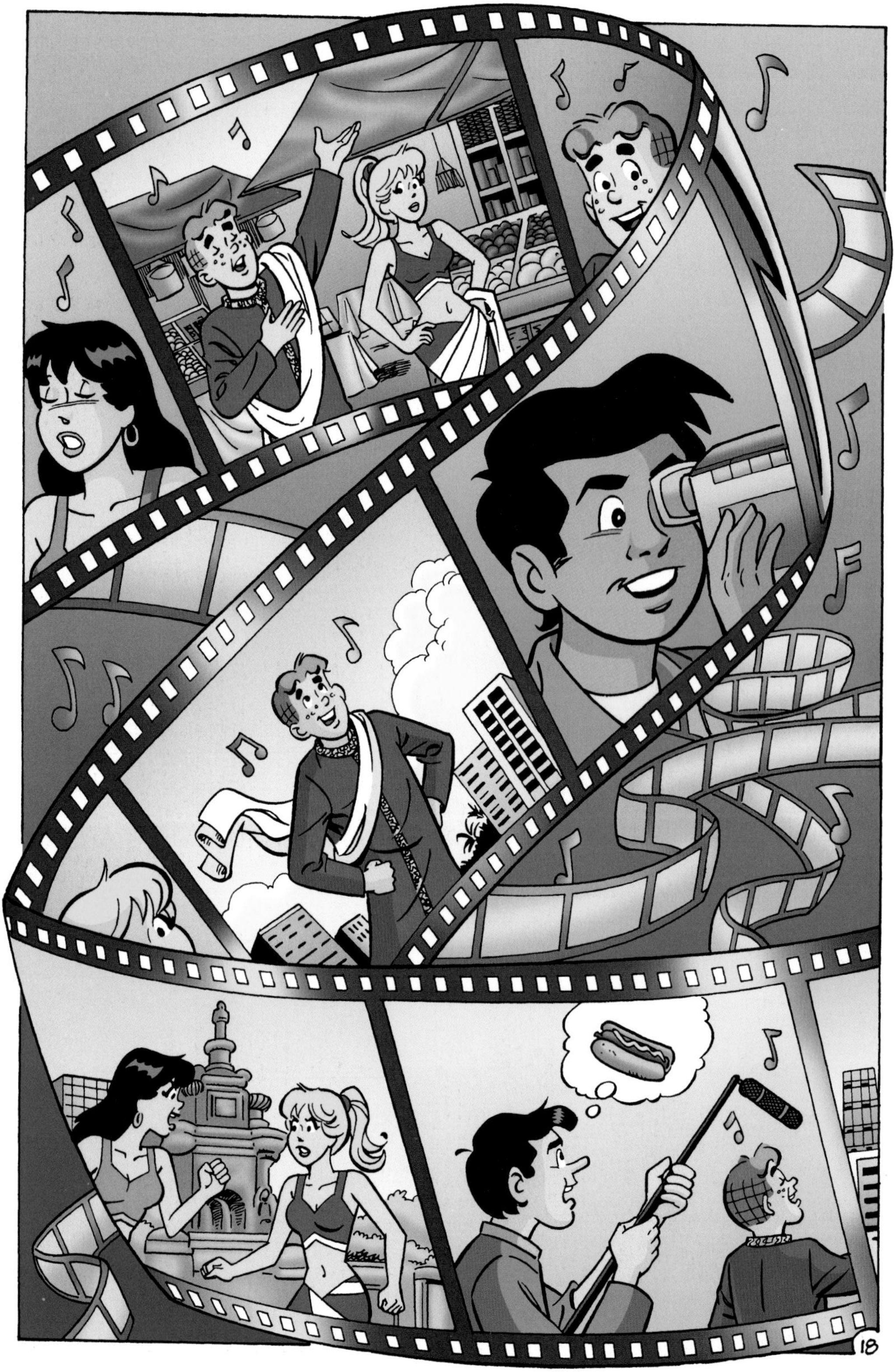
18

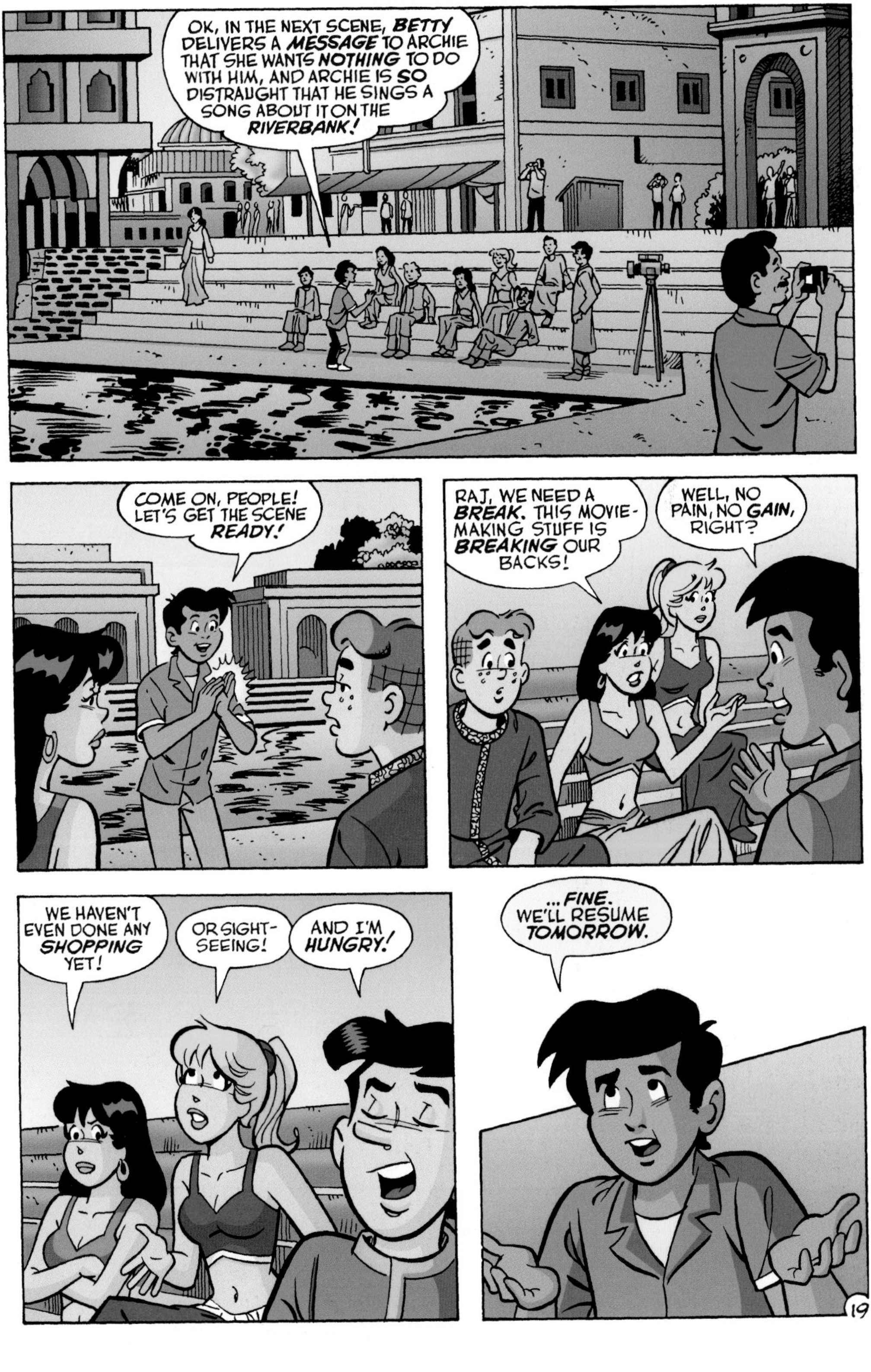
OK, IN THE NEXT SCENE, BETTY DELIVERS A MESSAGE TO ARCHIE THAT SHE WANTS NOTHING TO DO WITH HIM, AND ARCHIE IS SO DISTRAUGHT THAT HE SINGS A SONG ABOUT IT ON THE RIVERBANK!
COME ON, PEOPLE! LET'S GET THE SCENE READY!
RAJ, WE NEED A BREAK. THIS MOVIE-MAKING STUFF IS BREAKING OUR BACKS!
WELL, NO PAIN, NO GAIN, RIGHT?
WE HAVEN'T EVEN DONE ANY SHOPPING YET!
OR SIGHT-SEEING!
AND I'M HUNGRY!
...FINE. WE'LL RESUME TOMORROW.
19

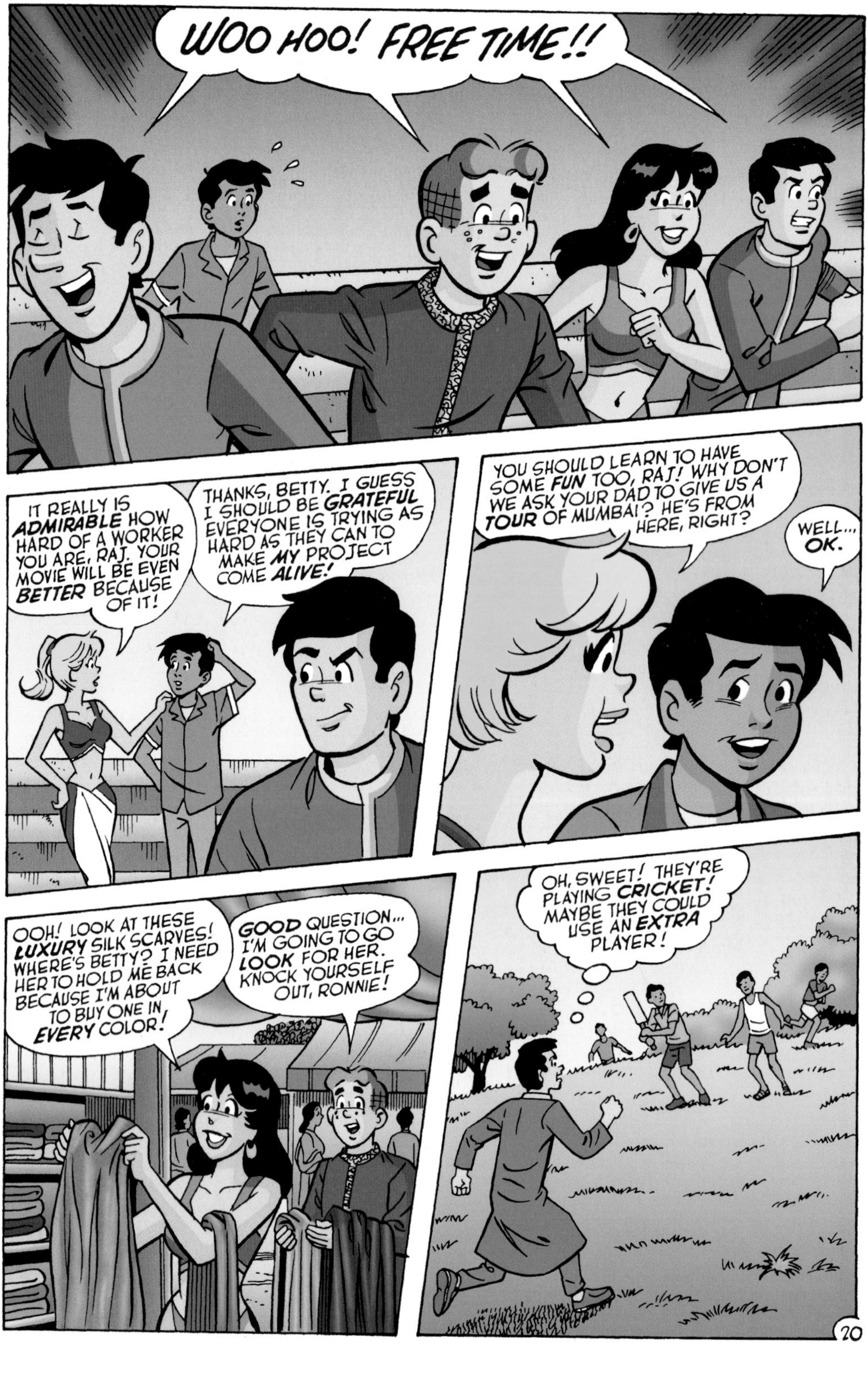
WOO HOO! FREE TIME!!
IT REALLY IS ADMIRABLE HOW HARD OF A WORKER YOU ARE, RAJ. YOUR MOVIE WILL BE EVEN BETTER BECAUSE OF IT!
THANKS, BETTY. I GUESS I SHOULD BE GRATEFUL EVERYONE IS TRYING AS HARD AS THEY CAN TO MAKE MY PROJECT COME ALIVE!
YOU SHOULD LEARN TO HAVE SOME FUN TOO, RAJ! WHY DON'T WE ASK YOUR DAD TO GIVE US A TOUR OF MUMBAI? HE'S FROM HERE, RIGHT?
WELL... OK.
OOH! LOOK AT THESE LUXURY SILK SCARVES! WHERE'S BETTY? I NEED HER TO HOLD ME BACK BECAUSE I'M ABOUT TO BUY ONE IN EVERY COLOR!
GOOD QUESTION... I'M GOING TO GO LOOK FOR HER. KNOCK YOURSELF OUT, RONNIE!
OH, SWEET! THEY'RE PLAYING CRICKET! MAYBE THEY COULD USE AN EXTRA PLAYER!
20

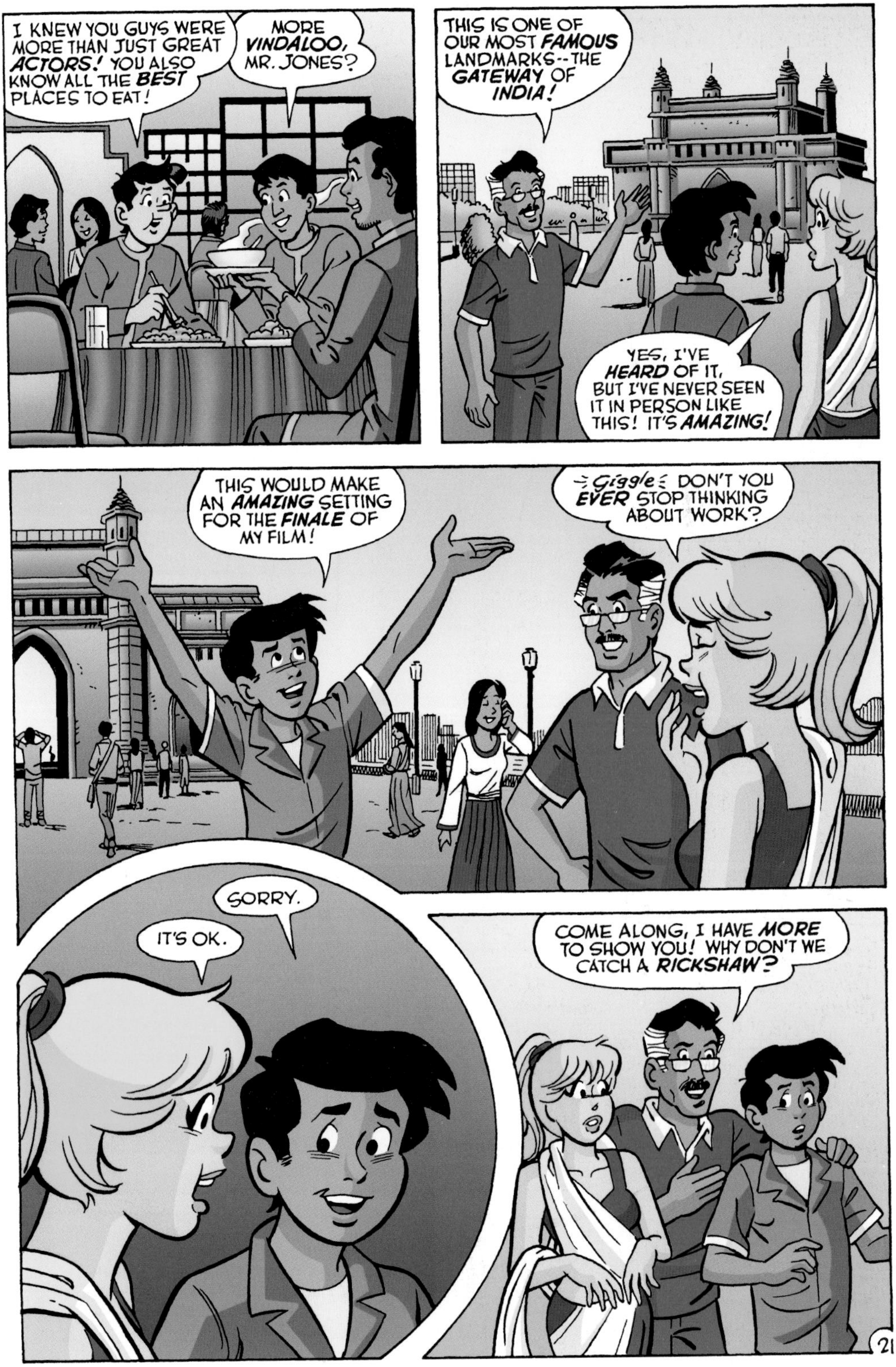
I KNEW YOU GUYS WERE MORE THAN JUST GREAT ACTORS! YOU ALSO KNOW ALL THE BEST PLACES TO EAT!
MORE VINDALOO, MR. JONES?
THIS IS ONE OF OUR MOST FAMOUS LANDMARKS--THE GATEWAY OF INDIA!
YES, I'VE HEARD OF IT, BUT I'VE NEVER SEEN IT IN PERSON LIKE THIS! IT'S AMAZING!
THIS WOULD MAKE AN AMAZING SETTING FOR THE FINALE OF MY FILM!
Giggle DON'T YOU EVER STOP THINKING ABOUT WORK?
SORRY.
IT'S OK.
COME ALONG, I HAVE MORE TO SHOW YOU! WHY DON'T WE CATCH A RICKSHAW?
21

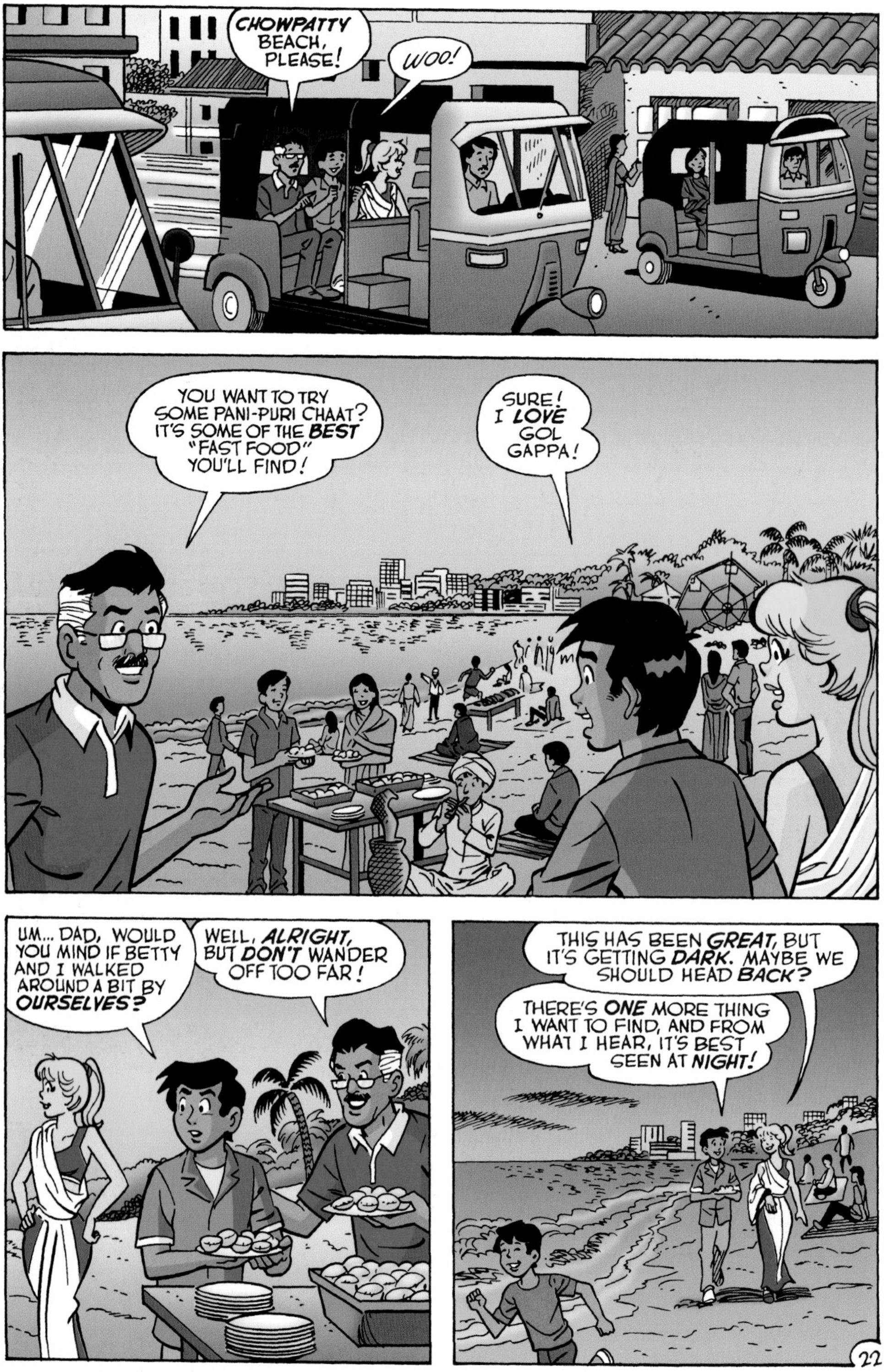
CHOWPATTY BEACH, PLEASE!
WOO!
YOU WANT TO TRY SOME PANI-PURI CHAAT? IT'S SOME OF THE BEST "FAST FOOD" YOU'LL FIND!
SURE! I LOVE GOL GAPPA!
UM... DAD, WOULD YOU MIND IF BETTY AND I WALKED AROUND A BIT BY OURSELVES?
WELL, ALRIGHT, BUT DON'T WANDER OFF TOO FAR!
THIS HAS BEEN GREAT, BUT IT'S GETTING DARK. MAYBE WE SHOULD HEAD BACK?
THERE'S ONE MORE THING I WANT TO FIND, AND FROM WHAT I HEAR, IT'S BEST SEEN AT NIGHT!
22

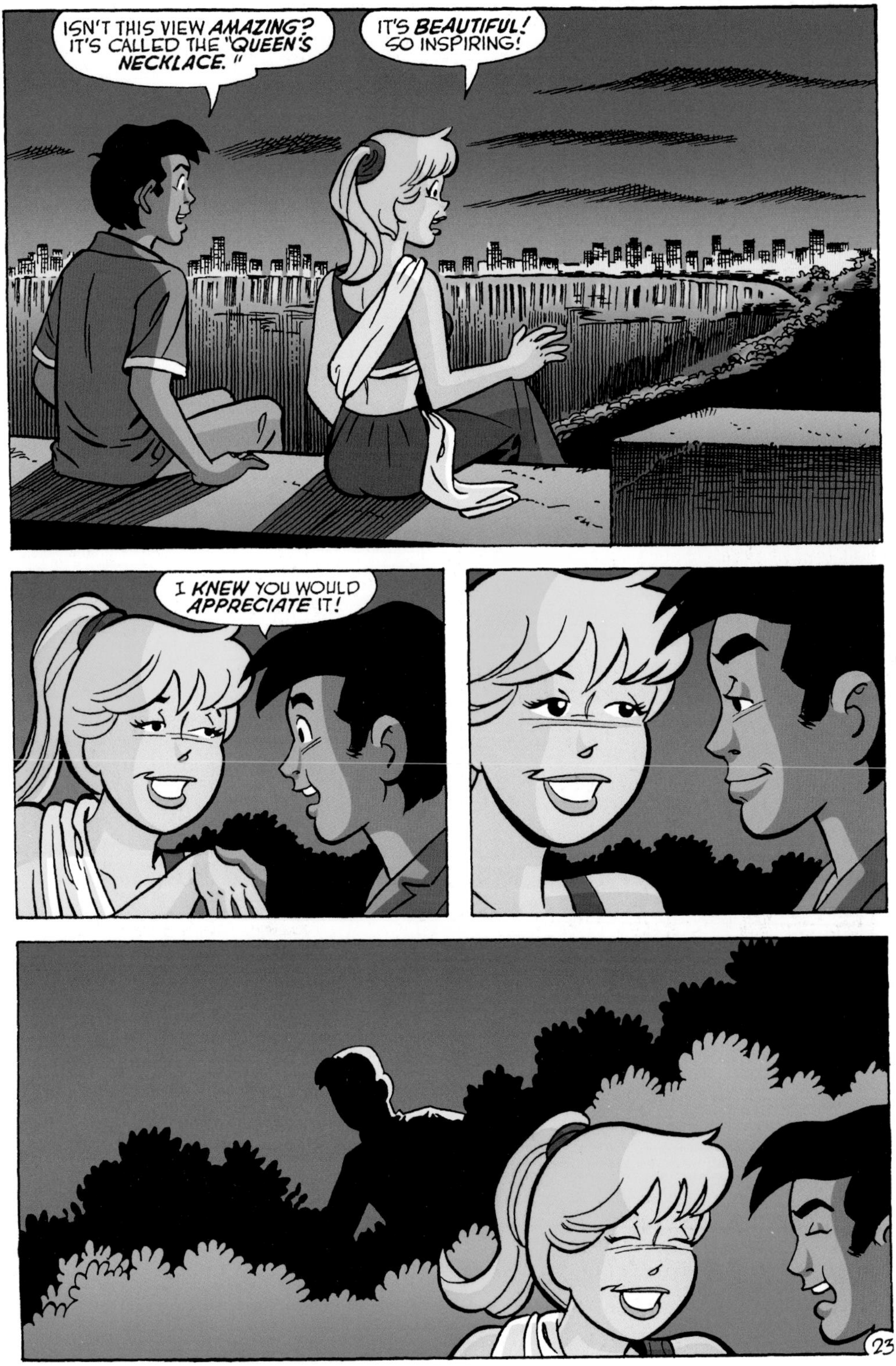
ISN'T THIS VIEW AMAZING? IT'S CALLED THE "QUEEN'S NECKLACE."
IT'S BEAUTIFUL! SO INSPIRING!
I KNEW YOU WOULD APPRECIATE IT!
23

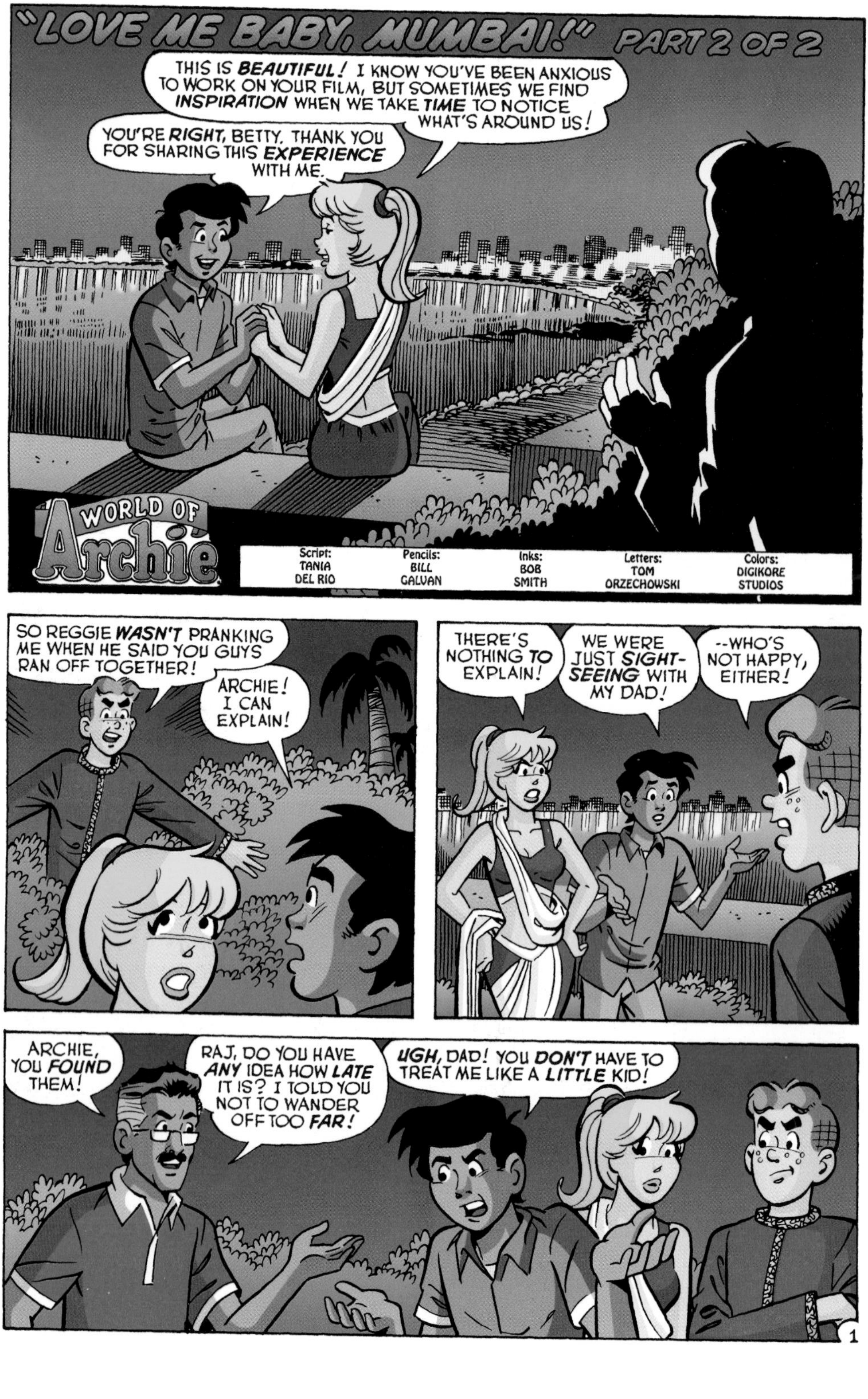
"LOVE ME BABY, MUMBAI!" PART 2 OF 2
THIS IS BEAUTIFUL! I KNOW YOU'VE BEEN ANXIOUS TO WORK ON YOUR FILM, BUT SOMETIMES WE FIND INSPIRATION WHEN WE TAKE TIME TO NOTICE WHAT'S AROUND US!
YOU'RE RIGHT, BETTY. THANK YOU FOR SHARING THIS EXPERIENCE WITH ME.
WORLD OF Archie
Script: TANIA DEL RIO
Pencils: BILL GALVAN
Inks: BOB SMITH
Letters: TOM ORZECHOWSKI
Colors: DIGIKORE STUDIOS
SO REGGIE WASN'T PRANKING ME WHEN HE SAID YOU GUYS RAN OFF TOGETHER!
ARCHIE! I CAN EXPLAIN!
THERE'S NOTHING TO EXPLAIN!
WE WERE JUST SIGHT-SEEING WITH MY DAD!
--WHO'S NOT HAPPY, EITHER!
ARCHIE, YOU FOUND THEM!
RAJ, DO YOU HAVE ANY IDEA HOW LATE IT IS? I TOLD YOU NOT TO WANDER OFF TOO FAR!
UGH, DAD! YOU DON'T HAVE TO TREAT ME LIKE A LITTLE KID!
1

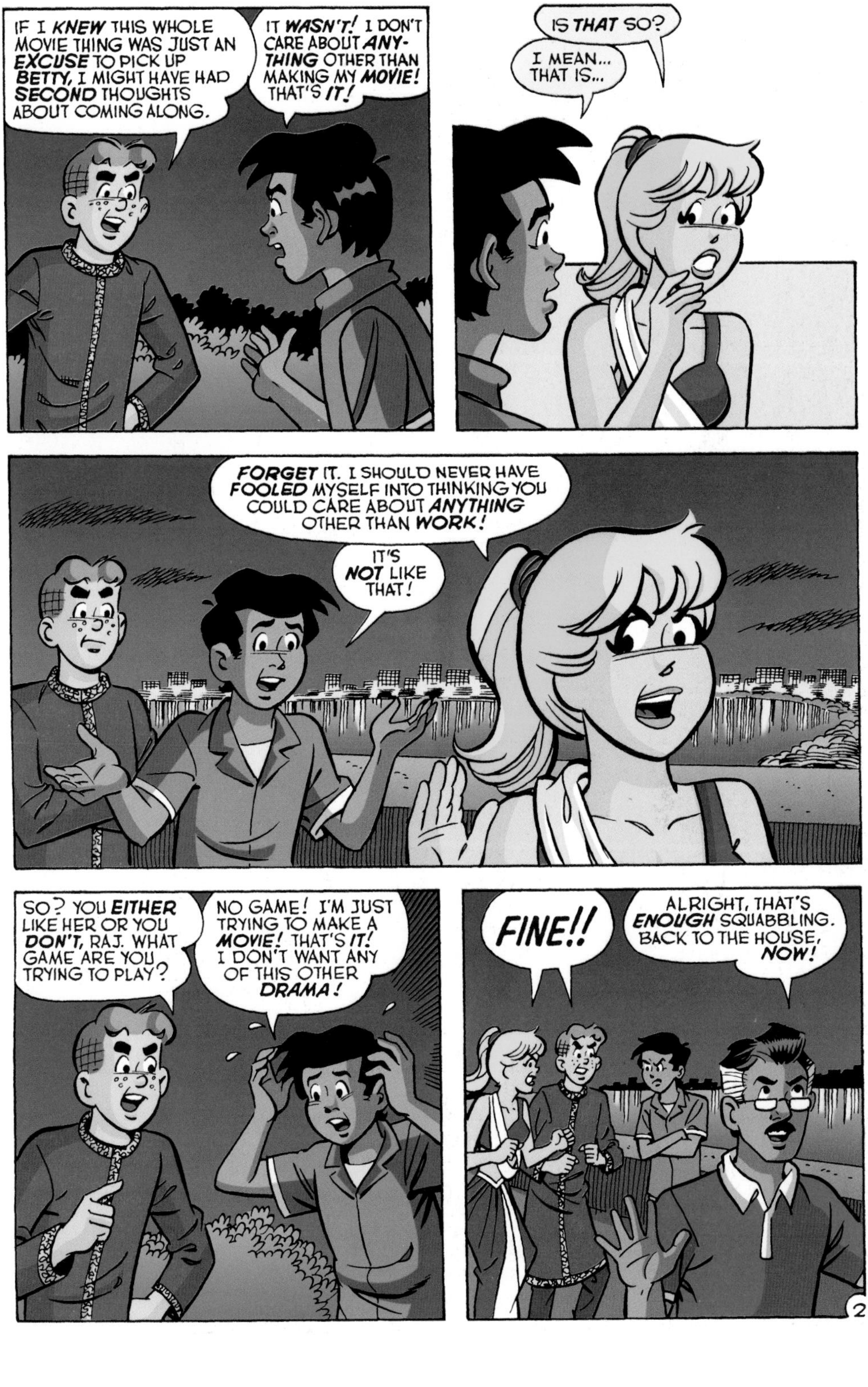
IF I KNEW THIS WHOLE MOVIE THING WAS JUST AN EXCUSE TO PICK UP BETTY, I MIGHT HAVE HAD SECOND THOUGHTS ABOUT COMING ALONG.
IT WASN'T! I DON'T CARE ABOUT ANY-THING OTHER THAN MAKING MY MOVIE! THAT'S IT!
I MEAN... THAT IS...
IS THAT SO?
FORGET IT. I SHOULD NEVER HAVE FOOLED MYSELF INTO THINKING YOU COULD CARE ABOUT ANYTHING OTHER THAN WORK!
IT'S NOT LIKE THAT!
SO? YOU EITHER LIKE HER OR YOU DON'T, RAJ. WHAT GAME ARE YOU TRYING TO PLAY?
NO GAME! I'M JUST TRYING TO MAKE A MOVIE! THAT'S IT! I DON'T WANT ANY OF THIS OTHER DRAMA!
FINE!!
ALRIGHT, THAT'S ENOUGH SQUABBLING. BACK TO THE HOUSE, NOW!
2

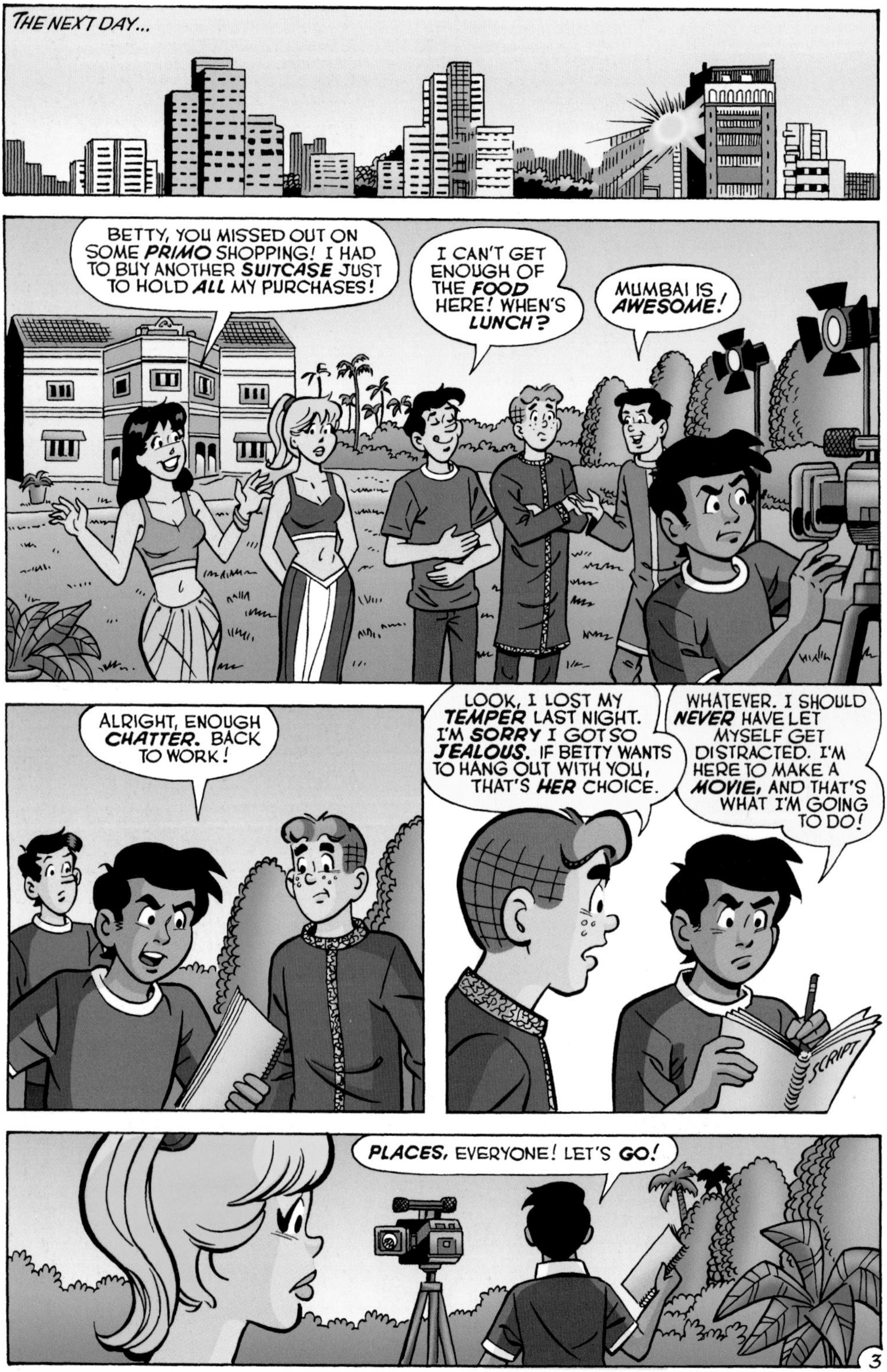
THE NEXT DAY...
BETTY, YOU MISSED OUT ON SOME PRIMO SHOPPING! I HAD TO BUY ANOTHER SUITCASE JUST TO HOLD ALL MY PURCHASES!
I CAN'T GET ENOUGH OF THE FOOD HERE! WHEN'S LUNCH?
MUMBAI IS AWESOME!
ALRIGHT, ENOUGH CHATTER. BACK TO WORK!
LOOK, I LOST MY TEMPER LAST NIGHT. I'M SORRY I GOT SO JEALOUS. IF BETTY WANTS TO HANG OUT WITH YOU, THAT'S HER CHOICE.
WHATEVER. I SHOULD NEVER HAVE LET MYSELF GET DISTRACTED. I'M HERE TO MAKE A MOVIE, AND THAT'S WHAT I'M GOING TO DO!
SCRIPT
PLACES, EVERYONE! LET'S GO!
3

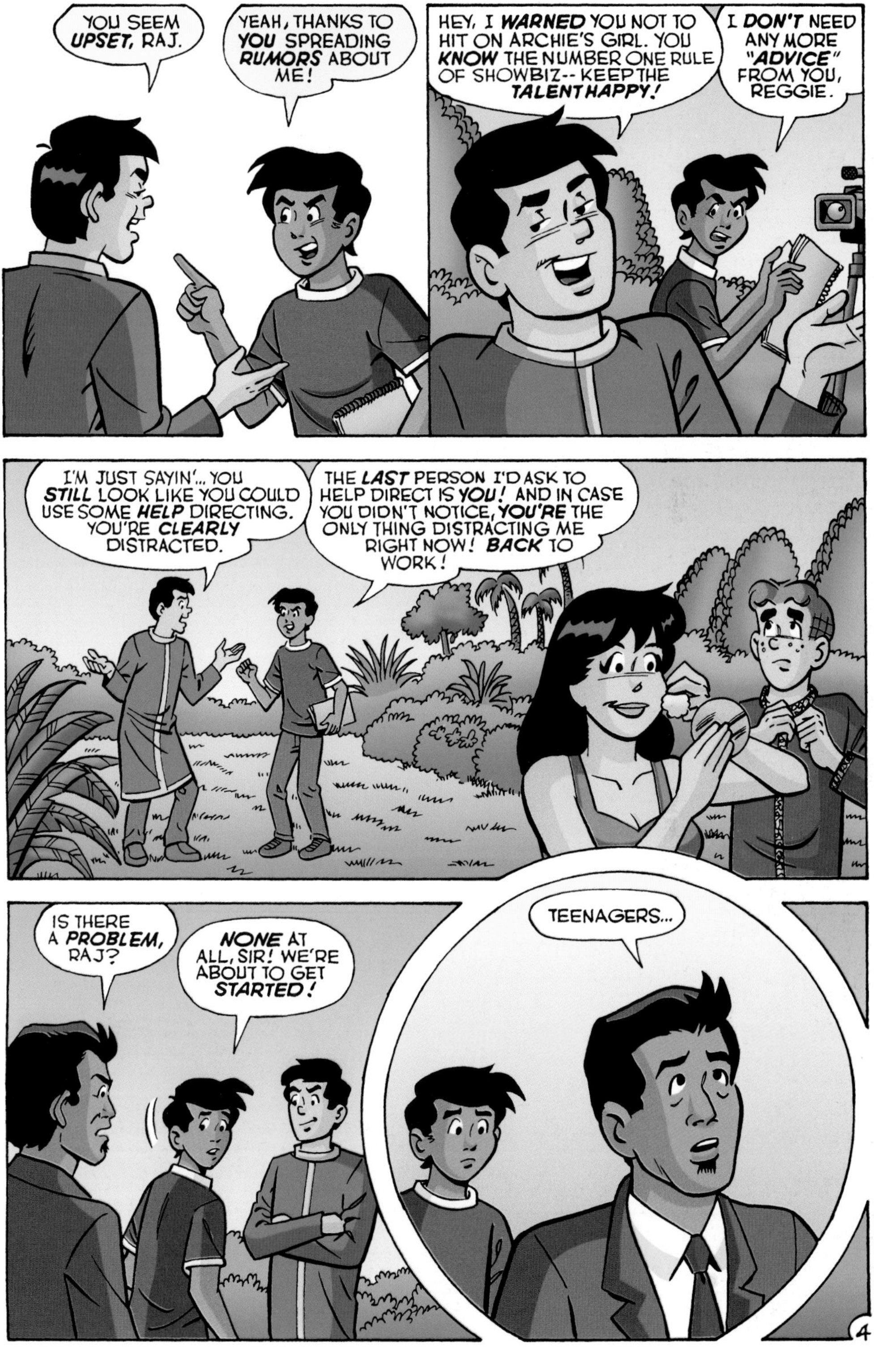
YOU SEEM UPSET, RAJ.
YEAH, THANKS TO YOU SPREADING RUMORS ABOUT ME!
HEY, I WARNED YOU NOT TO HIT ON ARCHIE'S GIRL. YOU KNOW THE NUMBER ONE RULE OF SHOWBIZ-- KEEP THE TALENT HAPPY!
I DON'T NEED ANY MORE "ADVICE" FROM YOU, REGGIE.
I'M JUST SAYIN'... YOU STILL LOOK LIKE YOU COULD USE SOME HELP DIRECTING. YOU'RE CLEARLY DISTRACTED.
THE LAST PERSON I'D ASK TO HELP DIRECT IS YOU! AND IN CASE YOU DIDN'T NOTICE, YOU'RE THE ONLY THING DISTRACTING ME RIGHT NOW! BACK TO WORK!
IS THERE A PROBLEM, RAJ?
NONE AT ALL, SIR! WE'RE ABOUT TO GET STARTED!
TEENAGERS...
4

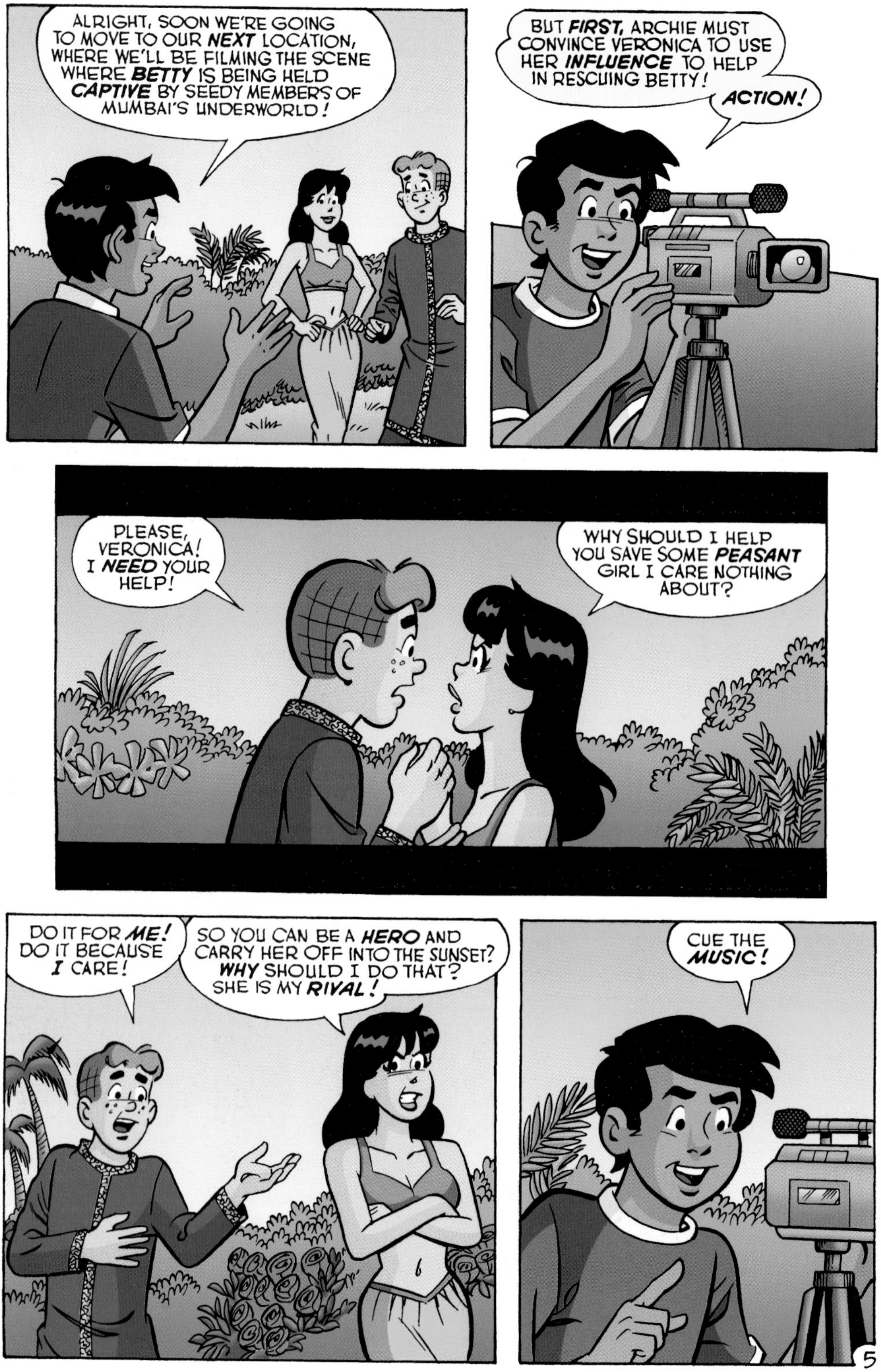
ALRIGHT, SOON WE'RE GOING TO MOVE TO OUR NEXT LOCATION, WHERE WE'LL BE FILMING THE SCENE WHERE BETTY IS BEING HELD CAPTIVE BY SEEDY MEMBERS OF MUMBAI'S UNDERWORLD!
BUT FIRST, ARCHIE MUST CONVINCE VERONICA TO USE HER INFLUENCE TO HELP IN RESCUING BETTY!
ACTION!
PLEASE, VERONICA! I NEED YOUR HELP!
WHY SHOULD I HELP YOU SAVE SOME PEASANT GIRL I CARE NOTHING ABOUT?
DO IT FOR ME! DO IT BECAUSE I CARE!
SO YOU CAN BE A HERO AND CARRY HER OFF INTO THE SUNSET? WHY SHOULD I DO THAT? SHE IS MY RIVAL!
CUE THE MUSIC!
5

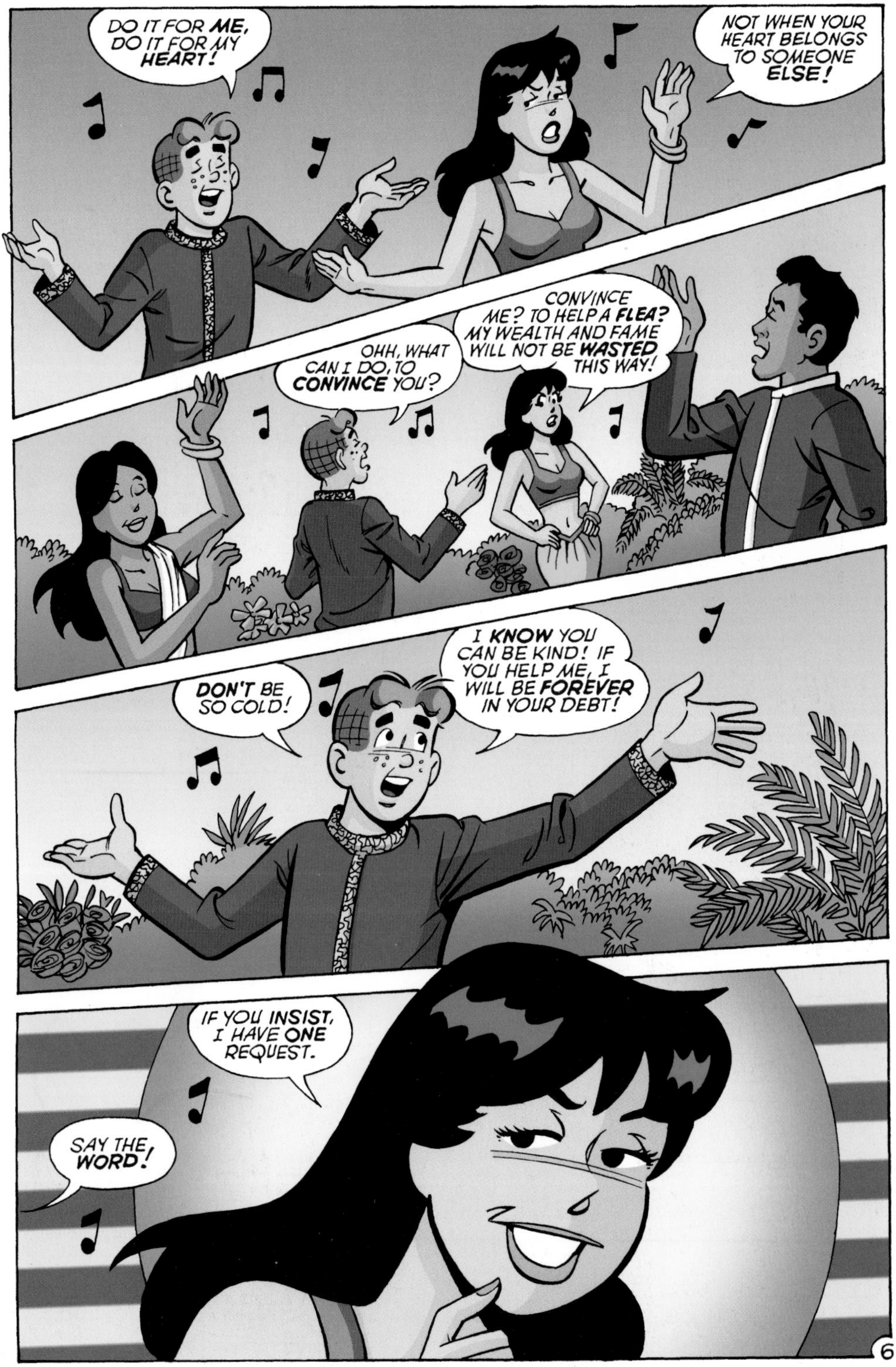
DO IT FOR ME, DO IT FOR MY HEART!
NOT WHEN YOUR HEART BELONGS TO SOMEONE ELSE!
OHH, WHAT CAN I DO, TO CONVINCE YOU?
CONVINCE ME? TO HELP A FLEA? MY WEALTH AND FAME WILL NOT BE WASTED THIS WAY!
DON'T BE SO COLD!
I KNOW YOU CAN BE KIND! IF YOU HELP ME, I WILL BE FOREVER IN YOUR DEBT!
IF YOU INSIST, I HAVE ONE REQUEST.
SAY THE WORD!
6

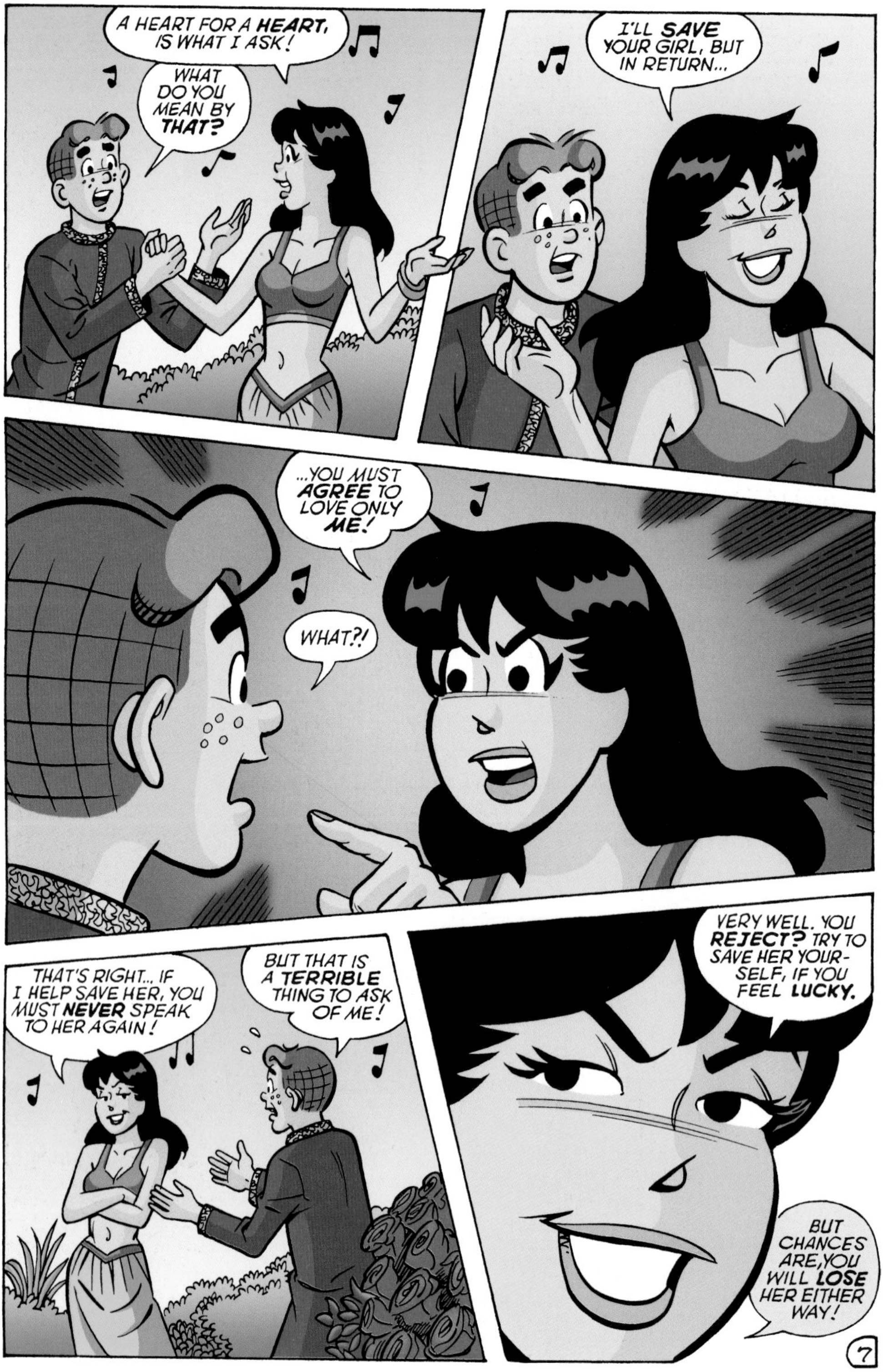
A HEART FOR A **HEART**, IS WHAT I ASK!
WHAT DO YOU MEAN BY **THAT?**
I'LL **SAVE** YOUR GIRL, BUT IN RETURN...
...YOU MUST **AGREE** TO LOVE ONLY **ME!**
WHAT?!
THAT'S RIGHT... IF I HELP SAVE HER, YOU MUST **NEVER** SPEAK TO HER AGAIN!
BUT THAT IS A **TERRIBLE** THING TO ASK OF ME!
VERY WELL. YOU **REJECT?** TRY TO SAVE HER YOUR-SELF, IF YOU FEEL **LUCKY.**
BUT CHANCES ARE, YOU WILL **LOSE** HER EITHER WAY!
7

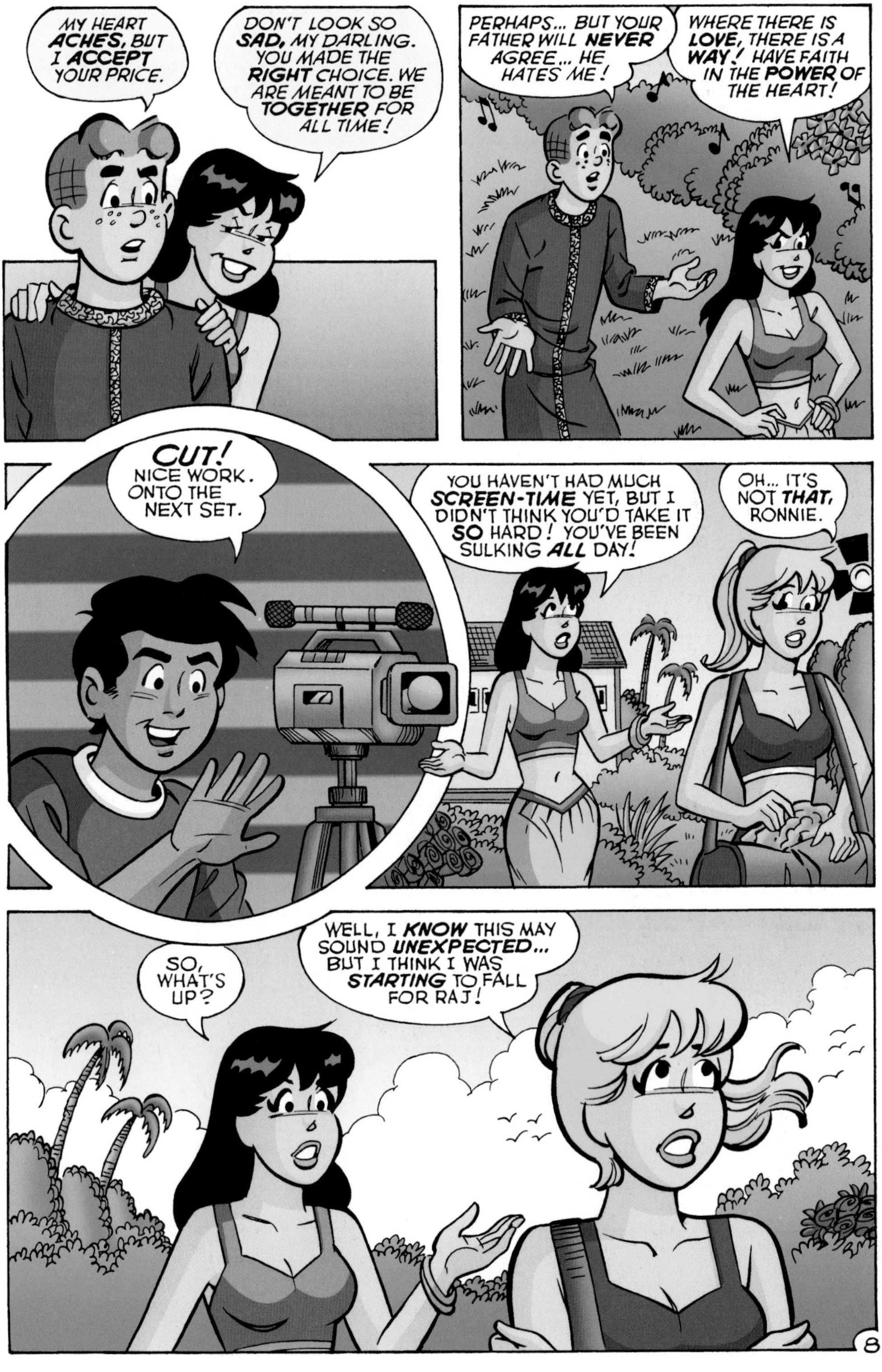
MY HEART ACHES, BUT I ACCEPT YOUR PRICE.
DON'T LOOK SO SAD, MY DARLING. YOU MADE THE RIGHT CHOICE. WE ARE MEANT TO BE TOGETHER FOR ALL TIME!
PERHAPS... BUT YOUR FATHER WILL NEVER AGREE... HE HATES ME!
WHERE THERE IS LOVE, THERE IS A WAY! HAVE FAITH IN THE POWER OF THE HEART!
CUT! NICE WORK. ONTO THE NEXT SET.
YOU HAVEN'T HAD MUCH SCREEN-TIME YET, BUT I DIDN'T THINK YOU'D TAKE IT SO HARD! YOU'VE BEEN SULKING ALL DAY!
OH... IT'S NOT THAT, RONNIE.
SO, WHAT'S UP?
WELL, I KNOW THIS MAY SOUND UNEXPECTED... BUT I THINK I WAS STARTING TO FALL FOR RAJ!
8

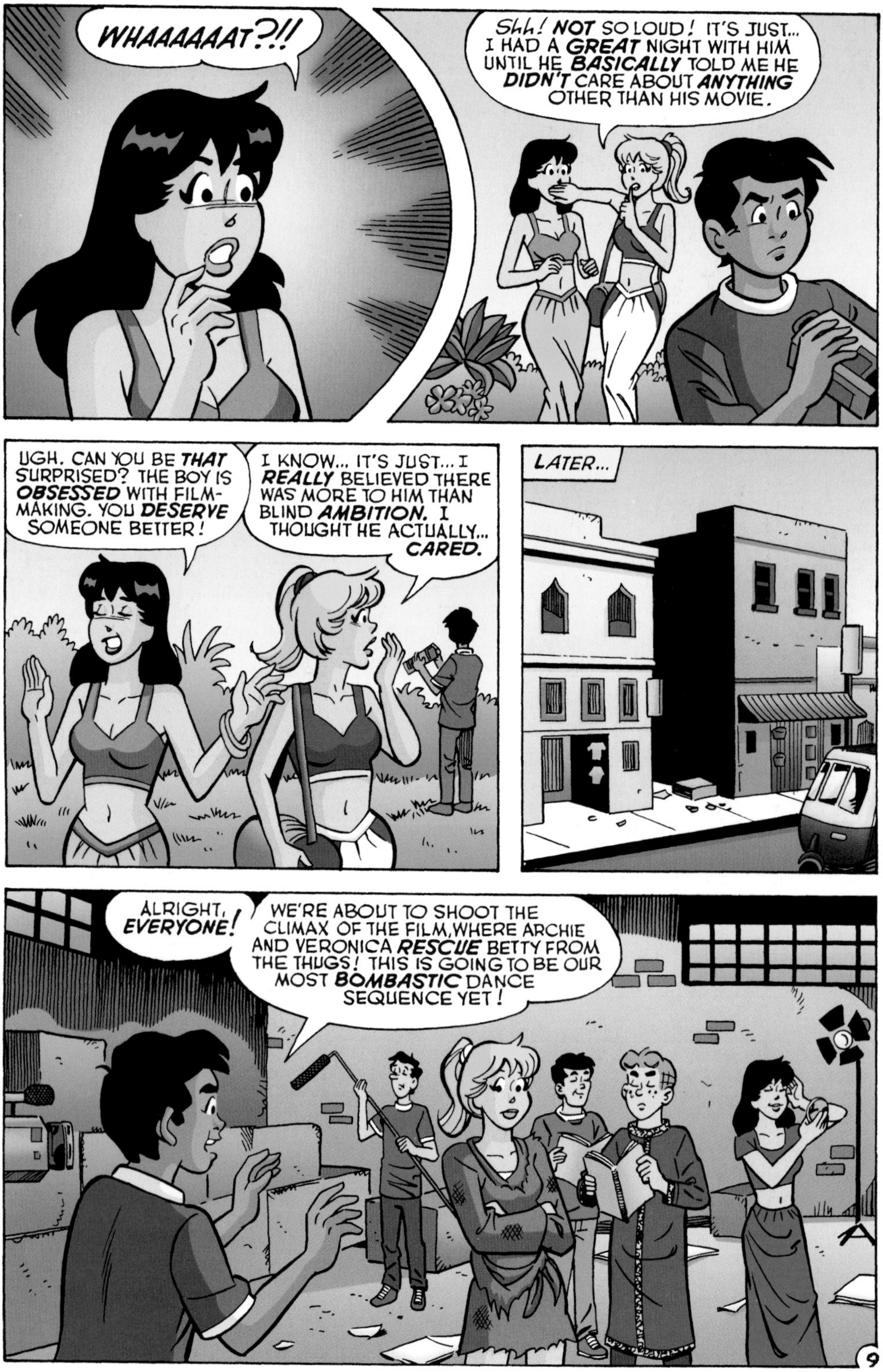
WHAAAAAAT?!!
Shh! NOT SO LOUD! IT'S JUST... I HAD A GREAT NIGHT WITH HIM UNTIL HE BASICALLY TOLD ME HE DIDN'T CARE ABOUT ANYTHING OTHER THAN HIS MOVIE.
UGH. CAN YOU BE THAT SURPRISED? THE BOY IS OBSESSED WITH FILM-MAKING. YOU DESERVE SOMEONE BETTER!
I KNOW... IT'S JUST... I REALLY BELIEVED THERE WAS MORE TO HIM THAN BLIND AMBITION. I THOUGHT HE ACTUALLY... CARED.
LATER...
ALRIGHT, EVERYONE!
WE'RE ABOUT TO SHOOT THE CLIMAX OF THE FILM, WHERE ARCHIE AND VERONICA RESCUE BETTY FROM THE THUGS! THIS IS GOING TO BE OUR MOST BOMBASTIC DANCE SEQUENCE YET!
9

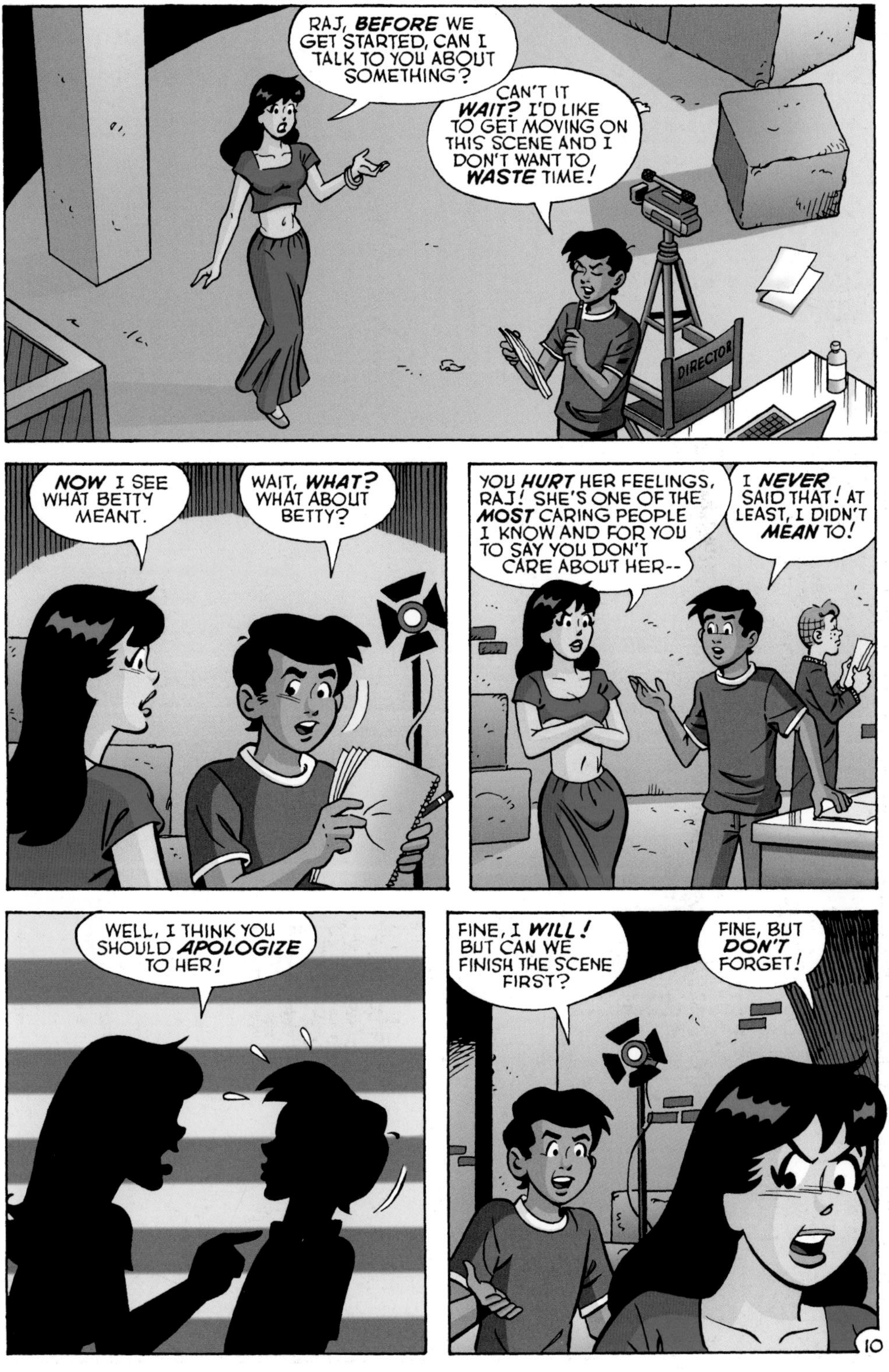
RAJ, BEFORE WE GET STARTED, CAN I TALK TO YOU ABOUT SOMETHING?
CAN'T IT WAIT? I'D LIKE TO GET MOVING ON THIS SCENE AND I DON'T WANT TO WASTE TIME!
DIRECTOR
NOW I SEE WHAT BETTY MEANT.
WAIT, WHAT? WHAT ABOUT BETTY?
YOU HURT HER FEELINGS, RAJ! SHE'S ONE OF THE MOST CARING PEOPLE I KNOW AND FOR YOU TO SAY YOU DON'T CARE ABOUT HER--
I NEVER SAID THAT! AT LEAST, I DIDN'T MEAN TO!
WELL, I THINK YOU SHOULD APOLOGIZE TO HER!
FINE, I WILL! BUT CAN WE FINISH THE SCENE FIRST?
FINE, BUT DON'T FORGET!
10

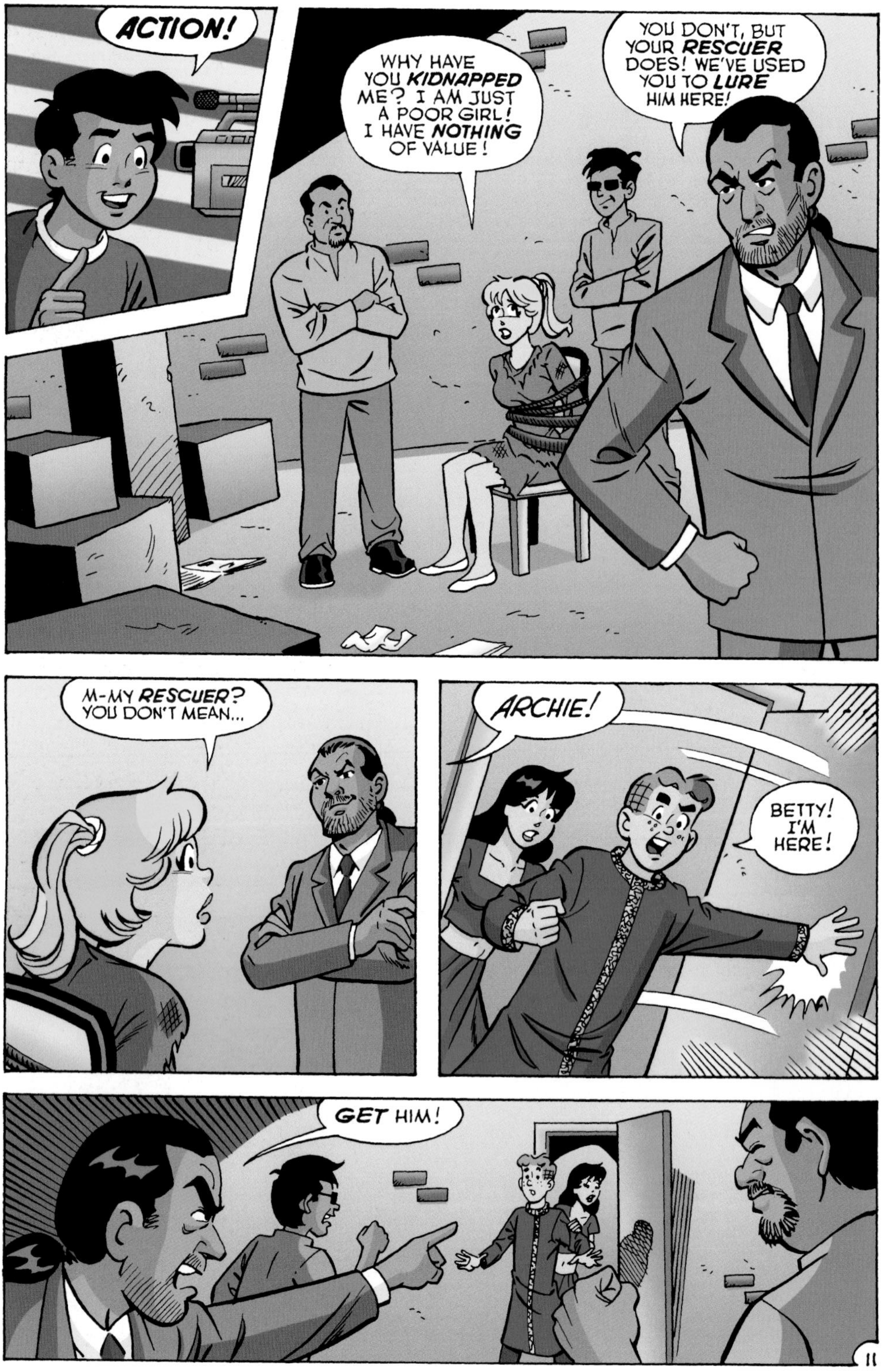
ACTION!
WHY HAVE YOU KIDNAPPED ME? I AM JUST A POOR GIRL! I HAVE NOTHING OF VALUE!
YOU DON'T, BUT YOUR RESCUER DOES! WE'VE USED YOU TO LURE HIM HERE!
M-MY RESCUER? YOU DON'T MEAN...
ARCHIE!
BETTY! I'M HERE!
GET HIM!
11

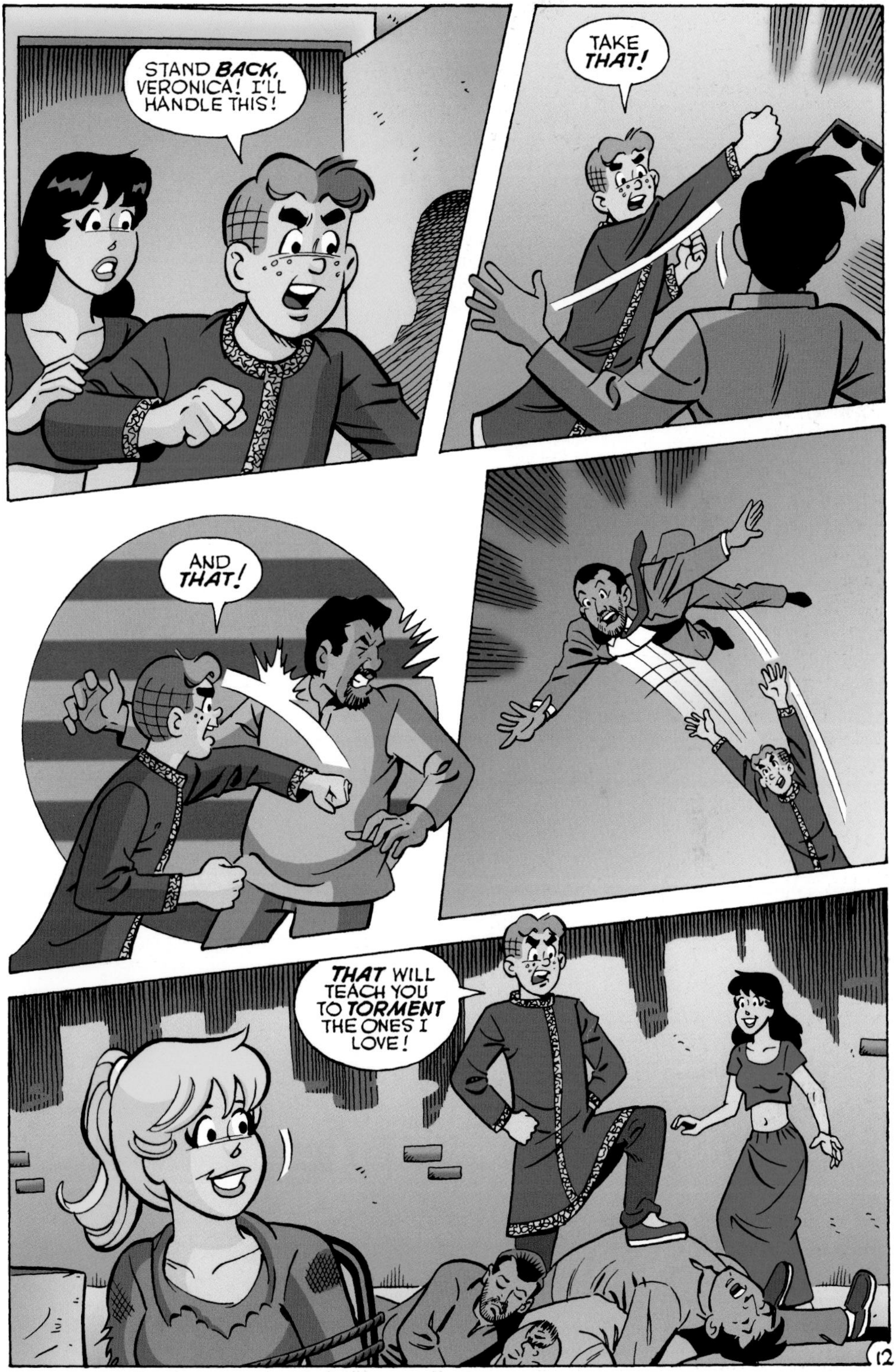
STAND BACK, VERONICA! I'LL HANDLE THIS!
TAKE THAT!
AND THAT!
THAT WILL TEACH YOU TO TORMENT THE ONES I LOVE!
12

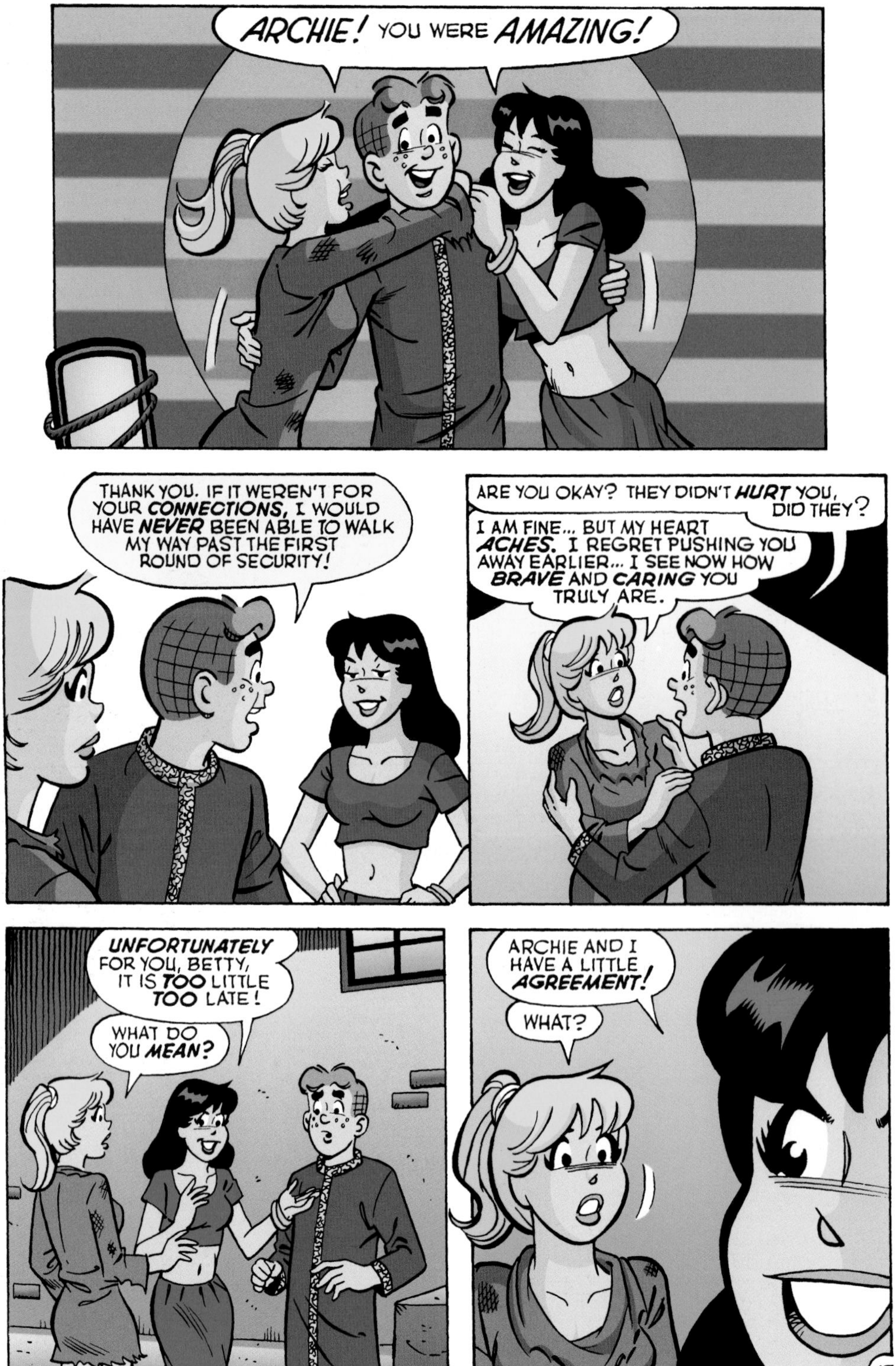
ARCHIE! YOU WERE AMAZING!
THANK YOU. IF IT WEREN'T FOR YOUR CONNECTIONS, I WOULD HAVE NEVER BEEN ABLE TO WALK MY WAY PAST THE FIRST ROUND OF SECURITY!
ARE YOU OKAY? THEY DIDN'T HURT YOU, DID THEY?
I AM FINE... BUT MY HEART ACHES. I REGRET PUSHING YOU AWAY EARLIER... I SEE NOW HOW BRAVE AND CARING YOU TRULY ARE.
UNFORTUNATELY FOR YOU, BETTY, IT IS TOO LITTLE TOO LATE!
WHAT DO YOU MEAN?
ARCHIE AND I HAVE A LITTLE AGREEMENT!
WHAT?
13

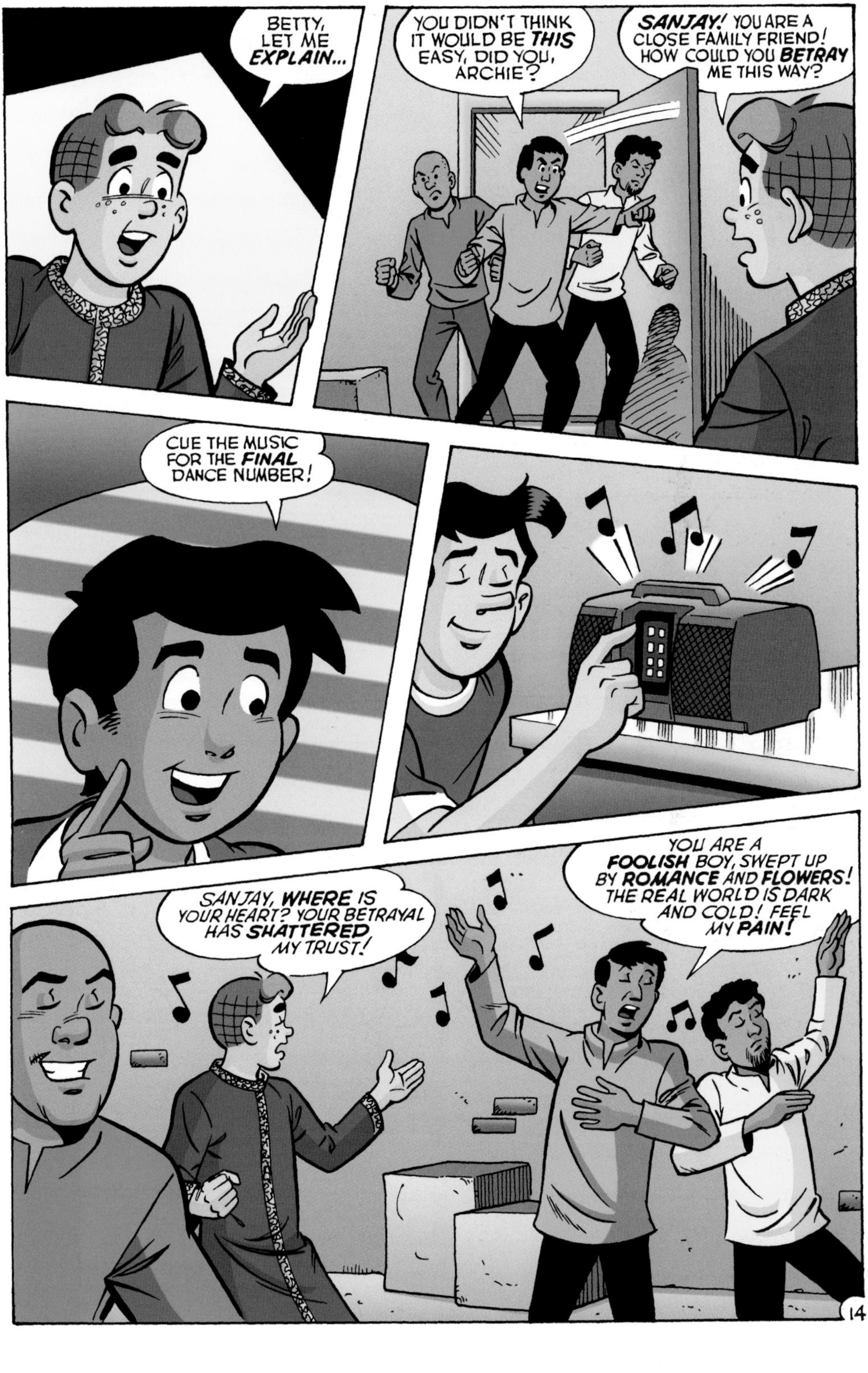
BETTY, LET ME EXPLAIN...
YOU DIDN'T THINK IT WOULD BE THIS EASY, DID YOU, ARCHIE?
SANJAY! YOU ARE A CLOSE FAMILY FRIEND! HOW COULD YOU BETRAY ME THIS WAY?
CUE THE MUSIC FOR THE FINAL DANCE NUMBER!
SANJAY, WHERE IS YOUR HEART? YOUR BETRAYAL HAS SHATTERED MY TRUST!
YOU ARE A FOOLISH BOY, SWEPT UP BY ROMANCE AND FLOWERS! THE REAL WORLD IS DARK AND COLD! FEEL MY PAIN!
14

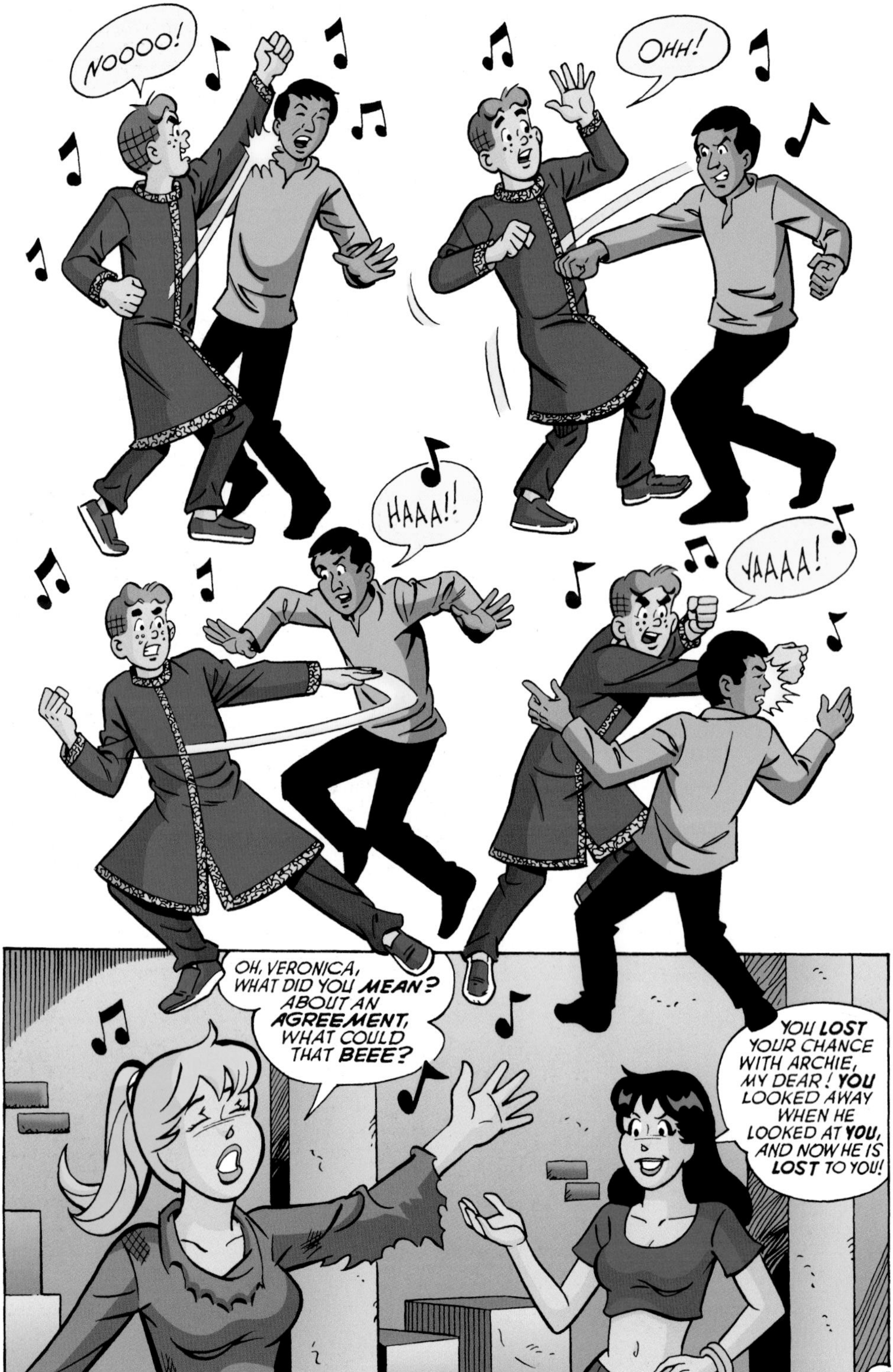
NOOOO!
OHH!
HAAA!!
YAAAA!
OH, VERONICA, WHAT DID YOU MEAN? ABOUT AN AGREEMENT, WHAT COULD THAT BEEE?
YOU LOST YOUR CHANCE WITH ARCHIE, MY DEAR! YOU LOOKED AWAY WHEN HE LOOKED AT YOU, AND NOW HE IS LOST TO YOU!
15

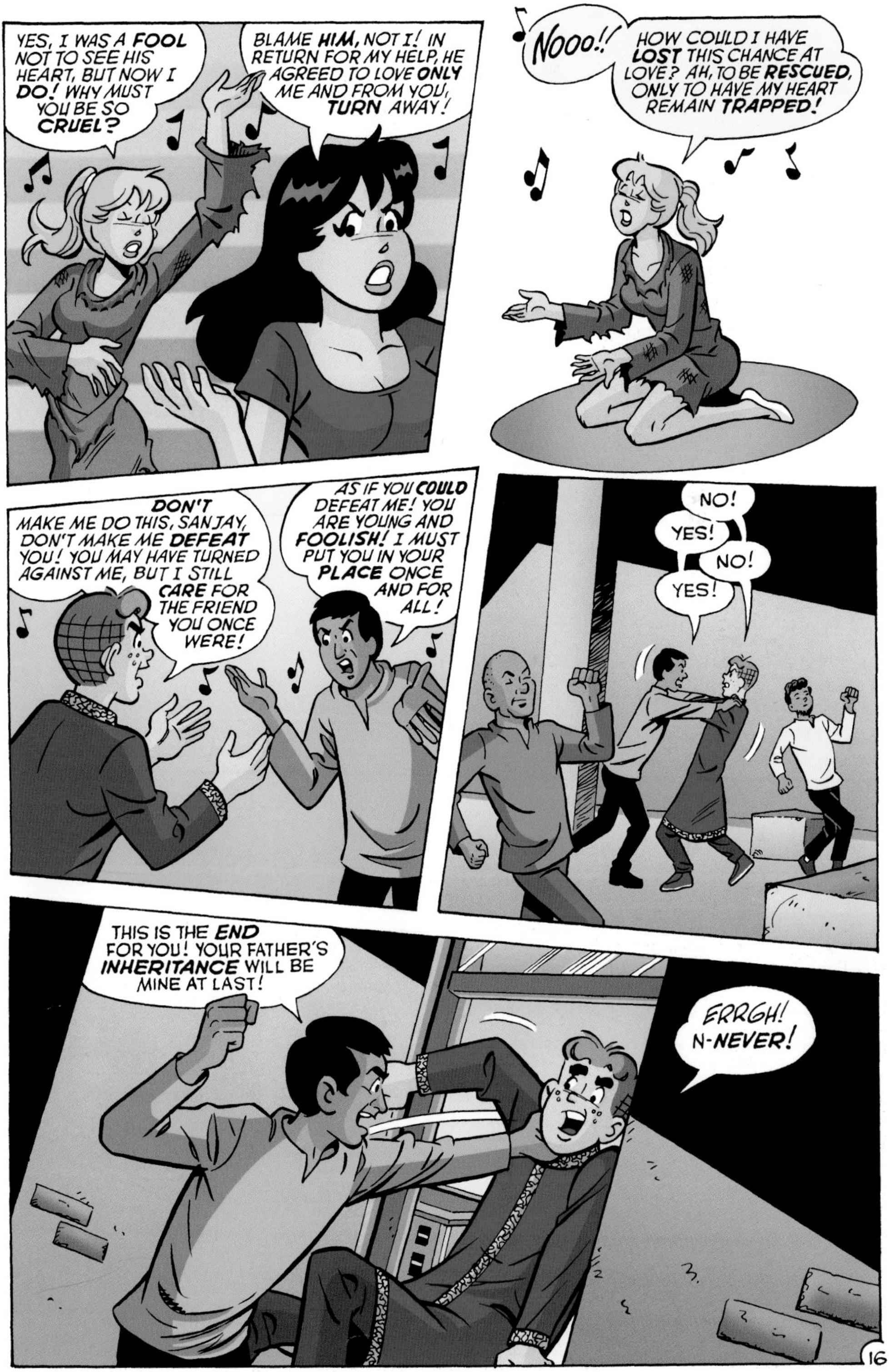
YES, I WAS A FOOL NOT TO SEE HIS HEART, BUT NOW I DO! WHY MUST YOU BE SO CRUEL?
BLAME HIM, NOT I! IN RETURN FOR MY HELP, HE AGREED TO LOVE ONLY ME AND FROM YOU, TURN AWAY!
Nooo!!
HOW COULD I HAVE LOST THIS CHANCE AT LOVE? AH, TO BE RESCUED, ONLY TO HAVE MY HEART REMAIN TRAPPED!
DON'T MAKE ME DO THIS, SANJAY, DON'T MAKE ME DEFEAT YOU! YOU MAY HAVE TURNED AGAINST ME, BUT I STILL CARE FOR THE FRIEND YOU ONCE WERE!
AS IF YOU COULD DEFEAT ME! YOU ARE YOUNG AND FOOLISH! I MUST PUT YOU IN YOUR PLACE ONCE AND FOR ALL!
NO!
YES!
NO!
YES!
THIS IS THE END FOR YOU! YOUR FATHER'S INHERITANCE WILL BE MINE AT LAST!
ERRGH! N-NEVER!
16

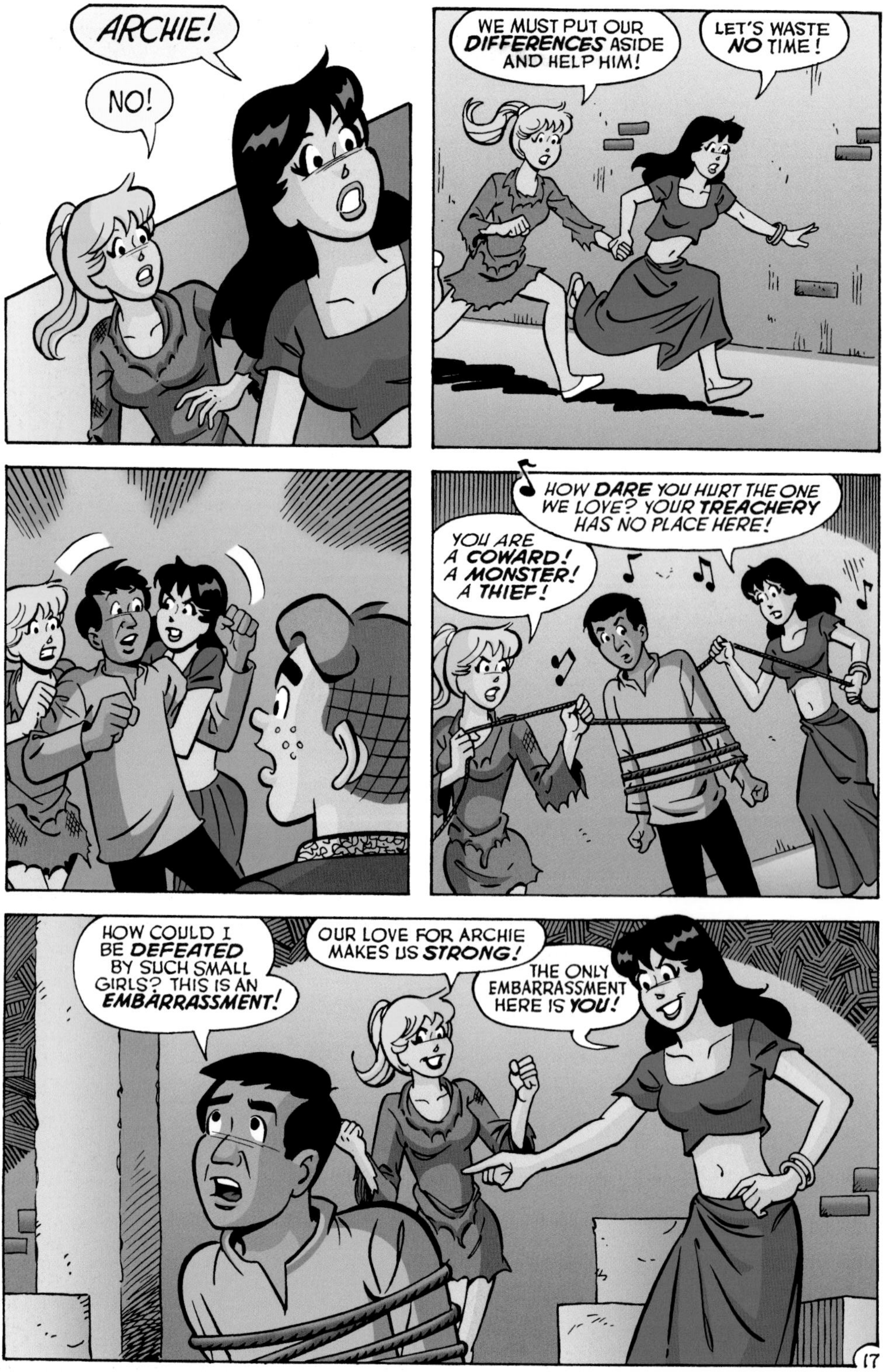

ARCHIE!
NO!
WE MUST PUT OUR DIFFERENCES ASIDE AND HELP HIM!
LET'S WASTE NO TIME!
HOW DARE YOU HURT THE ONE WE LOVE? YOUR TREACHERY HAS NO PLACE HERE!
YOU ARE A COWARD! A MONSTER! A THIEF!
HOW COULD I BE DEFEATED BY SUCH SMALL GIRLS? THIS IS AN EMBARRASSMENT!
OUR LOVE FOR ARCHIE MAKES US STRONG!
THE ONLY EMBARRASSMENT HERE IS YOU!
17

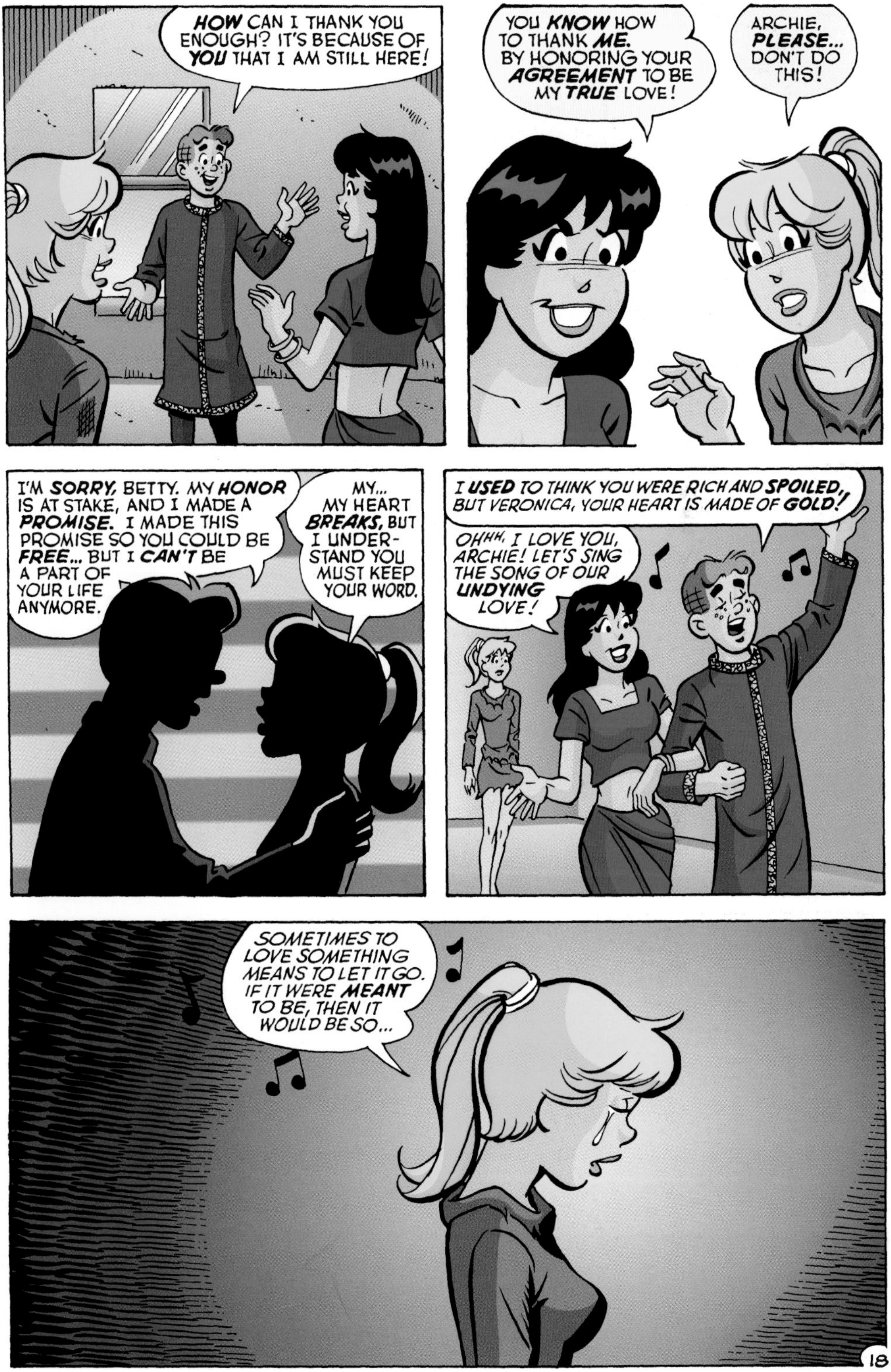
HOW CAN I THANK YOU ENOUGH? IT'S BECAUSE OF YOU THAT I AM STILL HERE!
YOU KNOW HOW TO THANK ME. BY HONORING YOUR AGREEMENT TO BE MY TRUE LOVE!
ARCHIE, PLEASE... DON'T DO THIS!
I'M SORRY, BETTY. MY HONOR IS AT STAKE, AND I MADE A PROMISE. I MADE THIS PROMISE SO YOU COULD BE FREE... BUT I CAN'T BE A PART OF YOUR LIFE ANYMORE.
MY... MY HEART BREAKS, BUT I UNDER-STAND YOU MUST KEEP YOUR WORD.
I USED TO THINK YOU WERE RICH AND SPOILED, BUT VERONICA, YOUR HEART IS MADE OF GOLD!
OHHH, I LOVE YOU, ARCHIE! LET'S SING THE SONG OF OUR UNDYING LOVE!
SOMETIMES TO LOVE SOMETHING MEANS TO LET IT GO. IF IT WERE MEANT TO BE, THEN IT WOULD BE SO...
18

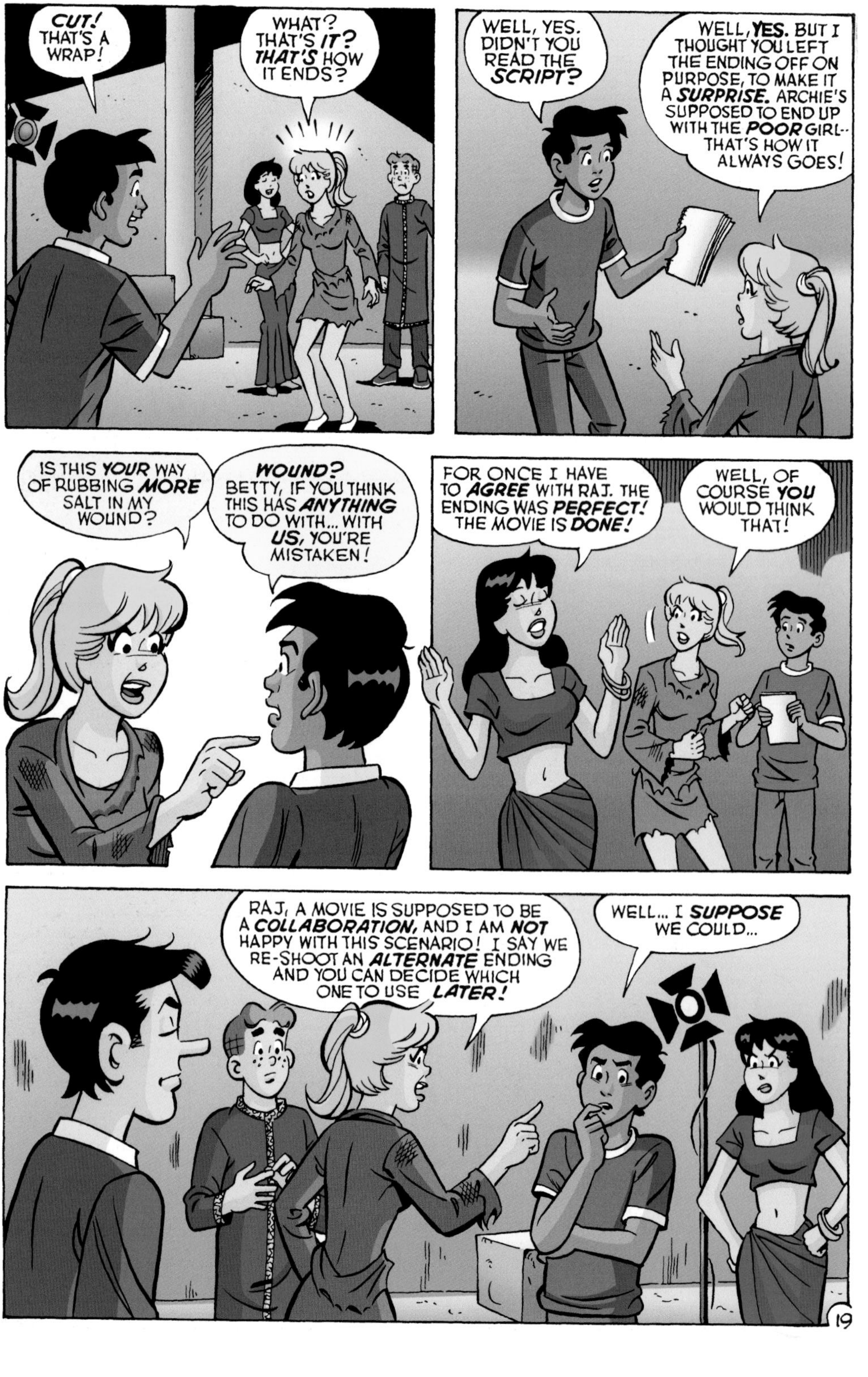
CUT! THAT'S A WRAP!
WHAT? THAT'S IT? THAT'S HOW IT ENDS?
WELL, YES. DIDN'T YOU READ THE SCRIPT?
WELL, YES. BUT I THOUGHT YOU LEFT THE ENDING OFF ON PURPOSE, TO MAKE IT A SURPRISE. ARCHIE'S SUPPOSED TO END UP WITH THE POOR GIRL-- THAT'S HOW IT ALWAYS GOES!
IS THIS YOUR WAY OF RUBBING MORE SALT IN MY WOUND?
WOUND? BETTY, IF YOU THINK THIS HAS ANYTHING TO DO WITH... WITH US, YOU'RE MISTAKEN!
FOR ONCE I HAVE TO AGREE WITH RAJ. THE ENDING WAS PERFECT! THE MOVIE IS DONE!
WELL, OF COURSE YOU WOULD THINK THAT!
RAJ, A MOVIE IS SUPPOSED TO BE A COLLABORATION, AND I AM NOT HAPPY WITH THIS SCENARIO! I SAY WE RE-SHOOT AN ALTERNATE ENDING AND YOU CAN DECIDE WHICH ONE TO USE LATER!
WELL... I SUPPOSE WE COULD...
19

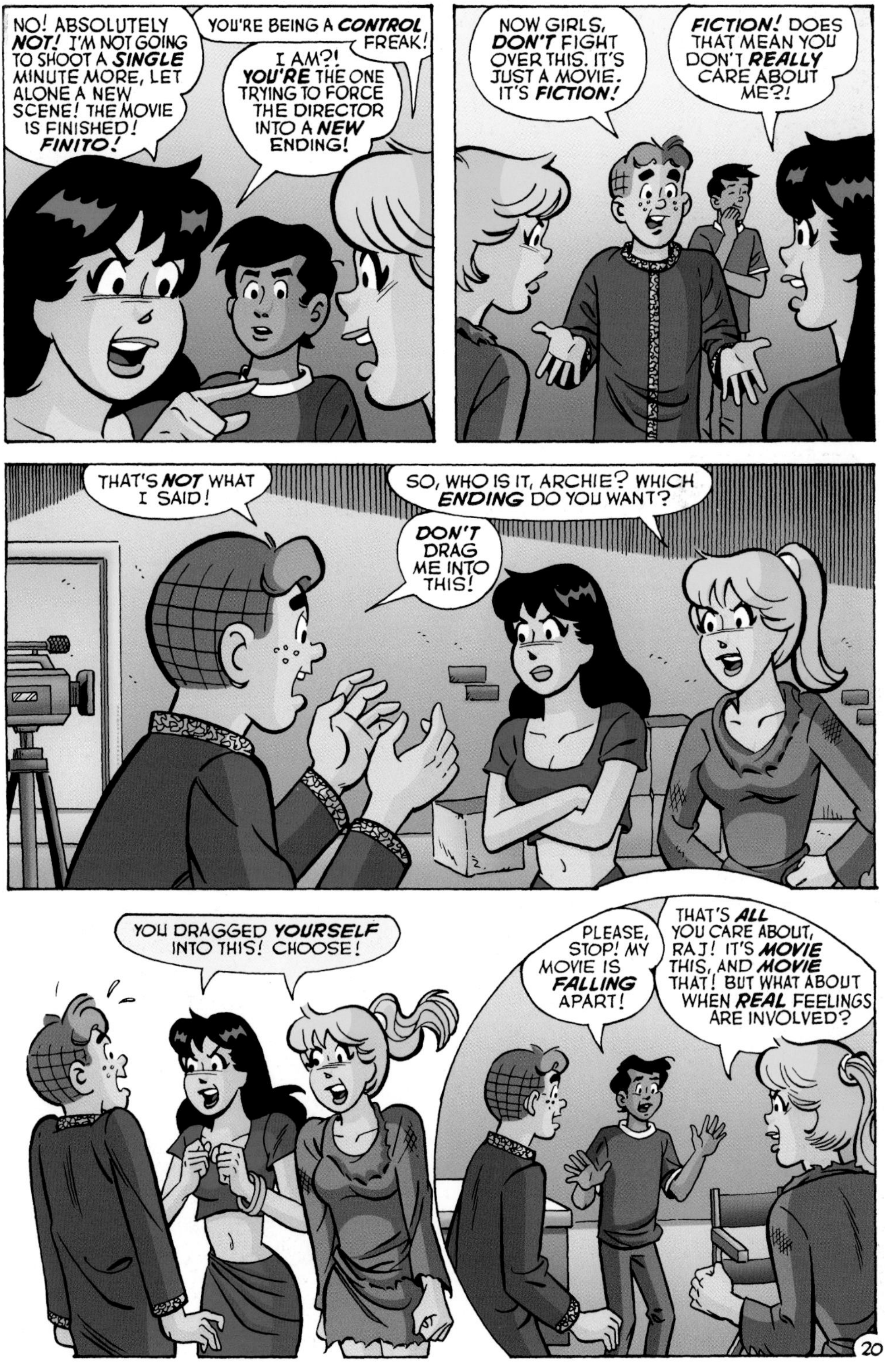
NO! ABSOLUTELY NOT! I'M NOT GOING TO SHOOT A SINGLE MINUTE MORE, LET ALONE A NEW SCENE! THE MOVIE IS FINISHED! FINITO!
YOU'RE BEING A CONTROL FREAK!
I AM?! YOU'RE THE ONE TRYING TO FORCE THE DIRECTOR INTO A NEW ENDING!
NOW GIRLS, DON'T FIGHT OVER THIS. IT'S JUST A MOVIE. IT'S FICTION!
FICTION! DOES THAT MEAN YOU DON'T REALLY CARE ABOUT ME?!
THAT'S NOT WHAT I SAID!
SO, WHO IS IT, ARCHIE? WHICH ENDING DO YOU WANT?
DON'T DRAG ME INTO THIS!
YOU DRAGGED YOURSELF INTO THIS! CHOOSE!
PLEASE, STOP! MY MOVIE IS FALLING APART!
THAT'S ALL YOU CARE ABOUT, RAJ! IT'S MOVIE THIS, AND MOVIE THAT! BUT WHAT ABOUT WHEN REAL FEELINGS ARE INVOLVED?
20

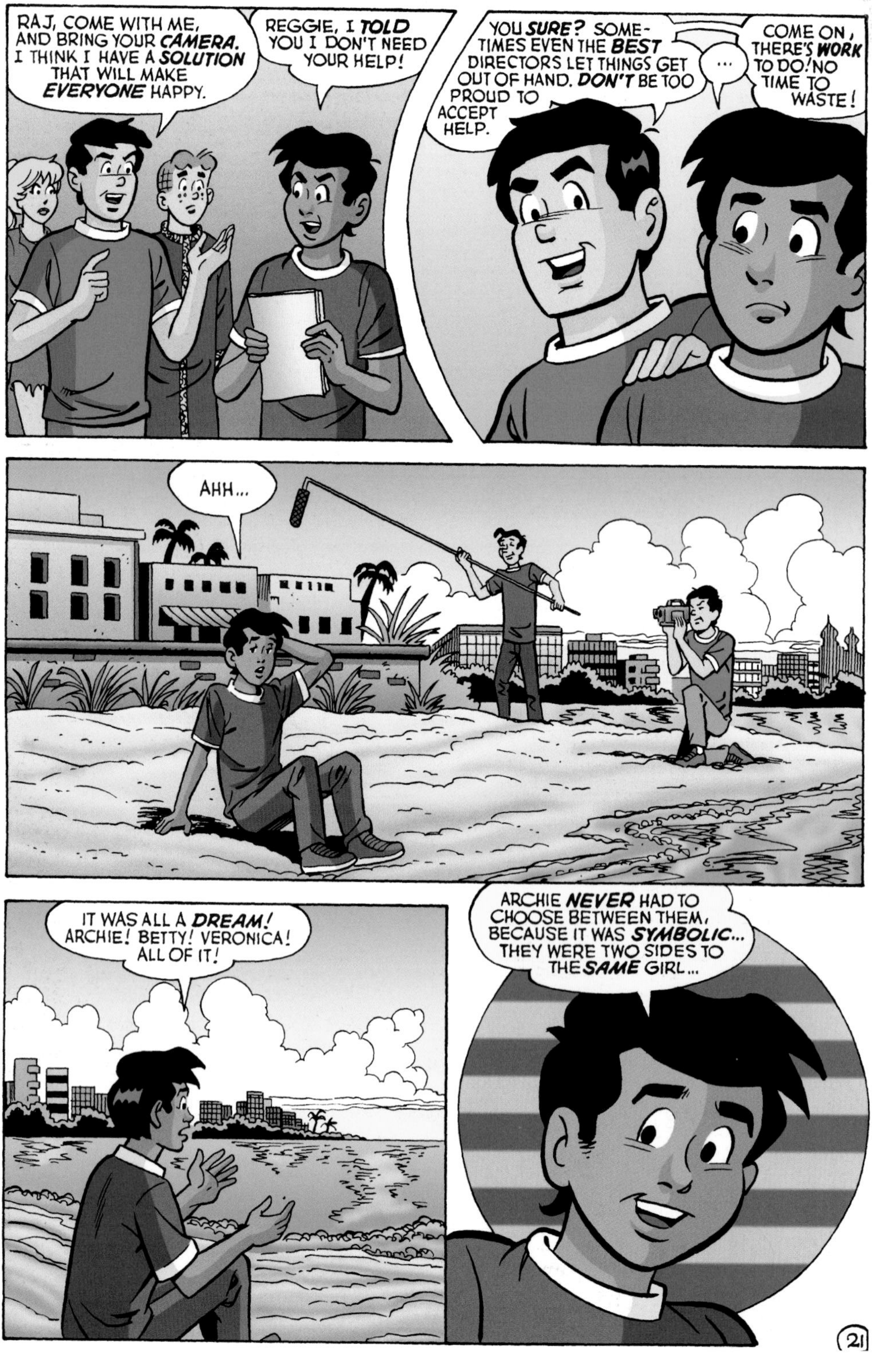
RAJ, COME WITH ME, AND BRING YOUR CAMERA. I THINK I HAVE A SOLUTION THAT WILL MAKE EVERYONE HAPPY.
REGGIE, I TOLD YOU I DON'T NEED YOUR HELP!
YOU SURE? SOMETIMES EVEN THE BEST DIRECTORS LET THINGS GET OUT OF HAND. DON'T BE TOO PROUD TO ACCEPT HELP.
...
COME ON, THERE'S WORK TO DO! NO TIME TO WASTE!
AHH...
IT WAS ALL A DREAM! ARCHIE! BETTY! VERONICA! ALL OF IT!
ARCHIE NEVER HAD TO CHOOSE BETWEEN THEM, BECAUSE IT WAS SYMBOLIC... THEY WERE TWO SIDES TO THE SAME GIRL...
21

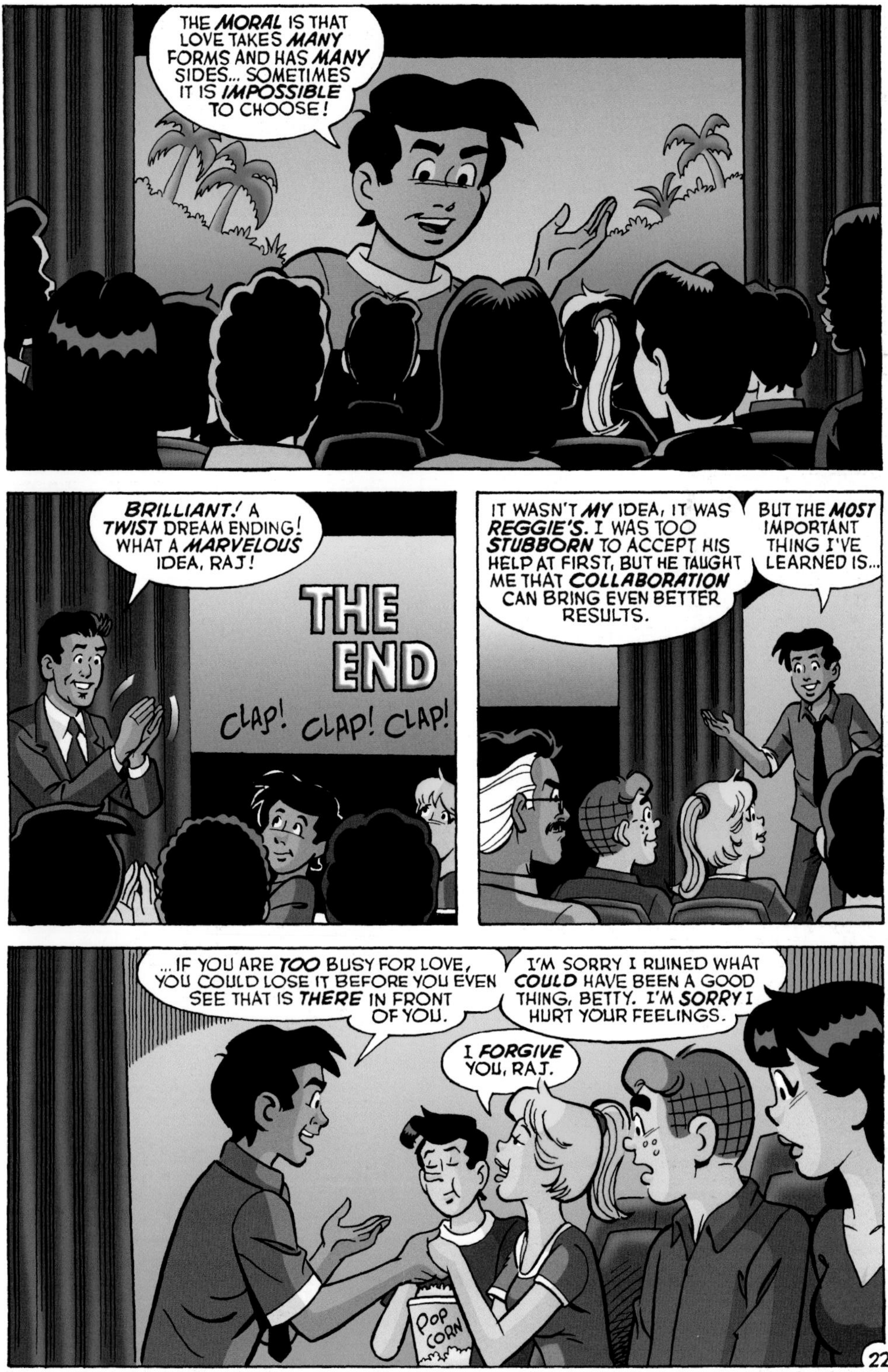
THE MORAL IS THAT LOVE TAKES MANY FORMS AND HAS MANY SIDES... SOMETIMES IT IS IMPOSSIBLE TO CHOOSE!
BRILLIANT! A TWIST DREAM ENDING! WHAT A MARVELOUS IDEA, RAJ!
THE END
CLAP! CLAP! CLAP!
IT WASN'T MY IDEA, IT WAS REGGIE'S. I WAS TOO STUBBORN TO ACCEPT HIS HELP AT FIRST, BUT HE TAUGHT ME THAT COLLABORATION CAN BRING EVEN BETTER RESULTS.
BUT THE MOST IMPORTANT THING I'VE LEARNED IS...
...IF YOU ARE TOO BUSY FOR LOVE, YOU COULD LOSE IT BEFORE YOU EVEN SEE THAT IS THERE IN FRONT OF YOU.
I'M SORRY I RUINED WHAT COULD HAVE BEEN A GOOD THING, BETTY. I'M SORRY I HURT YOUR FEELINGS.
I FORGIVE YOU, RAJ.
POP CORN
22

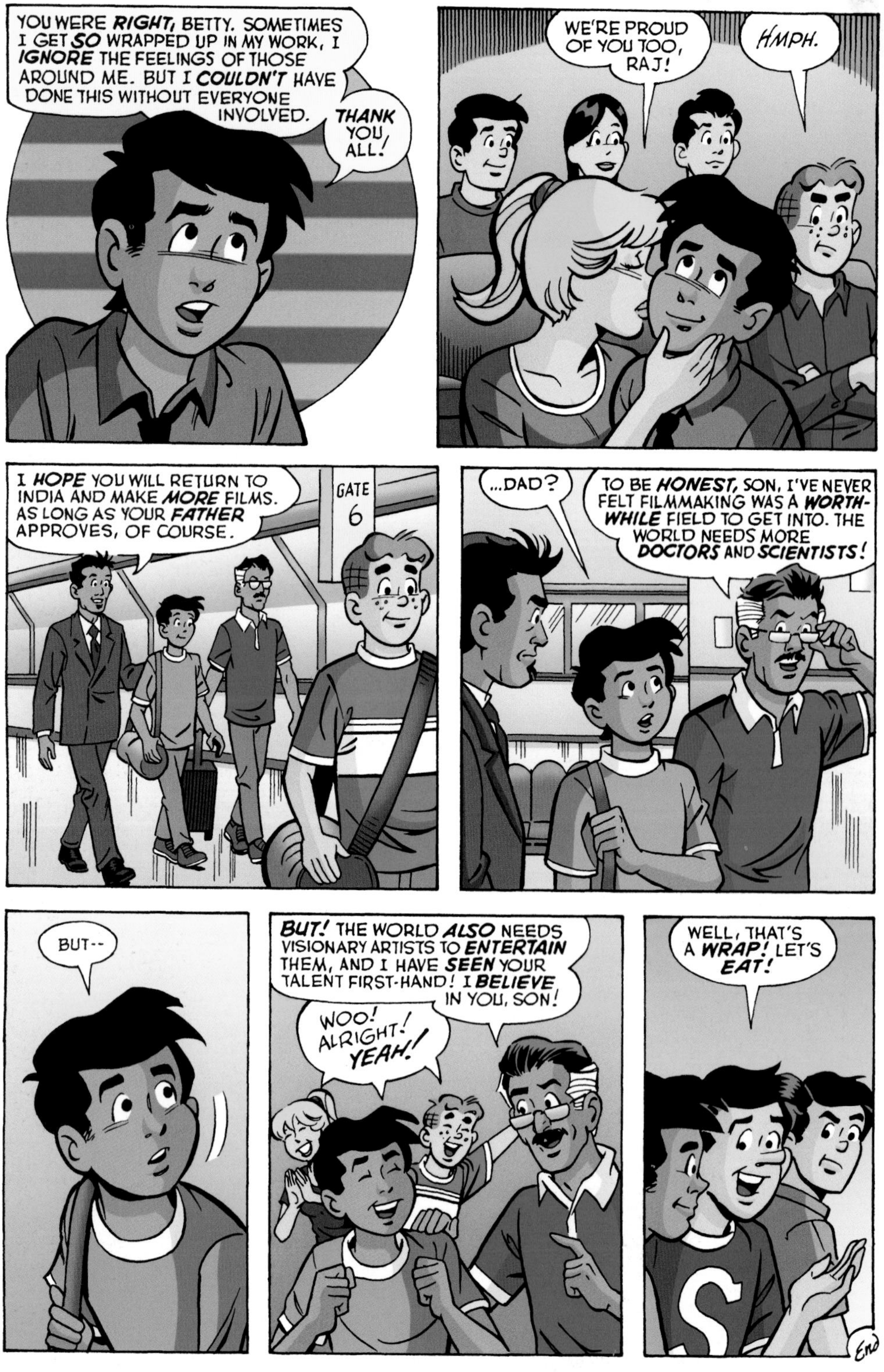

YOU WERE RIGHT, BETTY. SOMETIMES I GET SO WRAPPED UP IN MY WORK, I IGNORE THE FEELINGS OF THOSE AROUND ME. BUT I COULDN'T HAVE DONE THIS WITHOUT EVERYONE INVOLVED.
THANK YOU, ALL!
WE'RE PROUD OF YOU TOO, RAJ!
HMPH.
I HOPE YOU WILL RETURN TO INDIA AND MAKE MORE FILMS. AS LONG AS YOUR FATHER APPROVES, OF COURSE.
GATE 6
...DAD?
TO BE HONEST, SON, I'VE NEVER FELT FILMMAKING WAS A WORTH-WHILE FIELD TO GET INTO. THE WORLD NEEDS MORE DOCTORS AND SCIENTISTS!
BUT--
BUT! THE WORLD ALSO NEEDS VISIONARY ARTISTS TO ENTERTAIN THEM, AND I HAVE SEEN YOUR TALENT FIRST-HAND! I BELIEVE IN YOU, SON!
WOO! ALRIGHT! YEAH!
WELL, THAT'S A WRAP! LET'S EAT!
End

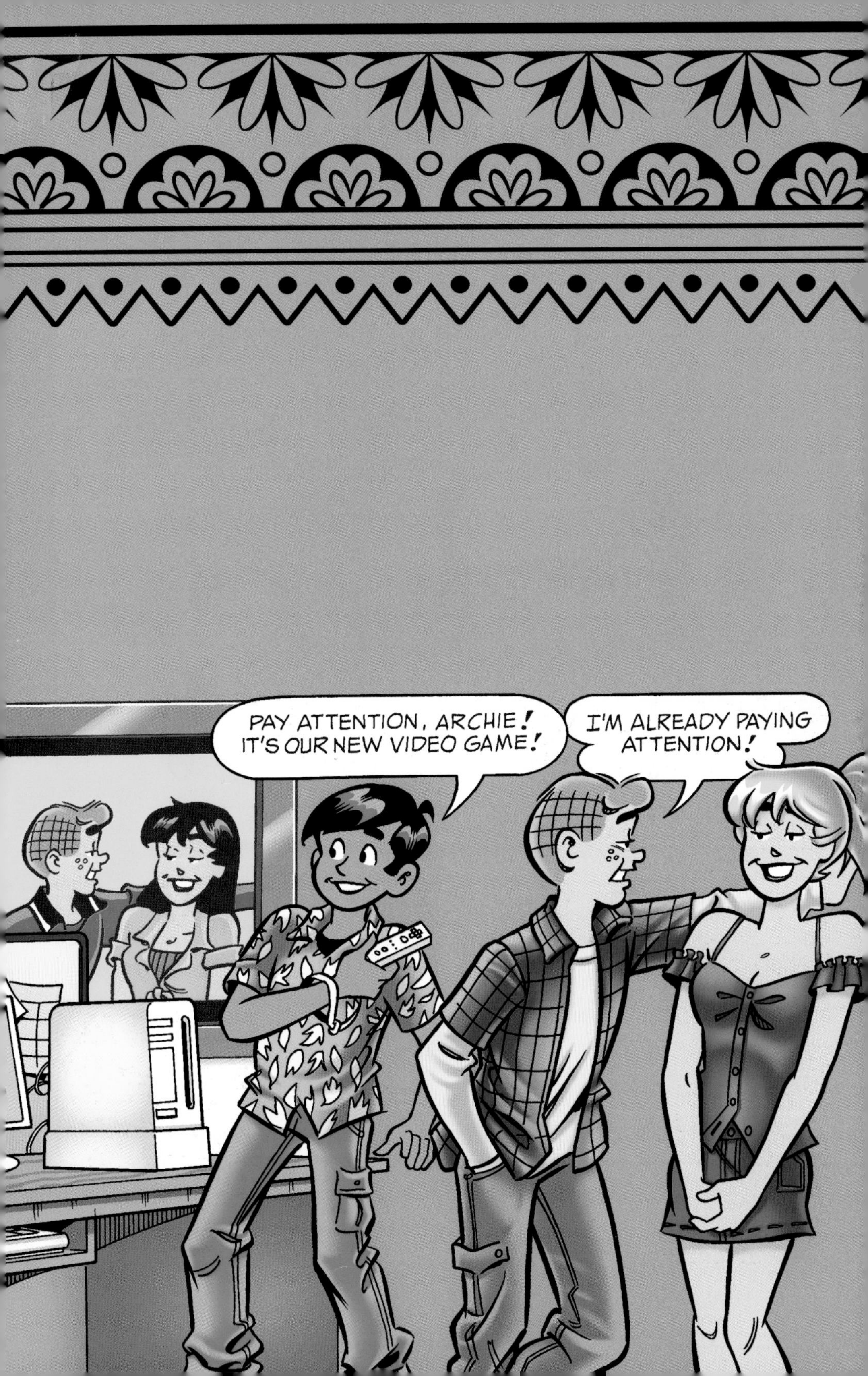
PAY ATTENTION, ARCHIE! IT'S OUR NEW VIDEO GAME!
I'M ALREADY PAYING ATTENTION!

Archie in HIGHSCORING HIJINKS

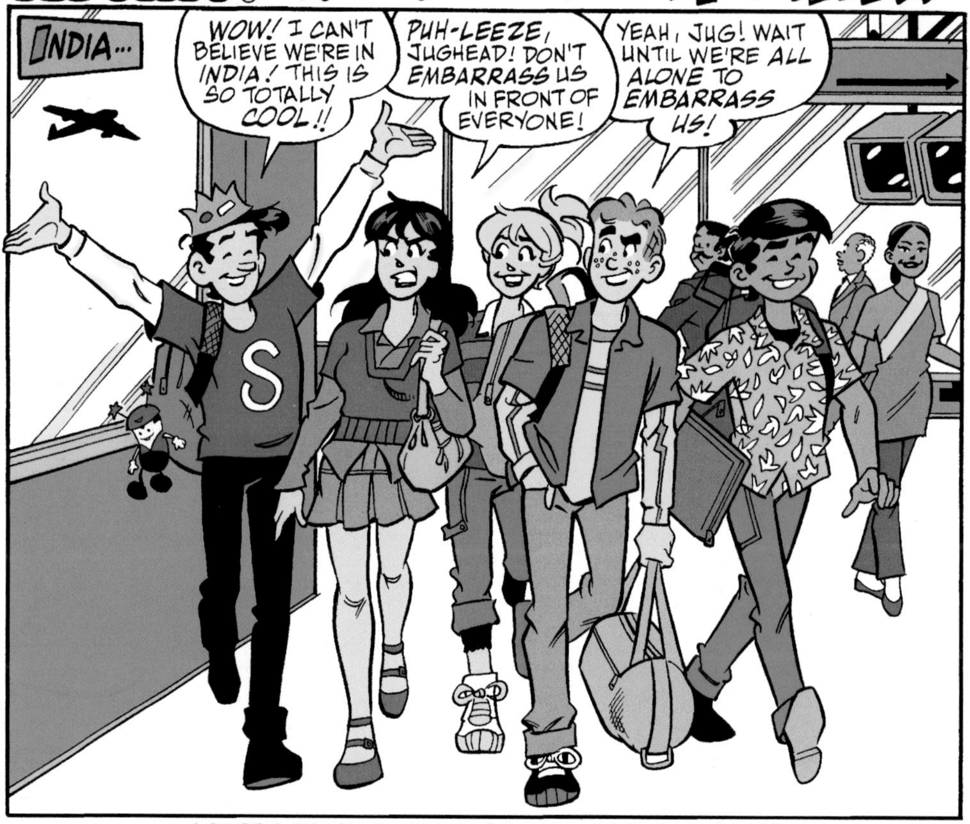
INDIA...
WOW! I CAN'T BELIEVE WE'RE IN INDIA! THIS IS SO TOTALLY COOL!!
PUH-LEEZE, JUGHEAD! DON'T EMBARRASS US IN FRONT OF EVERYONE!
YEAH, JUG! WAIT UNTIL WE'RE ALL ALONE TO EMBARRASS US!

SCRIPT & PENCILS: FERNANDO RUIZ INKS: BOB SMITH
COLORS: CARLOS ANTUNES LETTERS: JACK MORELLI

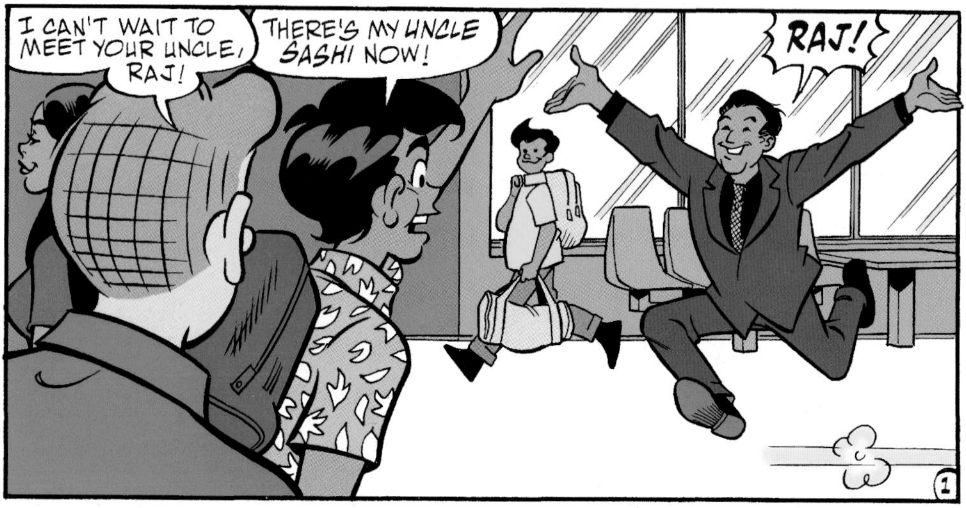
I CAN'T WAIT TO MEET YOUR UNCLE, RAJ!
THERE'S MY UNCLE SASHI NOW!
RAJ!
1

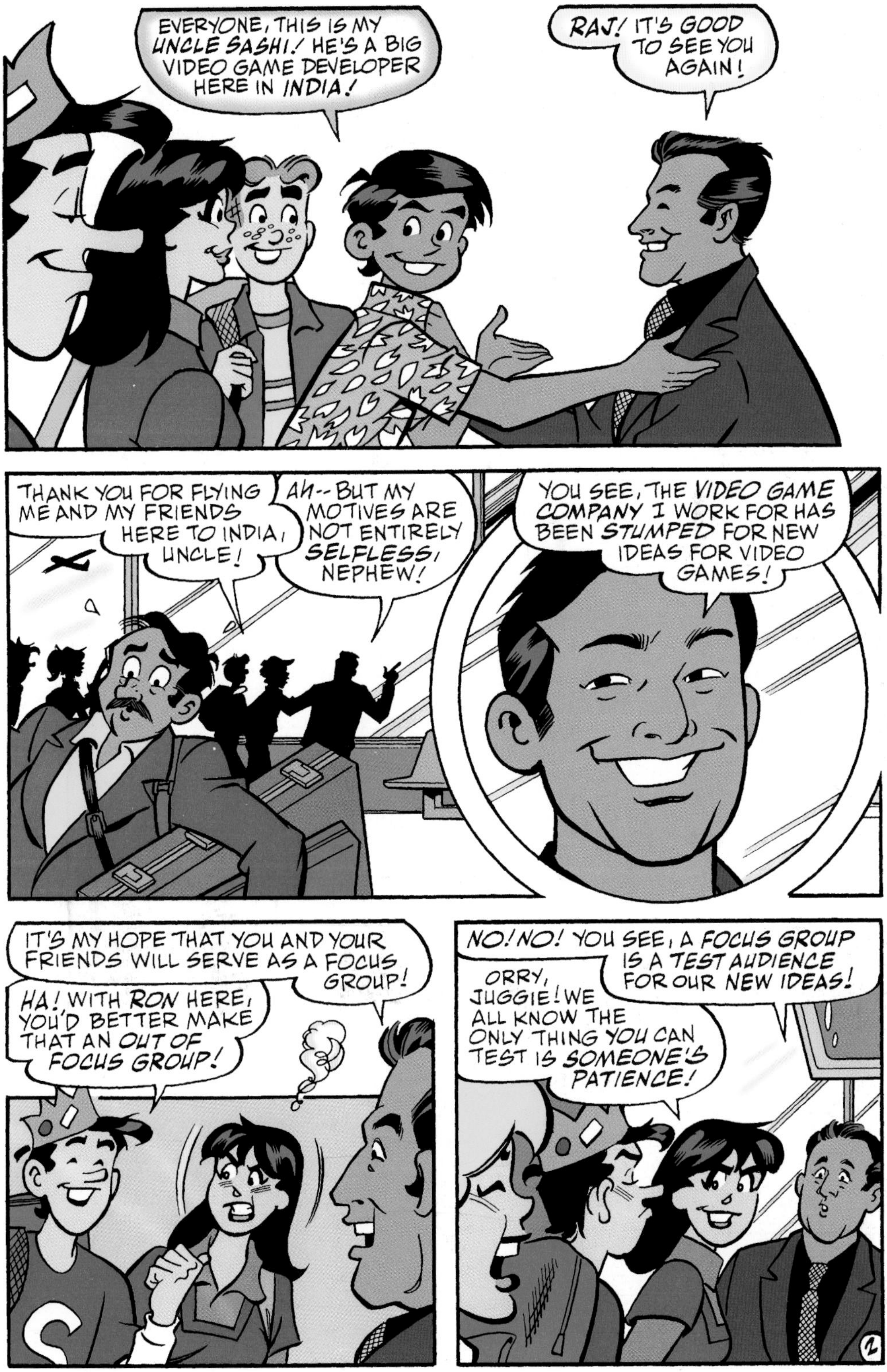
EVERYONE, THIS IS MY UNCLE SASHI! HE'S A BIG VIDEO GAME DEVELOPER HERE IN INDIA!
RAJ! IT'S GOOD TO SEE YOU AGAIN!
THANK YOU FOR FLYING ME AND MY FRIENDS HERE TO INDIA, UNCLE!
AH-- BUT MY MOTIVES ARE NOT ENTIRELY SELFLESS, NEPHEW!
YOU SEE, THE VIDEO GAME COMPANY I WORK FOR HAS BEEN STUMPED FOR NEW IDEAS FOR VIDEO GAMES!
IT'S MY HOPE THAT YOU AND YOUR FRIENDS WILL SERVE AS A FOCUS GROUP!
HA! WITH RON HERE, YOU'D BETTER MAKE THAT AN OUT OF FOCUS GROUP!
NO! NO! YOU SEE, A FOCUS GROUP IS A TEST AUDIENCE FOR OUR NEW IDEAS!
ORRY, JUGGIE! WE ALL KNOW THE ONLY THING YOU CAN TEST IS SOMEONE'S PATIENCE!

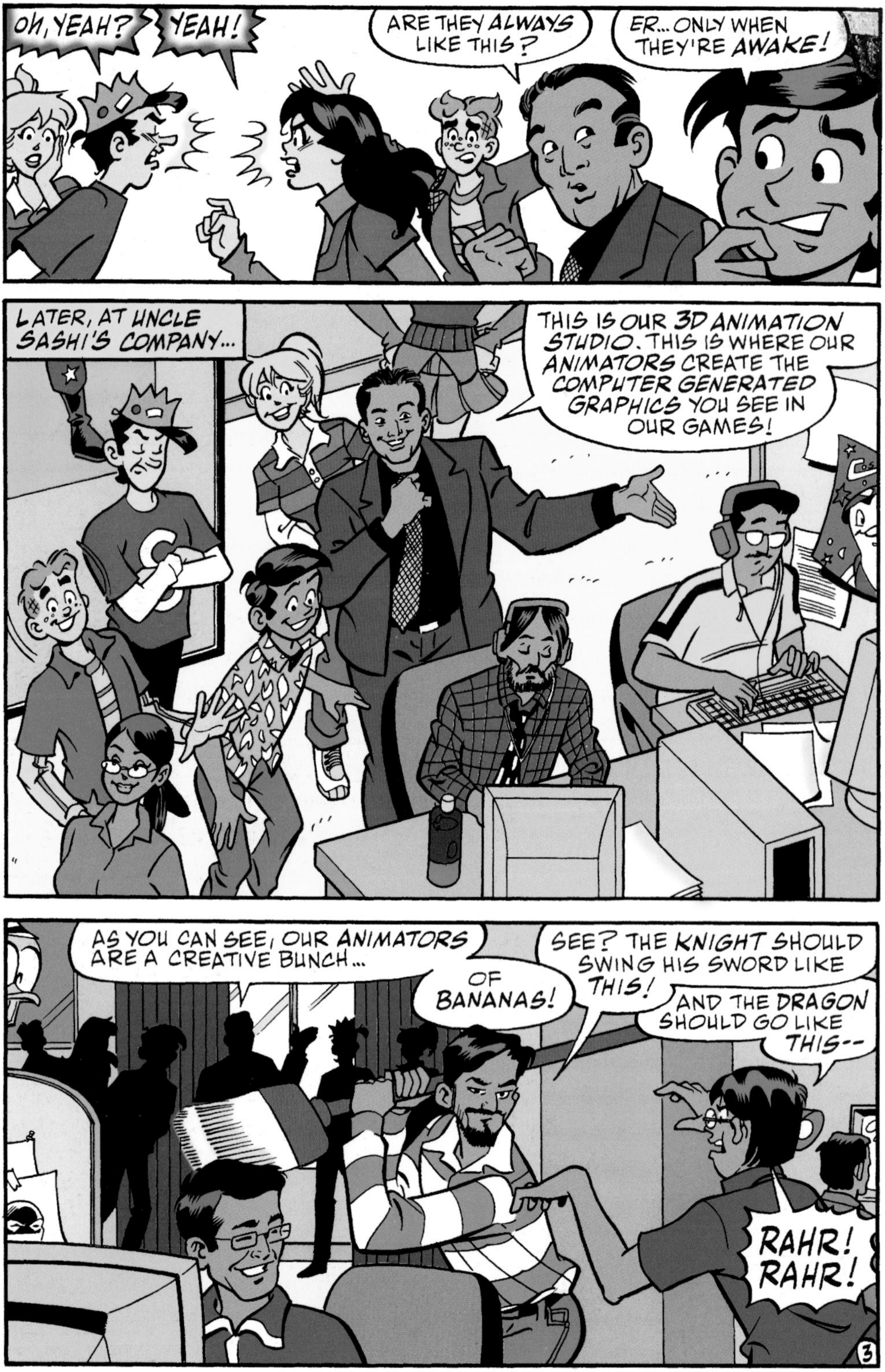

OH, YEAH?
YEAH!
ARE THEY ALWAYS LIKE THIS?
ER... ONLY WHEN THEY'RE AWAKE!
LATER, AT UNCLE SASHI'S COMPANY...
THIS IS OUR 3D ANIMATION STUDIO. THIS IS WHERE OUR ANIMATORS CREATE THE COMPUTER GENERATED GRAPHICS YOU SEE IN OUR GAMES!
AS YOU CAN SEE, OUR ANIMATORS ARE A CREATIVE BUNCH...
OF BANANAS!
SEE? THE KNIGHT SHOULD SWING HIS SWORD LIKE THIS!
AND THE DRAGON SHOULD GO LIKE THIS--
RAHR! RAHR!
3

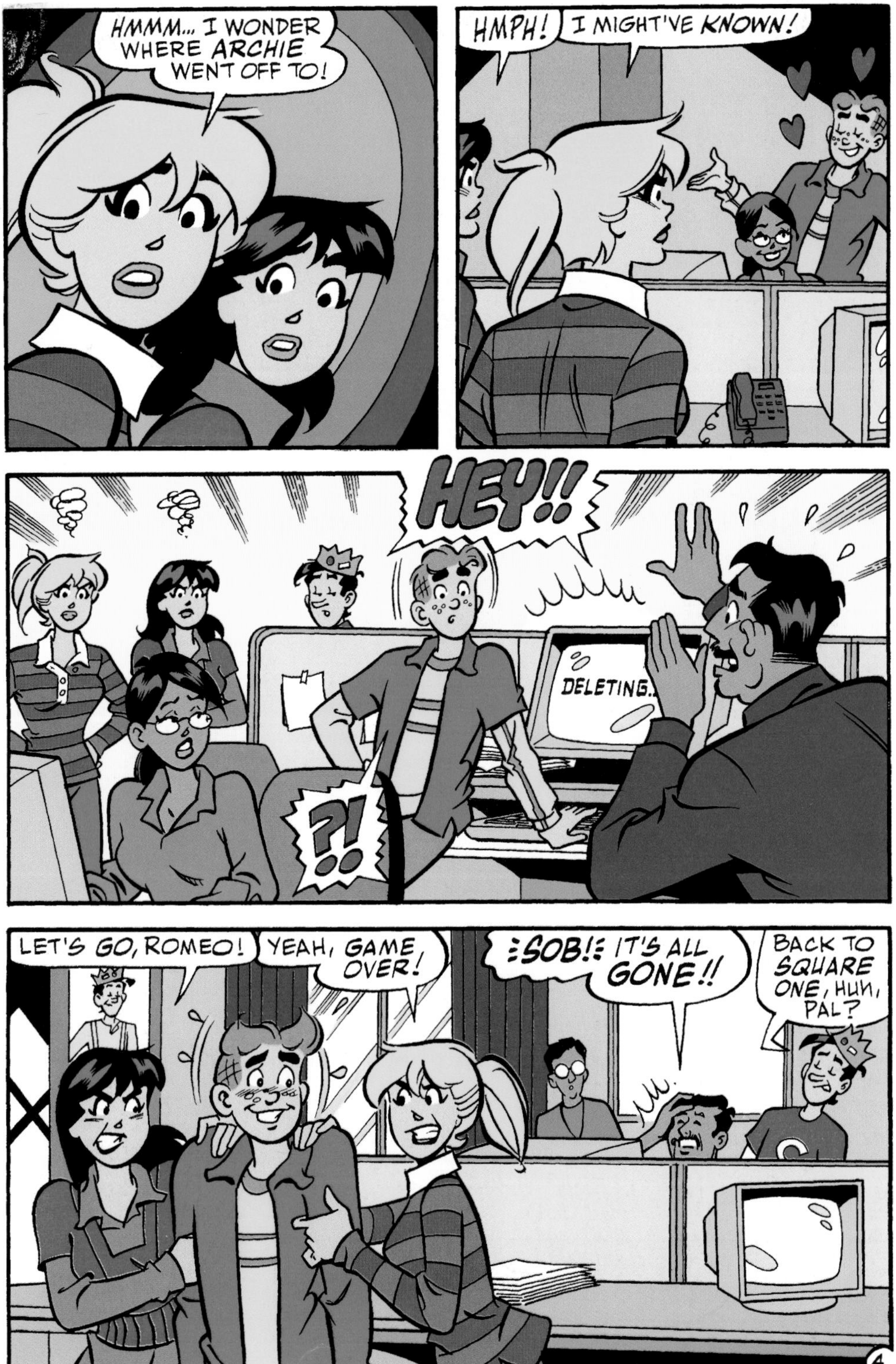
HMMM... I WONDER WHERE ARCHIE WENT OFF TO!
HMPH!
I MIGHT'VE KNOWN!
HEY!!
DELETING...
?!
LET'S GO, ROMEO!
YEAH, GAME OVER!
SOB! IT'S ALL GONE!!
BACK TO SQUARE ONE, HUH, PAL?
4

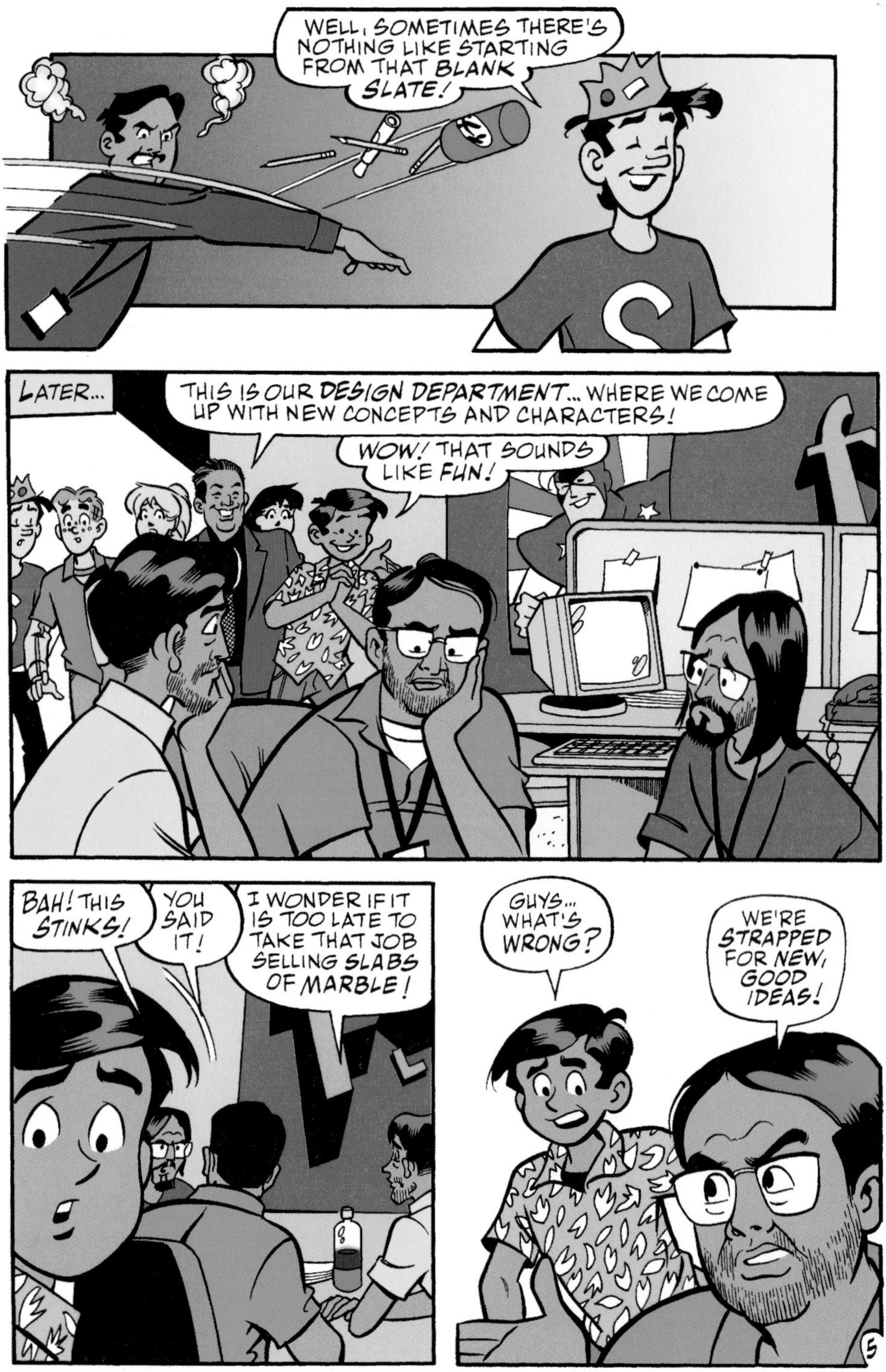
WELL, SOMETIMES THERE'S NOTHING LIKE STARTING FROM THAT BLANK SLATE!
LATER...
THIS IS OUR DESIGN DEPARTMENT... WHERE WE COME UP WITH NEW CONCEPTS AND CHARACTERS!
WOW! THAT SOUNDS LIKE FUN!
BAH! THIS STINKS!
YOU SAID IT!
I WONDER IF IT IS TOO LATE TO TAKE THAT JOB SELLING SLABS OF MARBLE!
GUYS... WHAT'S WRONG?
WE'RE STRAPPED FOR NEW, GOOD IDEAS!
5

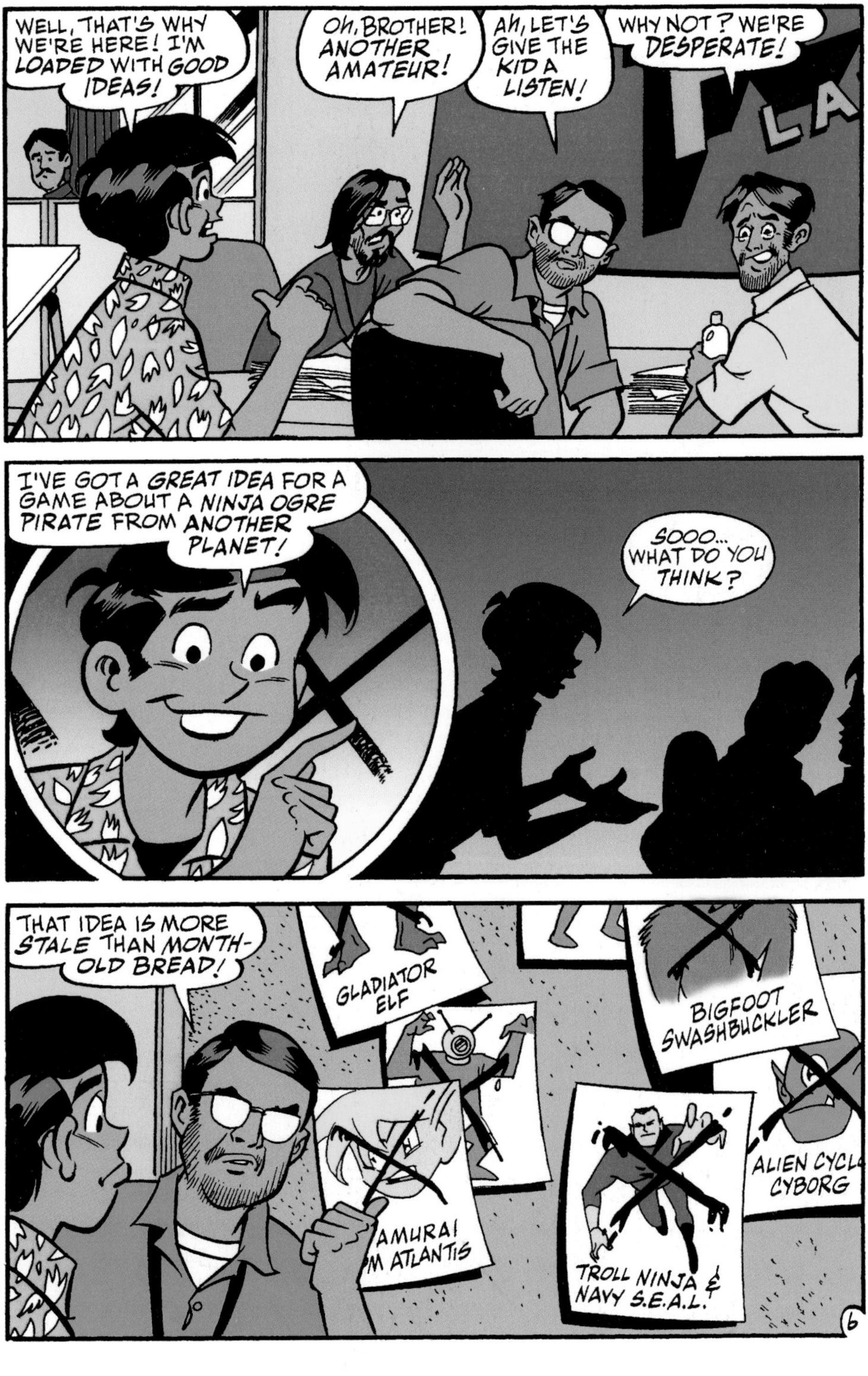
WELL, THAT'S WHY WE'RE HERE! I'M LOADED WITH GOOD IDEAS!
OH, BROTHER! ANOTHER AMATEUR!
AH, LET'S GIVE THE KID A LISTEN!
WHY NOT? WE'RE DESPERATE!
I'VE GOT A GREAT IDEA FOR A GAME ABOUT A NINJA OGRE PIRATE FROM ANOTHER PLANET!
SOOO... WHAT DO YOU THINK?
THAT IDEA IS MORE STALE THAN MONTH-OLD BREAD!
GLADIATOR ELF
BIGFOOT SWASHBUCKLER
ALIEN CYCL
CYBORG
AMURAI
M ATLANTIS
TROLL NINJA & NAVY S.E.A.L.
6

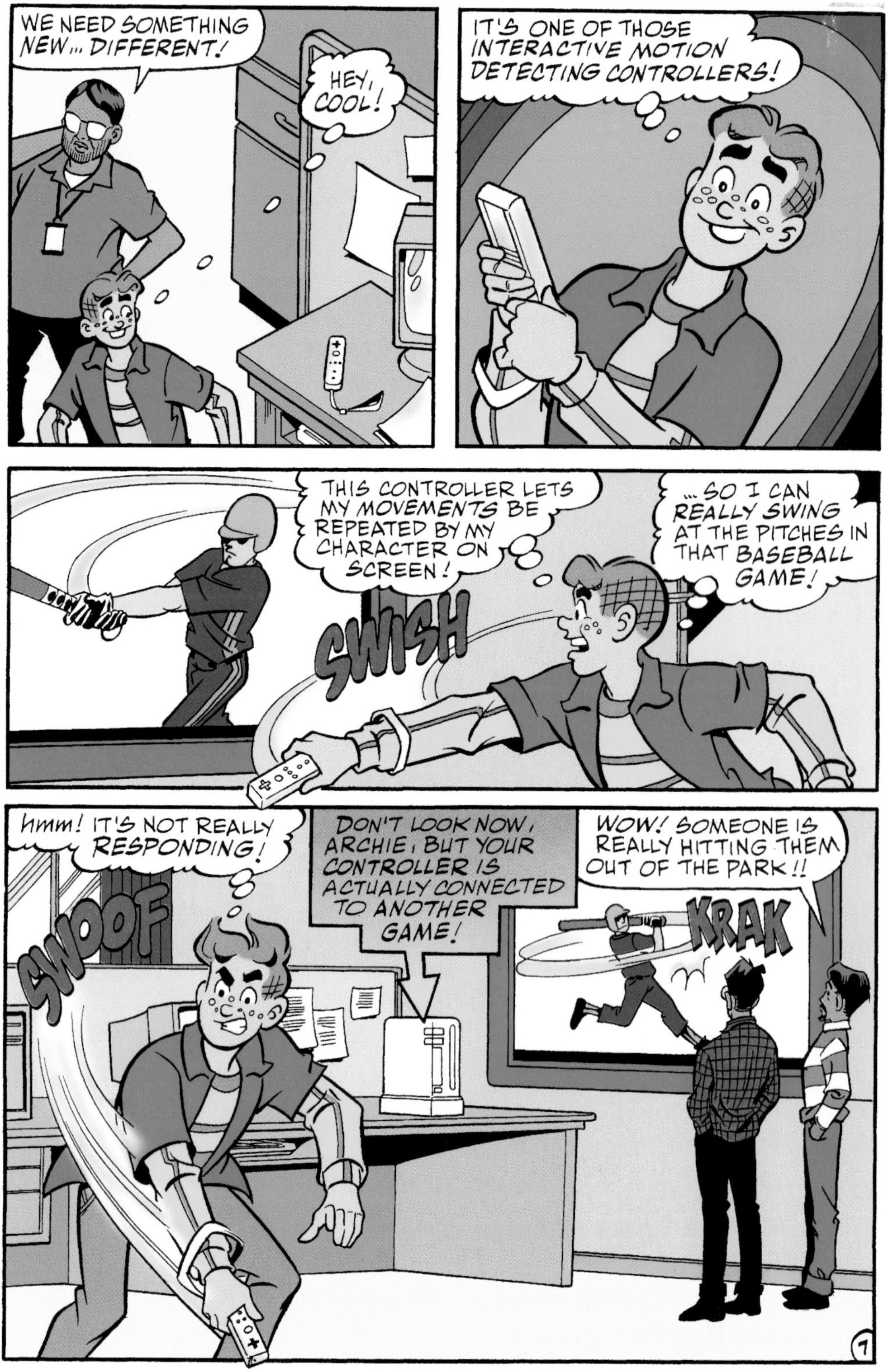
WE NEED SOMETHING NEW... DIFFERENT!
HEY, COOL!
IT'S ONE OF THOSE INTERACTIVE MOTION DETECTING CONTROLLERS!
THIS CONTROLLER LETS MY MOVEMENTS BE REPEATED BY MY CHARACTER ON SCREEN!
...SO I CAN REALLY SWING AT THE PITCHES IN THAT BASEBALL GAME!
SWISH
hmm! IT'S NOT REALLY RESPONDING!
SWOOF
DON'T LOOK NOW, ARCHIE, BUT YOUR CONTROLLER IS ACTUALLY CONNECTED TO ANOTHER GAME!
WOW! SOMEONE IS REALLY HITTING THEM OUT OF THE PARK!!
KRAK
7

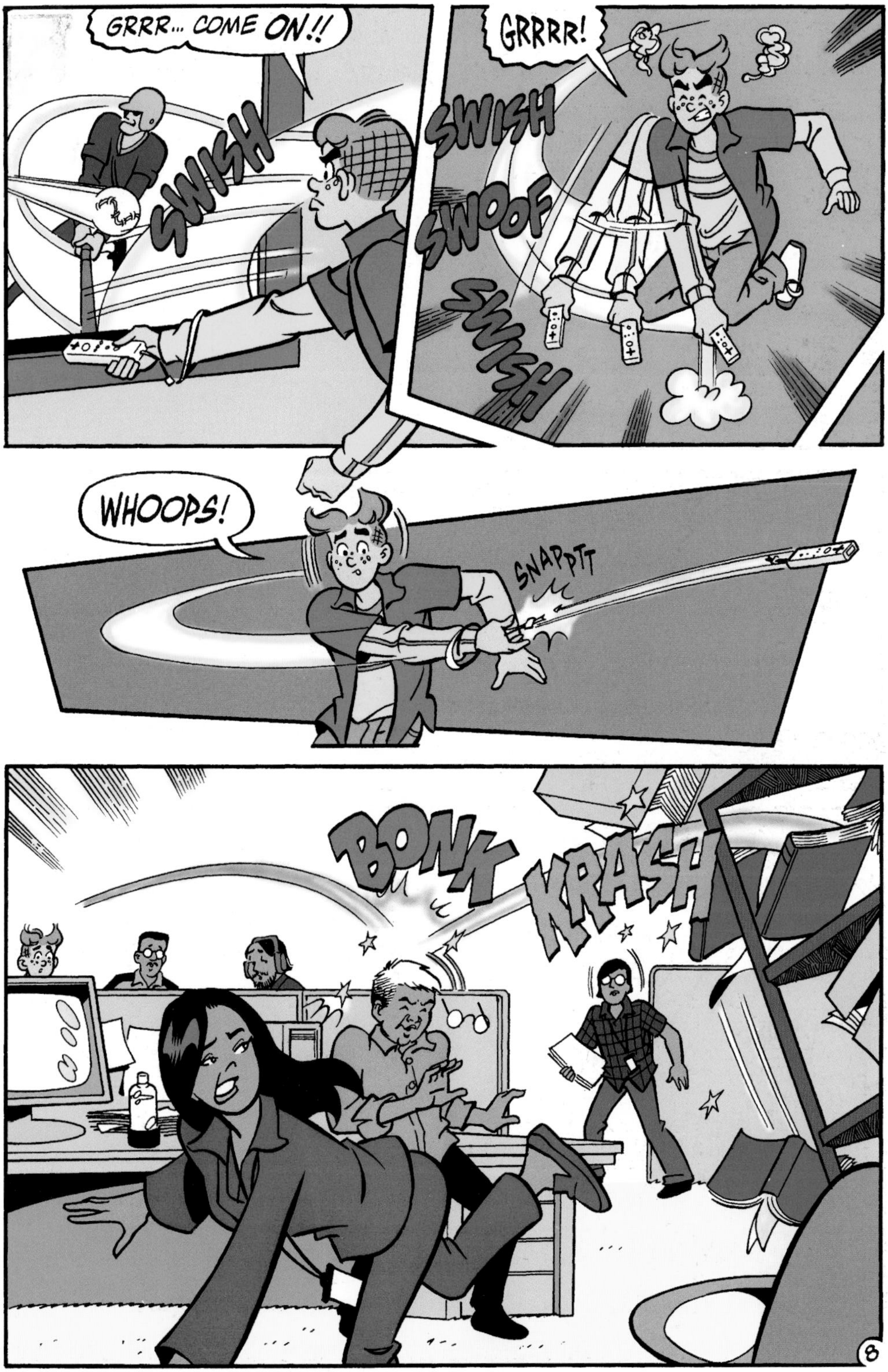
GRRR... COME ON!!
SWISH
GRRRR!
SWISH
SWOOF
SWISH
WHOOPS!
SNAPPTT
BONK
KRASH
8

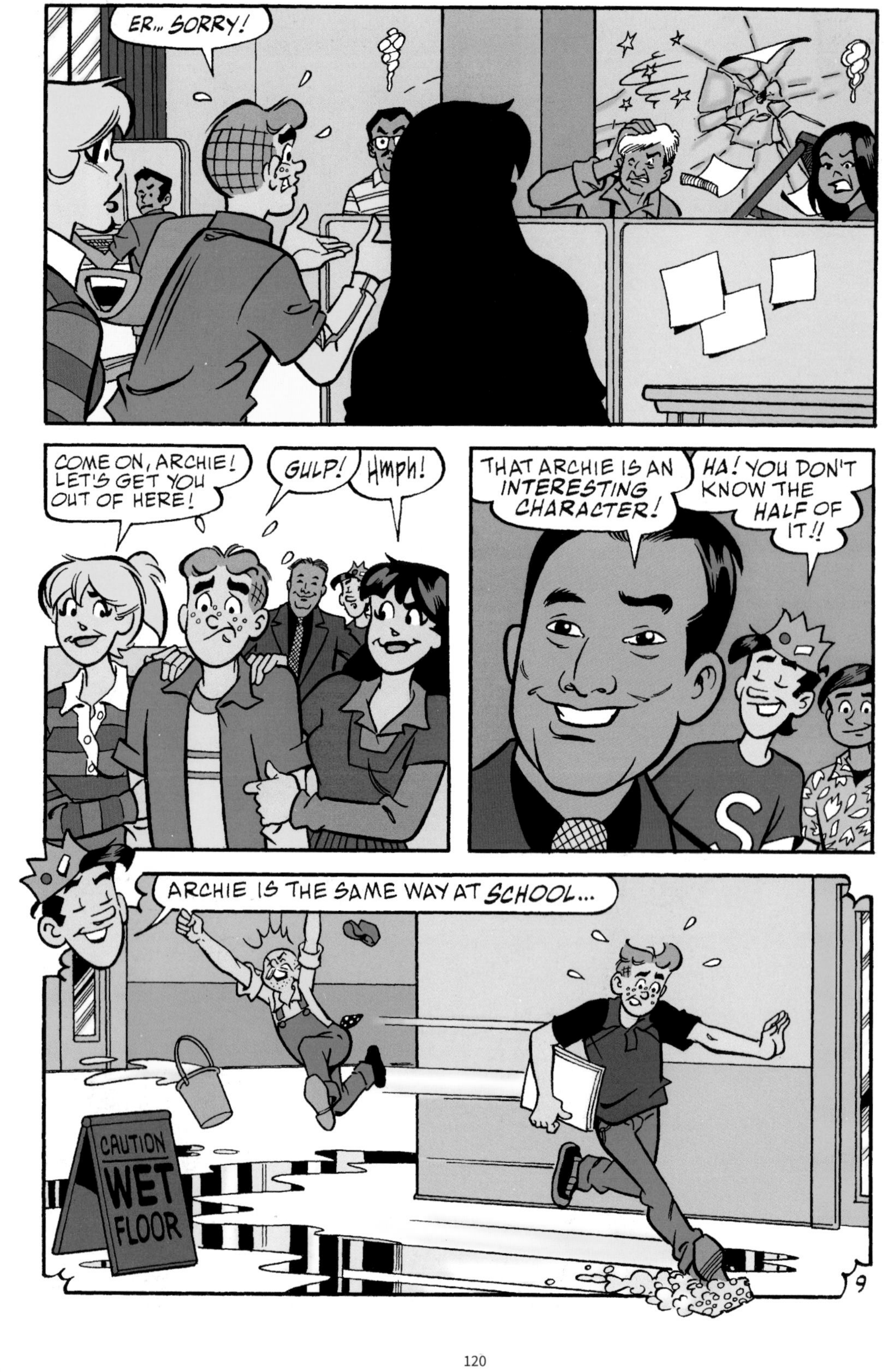

ER... SORRY!
COME ON, ARCHIE! LET'S GET YOU OUT OF HERE!
GULP!
Hmph!
THAT ARCHIE IS AN INTERESTING CHARACTER!
HA! YOU DON'T KNOW THE HALF OF IT!!
ARCHIE IS THE SAME WAY AT SCHOOL...
CAUTION
WET FLOOR
9

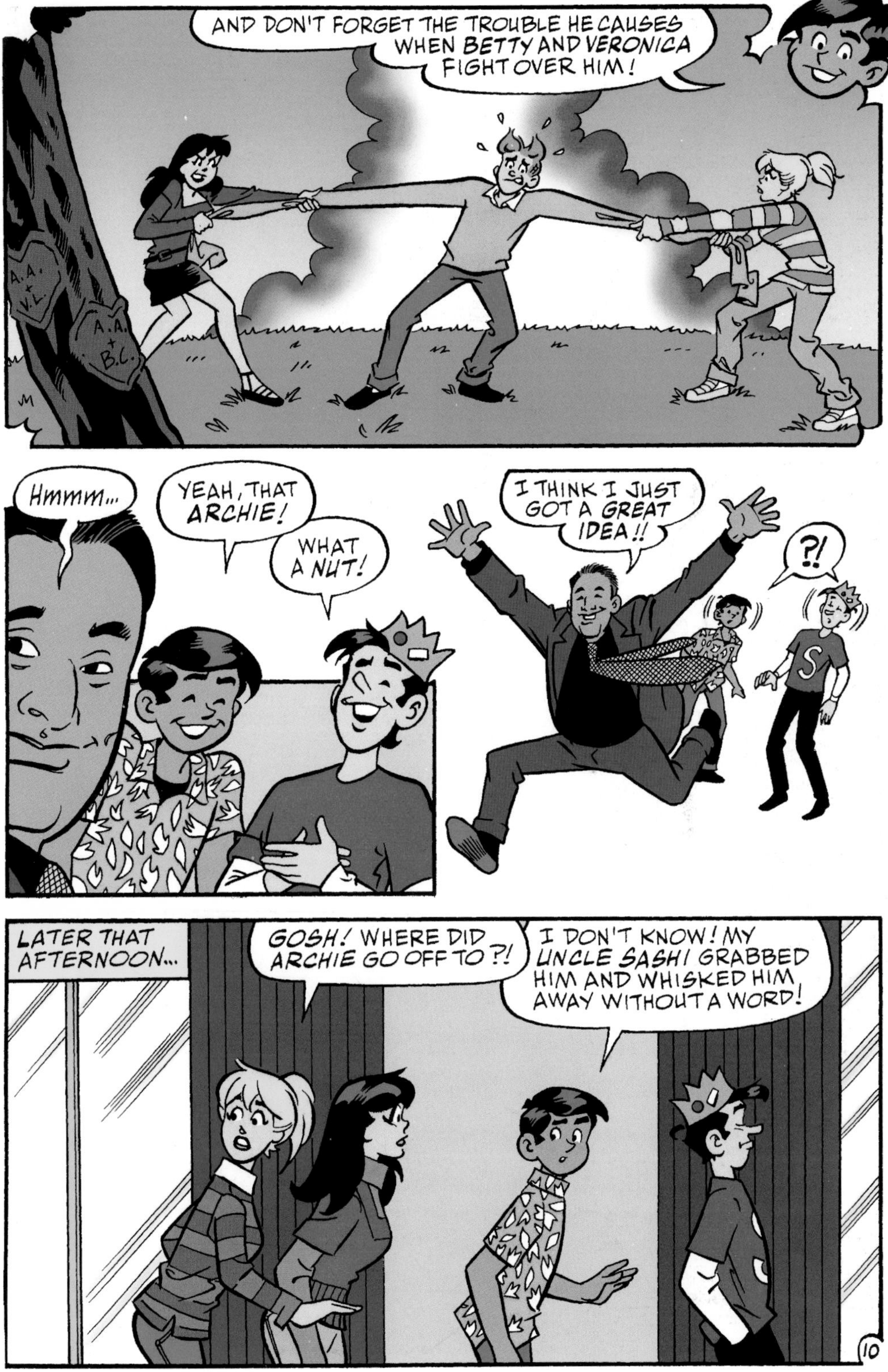
AND DON'T FORGET THE TROUBLE HE CAUSES WHEN BETTY AND VERONICA FIGHT OVER HIM!
A.A. + V.L.
A.A. + B.C.
Hmmm...
YEAH, THAT ARCHIE!
WHAT A NUT!
I THINK I JUST GOT A GREAT IDEA!!
?!
LATER THAT AFTERNOON...
GOSH! WHERE DID ARCHIE GO OFF TO?!
I DON'T KNOW! MY UNCLE SASHI GRABBED HIM AND WHISKED HIM AWAY WITHOUT A WORD!
10

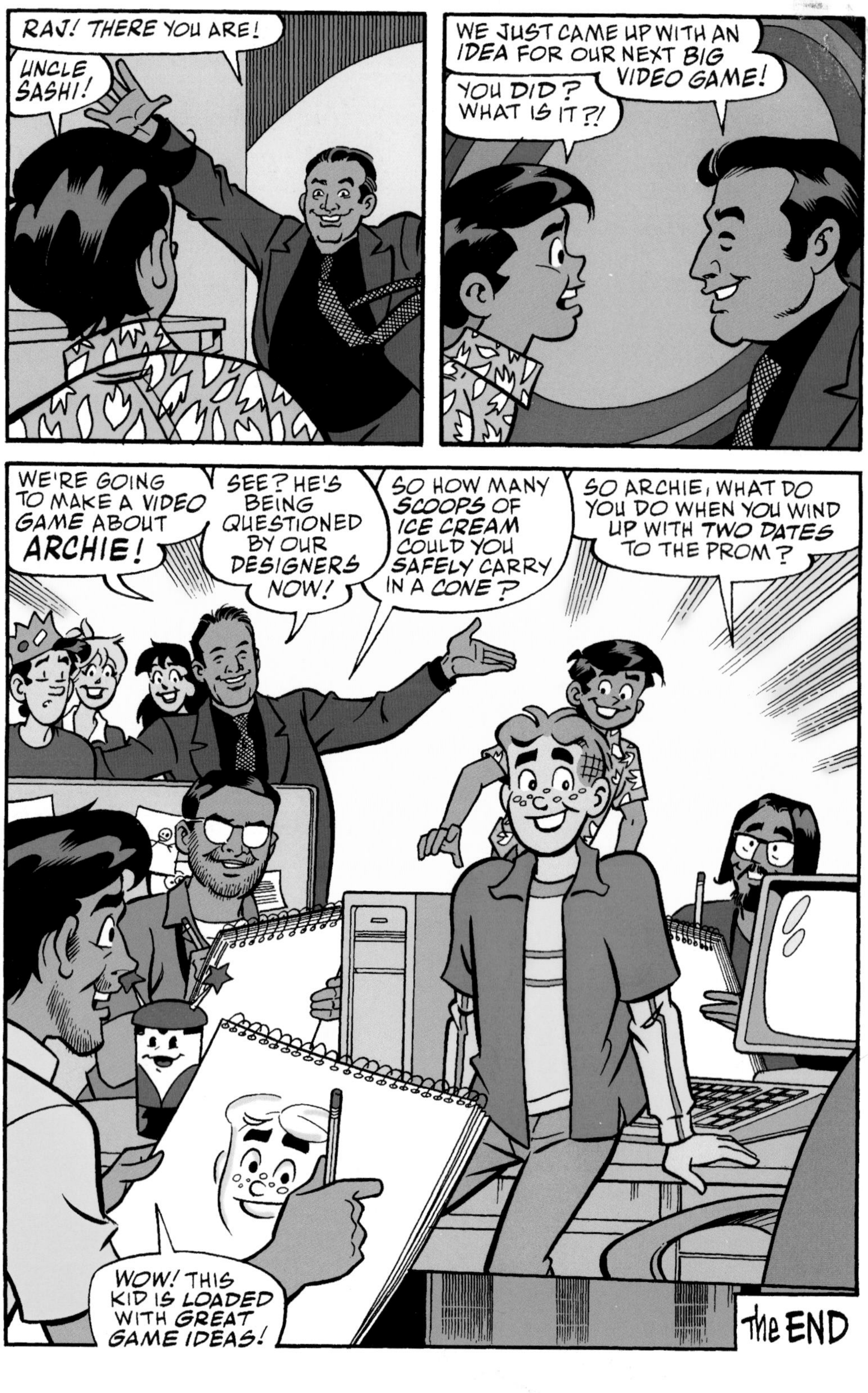
RAJ! THERE YOU ARE!
UNCLE SASHI!
WE JUST CAME UP WITH AN IDEA FOR OUR NEXT BIG VIDEO GAME!
YOU DID? WHAT IS IT?!
WE'RE GOING TO MAKE A VIDEO GAME ABOUT ARCHIE!
SEE? HE'S BEING QUESTIONED BY OUR DESIGNERS NOW!
SO HOW MANY SCOOPS OF ICE CREAM COULD YOU SAFELY CARRY IN A CONE?
SO ARCHIE, WHAT DO YOU DO WHEN YOU WIND UP WITH TWO DATES TO THE PROM?
WOW! THIS KID IS LOADED WITH GREAT GAME IDEAS!
The END

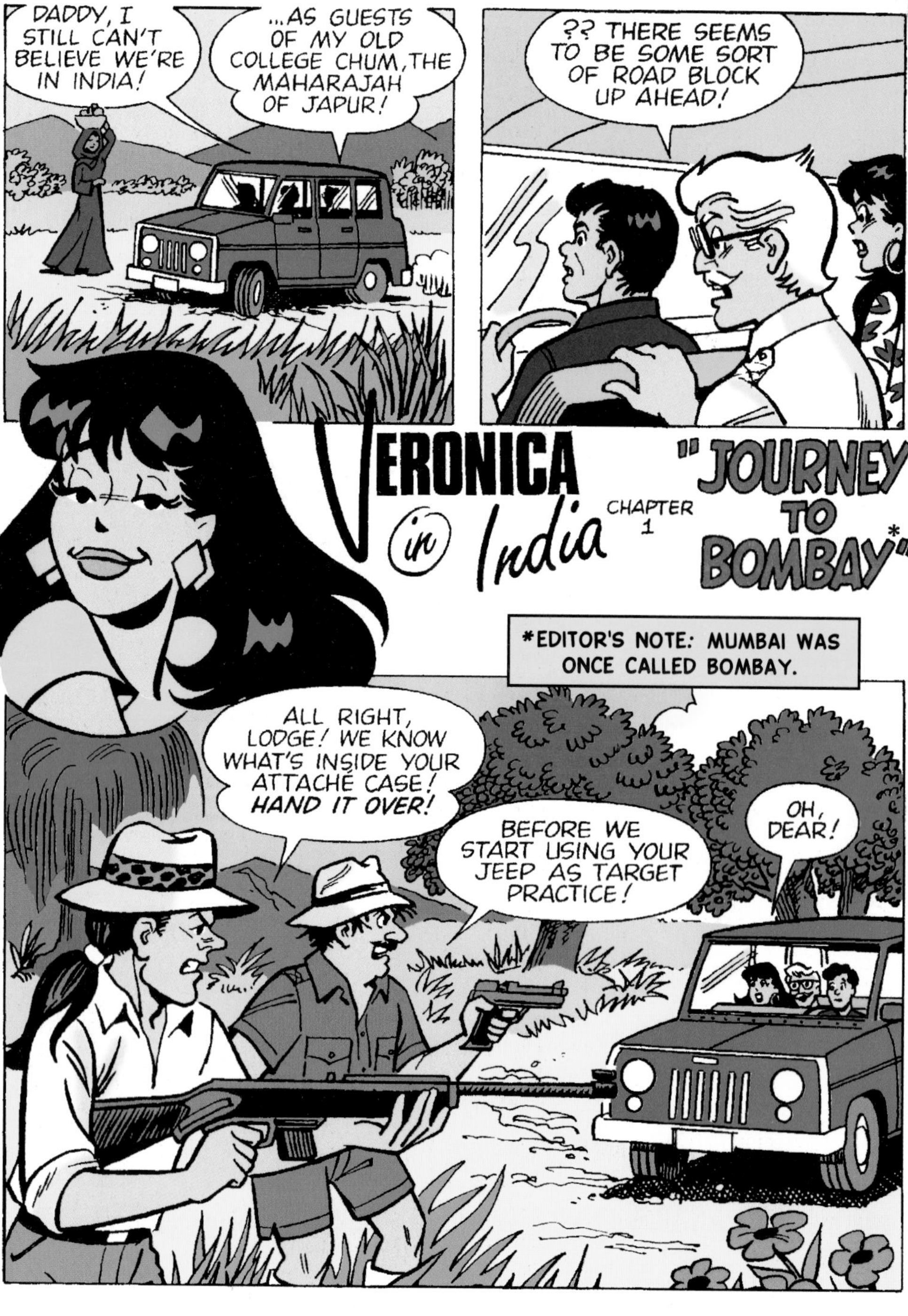
DADDY, I STILL CAN'T BELIEVE WE'RE IN INDIA!
...AS GUESTS OF MY OLD COLLEGE CHUM, THE MAHARAJAH OF JAPUR!
?? THERE SEEMS TO BE SOME SORT OF ROAD BLOCK UP AHEAD!
VERONICA in India
CHAPTER 1
"JOURNEY TO BOMBAY*"
*EDITOR'S NOTE: MUMBAI WAS ONCE CALLED BOMBAY.
ALL RIGHT, LODGE! WE KNOW WHAT'S INSIDE YOUR ATTACHÉ CASE! HAND IT OVER!
BEFORE WE START USING YOUR JEEP AS TARGET PRACTICE!
OH, DEAR!

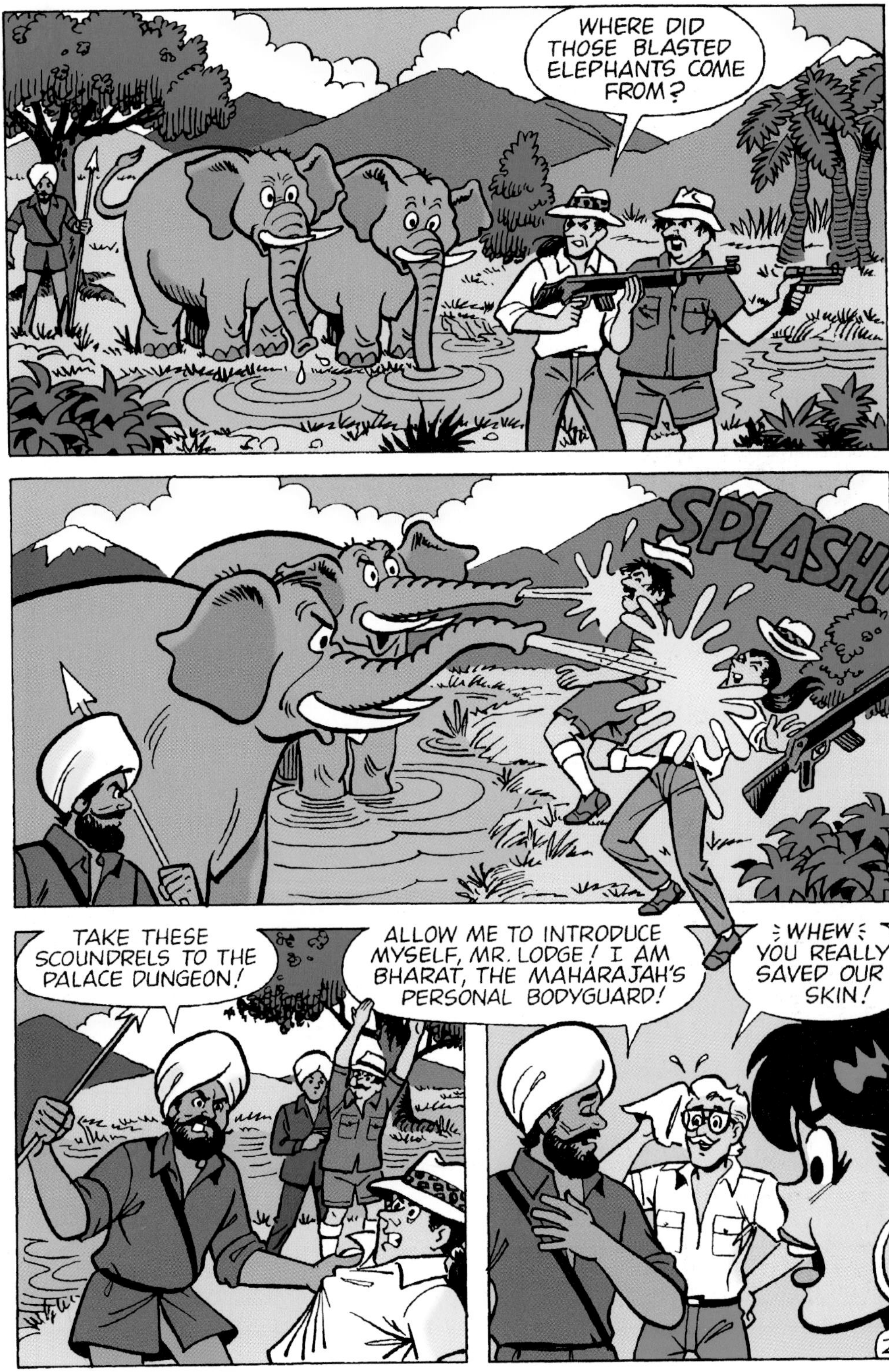
WHERE DID THOSE BLASTED ELEPHANTS COME FROM?
SPLASH!
TAKE THESE SCOUNDRELS TO THE PALACE DUNGEON!
ALLOW ME TO INTRODUCE MYSELF, MR. LODGE! I AM BHARAT, THE MAHARAJAH'S PERSONAL BODYGUARD!
WHEW YOU REALLY SAVED OUR SKIN!
2

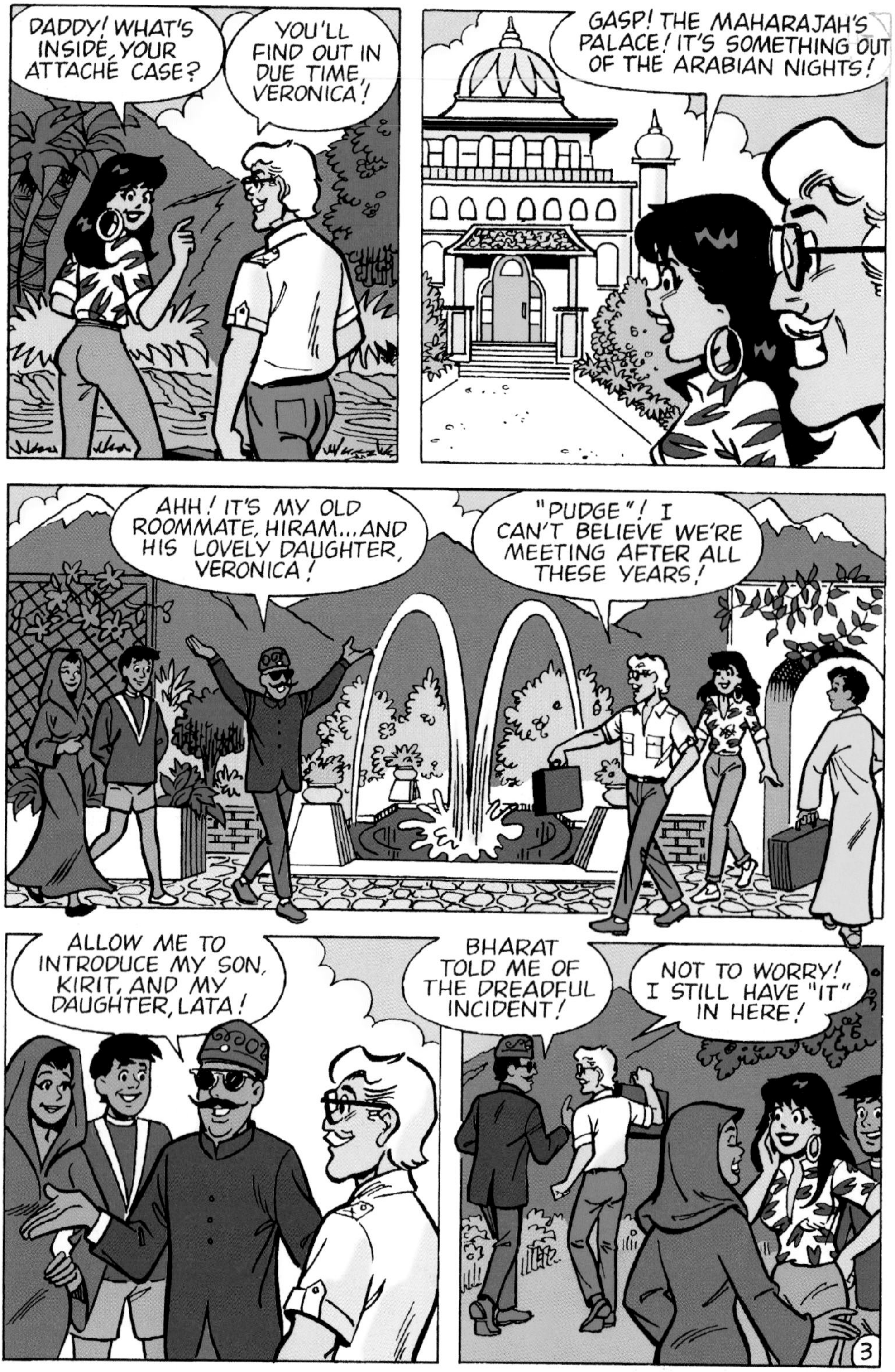
DADDY! WHAT'S INSIDE YOUR ATTACHÉ CASE?
YOU'LL FIND OUT IN DUE TIME, VERONICA!
GASP! THE MAHARAJAH'S PALACE! IT'S SOMETHING OUT OF THE ARABIAN NIGHTS!
AHH! IT'S MY OLD ROOMMATE, HIRAM...AND HIS LOVELY DAUGHTER, VERONICA!
"PUDGE"! I CAN'T BELIEVE WE'RE MEETING AFTER ALL THESE YEARS!
ALLOW ME TO INTRODUCE MY SON, KIRIT, AND MY DAUGHTER, LATA!
BHARAT TOLD ME OF THE DREADFUL INCIDENT!
NOT TO WORRY! I STILL HAVE "IT" IN HERE!
3

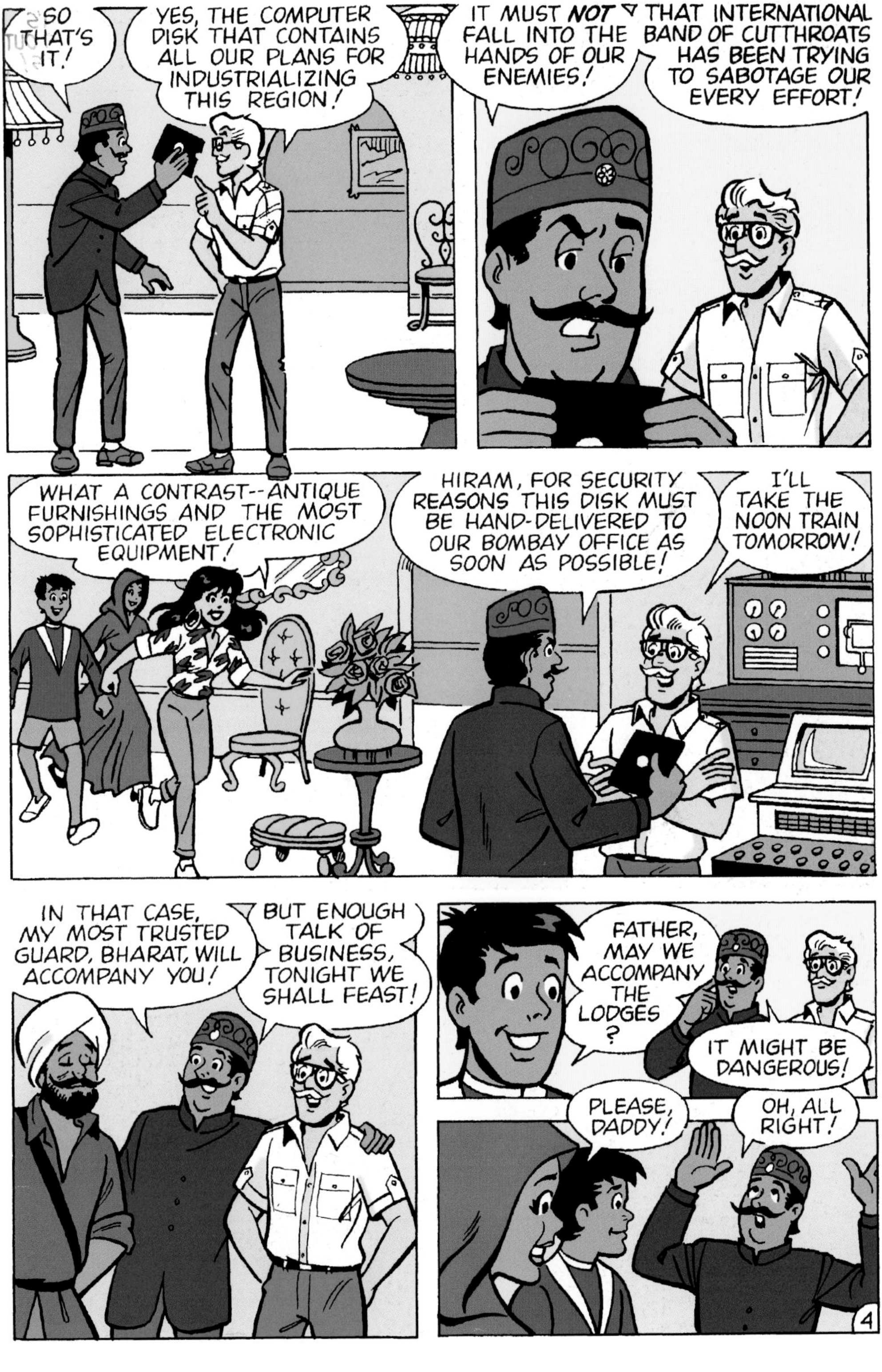
SO THAT'S IT!
YES, THE COMPUTER DISK THAT CONTAINS ALL OUR PLANS FOR INDUSTRIALIZING THIS REGION!
IT MUST NOT FALL INTO THE HANDS OF OUR ENEMIES!
THAT INTERNATIONAL BAND OF CUTTHROATS HAS BEEN TRYING TO SABOTAGE OUR EVERY EFFORT!
WHAT A CONTRAST--ANTIQUE FURNISHINGS AND THE MOST SOPHISTICATED ELECTRONIC EQUIPMENT!
HIRAM, FOR SECURITY REASONS THIS DISK MUST BE HAND-DELIVERED TO OUR BOMBAY OFFICE AS SOON AS POSSIBLE!
I'LL TAKE THE NOON TRAIN TOMORROW!
IN THAT CASE, MY MOST TRUSTED GUARD, BHARAT, WILL ACCOMPANY YOU!
BUT ENOUGH TALK OF BUSINESS, TONIGHT WE SHALL FEAST!
FATHER, MAY WE ACCOMPANY THE LODGES?
IT MIGHT BE DANGEROUS!
PLEASE, DADDY!
OH, ALL RIGHT!
4

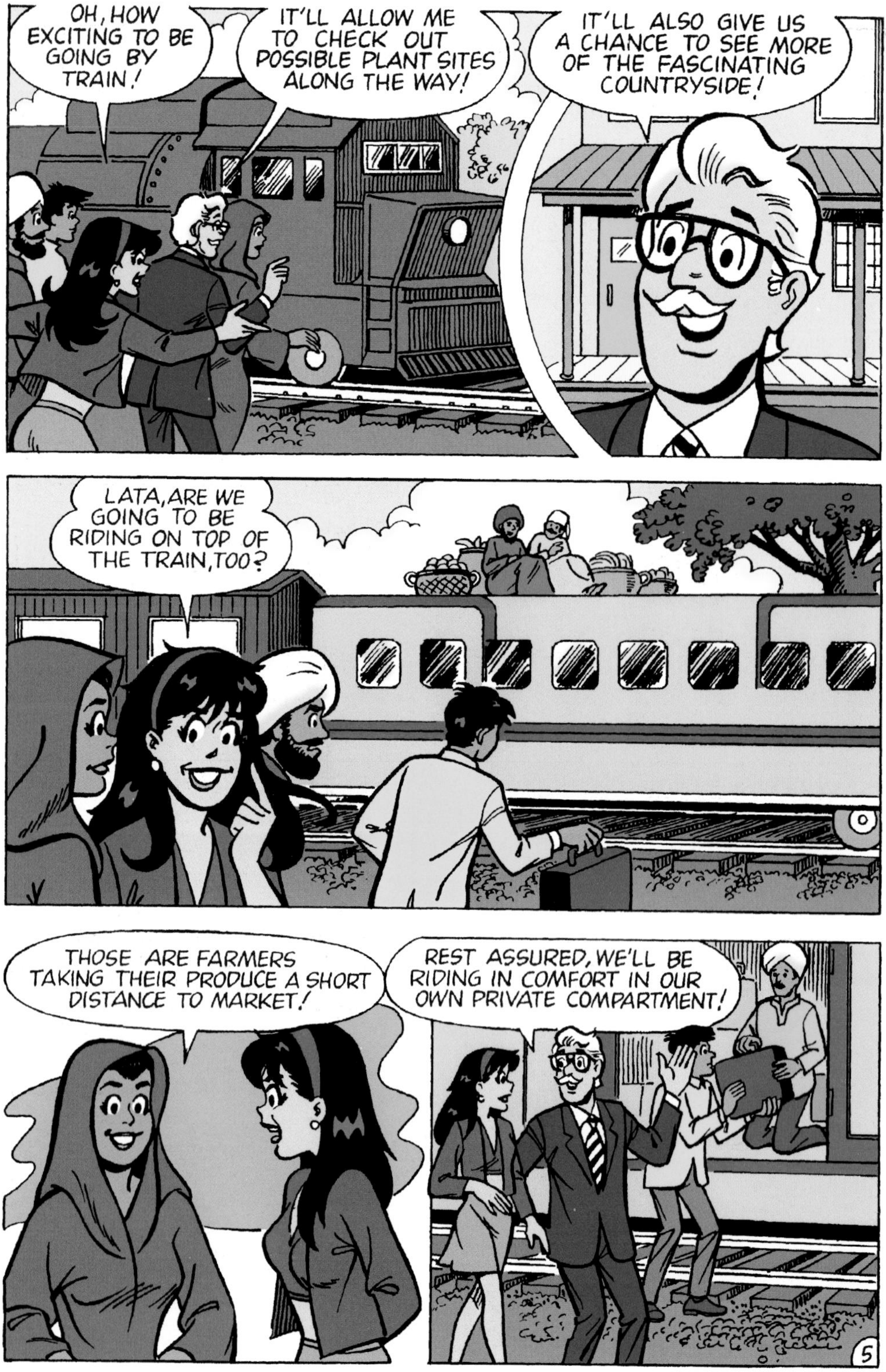
OH, HOW EXCITING TO BE GOING BY TRAIN!
IT'LL ALLOW ME TO CHECK OUT POSSIBLE PLANT SITES ALONG THE WAY!
IT'LL ALSO GIVE US A CHANCE TO SEE MORE OF THE FASCINATING COUNTRYSIDE!
LATA, ARE WE GOING TO BE RIDING ON TOP OF THE TRAIN, TOO?
THOSE ARE FARMERS TAKING THEIR PRODUCE A SHORT DISTANCE TO MARKET!
REST ASSURED, WE'LL BE RIDING IN COMFORT IN OUR OWN PRIVATE COMPARTMENT!
5

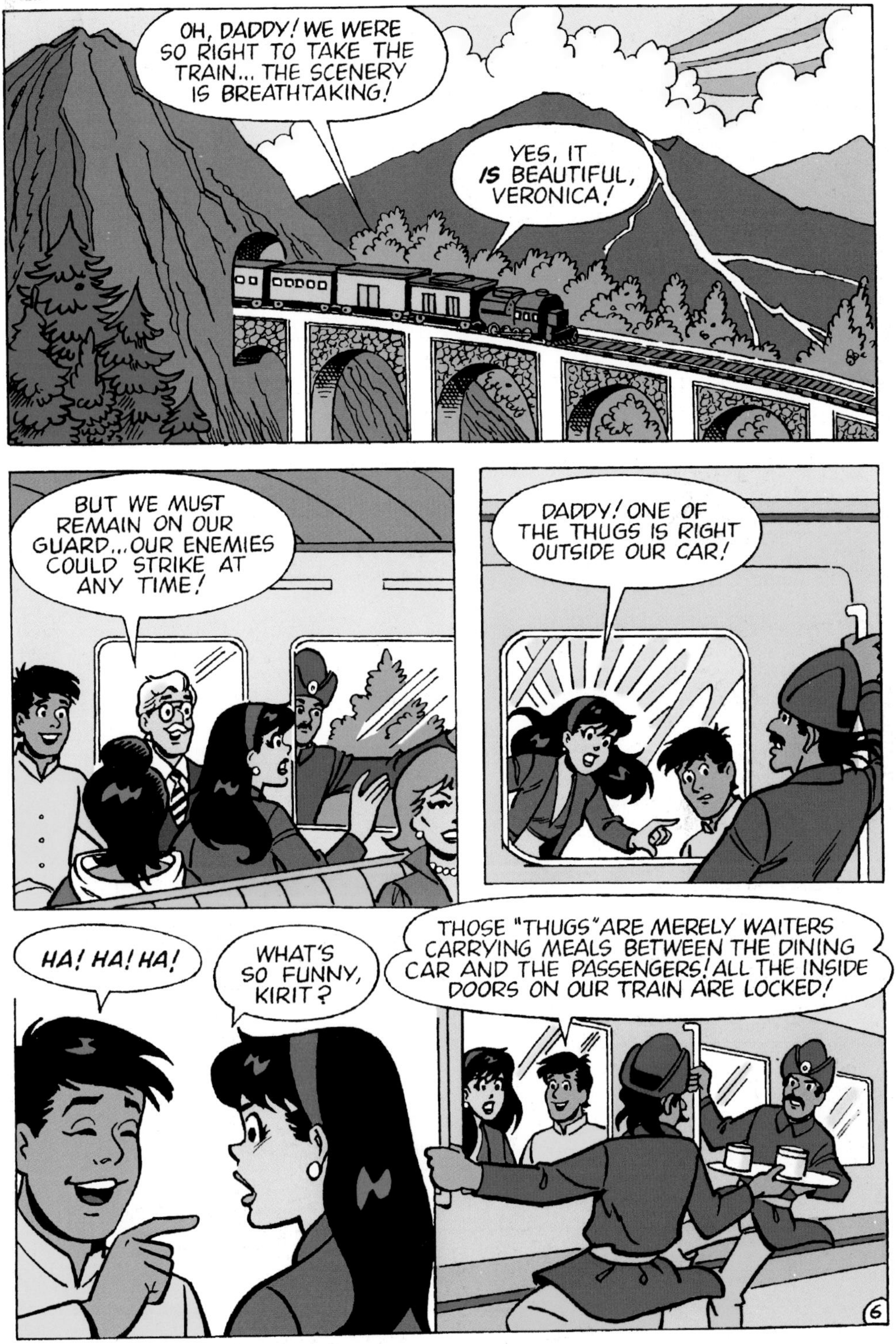
OH, DADDY! WE WERE SO RIGHT TO TAKE THE TRAIN... THE SCENERY IS BREATHTAKING!
YES, IT *IS* BEAUTIFUL, VERONICA!
BUT WE MUST REMAIN ON OUR GUARD...OUR ENEMIES COULD STRIKE AT ANY TIME!
DADDY! ONE OF THE THUGS IS RIGHT OUTSIDE OUR CAR!
HA! HA! HA!
WHAT'S SO FUNNY, KIRIT?
THOSE "THUGS" ARE MERELY WAITERS CARRYING MEALS BETWEEN THE DINING CAR AND THE PASSENGERS! ALL THE INSIDE DOORS ON OUR TRAIN ARE LOCKED!
6

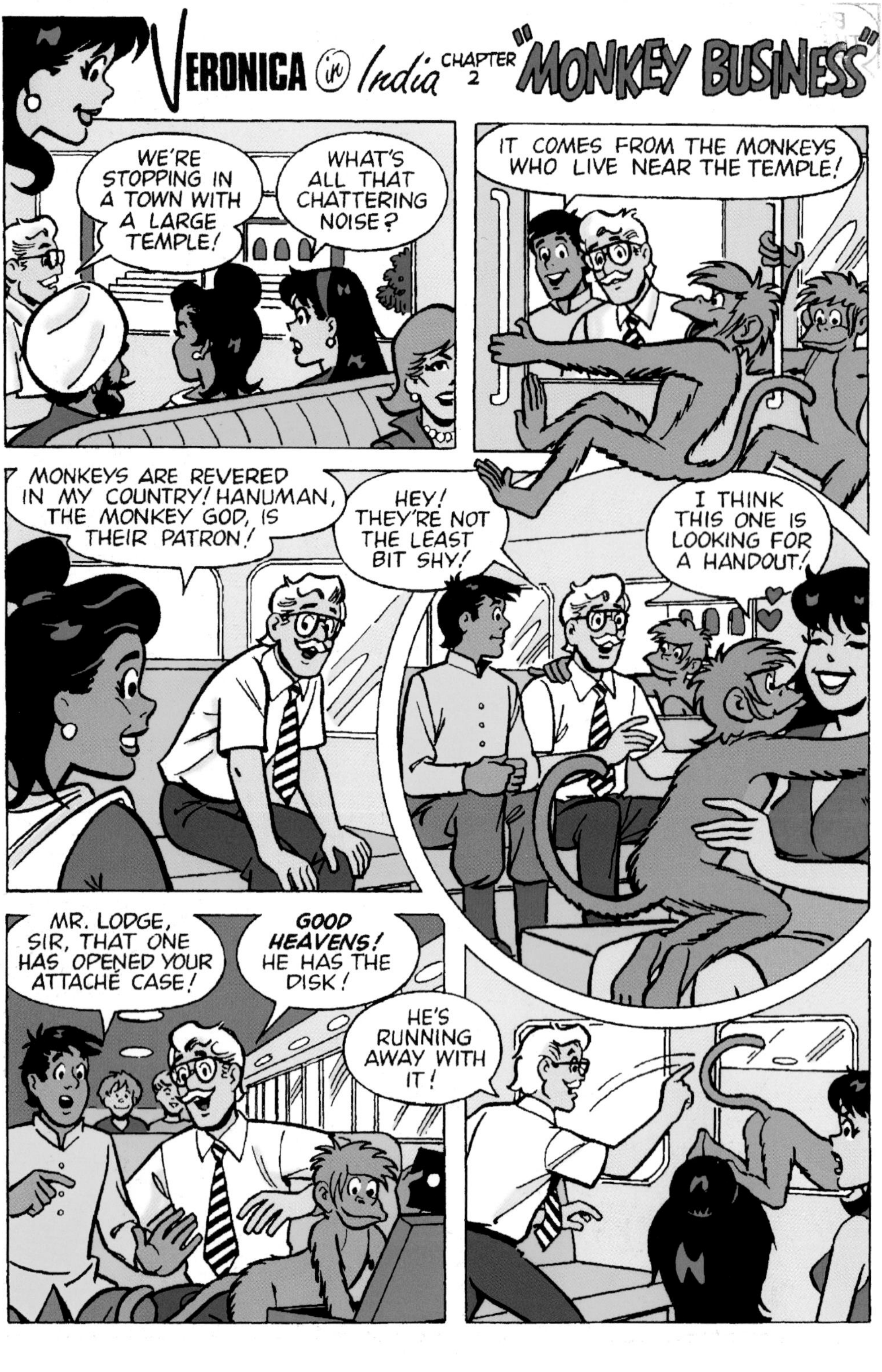
VERONICA in India CHAPTER 2 "MONKEY BUSINESS"
WE'RE STOPPING IN A TOWN WITH A LARGE TEMPLE!
WHAT'S ALL THAT CHATTERING NOISE?
IT COMES FROM THE MONKEYS WHO LIVE NEAR THE TEMPLE!
MONKEYS ARE REVERED IN MY COUNTRY! HANUMAN, THE MONKEY GOD, IS THEIR PATRON!
HEY! THEY'RE NOT THE LEAST BIT SHY!
I THINK THIS ONE IS LOOKING FOR A HANDOUT!
MR. LODGE, SIR, THAT ONE HAS OPENED YOUR ATTACHÉ CASE!
GOOD HEAVENS! HE HAS THE DISK!
HE'S RUNNING AWAY WITH IT!

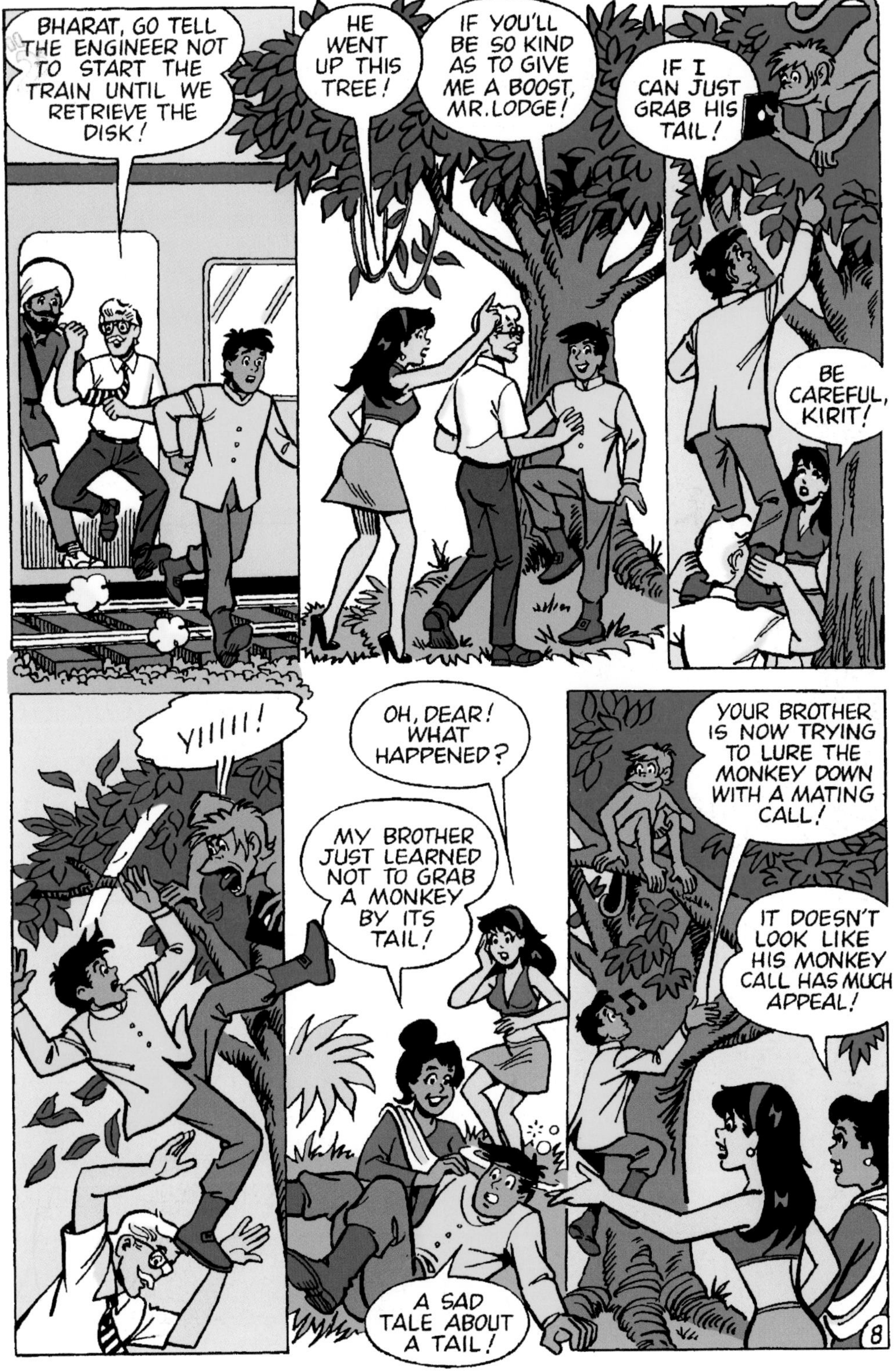
BHARAT, GO TELL THE ENGINEER NOT TO START THE TRAIN UNTIL WE RETRIEVE THE DISK!
HE WENT UP THIS TREE!
IF YOU'LL BE SO KIND AS TO GIVE ME A BOOST, MR. LODGE!
IF I CAN JUST GRAB HIS TAIL!
BE CAREFUL, KIRIT!
YIIIII!
OH, DEAR! WHAT HAPPENED?
MY BROTHER JUST LEARNED NOT TO GRAB A MONKEY BY ITS TAIL!
A SAD TALE ABOUT A TAIL!
YOUR BROTHER IS NOW TRYING TO LURE THE MONKEY DOWN WITH A MATING CALL!
IT DOESN'T LOOK LIKE HIS MONKEY CALL HAS MUCH APPEAL!
8

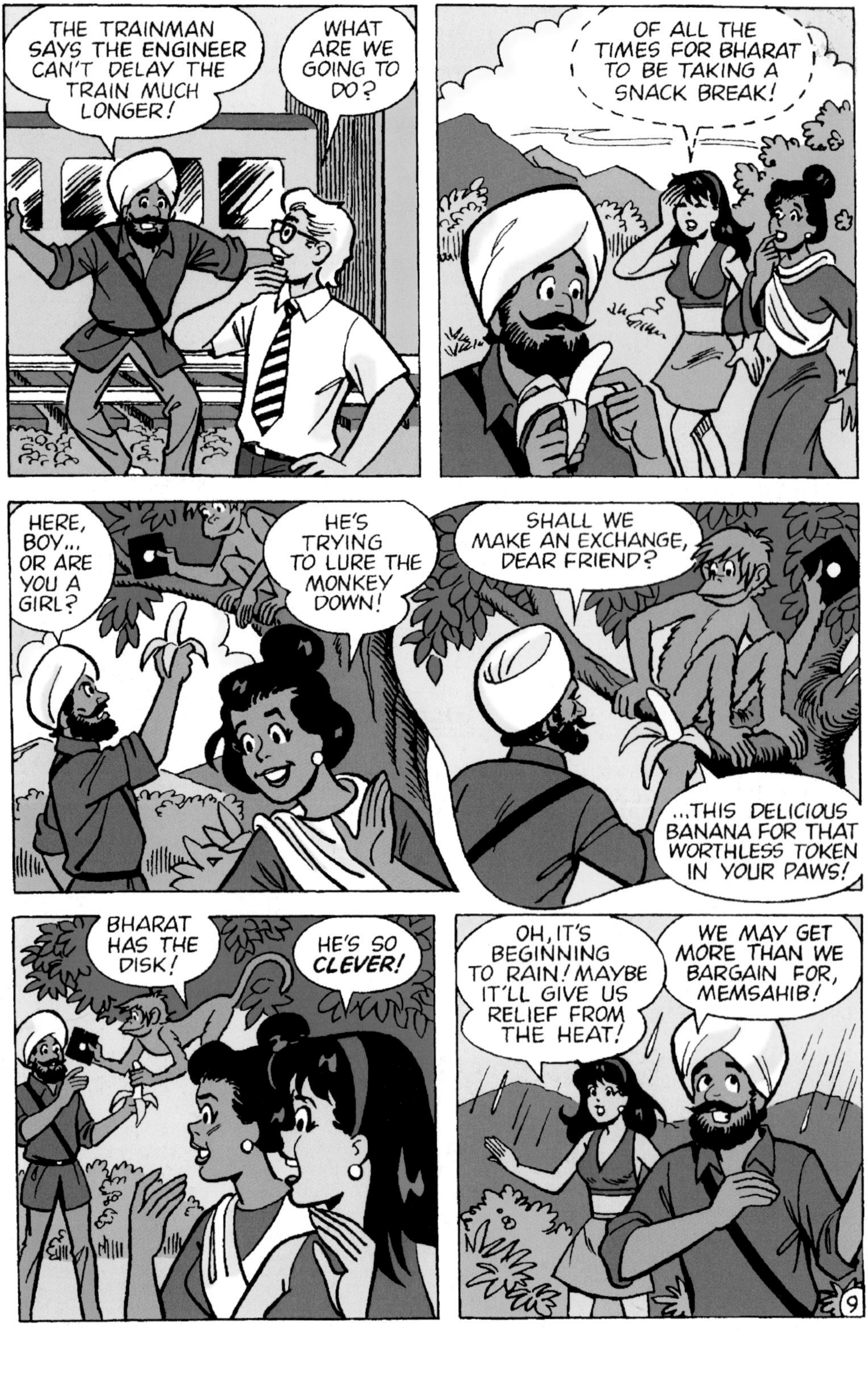
THE TRAINMAN SAYS THE ENGINEER CAN'T DELAY THE TRAIN MUCH LONGER!
WHAT ARE WE GOING TO DO?
OF ALL THE TIMES FOR BHARAT TO BE TAKING A SNACK BREAK!
HERE, BOY... OR ARE YOU A GIRL?
HE'S TRYING TO LURE THE MONKEY DOWN!
SHALL WE MAKE AN EXCHANGE, DEAR FRIEND?
...THIS DELICIOUS BANANA FOR THAT WORTHLESS TOKEN IN YOUR PAWS!
BHARAT HAS THE DISK!
HE'S SO *CLEVER!*
OH, IT'S BEGINNING TO RAIN! MAYBE IT'LL GIVE US RELIEF FROM THE HEAT!
WE MAY GET MORE THAN WE BARGAIN FOR, MEMSAHIB!
9

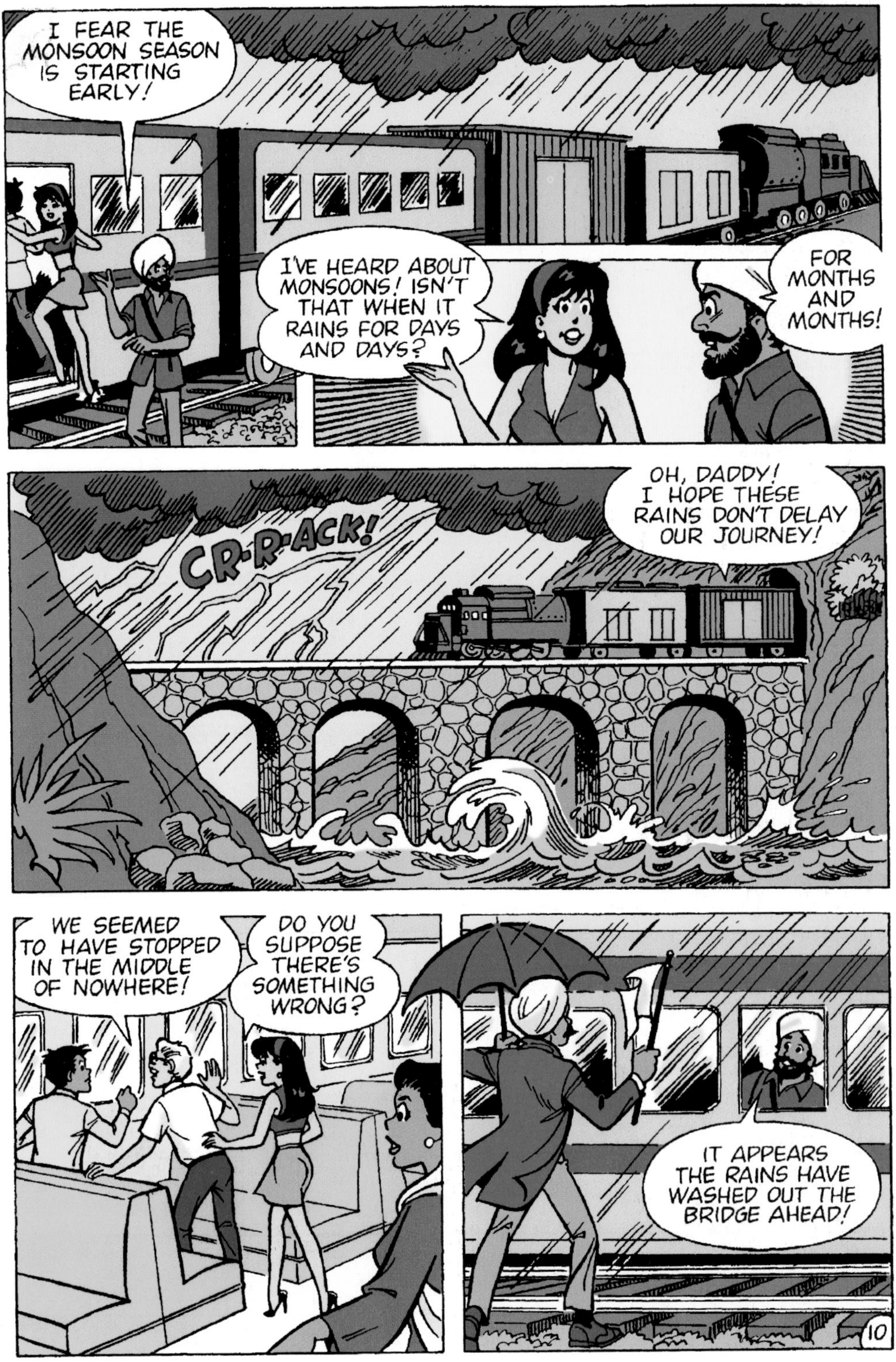
I FEAR THE MONSOON SEASON IS STARTING EARLY!
I'VE HEARD ABOUT MONSOONS! ISN'T THAT WHEN IT RAINS FOR DAYS AND DAYS?
FOR MONTHS AND MONTHS!
CR-R-ACK!
OH, DADDY! I HOPE THESE RAINS DON'T DELAY OUR JOURNEY!
WE SEEMED TO HAVE STOPPED IN THE MIDDLE OF NOWHERE!
DO YOU SUPPOSE THERE'S SOMETHING WRONG?
IT APPEARS THE RAINS HAVE WASHED OUT THE BRIDGE AHEAD!
10

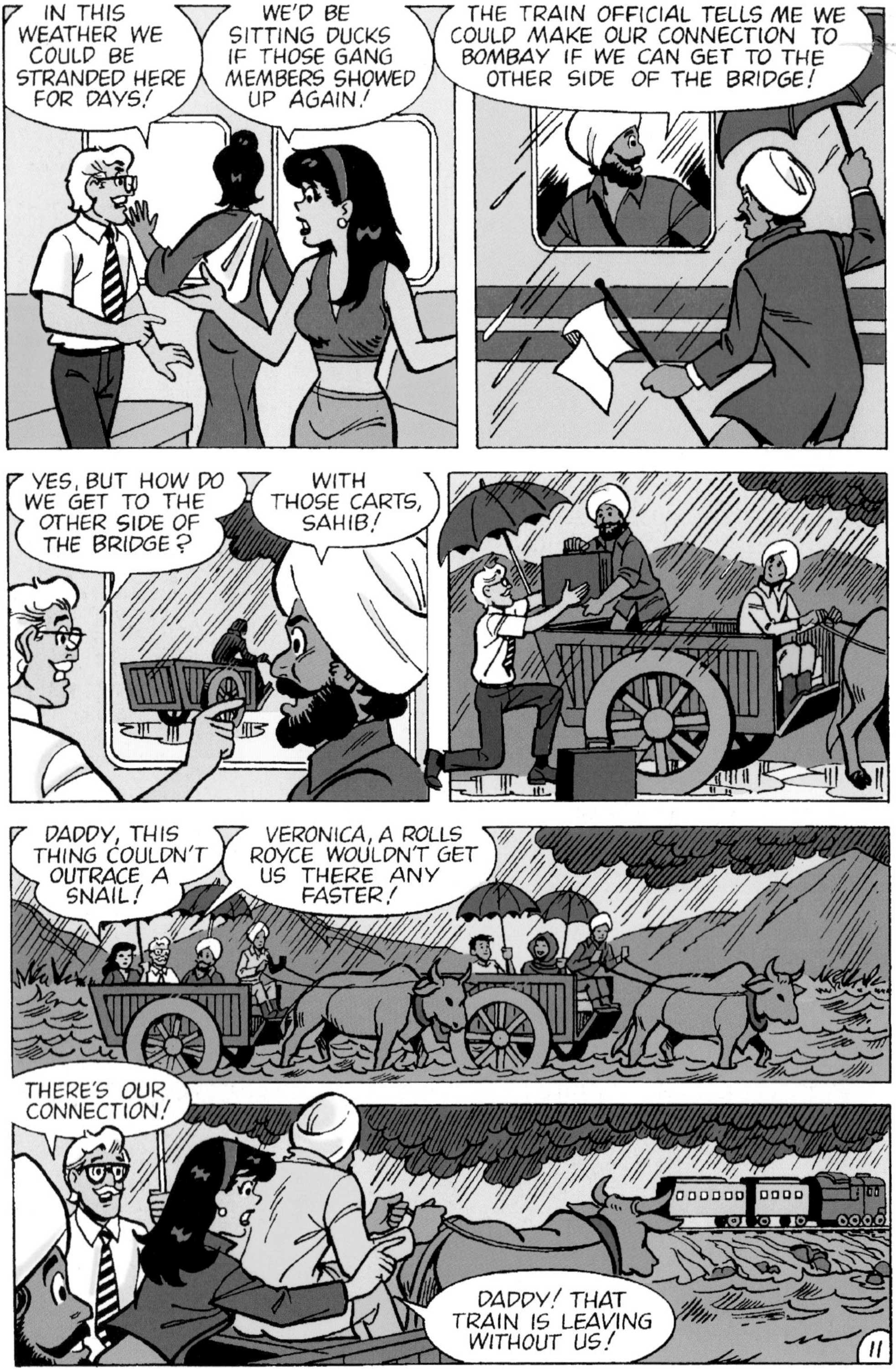
IN THIS WEATHER WE COULD BE STRANDED HERE FOR DAYS!
WE'D BE SITTING DUCKS IF THOSE GANG MEMBERS SHOWED UP AGAIN!
THE TRAIN OFFICIAL TELLS ME WE COULD MAKE OUR CONNECTION TO BOMBAY IF WE CAN GET TO THE OTHER SIDE OF THE BRIDGE!
YES, BUT HOW DO WE GET TO THE OTHER SIDE OF THE BRIDGE?
WITH THOSE CARTS, SAHIB!
DADDY, THIS THING COULDN'T OUTRACE A SNAIL!
VERONICA, A ROLLS ROYCE WOULDN'T GET US THERE ANY FASTER!
THERE'S OUR CONNECTION!
DADDY! THAT TRAIN IS LEAVING WITHOUT US!
11

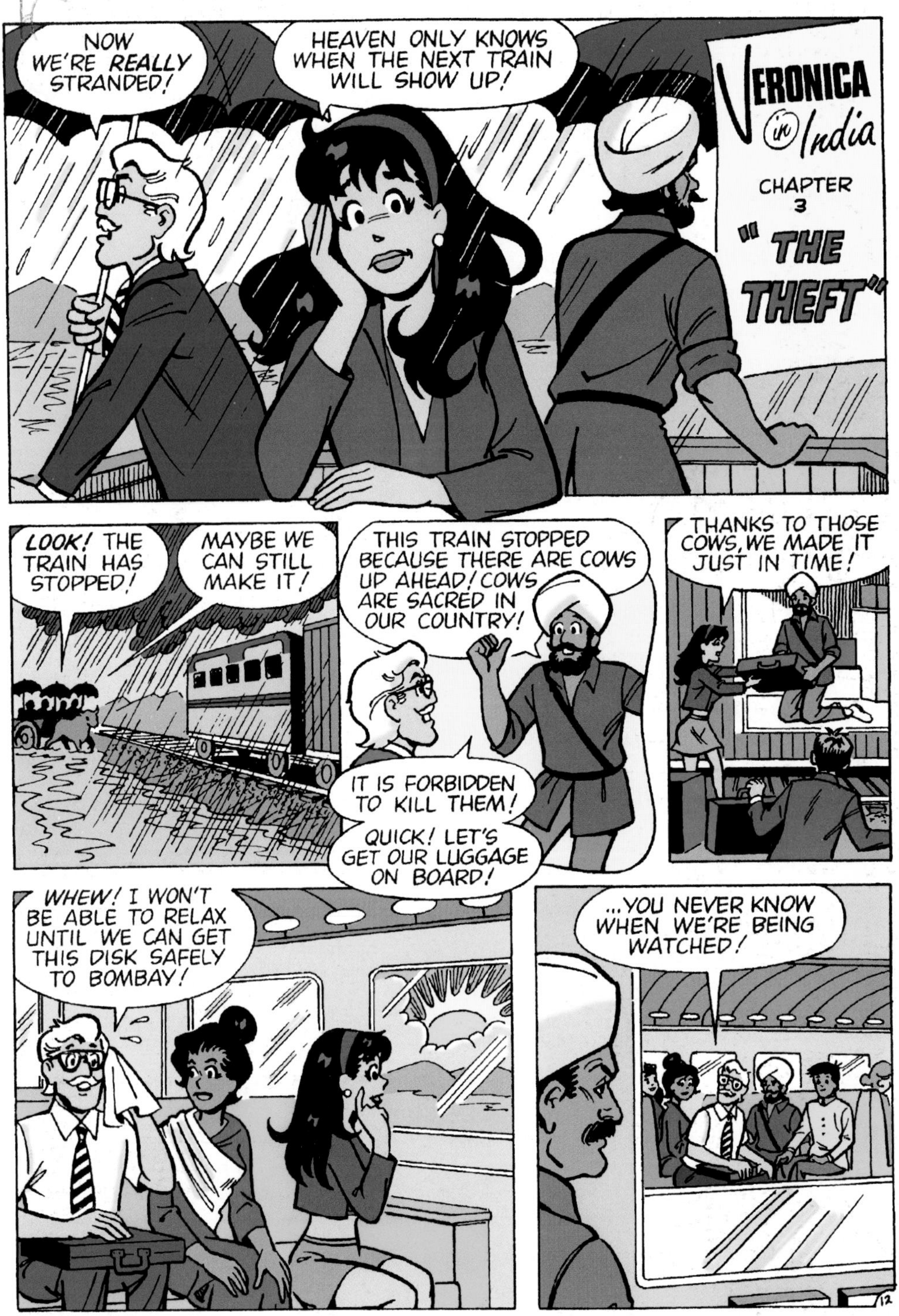
NOW WE'RE REALLY STRANDED!
HEAVEN ONLY KNOWS WHEN THE NEXT TRAIN WILL SHOW UP!
VERONICA in India
CHAPTER 3
"THE THEFT"
LOOK! THE TRAIN HAS STOPPED!
MAYBE WE CAN STILL MAKE IT!
THIS TRAIN STOPPED BECAUSE THERE ARE COWS UP AHEAD! COWS ARE SACRED IN OUR COUNTRY!
IT IS FORBIDDEN TO KILL THEM!
QUICK! LET'S GET OUR LUGGAGE ON BOARD!
THANKS TO THOSE COWS, WE MADE IT JUST IN TIME!
WHEW! I WON'T BE ABLE TO RELAX UNTIL WE CAN GET THIS DISK SAFELY TO BOMBAY!
...YOU NEVER KNOW WHEN WE'RE BEING WATCHED!
12

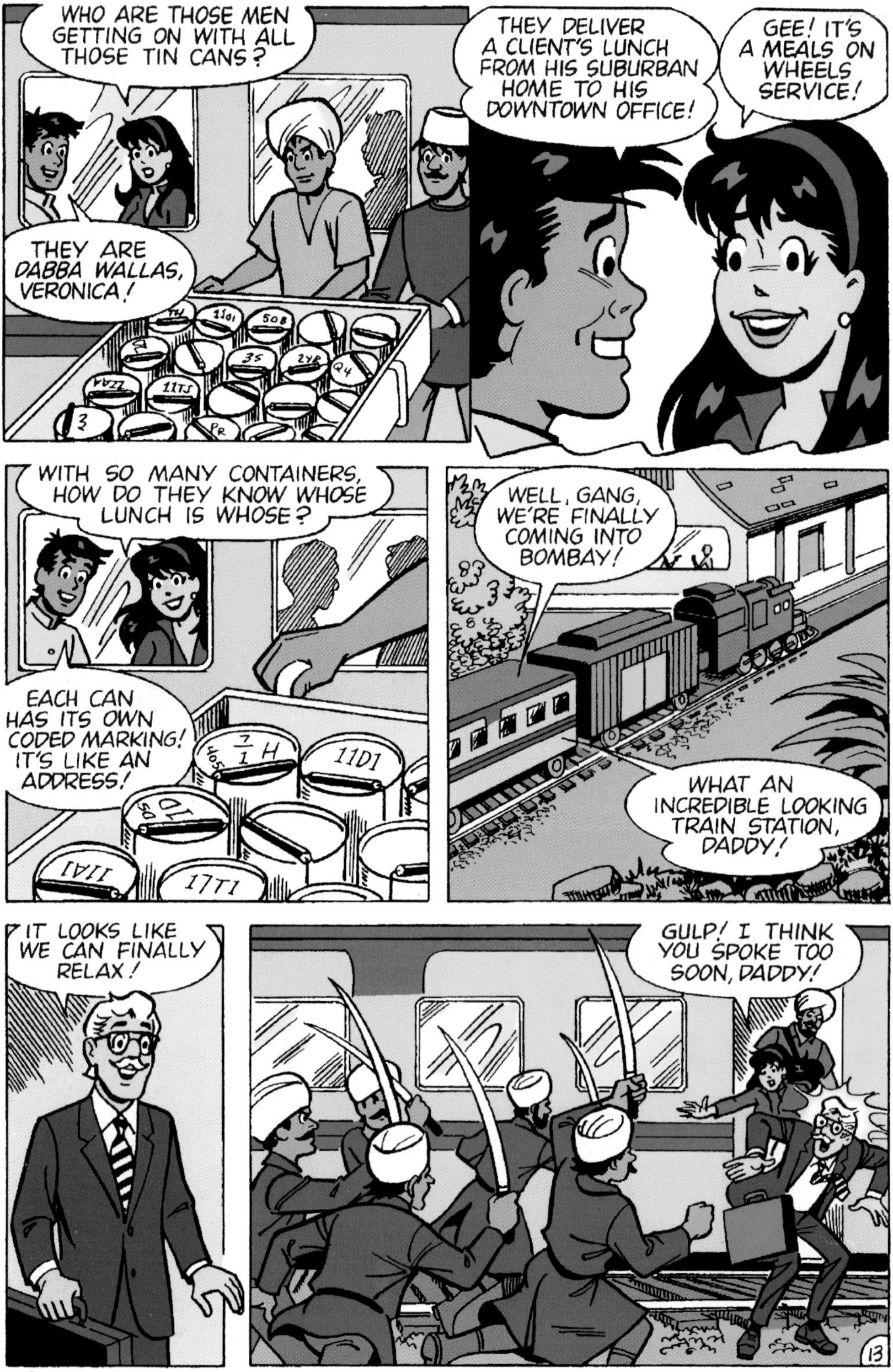
WHO ARE THOSE MEN GETTING ON WITH ALL THOSE TIN CANS?
THEY ARE DABBA WALLAS, VERONICA!
THEY DELIVER A CLIENT'S LUNCH FROM HIS SUBURBAN HOME TO HIS DOWNTOWN OFFICE!
GEE! IT'S A MEALS ON WHEELS SERVICE!
WITH SO MANY CONTAINERS, HOW DO THEY KNOW WHOSE LUNCH IS WHOSE?
EACH CAN HAS ITS OWN CODED MARKING! IT'S LIKE AN ADDRESS!
WELL, GANG, WE'RE FINALLY COMING INTO BOMBAY!
WHAT AN INCREDIBLE LOOKING TRAIN STATION, DADDY!
IT LOOKS LIKE WE CAN FINALLY RELAX!
GULP! I THINK YOU SPOKE TOO SOON, DADDY!
13

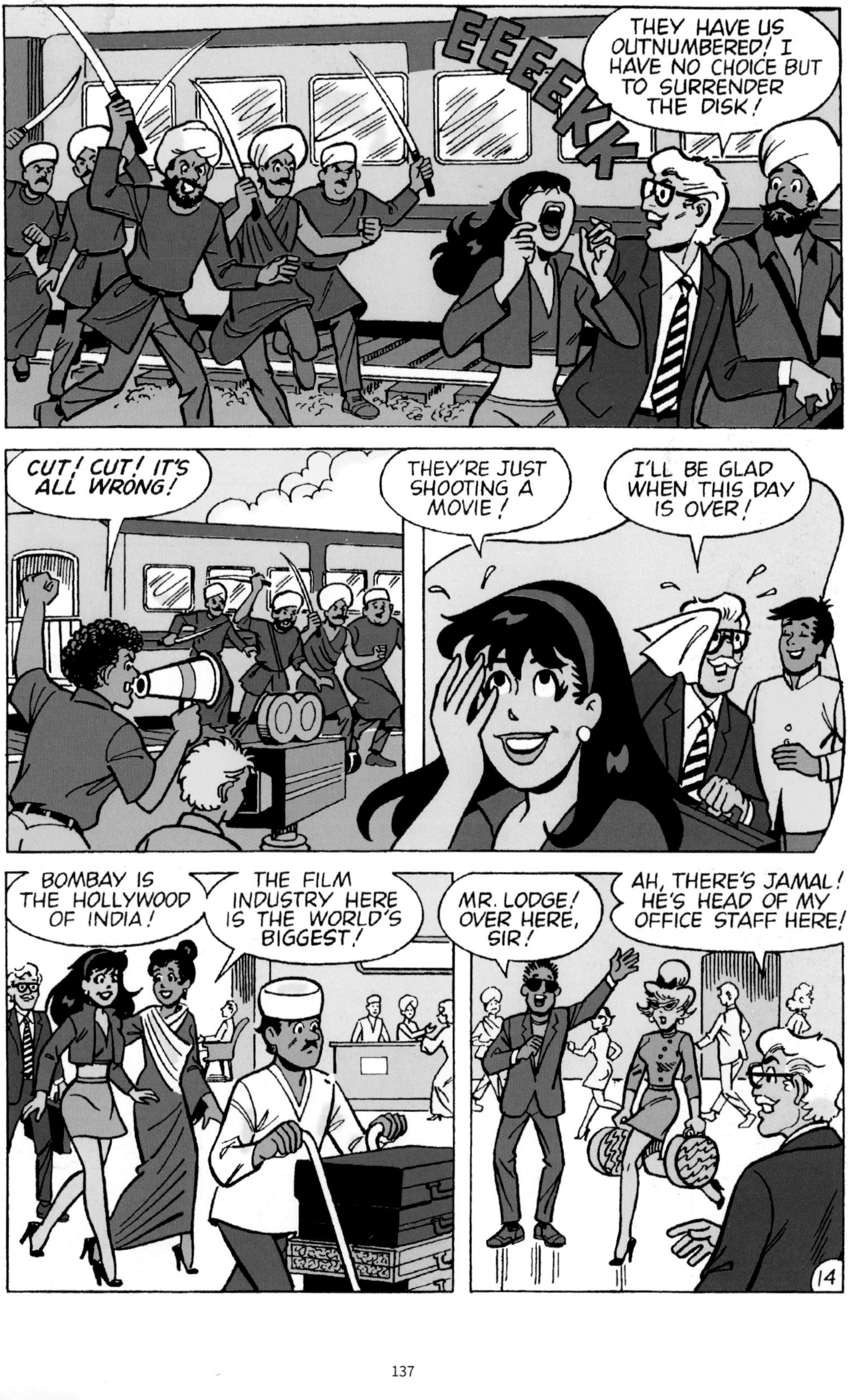
EEEEKK
THEY HAVE US OUTNUMBERED! I HAVE NO CHOICE BUT TO SURRENDER THE DISK!
CUT! CUT! IT'S ALL WRONG!
THEY'RE JUST SHOOTING A MOVIE!
I'LL BE GLAD WHEN THIS DAY IS OVER!
BOMBAY IS THE HOLLYWOOD OF INDIA!
THE FILM INDUSTRY HERE IS THE WORLD'S BIGGEST!
MR. LODGE! OVER HERE, SIR!
AH, THERE'S JAMAL! HE'S HEAD OF MY OFFICE STAFF HERE!
14

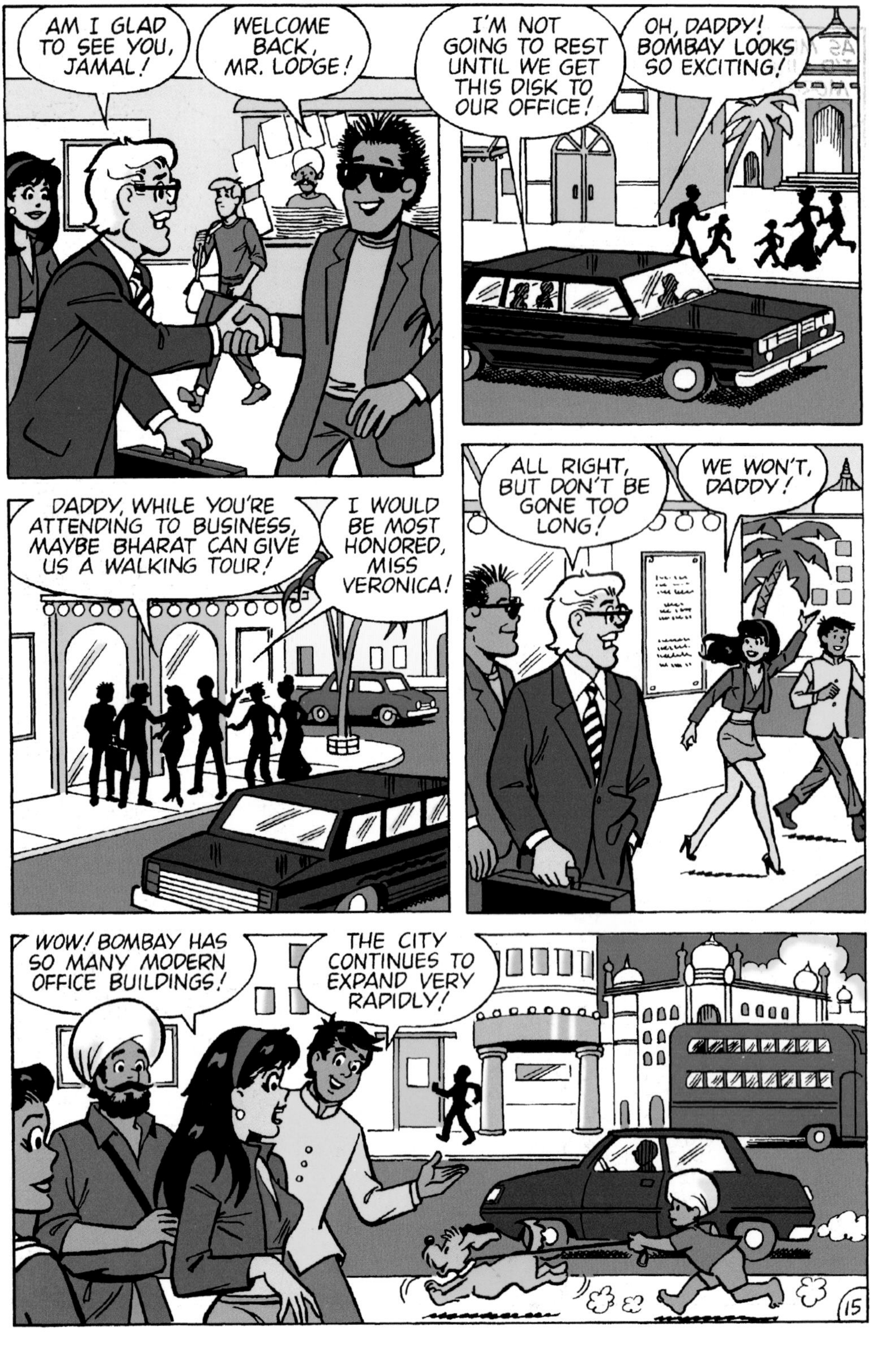
AM I GLAD TO SEE YOU, JAMAL!
WELCOME BACK, MR. LODGE!
I'M NOT GOING TO REST UNTIL WE GET THIS DISK TO OUR OFFICE!
OH, DADDY! BOMBAY LOOKS SO EXCITING!
DADDY, WHILE YOU'RE ATTENDING TO BUSINESS, MAYBE BHARAT CAN GIVE US A WALKING TOUR!
I WOULD BE MOST HONORED, MISS VERONICA!
ALL RIGHT, BUT DON'T BE GONE TOO LONG!
WE WON'T, DADDY!
WOW! BOMBAY HAS SO MANY MODERN OFFICE BUILDINGS!
THE CITY CONTINUES TO EXPAND VERY RAPIDLY!
15

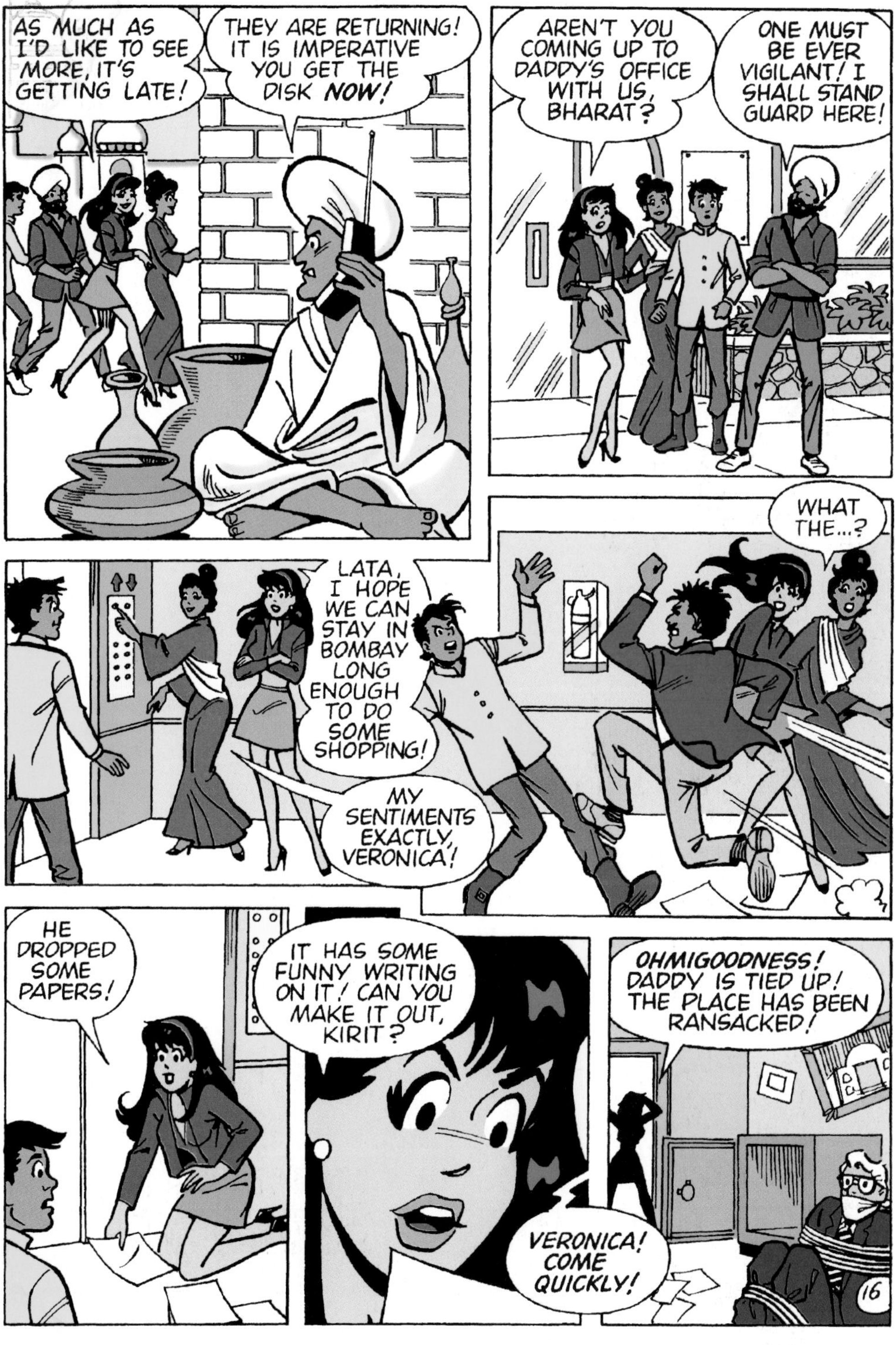
AS MUCH AS I'D LIKE TO SEE MORE, IT'S GETTING LATE!
THEY ARE RETURNING! IT IS IMPERATIVE YOU GET THE DISK NOW!
AREN'T YOU COMING UP TO DADDY'S OFFICE WITH US, BHARAT?
ONE MUST BE EVER VIGILANT! I SHALL STAND GUARD HERE!
LATA, I HOPE WE CAN STAY IN BOMBAY LONG ENOUGH TO DO SOME SHOPPING!
MY SENTIMENTS EXACTLY, VERONICA!
WHAT THE...?
HE DROPPED SOME PAPERS!
IT HAS SOME FUNNY WRITING ON IT! CAN YOU MAKE IT OUT, KIRIT?
VERONICA! COME QUICKLY!
OHMIGOODNESS! DADDY IS TIED UP! THE PLACE HAS BEEN RANSACKED!
16

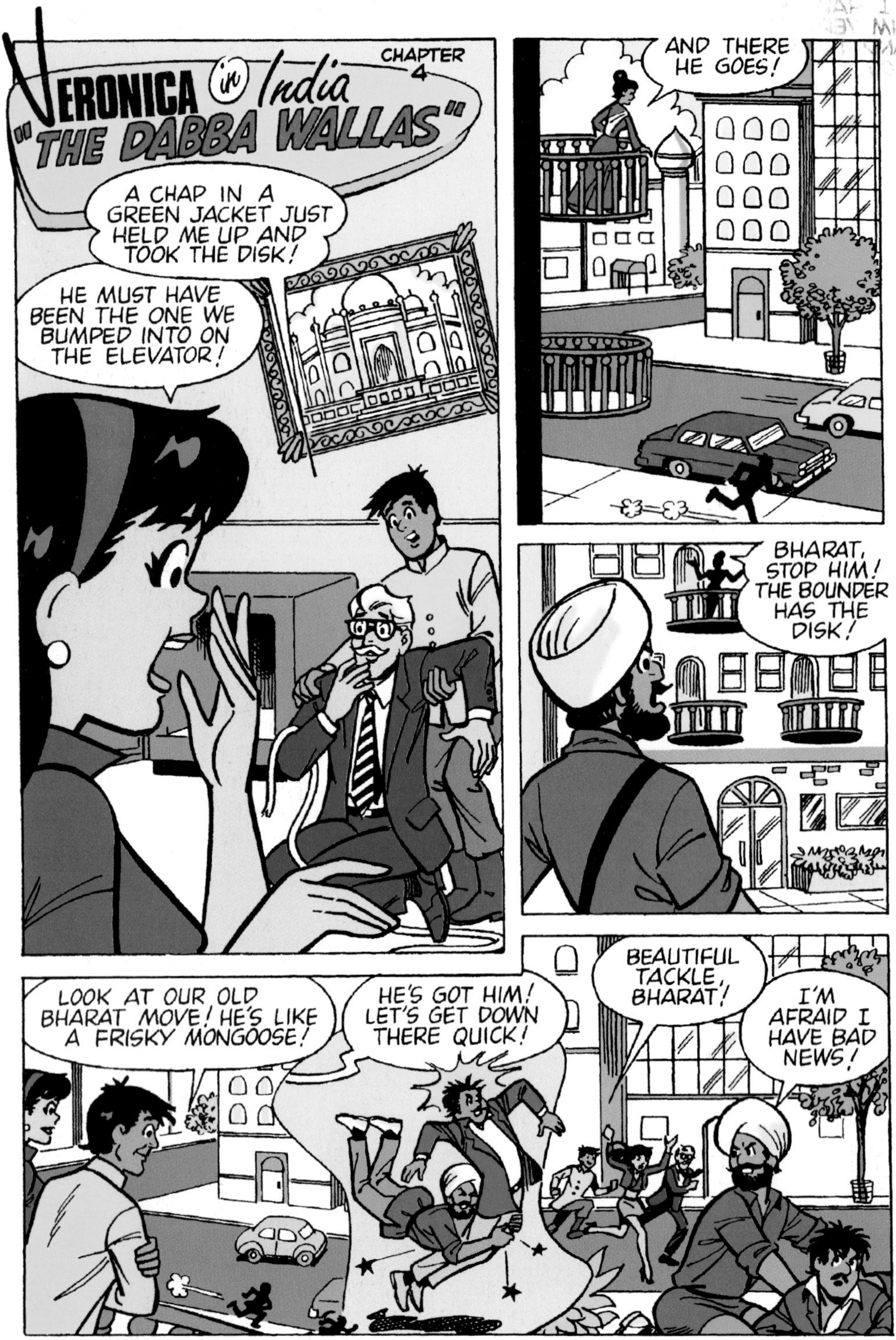
VERONICA in India
CHAPTER 4
"THE DABBA WALLAS"
A CHAP IN A GREEN JACKET JUST HELD ME UP AND TOOK THE DISK!
HE MUST HAVE BEEN THE ONE WE BUMPED INTO ON THE ELEVATOR!
AND THERE HE GOES!
BHARAT, STOP HIM! THE BOUNDER HAS THE DISK!
LOOK AT OUR OLD BHARAT MOVE! HE'S LIKE A FRISKY MONGOOSE!
HE'S GOT HIM! LET'S GET DOWN THERE QUICK!
BEAUTIFUL TACKLE, BHARAT!
I'M AFRAID I HAVE BAD NEWS!

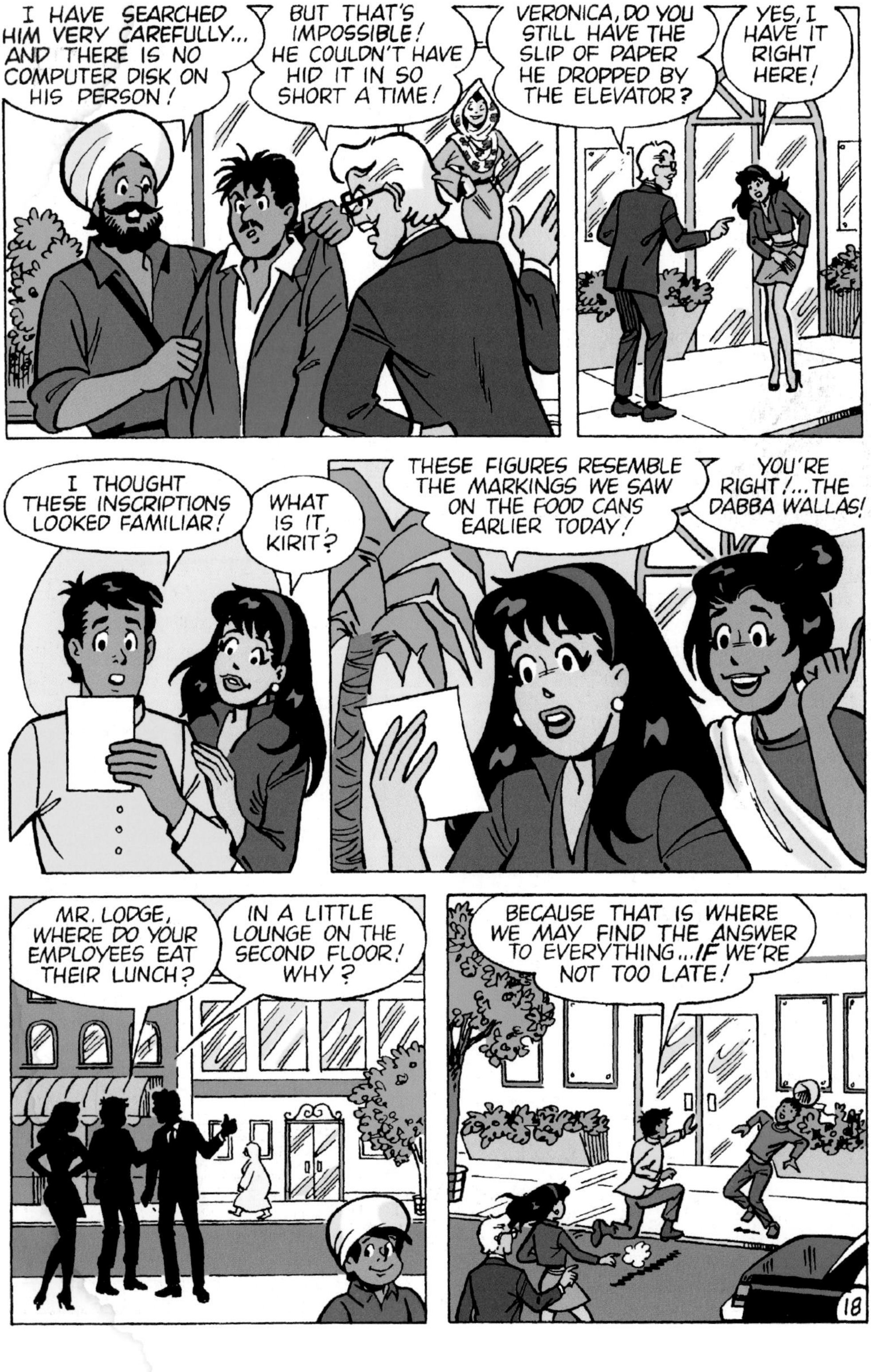
I HAVE SEARCHED HIM VERY CAREFULLY... AND THERE IS NO COMPUTER DISK ON HIS PERSON!
BUT THAT'S IMPOSSIBLE! HE COULDN'T HAVE HID IT IN SO SHORT A TIME!
VERONICA, DO YOU STILL HAVE THE SLIP OF PAPER HE DROPPED BY THE ELEVATOR?
YES, I HAVE IT RIGHT HERE!
I THOUGHT THESE INSCRIPTIONS LOOKED FAMILIAR!
WHAT IS IT, KIRIT?
THESE FIGURES RESEMBLE THE MARKINGS WE SAW ON THE FOOD CANS EARLIER TODAY!
YOU'RE RIGHT!...THE DABBA WALLAS!
MR. LODGE, WHERE DO YOUR EMPLOYEES EAT THEIR LUNCH?
IN A LITTLE LOUNGE ON THE SECOND FLOOR! WHY?
BECAUSE THAT IS WHERE WE MAY FIND THE ANSWER TO EVERYTHING...IF WE'RE NOT TOO LATE!
18

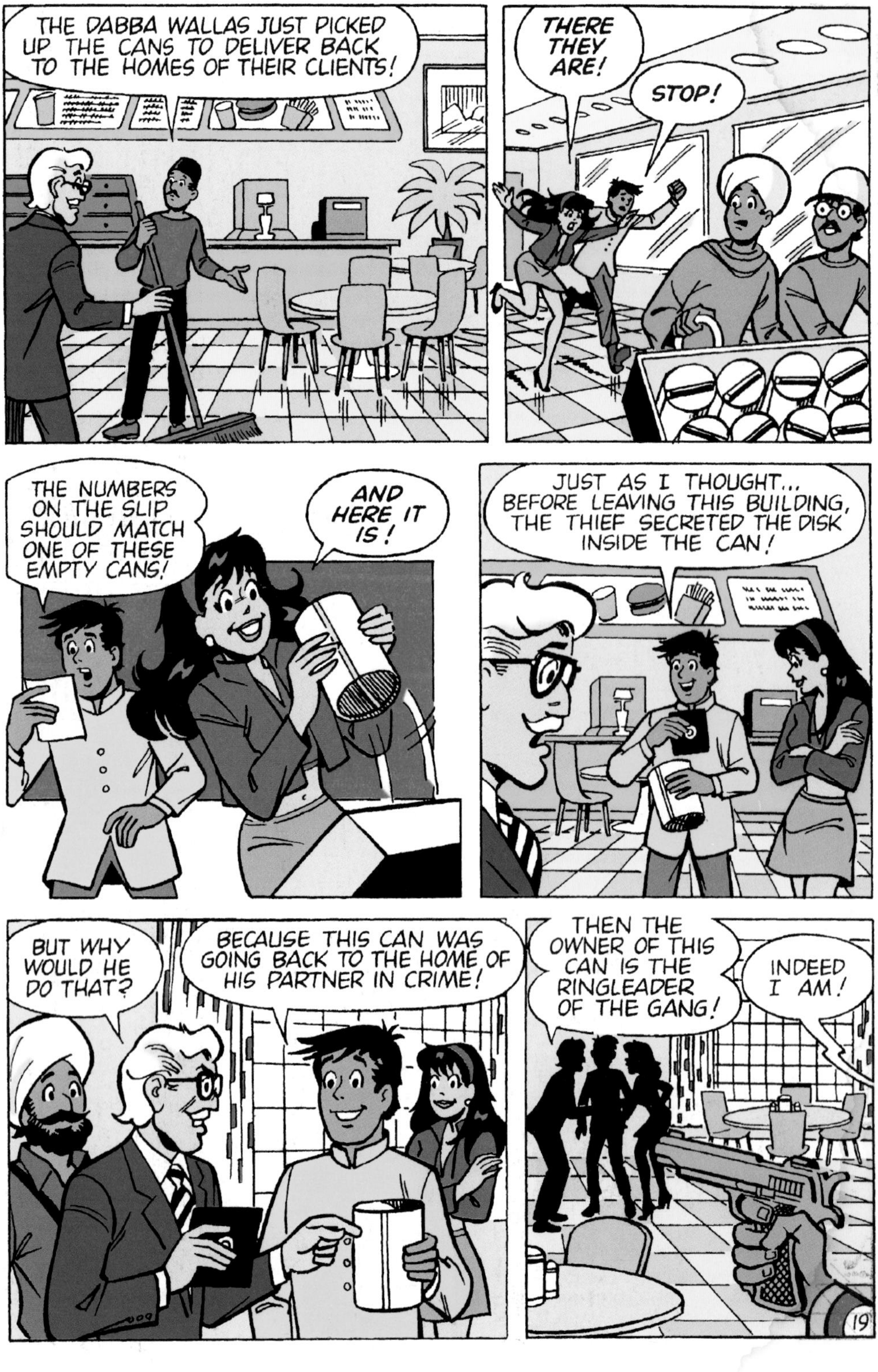
THE DABBA WALLAS JUST PICKED UP THE CANS TO DELIVER BACK TO THE HOMES OF THEIR CLIENTS!
THERE THEY ARE!
STOP!
THE NUMBERS ON THE SLIP SHOULD MATCH ONE OF THESE EMPTY CANS!
AND HERE IT IS!
JUST AS I THOUGHT... BEFORE LEAVING THIS BUILDING, THE THIEF SECRETED THE DISK INSIDE THE CAN!
BUT WHY WOULD HE DO THAT?
BECAUSE THIS CAN WAS GOING BACK TO THE HOME OF HIS PARTNER IN CRIME!
THEN THE OWNER OF THIS CAN IS THE RINGLEADER OF THE GANG!
INDEED I AM!
19

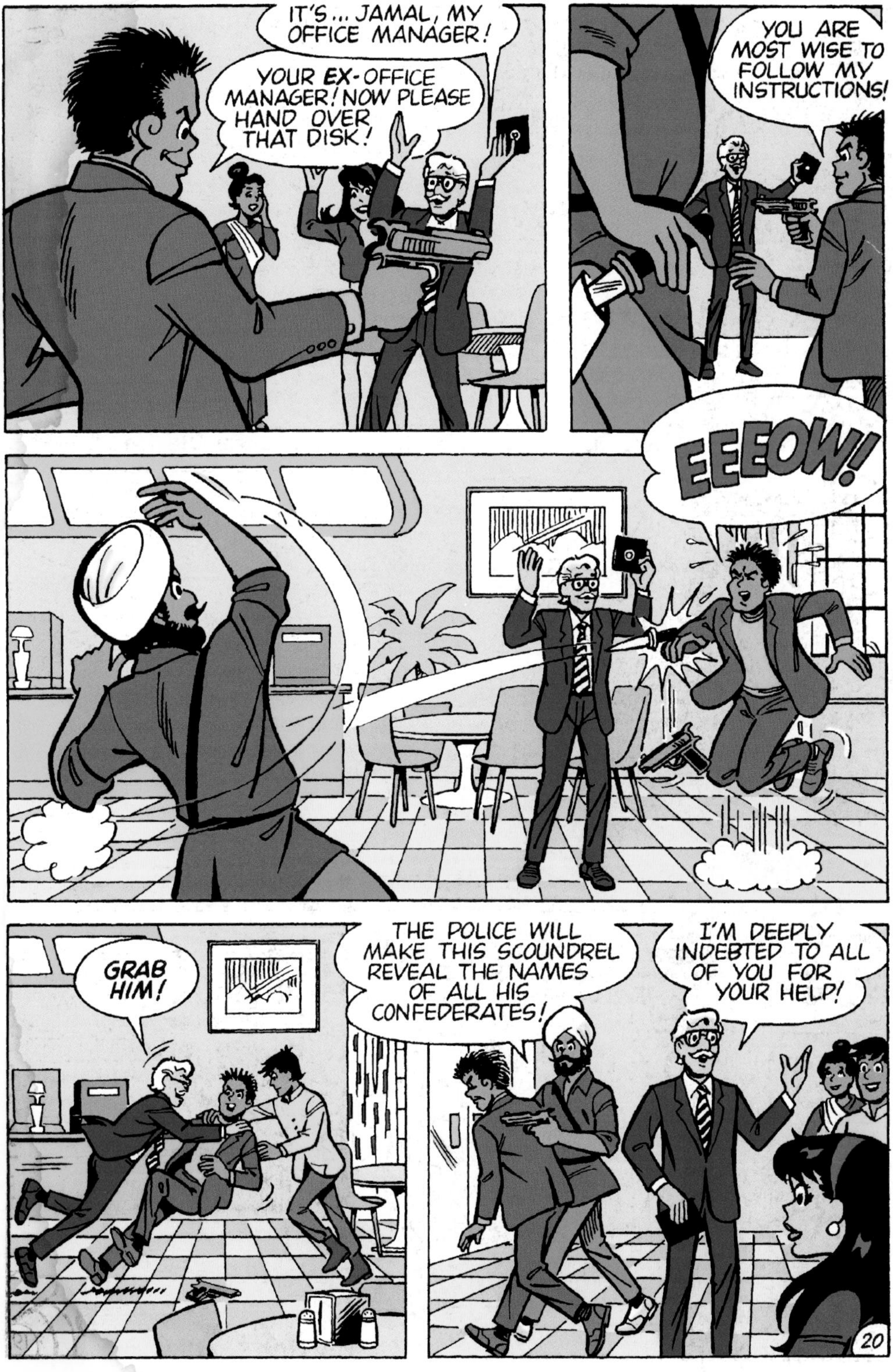
IT'S ... JAMAL, MY OFFICE MANAGER!
YOUR EX-OFFICE MANAGER! NOW PLEASE HAND OVER THAT DISK!
YOU ARE MOST WISE TO FOLLOW MY INSTRUCTIONS!
EEEOW!
GRAB HIM!
THE POLICE WILL MAKE THIS SCOUNDREL REVEAL THE NAMES OF ALL HIS CONFEDERATES!
I'M DEEPLY INDEBTED TO ALL OF YOU FOR YOUR HELP!
20

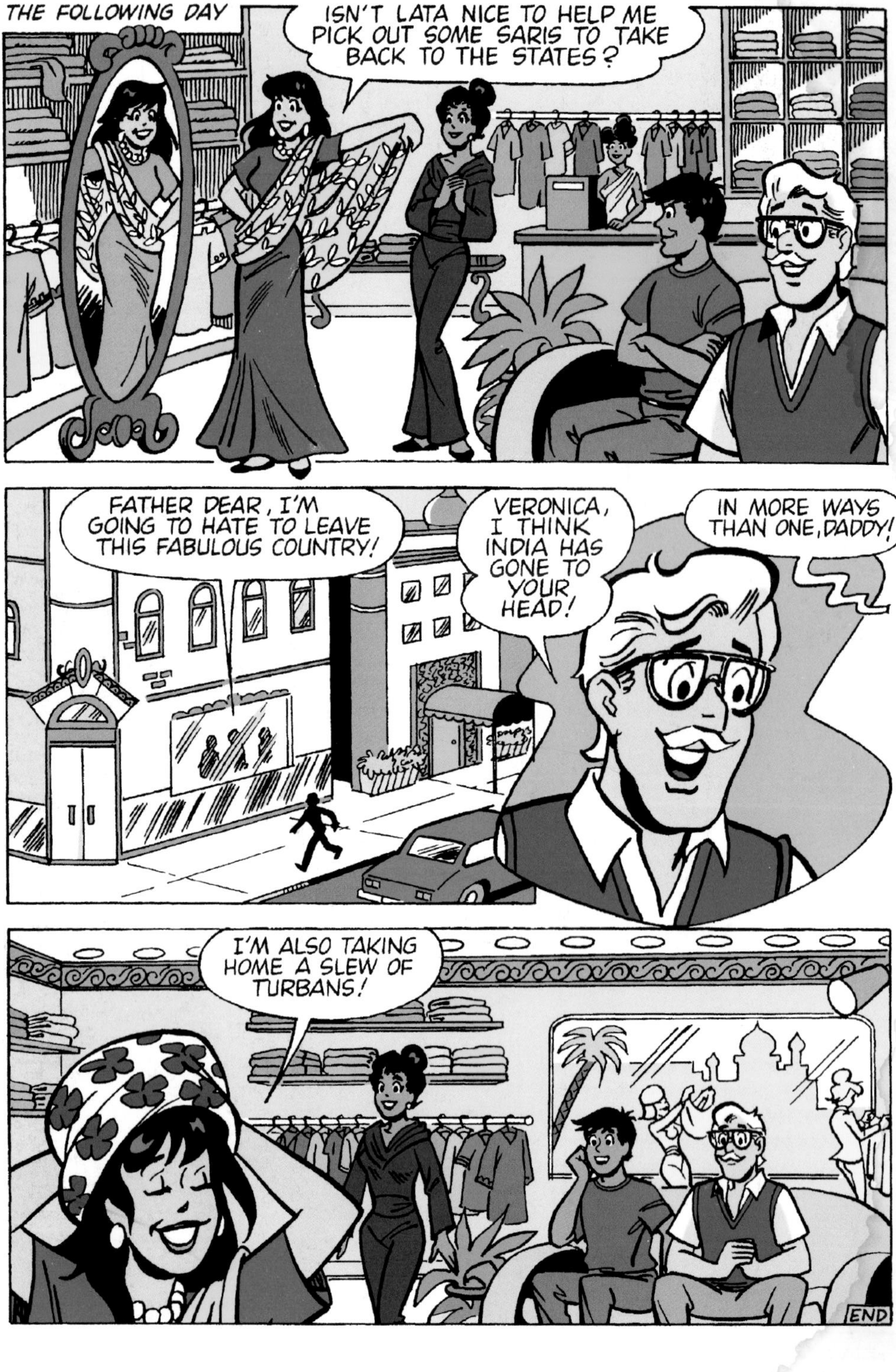
THE FOLLOWING DAY
ISN'T LATA NICE TO HELP ME PICK OUT SOME SARIS TO TAKE BACK TO THE STATES?
FATHER DEAR, I'M GOING TO HATE TO LEAVE THIS FABULOUS COUNTRY!
VERONICA, I THINK INDIA HAS GONE TO YOUR HEAD!
IN MORE WAYS THAN ONE, DADDY!
I'M ALSO TAKING HOME A SLEW OF TURBANS!
END